SNOWBOUND
SEDUCTION

SNOWBOUND
SEDUCTION

SARAH MORGAN
VICTORIA PARKER
SAMANTHA HUNTER

First Published in Great Britain 2017
By Mills & Boon, an imprint of HarperCollins*Publishers*
1 London Bridge Street, London, SE1 9GF

SNOWBOUND SEDUCTION © 2017 Harlequin Books S.A.

A Night of No Return © 2012 Sarah Morgan
To Claim His Heir by Christmas © 2014 Victoria Parker
I'll Be Yours for Christmas © 2010 Samantha Hunter

ISBN: 978-0-263-93168-6

9-1017

A NIGHT OF NO RETURN

SARAH MORGAN

USA TODAY bestselling author **Sarah Morgan** writes lively, sexy stories for both the Mills & Boon Modern and Medical lines. As a child, Sarah dreamed of being a writer and, although she took a few interesting detours on the way, she is now living that dream. With her writing career, she has successfully combined business with pleasure and she firmly believes that reading romance is one of the most satisfying and fat-free escapist pleasures available.

Sarah lives near London with her husband and two children. When she isn't plotting her next book, Sarah enjoys music, movies and any activity that takes her outdoors. Visit her website at www.sarahmorgan.com and look for her on Facebook and Twitter.

CHAPTER ONE

IT WAS the one night of the year he dreaded more than any other.

In the beginning he'd tried everything in a bid to escape it—wild parties, women, work—but he'd discovered that it didn't matter what he was doing or who he was doing it with, the pain remained the same. He chose to live his life in the present, but the past was part of him and he carried it everywhere. It was a memory that wouldn't fade. A scar that wouldn't heal. A pain that went bone-deep. There *was* no escape, which was why his favoured way of spending this particular night was to find somewhere he could be alone and get very, very drunk.

He'd driven the two hours from his office in London to the property he was restoring in rural Oxfordshire simply for the privilege of being alone. For once his phone was switched off, and it was staying that way.

Snow swirled in a crazy dance in front of the windscreen and visibility was down to almost zero. Huge white drifts were piled high at the side of the road, a trap for the nervous, inexperienced driver.

Lucas Jackson was neither nervous nor inexperienced and his mood was blacker than the weather.

The howl of the wind sounded like a child screaming and he clenched his jaw and tried to blot out the noise.

Never had the first glimpse of stone lions guarding the entrance to his estate been so welcome. Despite the conditions he barely slowed his pace, accelerating along the long drive that wound through acres of parkland towards the main house.

He drove past the lake, now frozen into a skating rink for the ducks, over the bridge that crossed the river and heralded the final approach to Chigworth Castle.

He waited to feel the rush of satisfaction that should have come from owning this, but as always there was nothing. It shouldn't have surprised him, he'd long since accepted that he wasn't able to feel in the way that other people did. He'd switched that part of himself off and he hadn't been able to switch it on again.

What he did experience as he looked at the magnificent building was a detached appreciation for something that satisfied both the mathematician in him and the architect. The dimensions and structure were perfect. A gatehouse presided over the entrance, its carved stonework creating a first impression that was both imposing and aesthetically pleasing. And then there was the castle itself, with its buff stonework and battlements that attracted the interest of historians from around the world. The knowledge that he was preserving history gave him a degree of professional pride, but as for the rest of it— the personal, emotional side—he felt nothing.

Whoever said that revenge was a dish best eaten cold had been wrong.

He'd sampled it and found it tasteless.

And tonight Lucas wasn't even interested in the historical significance of the house, just its isolation. It was miles from the nearest hint of civilisation and that suited him just fine. The last thing he wanted tonight was human contact.

Lights burned in a few of the upstairs windows and he frowned because he'd specifically instructed the staff to take the night off. He was in no mood for company of any description.

He drove over the bridge that spanned the moat, under the arch that guarded the entrance and skidded the last few metres into the courtyard, his tyres sending snow spinning into the air.

It occurred to him that if he hadn't left the office when he had, he might not have made it. He had staff capable of clearing the roads in the estate, but the approach to the house consisted of a network of winding country lanes that were a low priority for the authorities responsible for their upkeep. Briefly he thought of Emma, his loyal PA, who had stayed late at the office yet again in order to help him prepare for his coming trip to Zubran, an oil-rich state on the Persian Gulf. It was a good job she lived in London and wouldn't have far to travel home.

Abandoning the car to the weather, he strode across the snowy carpet and let himself in to the darkness of the entrance hall.

No housekeeper to greet him tonight. No staff. No one. Just him.

'Surprise!!' A chorus of voices erupted from around him and lights blazed.

Temporarily blinded, Lucas froze, shock holding him immobile on his own doorstep.

'Happy birthday to me!' Tara walked forward, a sway in her hips and a sly smile on her beautiful face as she hooked a finger inside his coat and lifted her scarlet painted mouth to his. 'I know you promised to give me my present next week, but I can't wait that long. I want it *now*.'

Lucas stared down into those famous blue eyes and still felt nothing.

Slowly, deliberately, he detached her hand from the front of his coat. 'What the hell,' he asked quietly, 'are you doing here?'

'Celebrating my birthday.' Clearly less than delighted with his chilly response, she produced her trademark pout. 'You refused to come to my party so I decided to bring the party to you. Your housekeeper let us in. Why haven't you ever invited me here before? I *love* this place. It's like a film set.'

Lucas lifted his gaze. He saw now that the grand hall with its magnificent paintings and tapestries had been decorated with streamers and balloons. Gaudily wrapped presents were stacked next to a large iced birthday cake. Open bottles of champagne stood on an antique table, mocking his black mood.

Never in his life had he felt less like celebrating.

His first thought was that he was going to fire his housekeeper, but then he remembered just how persuasive Tara could be when she wanted something. She was a master at manipulating emotions and he knew it frustrated her that she'd never succeeded in manipulating his.

'Tonight is not a good night for me. I told you that.' His voice sounded robotic but Tara simply shrugged dismissively.

'Well, whatever it is that is making you so moody, you need to snap out of it, Lucas. You'll forget about it once you've had a drink. We'll dance for a bit and then go upstairs and—'

'Get out.' His thickened command was greeted with appalled silence. Her friends—people he didn't know and had no desire to know—murmured their shock.

The only person who seemed unaffected by his response was Tara herself whose ego was the least fragile thing about her. 'Don't be ridiculous, Lucas. You don't mean that. It's a surprise party.'

But the surprise, apparently, was his. *Only Tara could hold a surprise party for her own birthday.* 'Get out and take your friends with you.'

Her eyes hardened. 'We all came by coach and it isn't coming back until one o'clock.'

'When did you last look outside? Nothing is going to be moving on these roads by one o'clock. That coach had better be here in the next ten minutes or you'll be snowed in. And trust me, you do *not* want that.' Perhaps it was his tone, perhaps it was the fact that he looked dangerous— and he knew that he must look dangerous because he *felt* dangerous—but his words finally sank home.

Tara's beautiful face, that same face that had graced so many magazine covers, turned scarlet with humiliation and anger. Those cat-like eyes flashed into his, but what she saw there must have scared her because the colour fled from her cheeks and left her flawless skin as pale as the winter snow blanketing the ground outside.

'Fine.' Her lips barely moved. 'We'll take our party elsewhere and leave you alone with your horrid temper for company. Now I know why your relationships don't last. Money, brains and skill in bed can't make up for the fact that you don't have a heart, Lucas Jackson.'

He could have told her the truth. He could have told her that his heart, once intact and fully functioning, had been damaged beyond repair. He could have told her that the phrase 'time heals' was false and that he was living proof that damage could be permanent. He could have described the relief that came from knowing he might never be healed because a heart already damaged could never be damaged again.

There was something beating in his chest, that was true, but it did nothing more than pump blood around his body, enabling him to get out of bed in the morning and go to work every day.

He could have told Tara all of that but she would have gained as little satisfaction in the listening as he would in the telling, so he simply strode past her towards the famous oak staircase that rose majestically from the centre of the hall.

Tonight the proportions and design gave him no satisfaction. The staircase was merely a means to escape from the people who had invaded his sanctuary.

Without waiting for them to leave, he took the stairs two at a time and strode towards his bedroom in the tower that overlooked the moat.

He didn't care that he'd shocked them.

He didn't care that he'd ended yet another relationship.

All he cared about was getting through this one night.

He was a cold-hearted, driven workaholic.

Her normal patience nowhere to be found, Emma struggled to keep the car on the road. It was Friday night and she should have been at home relaxing with Jamie. Instead, she was chasing her boss round the English countryside. After the week she'd had it was the last thing she needed. She had a *life*, for goodness' sake. Or rather, she would have liked to have a life. Unfortunately for her, she worked for a man for whom the concept of a life outside work didn't exist.

Lucas Jackson didn't have any emotional attachments and clearly didn't think his staff should have them either. He wasn't interested in her as a person, just in her contribution to his company. And there would have been no point in explaining her feelings because, as far as she could tell, he didn't have feelings. His life was so far removed from hers that sometimes when she drove into her space in the car park beneath the iconic glass building that housed the world-renowned architectural firm of Jackson and Partners, she felt as if she'd arrived on another planet. Even the building itself was futuristic—a tribute to cutting-edge design and energy efficiency, designed to maximise daylight and natural ventilation, a bold statement that represented the creative vision and genius of just one man. Lucas Jackson.

But creative vision and genius required focus and single-minded determination and that combination together created a driven, difficult human being. More machine than human, she thought moodily as she peered through the thick falling snow in an attempt to not end her days in a ditch.

When she'd started working for him two years previously she hadn't minded that their conversation was never personal. She didn't want or expect it when she was at work, so that suited her well. The one thing she would never, *ever* do was fall in love with her boss. But she'd fallen in love with her job. The work was interesting, stimulating and in every way that mattered Lucas was an excellent employer, despite the fact that his reputation had unnerved her to the point where she almost hadn't applied for the role. She'd found him to be professional, bright and a generous payer and it excited her to be involved with a company responsible for the design of some of the most famous buildings of recent times. He was undoubtedly a genius. Those were his positive points.

The negatives were that he was focused on work to the exclusion of everything else.

Take this week. Preparations for the official opening of the Zubran Ferrara Resort, an innovative eco hotel nestling on the edge of the warm waters of the Persian Gulf, had driven her workload from crazy to manic. Fuelled by caffeine, she'd stayed until the early hours every night in an attempt to complete essential work. Not once had she complained or commented on the fact that, generally, she expected to be fast asleep by two a.m. and preferably not at her desk.

The one thing that had kept her going had been the thought of Friday. The start of her holiday. Two whole weeks that she took off every year over the festive season. She'd visualised that time in the way a marathon runner might imagine the finish line. It had been the shining light at the end of a tunnel of exhaustion.

And then the snow had started falling. And falling. All week it had been snowing steadily until by Friday London was half empty.

All day Emma had been eyeing the weather out of the window. She'd seen staff from other office buildings leaving early, slithering and sliding their way through the snow to be sure of making it home. As Lucas's PA she had the authority to extend that privilege to other more junior staff and she had, until the only two people remaining in the building had been herself and her ruthlessly focused boss.

Lucas hadn't appeared to notice the snowstorm transforming the world into a death zone. When she'd mentioned it, he hadn't responded. That would have been bad enough and sufficient to have her cursing him for her entire journey home but just as she'd been about to turn out the lights, the last to leave as usual, she'd noticed the file sitting on his desk. It was the file she'd put together for his trip to Zubran and it included papers that needed his signature. A helicopter would be picking him up from his country house. He wouldn't be coming back to the office.

At first she didn't believe he could have forgotten it. Lucas never forgot anything. He was the most efficient person she'd ever worked for. And once she'd come to terms with the fact that for some reason his usual efficiency had chosen a frozen Friday night to desert him, she'd faced a dilemma.

She'd tried calling him, hoping to catch him while he was still in London, but his phone continually switched to voicemail, presumably because he was already talking to someone else. Lucas spent his life talking on the phone.

She could have arranged a courier, but the file contained confidential and sensitive information and she didn't trust it with anyone but herself. Did that make her obsessive? Possibly. But if it were to be mislaid she would be out of a job and she wasn't about to take that risk.

Which was why she was now, late on a miserable Friday night when no one else with any sense would be on the roads, heading west out of London towards his rural country house.

Emma squinted through the white haze. She didn't mind hard work. Her only rule was that she didn't work at weekends. And for some reason—maybe her references, maybe her calm demeanour, or just the fact that he'd lost six PAs in as many months—Lucas Jackson had accepted that one caveat, although he had once made a caustic comment about her 'wild social life'.

If he'd taken the trouble to find out about her, he would have known that there wasn't room for 'wild' in her life. He would know that the nearest she'd got to a party was through the pages of the celebrity magazines her sister occasionally bought. He would have known that after working a punishing week at Jackson and Partners her idea of a perfect weekend was just sleeping late and spending time with Jamie. Lucas would have known all that, but he didn't because he'd never asked.

She glanced briefly at the offending file on the passenger seat next to her, as if by simply glaring at it she might somehow manage to teleport the contents to its owner.

Unfortunately there was no chance of that. Her only choice was to take it to him. Never let it be said that she didn't do her job properly.

This launch was the most talked about event for a decade and the party itself would be a glittering gathering of everyone important. Emma had felt a wistful pang as she'd liaised with Avery Scott, the dynamic owner of Dance and Dine, the company in charge of organising the launch event. From her conversations with Avery, she knew that the international celebrity guest list would be indulging in vintage champagne in the glamour of a marquee designed as a Bedouin tent. Then they would enjoy a traditional Zubrani banquet under the stars and have the opportunity to explore the specially constructed 'souk', tempting the guests with various local delicacies and entertainment. To showcase the best of Zubran as a holiday destination there would be belly dancers, fortune tellers, falconry and the evening would conclude with what promised to be the most spectacular firework display ever witnessed.

This was probably how Cinderella had felt when she'd learned she would not be going to the ball, Emma thought gloomily.

Shivering in the freezing air that her inadequate heater didn't manage to warm, she sank deeper inside her coat and allowed herself a brief fantasy involving sunshine and palm trees. Just for a moment she felt envious. Right now this minute, the women on the guest list were probably deciding what to wear and packing for a break in the sun where all they were expected to do was look glamorous.

Emma pushed her hair away from her face with her gloved hand. She didn't need to look in the mirror to know she didn't look glamorous. She looked wrecked.

Forget celebrity parties. She'd be thrilled just to be able to get to bed before midnight. And if the weather carried on like this, she and Jamie would be spending their precious holiday trapped indoors.

She was struggling to keep the car on the icy road when her phone rang.

She thought it might be Lucas finally returning one of her many frantic messages, but it wasn't. It was Jamie.

Of course it was Jamie. He'd expected her over an hour ago.

'Where are you, Emma?' His concern was audible in his voice and she suddenly felt horribly disloyal for wishing she could have gone to Zubran and partied under the stars.

Not daring to drive and talk with the road conditions so bad, she pulled over, squashing down the guilt. 'I had to work late. I'm so sorry. I left you a message.'

'When will you be home?'

'Soon. I hope.' She stared doubtfully at the falling snow. 'But it might take me a while because the roads are terrible. Don't wait up.'

He didn't say anything and she knew he was upset with her.

His silence made her guilt worse. While he'd been worrying, she'd been imagining the perfect dress to wear to the party of the decade. 'We have the whole week-end to be together and next week,' she reasoned. When there was still no answer, she gave a sigh. 'Jamie, don't be upset. I have to work tonight. It's never happened before. You know I normally keep the weekends free but this is an emergency. Lucas left some really important papers and I have to take them to him.'

It was a difficult conversation and by the time she hung up she was cursing Lucas Jackson with words she never normally allowed herself to use. Why couldn't he have remembered the stupid file? Or why couldn't he at least get off the phone and pick up her calls? At least then she could have met him halfway or something.

Knowing that the only thing that was going to make her feel better was getting the job done and going home, she eased the car back onto the road. Her eyes felt gritty and her head throbbed. She couldn't wait to just crawl into bed and sleep and sleep.

She'd make it up to Jamie. They had two weeks together—the whole of the Christmas holidays. Two whole weeks while her high-flying boss was in Zubran, locked in business meetings with the Sultan and partying the night away under the stars. And she wasn't jealous. Absolutely not.

Visibility was down to virtually zero. She lost her way twice in the maze of country lanes that all looked the same and defeated her satnav. The only car on the road, she crawled her way along a snowy lane and finally found herself at the entrance to Chigworth Castle.

Two huge stone lions snarled down at her from either side of the open gates and she glared back at them, thinking that the house was about as friendly and welcoming as the man who owned it.

By the time she'd slithered and skidded her way down a drive that seemed as long as the road to London, the throb in her head was worse and she'd convinced herself she'd taken a wrong turn. This couldn't possibly be right. It was leading nowhere.

Where on earth was the actual house? Did one person really need this much land?

Her headlights picked out a wood and a lake and she drove over a bridge, tyres skidding, turned a corner and saw it. Floodlit with warm beams of light that illuminated honey-coloured stone and tall, beautiful windows, a small castle stood as it had no doubt stood for centuries, surrounded by a moat.

'Battlements,' Emma breathed, enchanted. 'It even has battlements.'

Snow clung to those battlements and smoke twirled from a chimney into the cold air. Lights shone from a tower in one corner of the building and her mouth literally fell open because she'd had no idea that he owned something like this. He was all about modern, cutting-edge design and yet this—this imposing, beautiful building was part of history.

It really was a castle. A small, but perfectly formed castle.

Small? Emma gave a choked laugh. Small was her rented room in one of the less salubrious areas of London. She had a single window that overlooked a train line and was woken every morning at five a.m. by the aeroplanes landing at Heathrow Airport. Idyllic living it was not. This, however, was. So much space, she thought enviously. Acres of gardens, now cloaked in white but easy enough to imagine them in the spring—carpets of bluebells stretching endlessly into the wood where currently there was nothing but layers of soft, unmarked snow.

It was truly beautiful.

For a moment her eyes stung and she wondered how a house could possibly make her want to cry.

It wasn't that perfect, was it?

For a start it was isolated. Realising just how isolated, Emma gave a shiver as she coaxed her little car forward over the bridge that spanned the moat. She might have been the only person on the planet.

And then through the archway she saw the sleek, familiar lines of Lucas's car, already almost obscured by the falling snow. So he'd made it, but he still wasn't answering his phone.

Resolving to buy him a phone that only she used and relieved to still be in one piece, she sat for a moment, waiting for her heart rate to slow down. When she was sufficiently recovered, she reached for the offending file.

Two minutes, Emma promised herself as she switched off the engine and stepped carefully out of the car. This was going to take her two minutes. As soon as she'd handed over the file, she'd get back on the road.

The moment her feet touched the ground, she slipped. Crashing down awkwardly in her attempt to protect the file, she bumped her elbow and her head. For a moment she lay there, winded, and then she rolled onto her knees and struggled back to her feet. Bruised, damp and angry, she picked her way gingerly towards the door, the snow seeping through her shoes.

She stabbed the bell with her finger and held it there, taking small comfort from that minor rebellion. There was no answer.

Snow trickled down from her hair to her neck and from there inside her shirt.

Emma shivered and rang the bell again, surprised that someone hadn't immediately opened the door. She'd assumed the place would be crawling with staff and Lucas was notoriously intolerant of inefficiency of any kind.

Someone, she thought, was going to be in trouble.

Having rung the bell for a third time and still received no response, she tried the door with no expectation that it would open.

When it did, she hesitated on the threshold. Walking into someone else's home uninvited wasn't a habit of hers, but she had a file he needed and she wasn't about to drive it all the way back to the office.

'Hello?' Cautiously, she peeped her head in through the door, bracing herself to set off an alarm. But there was no sound and she opened the door further. She saw dark wood panelling, tapestries, huge oil paintings and a sweeping staircase so romantic that it made a girl long for Rhett Butler to stride into the house and sweep her off her feet. When there was still no sign of life, she stepped inside.

'Hello?' She closed the door to keep the heat in—*how much did it cost to heat somewhere like this?*—and then noticed the open champagne bottles, the balloons and the streamers. And a cake. Something about the cake didn't quite seem right, but she couldn't work out what it was. Clearly a party was going on somewhere, except there was no sign of any guests, just an overpowering silence that was almost creepy. She half expected someone to jump out from behind the heavy velvet curtains and shout *boo*!

An uneasy feeling crept down her spine. For goodness' sake, it was just a house! A big house, admittedly, but there was nothing threatening about a house. And she wasn't alone. She couldn't possibly be alone. Lucas had to be here somewhere and a whole load of other people judging from the number of champagne bottles.

Hoping that an enormous guard dog wasn't about to bound out and close its jaws on a sensitive part of her anatomy, Emma walked over to a large oak door and pushed it open. It was a library, the walls lined with tall bookshelves stacked with books bound in various faded shades of old leather.

'Lucas?' She tentatively explored all the obvious rooms on the ground floor and then walked up the staircase. This was ridiculous. She couldn't search the whole house. Remembering the light she'd seen shining from the tower, she decided to just try there.

Hazarding a guess as to the correct direction, she turned right and walked along a carpeted corridor until she reached a heavy oak door.

She tapped once and opened it. 'Lucas?' A spiral staircase rose in front of her and she walked up it and found herself in a large circular room with windows on all sides. Logs blazed in a huge fireplace and out of the corner of her eye she caught sight of a huge four-poster bed draped in moss-green velvet, but her attention was on the low leather sofa because there, sprawled with his feet up on the arm and a bottle of champagne in his hand, was her boss.

'Lucas?'

'I thought I told you to get out.' His savage tone made her gasp and she took a step backwards and almost tumbled down the stairs. Not once in the years she'd worked for him had he spoken to her like that.

One glance told her that he was rip-roaring drunk and she so rarely saw him out of control that her initial reaction was one of surprise. The fact that he didn't make a habit of it did nothing to soothe her bruised feelings.

While her Friday night had been well and truly ruined, he'd been enjoying himself. He'd switched his phone off not because he was busy with an important business call, but because he was busy getting drunk. She'd risked her neck driving around the English countryside in a snowstorm, while all the time Lucas was warm and snug in front of a roaring log fire drinking champagne. Not only that, he had the gall to tell her to get out.

Emma's temper, usually slow to burn, began to glow hot.

She was about to slap the file down on the table and leave him to his solitary party when she suddenly realised that what he'd actually said wasn't *get out* but 'I thought I told you to get out.'

She frowned.

He certainly hadn't already told her to get out. Which could only mean that he thought she was someone else.

She remembered the balloons and the streamers. The abandoned champagne bottles. The cake.

'Lucas!' She spoke more clearly this time. 'It's me. Emma.'

For a moment she thought he hadn't heard her, and then his eyes opened.

Across the shadowy room she saw the lethal glitter that told her everything she needed to know about his mood. She was nowhere near him and yet it was as if he'd reached out and touched her. Her body warmed. She shifted uncomfortably. She'd never seen him like this before. The man she knew was always sleek and groomed. His suits were handmade in Italy, his shirts custom-made. He was a man who expected the best in everything. A sophisticated connoisseur of all things beautiful.

But tonight he looked dangerous in every way. In mood. In looks. His shirt was open at the neck, exposing a cluster of dark hair and a hint of powerful chest. Shadowy stubble darkened his strong jaw and, most disturbingly of all, she had the feeling that he was balancing on the very edge of control.

Sensing it, Emma reacted the way she would have

reacted had she suddenly been confronted by a snarling Rottweiler intent on ripping her throat out. She froze and tried to project calm. 'It's just me,' she said soothingly, 'only you seemed to think I was someone else, so I thought I ought to just clarify that…er…it's me.'

The silence stretched for such an agonizing length of time that she'd started to think that he wasn't going to answer when suddenly he stirred.

'Emma?' His voice was soft and deadly and did nothing to reassure her.

She discovered that her hands were shaking and that irritated her. This was Lucas, for goodness' sake. She'd worked with him almost every day for two years. He was tough, but he wasn't threatening. Not exactly kind, but not cruel either. 'I've been calling you for hours. Why didn't you pick up the phone?'

'Who the hell let you in?'

'No one. I rang the bell and no one answered so I—' She broke off and he raised an eyebrow.

'So you thought you'd just walk into my house? Tell me, Little Red Riding Hood, do you make a habit of walking through the forest when the wolf is loose?' Fierce blue eyes met hers and Emma felt as if she were being suffocated.

She lifted her hand and loosened the scarf around her neck. Maybe it was his tone. Maybe it was the look in his eyes, but suddenly her heart was pounding. 'I rang the bell. You didn't answer.'

'But you walked in anyway.' Those softly spoken words were a million times more disturbing than the hard tone he'd used to order her out.

She tried to rally herself. 'If you had answered your phone I wouldn't have had to walk in.'

'My phone is switched off. And I didn't answer the door because I wasn't looking for company.'

Something snapped inside her. 'You think I drove for over two hours in lethal conditions for the pleasure of your company? After the week we've had, when I've had your "company" for an average of fifteen hours a day? I don't think so.' The injustice of it stoked her temper. 'I drove here, at much personal inconvenience, I might add, to give you a file. The file that you forgot to pick up. The file you need tomorrow.'

'Tomorrow?' The way he said it made it sound as if that day were a lifetime away. A point somewhere in the future that might never come.

'Yes, tomorrow.' She looked at him in exasperation. Was he really that drunk? 'Zubran? The launch party? Your papers for the Ferrara meeting? Is any of this ringing any bells with you?' She'd been clutching the file to her chest like a shield but now she thrust it towards him and then decided that on second thoughts she didn't want him to move from the sofa, so instead she dropped it on the nearest table. 'There. My job is done. You can thank me when you're sober.'

Slowly, he put the champagne down on the floor. 'You drove out here to give me the file?'

'Yes, I did.' And suddenly she felt like a crazy person for doing that. 'You need it. I didn't want to trust it to a courier.'

'You could have given it to Jim.'

Jim was his driver. 'Jim has flown to Dublin for a long weekend.' Why hadn't he remembered that? *What was the matter with him?*

'So you chose to bring it in person.' His eyes glinted in the firelight and his gaze slowly travelled from her head to her toes as if he was seeing her properly for the first time.

'Yes, I brought it to you in person,' she snapped, hating herself for caring that she wasn't looking her best. It wasn't that she had any expectations of coming close to meeting his standards of visual perfection, but it would have boosted her confidence and made her feel businesslike. As it was, it was hard to feel businesslike with mud and snow streaked down her coat. 'Frankly I'm starting to wish I hadn't bothered, since the gesture clearly isn't appreciated.'

'Your head is bleeding. And your hair is wet. What happened to you?'

There was blood? Emma touched her head with her fingers and felt the bruise. Oh God, there *was* blood. How embarrassing. She rummaged in her bag for a tissue and pressed it against her head. 'I slipped walking from the car. It's fine.' Suddenly she was horribly aware that it was just the two of them in this enormous house. It didn't matter that she was often alone with him in the office. This felt different. 'I'm going now and I'll leave you to your party.' She thought again about the balloons and the cake and wondered where everyone else was. In a different part of the house?

'Ah yes, my party.' He gave a humourless laugh and his head dropped back against the sofa. 'Go, Emma. Someone like you shouldn't be here.'

She'd been about to retreat but his words stopped her. Offended, she tapped her foot on the floor. 'By "someone like me" I assume you mean someone who doesn't move in your lofty social circle.'

'I didn't mean that, but it doesn't matter.'

Stung, she stood still for a moment. 'Actually it does matter. I've just risked my neck and upset someone I love to bring you a file you don't even remember need-ing. A "thank you" would be nice. Manners are a good thing to have.'

'But I'm not nice. And I'm certainly not good.' His bitter tone shocked her. Her anger fizzled out.

'Lucas—'

'Get out, Emma.' This time he used her name so that there could be no mistake about whom he was address-ing. 'Get out and close the damn door behind you.'

CHAPTER TWO

OF ALL the ungrateful, rude, pig-headed… Emma stomped down the stairs, along the landing and down the main staircase, swept forward by rolling waves of righteous anger.

Get out, Emma.

Get out, Emma.

Those words rang in her ears and she set her teeth and walked faster.

Well, she was getting out. She couldn't get out fast enough.

She consoled herself that at least her conscience was clear. She'd done her job. She'd given him the file. No one could accuse her of behaving unprofessionally. Now she could relax and enjoy the holidays with Jamie without suffering a nagging worry that she should have done more. Lucas had made it clear that his personal life was his own business and that was just fine with her.

Her footsteps echoed in the magnificent hallway as she stormed towards the door. There was still no sign of anyone else and she wondered why a party would have finished so early.

I told you to get out!

His words played over and over again in her head. Who had he told to get out?

Telling herself that his manners were none of her business, she pulled open the door. The cold slammed into her and she gasped and huddled into her damp coat. Even in the comparatively short time she'd been inside, the weather had turned seriously ugly. The snow was falling twice as heavily. Already her footprints were covered and her car was an amorphous white blob.

Her head still aching from her last unscheduled contact with the ground, Emma picked her way gingerly to her car and knocked the worst of the snow off the windscreen with her glove. If that much snow had fallen since she'd been in the house then the bridge she'd crossed to get here would pretty soon be impassable. Her little car wouldn't be able to cope with the combination of the snow and the gradient.

With that thought in her head, she was about to slide into the driver's seat and start the engine when something about the smooth, untouched mound of snow on the roof made her think of the cake. And thinking of the cake made her realise what it was that had been bothering her. The cake was untouched. Whole. It hadn't been cut. Not a single slice had been taken from it.

Emma stood for a moment, one leg in the car, the other on the snowy ground, wondering about that. The celebration, whatever it was, had obviously stopped before they'd reached the part with the cake.

I told you to get out.

She tightened her lips and slid into the car. It wasn't any of her business. Wrapping her freezing fingers around the key, she started the engine. Maybe he didn't like cake. Maybe he didn't have a sweet tooth. Maybe—

'Drat and bother.' Switching off the engine, she thumped her head back against the seat. He'd told her to get out. If she had any sense she'd do just that.

Slowly she turned her head and looked back at the house.

He'd said he wanted to be alone so that was exactly what she should do. Leave him alone.

She tightened her hands on the wheel.

Whatever was wrong with Lucas Jackson wasn't any of her business.

Lucas stared blindly into the dying flames of the fire. He was drunk, but nowhere near as drunk as he wanted to be. The pain was as acute as ever. It was like lying down on the business end of a saw, feeling the teeth digging into every single part of him. Nothing he did could ease it.

Standing up, he walked to the basket of logs by the fire and pulled one out.

'You shouldn't be doing that. You'll burn the whole place down if you're not careful.' A female voice came from the doorway and he turned, wondering if he were hallucinating.

Emma stood there. Her cheeks were pink from the cold, snowflakes sparkled and clung to her dark hair and her eyes were frosty. He wasn't sure if he was seeing anger or defiance but he knew he was looking at trouble and he straightened slowly.

'I thought I told you—'

'—to get out. Yes, you did, which was very rude of you actually.' Her tone was brisk. 'For future reference, you *deserve* to be left on your own if that is the way you speak to people.' She lifted her hand and unwound her scarf from around her neck, sending snow fluttering onto the thick rug that covered the floor of the turret bedroom.

'That's what I want,' Lucas said slowly. 'I *want* to be left on my own.' He enunciated every syllable, aware that his emotions were dangerously close to the surface. 'I thought I'd made that clear.'

'You did.'

'So what are you doing here?'

'Sticking my nose into your business.' She tugged off a soaking-wet glove. 'For selfish reasons. I'm about to go on holiday. I don't want to spend that time worrying that you've fallen into the fire in a drunken stupor.'

'Why would that bother you?'

'If something happens to you I'd have to look for a new job and it's rubbish out there right now.'

'You don't have to worry.' Lucas tightened his hand on the log and felt the rough bark cut into his palm. 'I'm not that drunk, although I'm working on it.'

'Which is why I can't leave. When you stop "working on it" I'll be able to go.' The other glove went the same way as the first, the soaked fabric clinging to her skin. 'In the meantime, I don't want your death on my conscience.'

'I am not about to die.' He heard the anger in his voice and wondered why she couldn't hear it too. 'You can leave with a clear conscience. If you have any sense you'll do it. Right now.'

'I'm not leaving until you've told me why there seems to have been a party downstairs but you're on your own in the house.'

'Despite all my best attempts, I am *not* alone. *You're* here. And frankly I don't understand why. I've been rude to you. If you have any self-respect you should probably punch me and resign on the spot.'

'That only happens in the movies. In real life no one can afford to resign on the spot and only someone with your wealth would even suggest such a rash course of action.' Shivering, she unbuttoned her soaking coat and stepped closer to the fire. 'And self-respect means different things to different people. Dramatic overreaction isn't really my style, but if I walked away from someone in trouble *then* I'd lose all self-respect.'

'Emma—'

'And although it's true that you do lack empathy and certain human characteristics like a conscience, you are actually a reasonable person to work for most of the time so resigning would be a pretty stupid thing to do. Truth is, I love my job. And as for punching you—I've never punched anyone or anything in my life, although I did come close in the supermarket last week but that's another story. And anyway, my hands are so cold from scraping snow from the car I don't think I can even form a fist.' She flexed her fingers experimentally while Lucas watched with mounting exasperation.

Apparently wealth and success couldn't buy a man time alone when he wanted it.

'You love your job? In that case I am giving you a direct order,' he said in a thickened tone. 'Leave now or I *will* fire you.'

'You can't fire me. Not only would that be unfair dismissal but, technically, I'm now on my own time. Weekend time. How I spend it is my decision and no one else's.'

'Weekend time that previously you've always refused to work. Why pick this particular moment to break your unbreakable rule?' Anger exploded. 'Surely there is somewhere you need to be? What about this exciting life you live at weekends?' He remembered the one occasion, right at the beginning of her employment when she'd taken a personal call within his hearing. 'Why aren't you rushing home to Jamie?'

Her eyebrows rose in surprise. 'You know about Jamie?'

'Nothing to do with empathy or conscience.' Lucas was quick to dispel that possible thought before it even formed. 'I just have a good memory.'

'I didn't realise you knew about Jamie. And I will be going home, once I've assured myself you're OK.'

'I'm OK. You can see I'm OK.'

'There's no need to speak through your teeth and actually I don't see someone who is OK. I see a man who is drunk. On his own. A man who doesn't usually drink. Something seriously weird is going on.' She tapped her foot on the floor, a thoughtful look on her face. 'Why didn't anyone cut the cake?'

'Sorry?'

'The party downstairs. No one had bothered to cut the cake. And you only left the office just before me, so you didn't even have time for a party—' She stared at him as she worked it out. 'It was a surprise party, wasn't it? And you told them to get out.'

'Not all surprises are good ones. And now I'd like you to get out too.' His acid tone had no effect. She was like a barnacle, he thought, refusing to be chipped from the rock.

'I assume it was Tara and her hangers-on?' Her expression told him everything he needed to know about her opinion of the egocentric model. 'She should *not* have left you like this.'

'I ordered her to leave.'

'Then she shouldn't have listened. What was the occasion?'

'Her birthday.' He watched as her lips parted in astonishment. Soft lips, he noticed. Unpainted. She was wearing the same plain grey skirt she'd worn to work that day with a white shirt and a maroon sweater under her extremely damp coat. She looked sober and sensible. But then Emma always dressed soberly. Her hair was always smooth and neat, secured away from her face with a large clip that never failed her. She was the consummate professional in every way.

'She threw a surprise party for her *own* birthday?'

'I'd already told her this wasn't a good night for me. Tara isn't good at hearing no.'

'Why?'

Lucas gave a sardonic smile. 'Because she's a woman?'

'No—' her frown was impatient '—I mean, why isn't this a good night for you? I want to know why you're insistent on being on your own and why you're drinking your way through the entire contents of your cellar. Is it work? Has something gone wrong with the Zubran contract that I don't know about?'

'Why would you think it has anything to do with work?'

'Because work is the only thing that matters to you.'

Lucas stared at her for a long moment. Then he turned and threw the log he was holding onto the fire. The flames licked at it greedily, consuming it and delivering a sudden flare of heat.

He couldn't blame her for thinking that, could he?

She had no idea.

And that was a good thing. The last thing he was looking for was sympathy or understanding.

'You shouldn't be here, Emma.'

'But I am here. And I might be able to help.' She stood, straight and tall. Honest. Straightforward. A woman with a heart, innocent of how dark the world could be.

He made a point of avoiding women like her. Innocence had no place in his life. He was not a good guardian of innocence. Even thinking about it made his palms begin to sweat. 'You can't help.' Their relationship had always been strictly professional. For Lucas, business and pleasure didn't mix. He'd thought she felt the same way.

'Are you upset about Tara? Is that what's wrong? This isn't like you. In all the time I've worked for you I've never seen you remotely emotional about a woman. I've come to the conclusion that they're no more than an accessory to you. A bit like your cufflinks. You wear different ones, depending on the occasion.'

It was such a perceptive comment that had he not been struggling with his black mood, he might have laughed. He certainly would have been impressed. As it was, he just wanted her gone and if she was going to ignore his request for her to leave then it was time to employ other methods.

'Maybe it is like me. Maybe you don't know what I'm like. Maybe you don't know me at all.' Lucas prowled over to her, watching as she registered the threat in his tone. And because he was watching, because he was experienced, he sensed she was struggling not to step back.

'Don't intimidate me. I'm trying to help, Lucas.'

'And I don't want help. Not yours. Not anyone's.' *If nothing else would work, then this would.* Telling himself that he was doing her a favour, he flattened her back against the exposed brick of the wall. Her shallow breathing was the only sound in the room apart from the occasional crackle from the blazing fire. Next to them a window looked down at moonlit snow but his attention was on the soft curve of her mouth. Her hair smelled of flowers and wood smoke.

His body stirred, his response to her primitive, powerful and entirely inappropriate.

Her eyes were fixed on him, wide and shocked.

And he couldn't blame her for that. He was shocked too. Shocked by the concentrated rush of raw desire that ripped through him, shocked by the degree of control he had to exert over himself to prevent himself from doing what he was suddenly burning to do.

In a few brief seconds the nature of their relationship had shifted. Here, outside the glass walls of his office, the barrier had lowered.

Not boss and employee.

Man and woman.

He hadn't expected that. He certainly didn't want it. Not tonight and not with this woman.

It was the drink, he thought. Damn the drink, because he didn't want that barrier lowered. Not just because that was a line he never crossed with someone who worked for him, but because he knew that what he had to give wasn't what she would want.

Not trusting himself to be this close to her, he was about to step back when she pushed at his chest and escaped from his grasp. 'I'll leave you to sober up.'

She seemed as brisk and efficient as ever, but Lucas knew that she wasn't. He heard the shake in her voice and saw the way her hands clutched at her wet coat as if she were trying to hold herself together.

He'd unsettled her.

Maybe he'd even scared her a little.

And that had been his intention, hadn't it? He'd wanted her to walk away.

So why, in those few tense seconds as she stalked towards the door, did he find himself noticing things he hadn't noticed before? Like the fact that her hair was the same rich glossy brown as the wood panelling in the tower bedroom and that she was one of the only women he knew who was still capable of blushing.

He found himself wondering about Jamie, the man she was rushing home to.

All he knew about the guy was that she'd been with him for the whole time she'd worked for him. Two years. And that confirmed everything he already knew about her.

Emma believed in love.

And with that thought he reached for another bottle of champagne.

For the second time that evening, Emma stomped down the stairs into the main hallway. The only difference was that this time she was shaking. Her knees shook, her fingers shook. Even her stomach shook.

From the first day she'd taken the job, she'd tried not to think of Lucas Jackson as a man. He was her *boss*. Her employer. Someone who paid her salary. Of course she couldn't help but be aware of his appeal to women because she fielded his calls—and she fielded a *lot*— but somehow she'd managed to view his sex appeal in a detached way, a bit like admiring a valuable painting in a gallery that you knew you'd never be able to hang on your own wall.

And then suddenly, out of nowhere, had come this rush of sexual awareness that she absolutely didn't want to feel. She was happy with her life. Happy doing her job and going home to Jamie. She didn't want to jeopardize any of that. She couldn't *afford* to jeopardize any of that. Especially not for a rude, totally selfish human being like Lucas Jackson.

Sexy eyes, a great body and a brilliant mind didn't make up for serious deficiencies in his personality. He didn't care about anyone. And that, she told herself firmly, was not an attractive trait.

And she was well aware that the incident back in the cosy turret bedroom had been about control, not chemistry.

He'd been trying to unsettle her. Trying to get her to back off. Well, that was fine. She'd backed off, hadn't she?

But she wasn't leaving. There was no way she could leave another human being in that state.

Trying to forget the way he'd looked at her as he'd pinned her to the wall, Emma reached the bottom of the stairs and stared at the decorations, so tacky and out of place in the elegant hallway. Something about the surprise party had upset him. Or maybe he'd been upset before he'd arrived home. Whichever, it was the first time she'd ever seen him drunk.

Deciding that the decorations were presumably as unwelcome as the party, she set about removing them. As she liberated a streamer that had been twisted around the ornate frame of a painting, a memory came at her from nowhere.

It wasn't the first time she'd seen him drunk, was it? It was the second time. And the first time would have been—when? Trying to remember, she twisted the streamer between her fingers. There had been snow on the ground then too. It would have been around the same time of year as this.

Last year.

She'd worked late and assumed she was on her own in the building apart from Security, but when she'd walked into his office Lucas had been there, sprawled on the sofa with an empty bottle of whisky next to him.

He'd been asleep and she hadn't woken him.

Instead, she'd covered him with a blanket and checked on him a few times while she quietly got on with her work.

He probably didn't even know who had put the blanket there. Either way, neither of them had ever referred to it.

Reaching up, she removed the rest of the streamers and the balloons.

It had been exactly this week. It might even have been the same date. She remembered because it was the same time that she took her holiday every year.

She stood, holding a bouquet of unwanted festivity as she thought it through.

Was it a coincidence that he was drunk again? Yes, probably. It was a busy time and everyone was entitled to let their hair down from time to time. Even the ruthlessly focused Lucas.

Emma clenched her jaw and stabbed the balloons with her car keys until they popped. *It was none of her business.*

But what if it wasn't coincidence that he'd chosen to drink alone on the same night last year? What if it wasn't coincidence that a man who forgot nothing chose this night to forget important documents?

She gathered up the last of the streamers until the only remaining evidence of the unwanted party was the uncut cake and the empty glasses.

With a murmur of frustration, she glanced over her shoulder towards the stairs.

This was one of those situations where she couldn't win. If she left she'd worry and if she stayed she ran the risk of being shouted at again. Or worse.

Her cheeks heated. What if he thought she'd stayed for a different reason? She wasn't stupid enough to think he hadn't noticed the way she'd reacted to him earlier. Lucas

Jackson had far too much experience with women not to have noticed. Her only hope was that he was too drunk to remember. That, by morning, the single breathless moment when she'd forgotten to think of him as her boss would have been drowned out by other more important memories. And if he did happen to remember it, with luck he'd dismiss it as a figment of his imagination. A memory spun by alcohol, not reality. Her own behaviour would support that belief because at work she was always careful never, *ever* to stray into the realms of personal.

Looking out of the window, she saw that the snow was still falling.

She'd stay another half an hour, she decided. She'd check on him one more time, hopefully without him even noticing her, just as she'd done the last time. And then she'd leave him to his snowy solitude.

CHAPTER THREE

LUCAS stood under the shower while needles of icy water stung his skin. He was undoubtedly drunk but, instead of being numbed, his senses appeared heightened. He was having thoughts he absolutely should *not* be having and he blamed that on the champagne. Thank goodness Emma had walked out when she had, otherwise he might have been tempted to seek an entirely different form of oblivion.

He gave a growl of self-disgust.

Since when had he imagined his PA naked? Never. Not once. But suddenly he found himself tormented by thoughts of dark, shiny hair. He'd wanted to yank out that damn clip and let it tumble free. He'd wanted to sink his hands into it and drown in the softness. He'd wanted to twist it around his fingers and hold her captive while he drank from that soft, innocent mouth to see if she were the cure he'd been looking for.

And he shouldn't want any of those things.

Cursing softly, he leaned his shoulders against the cool tiles, closed his eyes and let the water slide over his head.

He shouldn't want to touch her hair and he definitely shouldn't be thinking about kissing that mouth. Emma worked for him and he wanted her to continue to work for him. And there was no cure for what he was feeling.

It had been a rocky road finding someone suitable to fill the role of his personal assistant—a role that required a multitude of skills. Before Emma he'd had a series of giggling girls for whom work was nothing more than a way to fund their social life. He'd had girls who were overawed by him, girls whose only reason for working late was the wistful hope that their relationship with him might turn into something more intimate. He'd had a male PA who had sadly struggled with the sheer volume of simultaneous projects he'd been expected to handle and an older woman who was a grandmother four times over, but she hadn't had the stamina to handle the heavy workload and had resigned after a month.

And then he'd discovered Emma. Emma, with her serious brown eyes and her astonishing ability to juggle any number of projects at the same time without complaint. Emma, who never worked with one eye on the clock and had an admirable way of soothing the most frayed of tempers. She was the ultimate professional and it was that dedication to her job, her understanding of the importance of attention to detail, that had brought her out here tonight.

She was a gem.

And he'd shouted at her. And worse, he'd scared her.

His head spinning, Lucas swore under his breath and wondered if he'd remember to send her flowers when he was sober. The irony was, he never sent a woman flowers. Emma did it for him. But he'd have to do *something* because the last thing he wanted was for her to resign.

Hopefully they would both be able to ignore that single moment when their view of each other had changed and re-establish the normal parameters of their relationship.

Switching off the shower, he grabbed a towel.

He dried himself briefly and then tried to tie the towel around his waist but his fingers were clumsy and un-coordinated so in the end he gave up and dropped the towel on the floor with a frustrated laugh directed to-wards himself. Too drunk to secure a towel, apparently, but not drunk enough to forget.

Never drunk enough to forget.

The pain was lodged under his ribs like shrapnel that couldn't be removed. Nothing eased the ache.

Surprised that he could still walk in a straight line, he returned to the bedroom and stopped dead because Emma was standing there.

For a moment he assumed that she was nothing more than a vivid image conjured by an intoxicating mixture of champagne, wishful thinking and inappropriate thoughts.

And then he heard a soft sound escape from her throat.

Her shocked eyes slid down his naked body and wid-ened.

'Oh my God—' With a gurgle of horror she slapped her hand over her eyes and turned her head away. 'Sorry! I'm so *sorry*. I… What are you doing walking around naked? I can't believe you just…and I…' She broke off, hideously embarrassed, and it was that embarrassment that penetrated his fuzzy brain.

Not an image, he thought. An image wouldn't turn scarlet and have her hands over her eyes.

And he didn't trust himself to move because suddenly all he wanted to do was give in to that most primitive part of himself, throw her down on the bed and explore a different way of getting through this one night. He wanted her to be the heat that melted the chill inside him. He wanted her warmth and all that was real about her. Instead of being surrounded by ghosts, he wanted human contact. Flesh and blood. *Emma.*

Hands clenched by his sides, he channelled all his power and strength into standing still. 'I thought you'd left.'

'No! I just went downstairs to tidy up and give you some space and—' Her hand still over her eyes, she snatched in a breath. 'Are you decent yet?'

'For God's sake, Emma, stop overreacting.' Tension made his voice rougher than he intended. 'You must have seen a naked man before.' *Jamie*, he thought bitterly. *She'd seen Jamie.*

'You're my boss—' her voice was muffled '—I don't think of you as a man. Or at least I didn't until… Please can you just get dressed or something? This is *not* good.'

In other circumstances he might have smiled at her confusion, but a smile was nowhere near his grasp. Instead he walked into the small anteroom he used as a dressing room and grabbed a robe. Any benefit derived from the cold shower had been instantly wiped out by the sight of her. Raw lust mixed uncomfortably with the knowledge that this was one woman he couldn't have.

He needed to switch it off. He *had* to switch it off.

However much he'd drunk, this was *not* going to happen. She was the last woman in the world he wanted to see as—well, as a woman.

Dragging his hand through his wet hair, he prowled back into the room. 'I presume you came back to tell me you're snowed in?'

'I have no idea if I'm snowed in. I haven't tried to leave.' Her hand was still over her eyes and Lucas sighed and knotted the cord around his robe firmly. Then he closed his hands over her wrists and tugged firmly at her hands. She kept her eyes screwed tightly shut. 'Really, I don't want to—'

'I'm decent.' At least on the outside. His thoughts were

far from decent but as long as she couldn't read minds, everything would be fine. Trying to ignore the warmth and softness of her skin against his palms, he let go of her wrists and stepped back for no other reason than the fact he knew he wasn't sober enough to make good decisions. *Distance*, he thought. *All he had to do was keep his distance.* 'If you're not snowed in, why are you still here? You left half an hour ago.'

'I told you, I was clearing up all those balloons and things. I assumed you didn't want them. And I was worried about you.' Cautiously, she half opened her eyes and when she saw the robe she relaxed and opened them properly. 'I was worried that you'd carry on drinking your way through all that champagne, fall face down in the fire and die a hideous death.'

'Worrying about your job again?'

'Of course.' Avoiding his gaze, she pushed strands of damp hair away from her face. 'And possibly my conscience. I want to be able to sleep at night.'

Distracted by all that lush, dark hair, Lucas found it hard to keep his mind focused. 'Maybe I'm more drunk than I think I am, but why would that be on your conscience?'

'Because I would have been the last person to see you alive.' Wrapping her arms around herself, she gave a little shrug and backed towards the staircase. 'But if you're sober enough to take a shower without drowning, I expect you're safe to be left so...I'll just go.'

He was used to her being brisk and confident in all things. He'd never seen her like this. 'Why aren't you looking at me?'

'Because I still haven't recovered from the shock of the last time I looked at you. Seeing your boss naked isn't something that happens every day of the week.' She was stammering and flustered. 'I may need therapy. And this time I really am going.' She felt for the handrail at the top of the spiral staircase, her gaze everywhere except on him even though his robe was firmly secured around his waist.

Her unsophisticated response simply fuelled his libido and he felt a rush of frustration because what he had to do was in direct conflict with what he wanted to do. 'You're not going anywhere, Emma.' He watched as her pale throat moved as she swallowed hard.

'Yes, I am. You're obviously fine to be left so—'

'When did you last look outside?'

The tension in the air built around them. It didn't help that the turret bedroom was designed for seduction with its huge four-poster bed, flickering fire and windows that gave a perfect view of the estate. The snow reflected the moon and sent a ghostly silver light over the wood and the lake, producing a view that was both ethereal and romantic.

The irony was that he never had seduced a woman here. With the exception of Tara's impromptu, unwanted visit earlier, no woman had ever visited him at Chigworth.

But Emma was here now, and she was clearly regretting her earlier decision to stay around.

'It will be fine,' she said firmly. 'I'm good in the snow. If I drive carefully I'll be able to get to the end of the road. The gritting lorries were already working on the motorway so I shouldn't have any trouble getting home once I get to the main roads.'

'And do you know how far it is to the main roads from here? Even if you make it out of the estate, which I doubt that you would, you have five miles of country roads that are always low on the priority list for whoever decides which part of our little island is gritted in bad weather.'

'Well, I'll give it a try anyway.'

'I may be drunk,' Lucas drawled, 'but I'm not so drunk that I can't recognise a truly bad idea when I see it. Call me selfish, but I don't want to spend the rest of tonight trying to locate your frozen corpse. Nor do I want to find myself recruiting a new PA. I can't stand the interview process.'

Her lips twitched as she tried to hold back a smile. 'It's all about you, isn't it?'

'Absolutely. I'm the most selfish bastard you'll ever meet, you know that.' *So don't look at me with those soft brown eyes. Don't show me that you care.*

But she'd already done that, hadn't she? The moment she'd discovered that he hadn't wanted a party, she'd set about quietly removing the evidence.

Hands clasped in front of her, she stared at the floor. 'I was stupid, wasn't I, coming here in the first place.'

'Not stupid, no.' Because he could barely keep his hands off her, Lucas strolled over to the fire and kept his back to her. 'You were dedicated. Professional. Which is no more than I would have expected from you. It's just unfortunate that you chose tonight.' He didn't state the obvious. That if it hadn't been for what this night did to his mind, he wouldn't have forgotten the damn file in the first place.

'Lucas—'

'This is what we're going to do.' Taking control, he turned, interrupting her before she could ask the question he knew she was going to ask. *The question about why exactly this night was so painful for him.* 'You are wet, cold and, presumably, very tired. I'm going down to the kitchen to make us some soup and while I do that you are going to have a hot bath or shower—whichever—and then help yourself to whatever clothes take your fancy from my dressing room. Nothing will fit, but you're a practical enough person to improvise, I'm sure. We'll hang yours up and they'll be dry in the morning.'

'Lucas, I can't—'

'I'm going to light a fire in one of the other bedrooms, then it will be warm once you're ready to sleep.' Without looking at her, he strode towards the staircase, keeping his hands to himself. 'There are plenty of warm towels in the bathroom. Help yourself.'

She should have argued, but one glance through the pretty arched window convinced her that he was right. In the half hour she'd spent clearing up downstairs, killing time until she could check on him again, it seemed as if half a ton of fresh snow had fallen. It glistened in the moonlight, a sparkly, silvery deathtrap. The decision whether or not to stay was out of her hands. She wasn't going to be going home any time soon. She was stuck here with a man who clearly didn't want her around when all she wanted was to be home with Jamie.

What she should have done was leave when it had been possible to do so, instead of putting him in a position where he had no choice but to offer her accommodation. And if there were other feelings sloshing around inside her, then she chose to ignore them, just as she was trying to ignore the recurring images of that one dangerous glimpse of him naked.

It was a shame he wasn't flabby, she thought gloomily. A seriously out of shape boss would have been so much easier to forget than a boss with rock-hard abs and—

Emma squeezed her eyes shut and reminded herself that a luscious body didn't maketh a man.

And there was no point in going back over what she could have done or should have done because she was stuck here now so she just had to make it work.

Resigned to the inevitable, she started by calling Jamie to tell him she wouldn't be home. It was a call she dreaded making and she breathed a sigh of relief when the phone went to voicemail.After she'd left a brief message explaining the facts and promising to call the next morning once she'd had a chance to check the weather and road conditions, she eased off her soaking-wet shoes and put them close to the fire to dry off.

Shivering now, she realised just how wet she was. Shrugging off her coat, she draped it over the back of the chair, checking it was far enough away from the fire to be safe from sparks. Then she walked towards the bathroom.

She was far too cold to argue with his suggestion that she have a hot bath. She needed to warm up and change into dry clothes.

Despite the age of the castle, the bathroom was the last word in luxury and Emma gave a moan of pleasure as she slid her freezing cold limbs into the warm, scented water. She never did this. She usually took a shower because it was faster. Everything in her life was dictated by speed and efficiency. Her life was such a crazy whirl that it was all about racing on to the next thing on her list, never about just enjoying a moment of self-indulgence. But she enjoyed it now, so tired after her week at work that she didn't dare allow herself to lie back and close her eyes for long in case she slept.

She could have stayed there for ever, but in the end stayed just long enough to thaw her frozen limbs. Then she let her hair down and lathered it clean, feeling the hot water stinging her scalp as she rinsed away the evidence of her fall in the snow.

It felt blissful to be clean and warm. Only the knowledge that if she didn't reappear he'd come looking for her was enough to eject her from the water. Grabbing two towels, Emma dried herself with one and then wrapped the other around her head. Then she popped her head round the door. Relieved that there was still no sign of him, she walked into his dressing room wondering what on earth she was likely to find to wear. A sweater would be fine, she thought. Or a shirt of some sort to sleep in. Anything, really, as long as it was decent.

Ignoring the rows of suits, she instead selected a white shirt. It would be much too big for her but she could just roll up the arms. Now all she needed was to find something to wear on her bottom half so that she didn't freeze to death or expose herself. Didn't the man own sweatpants or something? Pyjamas?

Deciding that everything on the rails was too formal, she instead focused on the drawers. Opening the top one, she found socks. Deciding that socks might be useful, she pulled out a pair and then opened the next drawer.

But Lucas Jackson didn't appear to own either pyjamas or anything suitably casual and she was just about to give up on the final drawer when her fingers brushed against something hard. Shifting aside the neatly folded T-shirt, she saw a photograph in an antique silver frame.

Wondering why a photograph would be buried in the bottom of a drawer, she picked it up. As she stared at the faces in the picture, she held her breath.

This photograph hadn't been buried by accident, she thought numbly. It hadn't tumbled there or been stowed away in a moment of de-cluttering. It had been hidden there intentionally by someone who couldn't bear to look at it, but equally couldn't bear to part with it. For some reason she didn't yet understand, that image represented pain.

'Emma?' Lucas's voice came from outside the bedroom and she jumped guiltily. Whether or not she would have replaced the photograph she didn't have a chance to find out because one minute she was alone with his secrets and the next he was standing in the doorway, witnessing her trespass into a private part of his life that he'd clearly labelled 'no admittance'.

His eyes flickered to the frame in her hands and the change in him was instantaneous. The colour literally drained from his face, the sudden pallor emphasising the dark shadows that lurked in his eyes. And she knew immediately that what she held in her hands held the clue to the source of those shadows. Across that narrow distance she *felt* his agony and she wanted to offer comfort but how could she when she didn't even know what she was offering comfort for? And how could she discuss something this personal with someone who didn't encourage personal? The nature of their relationship would be for ever shifted.

But it already was, she thought. Even if she said nothing, she knew now that Lucas *did* have a personal life. That he was so much more than the man she'd thought she knew.

And this was worse, far worse, than seeing him naked, she realised. This was more intimate. More intrusive. And he obviously thought so too because there was no sign now of the indifference with which he'd treated her unexpected appearance in his bedroom. No trace of amusement in those cold blue eyes. His unsmiling gaze travelled from the towel tied around her head to the towel wrapped around her body and Emma lifted her hand instinctively to the knot, even though she knew it was tied firm.

'I…I was just looking for something to wear. I didn't mean to pry.' Feeling the heat pour into her cheeks, she slid the photograph back where she'd found it. But it was too late, of course. The damage was done and it couldn't be undone. 'I'm sorry.' The words left her in a stumbled rush. 'I didn't know it was there. You told me to help myself to clothes and that was what I did, and…maybe I shouldn't have looked at it, but I didn't know it was significant until I looked and—' She broke off, waiting for him to speak, but he said nothing.

He was as cold and inhospitable as the snow and ice clinging to the trees outside, his emotions as frozen as the moat.

And Emma had no idea what she was supposed to do now. What to say. So in the end she just said the obvious thing. 'You have a daughter.' Her voice was barely audible. 'And she looks exactly like you.' And the moment she said it, she knew that the obvious thing had been the wrong thing.

The silence stretched for so long she was about to mumble an apology when he finally spoke.

'I *had* a daughter.' This time his tone wasn't harsh or angry. In fact it was oddly flat, as if all the emotion had drained out of him. 'She died, four years ago tonight, and it was my fault. She died because of me.'

CHAPTER FOUR

SHE'D found the photograph. The photograph he couldn't bear to look at.

Lucas stood by the window of the tower with his back to the room. His chest ached. He felt raw, as if his flesh had been ripped from his bones, every last layer of protection stripped from him.

He had no idea how to ease the pain.

He was a man who prided himself on his control and yet right now it was nowhere within his grasp. His hand curled into a fist and he pressed it against the wall and closed his eyes, trying to pull together the torn edges of his self-control.

From the dressing room he could hear a soft rustle as she dressed. He guessed she'd managed to find clothes but she was taking her time and it was all too easy to understand why. The expression on her face stayed with him, the impact of his raw confession a million times more shocking than the moment she'd seen him naked.

And in a way she had.

She'd seen a part of him he'd never shown to anyone else. A part of him he guarded fiercely. He had no issues with her having seen him without his clothes on. He had plenty with the fact she'd seen that photograph.

And he was willing to bet she was as appalled as he was.

It was ironic, he thought, that it had taken this to finally give him what he'd been hoping for. Solitude. Because he had no doubt that now she'd leave him alone. Given the choice of waiting out the weather in the warm bedroom downstairs or with him in his own private version of hell, he had no doubt which option she'd pick.

He was so sure that would be her choice that it was a shock to hear her soft tread on the wooden floor.

'So is this what you do every year?' Her soft voice brushed over his nerve endings. 'Shut yourself away and drink? Does that help you get through the night?'

Because he wanted her to leave, he didn't turn. 'Nothing helps.'

'No. I can imagine that it wouldn't.' He felt her sympathy and her compassion and rejected both because he knew he deserved neither.

'I appreciate your dedication in bringing the file here tonight, but your job is done, Emma.' He knew he sounded brutal but he didn't even care. 'Your responsibility doesn't extend to any other part of my life. The bedroom downstairs is warm and comfortable. I've left a tray of food there. Eat and then get some rest.'

'What about you? What will you do?'

What he always did. Put one foot in front of the other and keep on living even though others didn't. 'I'll be fine. Eat the food while it's hot.'

There was a brief pause. 'Instead of getting through it on your own, you could try another way.'

He didn't hear her move but suddenly her hand was on his shoulder. He stiffened his muscles against that gentle touch, surprised that she couldn't sense the violence in him. Or maybe she did and chose to ignore it. He knew she was no coward. If she were, she would have driven off the first time instead of coming back to check on him. 'You need to leave, Emma. Now.'

'If it's about finding ways to get through a hideous, horrible night then there has to be a better way than drinking. Or at least a way that won't have you waking up feeling even worse in the morning.'

'What better way?' He turned, slowly, the effort of fighting suddenly too much. His eyes found hers. She was wearing one of his white shirts and it fell to mid-thigh exposing a long, tempting length of leg. Part of him was clearly still functioning normally because he found himself wondering how he could possibly have missed the fact that Emma had fabulous legs and then realised that her office dress was always businesslike, never provocative. Intentional, perhaps, if this was what she was hiding under grey wool.

The inappropriateness of his thoughts almost made him laugh.

Was this really the only feeling of which he was capable? Surely it should be gratitude, or some other equally bland and harmless emotion. What he was feeling definitely wasn't harmless. It was raw, dangerous and powerful and it threatened to burn up anything or anyone standing in his path.

And she sensed it.

He saw the exact moment she read his mood. The expression in her brown eyes shifted from warmth to something different. Her certainty seemed to falter and her hand fell from his shoulder.

A cynical smile touched his mouth. 'Exactly.' He softened his voice in an attempt to snap the tension that was brewing in the air. 'You need to be more specific when suggesting alternatives or your generosity might be misconstrued. Especially when you're wearing nothing more than one of my shirts.'

'You date women who wear nothing but designer couture. You expect me to believe that seeing your PA in one of your own shirts is going to send your libido into the danger zone? I don't think so.' Her tone was light but it was the sort of lightness that took effort to produce and her cheeks were streaked with pink. 'You're not that desperate.'

'Maybe I am.' His voice thickened by emotion that had been simmering all day, Lucas slid his hand round the back of her head and forced her to look at him. 'Maybe I'm so desperate I don't care what I do tonight. Or who I do it with. And maybe that makes this the worst place you could be right now, Emma.' He could feel her pulse galloping under his fingers. Sensed that she was afraid to breathe in case she upset the delicate balance that existed between them. She was afraid she was going to tip him over the edge and he found himself incapable of reassuring her. He'd always thought of her as sturdy and robust but the thin silk of his shirt revealed slender, flowing lines and everything fragile.

And he wasn't to be trusted with fragile, was he?

He'd already proved that.

The thought was like a shower of cold water.

His hand dropped.

Disgust was a bitter taste in his mouth. Was he really so desperate that he'd risk hurting one of the few genuine people in his life? 'You should leave. Now. Go downstairs and lock your door.' He wondered why she couldn't sense the urgency. Or was it just that she had no sense of danger?

Either way, she didn't move. 'There's no way I'm leaving you like this.'

'You should have left hours ago when I told you to and then we wouldn't have found ourselves in this position.'

'I'm glad I didn't. You shouldn't be on your own to-night.'

'Because you're worried about your job?'

'No. Because I'm worried about *you*.'

'You just don't get it, do you?' The violence in him was so close to the surface that he could taste it. He stepped towards her, her subtle perfume sliding over his senses and disturbing the balance of his control. 'I *should* be on my own. It's the only way that works.' He expected her to step back but she didn't even flinch.

'It doesn't look as if it's working to me. Perhaps it's time you considered a different way. Perhaps, instead of alcohol and oblivion, you might try friendship and comfort.'

'Friendship?' The word chafed against his raw feelings. 'You think right now I have *friendship* on my mind?'

'No. I don't think that. I'm not stupid. But I think you are hurting so badly all you want to do is make it stop. You want a rest from the pain. And I made that pain worse by finding that photograph,' she said quietly, 'and I'm sorry for that.'

'You have no reason to be sorry. Now go.'

'No. We can find another way to do this.'

He shouldn't have been surprised by her stubbornness because she showed the same indomitable spirit at work. 'There is no "we" in this, Emma. And as for friendship—' it seemed imperative to smash her illusions about that '—I don't have friends. I have people who want something from me and people who work for me.' His harsh analysis didn't seem to surprise her. *Maybe she wasn't as naïve as he thought she was.*

'You only think like that because of the company you keep. But you shouldn't judge everyone based on the actions of Tara Flynn. She shouldn't have left you alone tonight. That was wrong of her.'

At another time he would have been amused that she thought Tara capable of the sort of care she was describing. 'Perhaps she was sensible. Perhaps she realised that it wasn't safe to stay'

The heat of the fire had dried her hair curly and it tumbled in thick, dark waves over the snowy white of his shirt, which was proving woefully inadequate as a cover-up. The flickering light from the fire shone through the thin fabric, clearly outlining the dips and curves of her body and suddenly it was becoming harder and harder to do the right thing and send her away.

'It's true that I work for you. But it's wrong to dismiss that relationship as a purely economic arrangement. I've worked closely with you for two years. I care.' She bit her lip. 'I was with you this time last year when you emptied a bottle of whisky and slept in your office, although I doubt you remember.'

It came back to him instantly. The blanket. She was the one responsible for the blanket. It was a question that had bugged him on and off over the past twelve months and now he had the answer.

Emma.

She hesitated and then held out her hand. 'Stop drinking, Lucas. You've tried that and it hasn't worked. We're going to find another way to get through tonight. And before you make another caustic comment involving all sorts of physical alternatives, I should point out that there are a million other options that aren't going to make it embarrassing to bump into each other in the morning.'

'What options?' His mind had been so full of those

physical alternatives that it took him a minute to focus on what she'd said.

She pursed her lips thoughtfully. 'We could play chess?'

'Chess?' Did she even realise that he could see through the shirt? No, presumably not or she wouldn't have been standing there so confidently.

'I'm a brilliant chess player.' Her fingers closed over his, soft and warm, her grip surprisingly firm.

Instead of removing his hand from hers as he should have done, Lucas found himself staring at her mouth. 'You don't want to challenge me to chess. It would end in tears.'

'*Your* tears, I presume.' A half smile tilted that mouth at the corners. 'There's no need to make excuses. If you're too scared to play, I understand. There's always Scrabble. But I should warn you that I know all the words in the Chambers dictionary containing Z and X and I'm a ruthless player. I will not hesitate to use a Q on a triple word score.'

Ruthless? He looked down at her sweet face and almost laughed. She wouldn't know ruthless if she passed it in the street. 'These are your best suggestions for distraction? Chess and Scrabble?'

'Unless you're up for an all-nighter, in which case I'm a whizz at Monopoly.'

'You think it's wise to play Monopoly with an architect?'

'Why not? If you're trying to scare me you won't succeed. If you were a building contractor, perhaps I'd be nervous of your capacity to build large hotels on your property, but an architect like yourself who is capable of nothing more impressive than pretty drawings—' she shrugged '—no challenge. So—which is it to be? Chess, Scrabble or Monopoly? Do you want to play?'

Yes, he wanted to play.

But none of the games she was suggesting. The game he wanted to play was far, far more dangerous. He wanted to play with fire. He wanted to kiss that mouth, strip off that shirt that barely covered her and seek oblivion in the most basic way known to man. And he wanted to do it again and again until his mind was wiped of everything except her. Until he forgot. Until the pain was drowned out by other sensations.

Why not? Nothing else had worked. Nothing else had helped.

And then he remembered that this was Emma.

And that she was absolutely and completely off-limits.

He forced himself to extract his hand from hers. 'I've never met anyone who could beat me at chess,' he said coldly, 'and I can't think of anything worse than property development with toy money. I put a bowl of soup in your room. If it isn't enough then help yourself to anything you find in the kitchen.' He turned his back to her and waited to hear the outraged tap tap of her footsteps retreating towards the stairs as she responded to his rude rejection.

Instead he felt her arms come round his waist. 'I don't know what happened,' she said hesitantly, 'but I know it couldn't have been your fault. I *know* that. She didn't die because of you.'

Something inside him snapped. 'You don't know anything.' His voice savage, he turned so violently that her hands dropped. 'You have no idea what you're talking about and you have to leave this alone. You have to leave *me* alone.' Somehow his head was close to hers, his stance so threatening that she should have instantly backed off but she didn't move.

'I won't leave you alone.'

'No? Then maybe this will change your mind. There is only one other form of distraction I'm willing to try. Are you willing to play that game, Emma?' Somehow his hands had buried themselves in her hair, the softness of it engulfing his fingers and flowing over his wrists. Without pause or hesitation he took her mouth, his kiss rough and demanding, hard against soft, bitter against sweet. He was driven not just by lust, but by desperation. By some deep, primitive need to try and drive out the agony that possessed him. He was drawn to her warmth, as if being close to her might somehow melt the thick layer of ice inside him. As if something in her might be able to heal that damaged part of him even though everything else had failed. He took greedily, selfishly, ruled by his feelings, by the pain, by the need to seek oblivion wherever it was offered. He could feel her shivering against him and he had no idea if she was cold or whether some other more complicated emotion was responsible for the tremors. His thinking wasn't clear enough to make sense of it. All he knew was that he wanted this and he wanted it right now and, unless she stopped him, he wasn't stopping.

His mouth still on hers, one hand still in her hair, he used his free hand to untie his robe. Still kissing her, he shrugged it off and when her arms came round his neck he scooped her off her feet and lowered her to the rug in front of the fire. Part of him, a small distant part that had virtually no voice in the madness that engulfed him, told him to slow down, to take his time, to think of her—but there was only him and the madness inside him. He didn't want to think of her. He didn't want to think of anything.

He wasn't interested in a slow seduction.

With hands that shook, he ripped the shirt from neck to hem, exposing her completely. Somewhere in the depths of the madness that streaked through him he heard her gasp but he blocked that out as he parted her thighs.

'Lucas—' She whispered his name and he lifted his head, his vision hazy as he tried to focus on her.

The warmth of the fire had given her cheeks a rosy glow, or perhaps she was embarrassed by the intimacy with which he touched her. Either way, her body offered up a sinuous, sensual invitation, an erotic escape from his own painful brand of reality. But even in forgetting, there was one thing he remembered, and that was to grope in his robe for the contraception that had never once been out of his reach for the past five years.

His mouth was hungry on hers and then he slid his hand down her sleek body, losing himself in her curves and her softness. His touch was bold and explicit, the sexual urge so shockingly powerful that it drove aside every other emotion and drowned out the ache. Part of him knew that he was taking this too fast, but she was like a drug. The more he consumed the better he felt and the better he felt the more he wanted. He was out of control and he knew it. He knew it as he spread her legs and heard her soft intake of breath. He knew it as he slid his hand under her and lifted her and he knew it as he thrust into her body, propelled by an almost desperate urgency that didn't allow him to hold back.

Heat engulfed him. A heat intensified a thousand times by the tightness of her body gripping his shaft. He felt every ripple of her body in the most intimate way possible. Never before had he experienced anything like it.

'God, Emma—' Her body clasped his and he wanted to pause, to make it last and prolong the moment, but he couldn't hold back. Physically he was stronger than her. Much stronger. And he used that strength as he surged deep. Through the heat that blurred his brain he heard her moan his name. Felt her fingers grip his back and heard the breath catch in her throat. Perhaps he should have slowed things, whispered soft words or gentle endearments but Lucas could no longer access soft or gentle. He was deaf and blind to everything except his own need. He felt slick silken muscle tightening around him and he gave into it, gave into the rhythm and the wildness, his performance driven by instinct, not technique. Everything about it was raw and primitive, each sure thrust of masculine possession designed for his own gratification. The bite of his hand on her soft skin held her where he wanted her. The scent of her made him dizzy and the softness of her skin drove him wild. He took greedily, he plundered all that she offered and more and, in that single moment, those few suspended seconds of sexual oblivion, he was aware of nothing but the pleasure of release. And as his body emptied, so did his brain. Emptied of everything except this woman.

It took a while for reality to return.

Lucas became aware first of the heat of the fire burning his skin, and finally of the warmth of the woman still wrapped around him. Not any woman, he thought.

Emma.

Emma, his PA. Sweet Emma who deserved so much more than a one-night stand with a selfish bastard like him.

Closing his eyes, he rolled away from her onto his

back feeling a rush of self-disgust, wondering what insanity had possessed him. More alcohol would have been a better option. At least then he would have woken in the light of day with no apologies owing. There would be a price, he thought. There was always a price for everything.

The only question was how high it would be this time.

Emma woke to find herself alone in the huge four-poster bed. The first fingers of cold winter daylight shone through the windows and all that remained of the fire in the hearth that had warmed their night of loving was a sprinkle of glowing embers.

It was morning, the dawn of another day, the agony and anguish of the night before nothing more than a cold memory.

But it wasn't all forgotten, was it?

Her body ached in ways that were new to her. She felt—

Emma rolled onto her back and stared up at the canopy of the four-poster bed.

Incredible. She felt incredible. And with that thought came guilt. It seemed thoroughly wrong that what felt like the best night of her life had been the worst night of his.

For him, it hadn't been special, had it? It hadn't really been about *her* at all, even though it had been her name he'd spoken in the heat of the moment. She wasn't foolish enough to pretend it had been personal. For him, it had been nothing more than a temporary escape. She'd offered distraction at a time when he'd needed it most, a woman who'd happened to be there when he was in trouble. She was his employee—

Emma's smile vanished and she felt a sudden rush of panic as reality bloomed.

Oh God, she'd slept with her boss. What had she been *thinking*?

Sleeping with the boss wasn't incredible, it was stupid. *Stupid, stupid, stupid.*

She, of all people, knew just how foolish that was. How could she have been so reckless? She was always professional. *Always.* She was always careful not to step over that line.

Emma shot out of bed on legs that shook and grabbed the clothes she'd left drying in front of the fire. Afraid that he might reappear at any moment she dressed in a flash, a surprising achievement considering that her hands were shaking as much as her legs. Switching on her phone, she saw that it was eight a.m. And she already had five missed calls from Jamie.

Oh God, *Jamie.*

It was like a thump in her stomach. The warm glow that had surrounded her when she'd woken had vanished and all that was left was cold panic.

What had she done? From the moment she'd put her hand on Lucas's shoulder, she hadn't given her life a single thought. It had all been about the moment, not about what would happen afterwards. With a groan of remorse, she sank onto the edge of the bed.

'This looks like a serious case of morning-after regret to me.' A dark male drawl came from the doorway and Emma gave a start because she'd been hoping for some time to pull herself together before having to face him and now there was no hope of that.

This was a scenario she'd never had to handle before and she was clueless.

She looked at him and felt her stomach drop. He was

insanely attractive. Not just good-looking, but truly gorgeous in a deliciously sexy, bad boy sort of way, with those strands of dark hair flopping over his forehead and his jaw unshaven. Was it wrong to wish he hadn't decided to leave the bed before she woke? Wrong to wish they'd woken together?

Sex with him had been unforgettable.

And that was the problem.

He was her boss. She *had* to forget it. She had to ignore that tiny, ridiculous part of her that just wanted to resign on the spot and see if this thing between them could go somewhere. She had to ignore that part of her that wanted to forget the professional so that they could pursue the personal. That would have been crazy and impulsive and she was neither of those things. She had responsibilities. Commitments. She always made sensible decisions and the sensible decision was to lock last night away in her brain and forget it had ever happened. She had to forget everything personal that she knew about him.

The question was—*how?*

She wondered if he was asking himself the same question but one glance at his face told her that he wasn't. There was no doubt or uncertainty there. Nothing that suggested that what they'd shared had meant anything to him but a way of getting through a bad time. There was no evidence now of the unspeakable agony she'd witnessed the night before. Whatever dark, savage emotions had gripped him in the bitter cold of the night had been chased away by the morning light. Lucas Jackson was back in control, those secrets buried deep under layers of self-discipline.

She, however, felt emotionally and physically wrecked.

He was already dressed, in black jeans and a black

sweater that added emphasis to powerful shoulders. His choice of clothes was casual, and yet there was still an innate sophistication about him, an effortless style that was evident in everything he did.

Through her moment of panic came the memories. Memories of how those shoulders had felt under her fingers, the ripple of male muscle and hard strength. Memories of how it had felt to touch him and be touched. Strange, she thought, how even that unscheduled glimpse of vulnerability hadn't seemed like weakness. There was nothing weak about this man.

They hadn't even talked about it, she realised. Not really. All she knew was that he blamed himself for the death of his daughter. Other than that she had no details and, judging from the grim set of his mouth, he had no intention of offering any.

This was the man she knew. The Lucas Jackson she recognised. And of course that made it worse, because *this* man was her boss.

Which really only left her with one course of action.

Emma stood up slowly, as if by taking her time a miracle might happen and she might somehow know what to say. And he was obviously waiting for her to speak. That intense blue gaze, always more perceptive than most people's, held hers for longer than was comfortable. And although it seemed shallow to care about such things, she was acutely conscious of how appalling she must look. She had that exhausted, gritty-eyed feeling that followed a night of seriously reduced sleep so she knew she'd be pale. And she knew she'd look rumpled because, although she'd pulled on clothes, she hadn't had time to do more than smooth her hair and after the way he'd treated it the night before it tumbled in a wild mess over her shoulders.

As awkward moments went, this one reigned supreme.

'Hi. Good morning—' Oh God, this was *awful*. She cleared her throat, thinking that it was impossible to sound businesslike when faced with a man who had intimate knowledge of every part of your body. 'I just need to make a quick phone call and then I'll be out of your way.'

The last thing she wanted was to talk about what had happened, so she was relieved when he said nothing. Instead, he continued to study her as if he were seeking an answer to something. And Emma soon discovered that his scrutiny was every bit as uncomfortable as any conversation would have been. The way he was looking at her unsettled her so badly that in the end she turned away and rescued her shoes from their place in front of the fire. The snow had made a mess of them, but at least they were dry and putting them on gave her something to do and made her feel more *dressed*, somehow.

Wanting to escape as fast as possible, knowing that she was already going to be in trouble, she dug her hand in her bag and pulled out her phone. 'I need to call Jamie,' she muttered, 'and tell him I'll be back later. He'll be worried that I didn't make it home last night. He's already called this morning but my phone was off.'

'Are you sure he'll be worried? You're that close, are you?' His hard tone held a hint of scepticism and she looked up, shocked and confused by the question.

Was this just about the fact he was annoyed with her for staying when he'd wanted to be alone? Was he cross that he'd woken to find that someone was the wrong side of his castle moat?

'Of course. I did tell him I'd be late but he wasn't expecting me to not make it home at all.'

Those blue eyes didn't shift from her face. 'And how is he going to feel when he finds out you had sex with me?' His blunt question was so unexpected she gave a soft gasp.

'Well, obviously I won't be mentioning that part.'

One dark eyebrow lifted and the faintest of smiles touched his hard mouth. That same mouth that had kissed her to oblivion the night before. *The same mouth that had caressed its way down her shivering, compliant body.* 'If that's your plan then you'd better learn not to blush or he'll see right through you.'

Suddenly she was angry with him. And yes, with herself. It was embarrassingly unsophisticated to have a morning-after encounter with a face the shade of a tomato, especially when he seemed to be treating the whole episode with something that came close to indifference. No romantic words then, she thought numbly. No soft smiles or gentle touches to smooth the transition from passionate to professional. And maybe she should be grateful for that, Emma thought, as she strived to match his detached approach. She would have liked to look calm and businesslike and sail out of his life with her dignity intact but she knew there was very little chance of that. 'Jamie doesn't think the way you do.'

'No?' His expression revealed nothing of his thoughts. 'What if you're wrong? What if he guesses?'

'Why would he guess? It's not exactly the sort of thing we talk about.'

'And yet you claim to be close?'

'We're close but I'm hardly going to tell him I slept with you, am I?'

'I'm no expert on relationships, but I can imagine that would make things pretty awkward.' His tone was scrupulously polite, as if they were in the office discussing a project. 'And if that's the way you want to play it, that's fine with me. But I do have one question before we turn to more practical matters.'

Practical matters? 'What question?'

There was silence, and that silence stretched from seconds to a full minute. A full minute that she counted out with each beat of her heart. And not once in that time did he stop looking at her. Not once did his gaze flicker from hers.

When he finally broke that silence, his voice was soft. 'If your relationship with Jamie is "close",' he drawled, 'why did you have sex with me?'

CHAPTER FIVE

HE WATCHED as the colour deepened in her cheeks. On one level she fascinated him because everything about her was fresh and unexpected. Or perhaps it was just that he was jaded and cynical. Too jaded and cynical for someone like her. If circumstances had been different then perhaps, just perhaps, the conversation they were about to have would also have been different. But he couldn't change the way he felt. Or rather, the way he didn't feel.

If he hadn't already regretted the madness that had driven him to take what she'd offered in the dark of the night then he regretted it now because it was all too easy to guess how she was feeling. It was written all over her face.

For her, it hadn't been about living in the moment. It had been significant. And if there was one thing he didn't look for in a relationship, it was significance. He was quite possibly the worst man she could have found herself trapped with in a snowstorm. And perhaps she knew that because right now she wasn't looking at him. All he could see was her profile. The curve of her cheeks, slightly pinker than usual, the swoop of those dark eyelashes as she focused her gaze on the snowy landscape that isolated them as effectively as any moat.

It was up to him to unravel the mess.

'Emma?' He kept his voice neutral, knowing that the way he played the next few minutes was crucial. He didn't want her to misinterpret what had happened between them. He didn't want her yearning for something that wasn't going to happen. Most of all he didn't want her ending her relationship over it, even if that relationship seemed pathetically lacking to him. 'Emma?' He repeated her name more firmly and this time she turned, her expression confused.

'I don't really understand your question.'

Which left him with no choice but to take over both sides of the conversation. 'Jamie. You've been with him for two years so it must be serious.'

She was eyeing him as if he were an alien. 'I think there's been a bit of a misunderstanding,' she said slowly and Lucas frowned because he knew there was no 'misunderstanding'.

He was plain-speaking to the point of blunt and he saw no reason to modify that trait now. Determined to extract the truth, he took her face in his hands, feeling the soft skin of her cheeks against his rough palms, noticing for the first time the flecks of green in her brown eyes.

'He's obviously someone who means a lot to you if you've been together for two years.' He heard the cynicism in his own voice and thought bitterly that he had to stop judging other people's relationships. What did he know about sustaining a long-term partnership? About as much as he knew about love. Which was precious little. His hands dropped to his sides.

Someone like him shouldn't be touching her. He shouldn't have touched her the night before and he shouldn't be touching her now.

It was wrong on every level.

She was looking at him steadily. 'I've been with him

longer than two years. Jamie and I have been together for nine years. Which is basically the whole time he's been alive. Jamie is my little brother. His current obsession is Star Wars Lego.'

It took a moment for those words to sink in.

Brother? *Brother?*

'Lucas?' She was still watching him. Carefully, as if his every reaction was a mystery to her. 'I don't know where you got the idea Jamie was my—I don't know—significant other. You were the one who mentioned him earlier, so I assumed you knew who he was. It didn't occur to me that I needed to explain.'

'I heard you on the phone to him and—' Lucas breathed deeply and dragged his hand over the back of his neck as he confronted the depth of his error. 'Your *brother*?'

'Yes.'

'How can you have a brother who is nine years old?'

There was a hint of humour in her eyes. 'I think you can probably work that out for yourself.'

'But you're—'

'Twenty-four. And he's a lot younger than me. Welcome to the world of complicated families.' She shrugged. 'Jamie lives with my sister and me. Or rather, he lives with my sister and I join them at weekends and holidays.'

'But you live in London.'

'During the week. On Friday nights I drive to them and take over so that Angie—that's my sister—can have some time to herself. We're sort of sharing the parenting. I suppose you could say I'm the main breadwinner.'

And with that simple statement it all fell into place.

Suddenly he understood her rule that she wouldn't work on a Friday and never at a weekend. He realised how much he'd assumed and just how wrong he'd been.

'I thought you kept your weekends free because you were having a wild social life.'

'You must be confusing me with Tara,' she said lightly. 'I'm a normal person, with a normal person's life. A life that I happen to like very much. But I confess it isn't full of parties. It's a pretty routine existence.'

Lucas was stunned. 'Caring for your little brother isn't exactly a routine existence. It's an enormous sacrifice on your part.'

Her gaze cooled. 'It's not a sacrifice at all. I consider myself very lucky to have such a lovely family. I just wish we could live in the same place all the time. It's pretty lonely for me during the week stuck in London by myself.'

'I've offended you and I apologise; it's just that I thought—' He broke off, reminding himself that his own thoughts were irrelevant. His life experience was irrelevant too. He came from a background where family ties were seen as something to be cut with a sharp blade. 'Never mind what I thought. So if you're lonely, why can't you live in the same place as them? Why London? Enlighten me.'

'We can't afford a big enough place in London, and I can't afford to work out of London because the pay isn't good enough, so this is our compromise.' She tucked a strand of hair behind her ear. 'Angie is a teaching assistant, which means she can be there for after-school care and holidays when I'm not around. It works well. Or at least, it did.'

'You mean until you got snowed in because your selfish boss kept you late at the office.'

'That wasn't really what I meant, no. Lately it's been—' She broke off and smiled. 'Never mind. None of that is relevant.'

Lucas cursed softly and paced back to the fireplace. 'Why the hell didn't you tell me? I had no idea you had responsibility for your brother. I'm not such a monster that I would have kept you that late in the office every night if you'd explained.'

'There was nothing to explain. You pay me to do a job, and you pay me well. You have a right to expect the job done well. And I don't need to leave early during the week. I rent a room in an area of south London that couldn't exactly be described as a hub of activity. There's not a lot to go back to and anyway, I love my job.'

He dimly remembered her saying that to him the night before. 'Where exactly do you live?'

When she told him, Lucas didn't even bother trying to hide how appalled he was. 'If I'd known that I never would have let you work until two in the morning.'

'You always arranged for me to have a lift home so it was never a problem.'

'You still had to walk from the car to your house.' And the thought of her doing that horrified him. She could have been mugged. Or worse.

'You're overreacting. More often than not the driver would wait until I put my key in the door, but honestly, Lucas, I was fine.'

He looked at her cheeks, pale as chalk, and knew she wasn't fine now.

And not because of some random mugger who had attacked her in the street, but because of him. And he was about to make it a thousand times worse. He wasn't about to offer up soft words and promises of happy ever afters. He wasn't about to give her anything except a major dollop of pain.

What they'd shared was the sexual equivalent of a hit-and-run.

'We have to talk about last night.' His voice was rougher than he intended and she looked as uncomfortable as if he'd just suggested she strip naked and pose for him.

And she'd already done that.

He had a vivid image of her body, creamy skin warmed by the firelight, her curves both a sensual invitation and a balm to a man seeking oblivion.

He no longer had to wonder what she looked like under her ultra conservative clothing. He knew. *And he had to wipe it from his mind.*

'Honestly, I'd rather not.' Her hands were clasped in front of her, her knuckles white. 'Just tell me whether you want me to hand write the letter now or type it up and email it to you.'

Lucas dragged his mind away from thoughts that could only be described as shocking. 'What letter?'

'My letter of resignation. Or I suppose you could lend me a computer and I can just type it here if you like.'

'Resignation?' It was the last thing he'd expected her to say. 'What are you talking about? Why would you resign?'

'Er…because that's the only option?'

'Well, it's not an option that works for me,' Lucas thundered, the sudden rush of anger surprising him almost as much as her unexpected proposal. His emotions were all over the place and that shocked him too because he wasn't used to having to struggle for control. Usually it wasn't concealing emotion that was his problem, it was expressing it. 'I don't know why you would even suggest it when you've just spent five minutes telling me how much you love your job and how much you need the money. You're not resigning and that's final.'

Her eyes widened. 'That's my decision.'

'Well, you're making the decision for the wrong reasons so I'm not accepting it.'

'You honestly think we can still work together after last night?'

'Yes. Because last night was a one-off and is never going to happen again.' He knew from experience that it was better to spell it out but if he'd expected her to wilt then again she surprised him.

'I know that. But knowing that doesn't make it any easier to work together. It would be horribly, hideously awkward. It's already horribly, hideously awkward and since you obviously prefer to be blunt about the whole thing, I'll be blunt too. I cannot believe I had sex with my boss. I cannot believe I was so unprofessional.' She fiddled with the edge of her sweater and then turned away from him but Lucas wasn't having that.

'Why are you blaming yourself?' He closed his hands around her shoulders and spun her round to face him, forcing her to look at him. 'What happened last night was my responsibility, not yours.'

'That isn't true. You didn't know what you were doing.' She looked pale and tired and suddenly he remembered the nightmare drive she'd had to reach him the night before. That alone must have been exhausting. And then there had been everything that had happened afterwards.

He gave a humourless laugh. 'Emma, I knew *exactly* what I was doing.' *Escaping*. Taking ruthless advantage of a decent young woman who ordinarily wouldn't have found herself anywhere near a man as damaged as him.

'It *was* my fault. You were out of your mind with grief,' she said softly. 'I handled it badly.'

'No, you didn't.'

'You told me to go away. Over and over again you told

me to go. And did I listen? No, of course not.' Her tone
was loaded with self-recrimination. 'It was so arrogant
of me to think I could help. Stupid. There was nothing
that could have helped, I see that now.'

'You did help.' And that had come as a surprise. For
those moments in front of the flickering fire, the pain
had eased. But at what cost? Guilt gnawed at him. 'I owe
you an apology.'

'For what?'

'I used you.' His brutal honesty made her flinch.

'That isn't the way I see it.'

'Well, it's the way it was.' He refused to gild the truth
and when she tried to pull away he tightened his grip,
refusing to let her duck the subject. With that in mind
he asked the question that had been playing on his mind
since waking. 'I was rough. Did I hurt you?'

'No! You were amazing. The whole thing was incredible. To be wanted like that and—oh God, I can't believe
I just said that—' She covered her face with her hands,
her moan muffled. 'Please, just shoot me right now. Shoot
me and end this. This has to be the single most embarrassing moment of my life. Please—if you're a nice man
you'll accept my resignation and then I'll never have to
face you again.'

There was something so hopelessly endearing about
her that had the situation not been so serious, he would
have smiled. 'I'm not a nice man and you'll be facing me
on a daily basis, so you might as well get used to it.' He
tugged her hands away from her face. 'And because I'm
not a nice man I'm going to embarrass you even more by
asking when you last had sex with someone.'

'That is *such* a personal question—' And then she
caught the ironic lift of his eyebrow and turned vivid

scarlet. 'You're thinking that we've already made this personal—'

'Just a little.' He made a concerted effort to delete thoughts of the way her lithe, naked body had felt under his. 'So when?'

'I don't know. It's been a while.'

Which confirmed all his worst fears. 'Why?'

'Meeting people isn't as easy as it looks in the movies. During the week I only meet people at work and I don't want to have a relationship with someone I work with—' she caught his eye and turned fiery red '—and before I took the job with you…well, there *was* someone actually,' she admitted reluctantly, 'but it didn't work out and that's probably a good thing because although I thought I was in love with him, it turned out I wasn't.'

Love.

Hearing the word was enough to make him release her but she looked so miserable that he felt the need to lighten the atmosphere. 'So let me guess—you met this loser at school and when he fumbled under your skirt you hit him with your pencil case and after that he could never father children.' He was rewarded by a gurgle of laughter.

'Close.'

'It was a school bag and not a pencil case?' Tara would have been bitching about how tired she was, he thought. He would have been treated to sulks and moods, not a sweet smile. And never in a million years would Tara have let him see her without make-up.

'It was a little more mundane than that. And it wasn't at school. I didn't have time for boys when I was at school.' Avoiding his gaze, she turned back to the window, staring down at the acres of parkland and woodland that wrapped itself around the castle. 'I was fourteen when Mum got pregnant. When other girls were discovering make-up and dating, I was helping with a baby.'

'Why? Where was your mother?'

'She died.' Slowly, she turned her head, her eyes uncertain as she looked at him. 'This is way too much information. Do you honestly want to hear it?'

'Yes.' Lucas surprised himself by saying that. 'All of it.'

She gestured awkwardly. 'It's just that we don't normally do the whole personal conversation thing—'

'Well, we're doing it now. I think we've already overstepped what might be considered personal boundaries and we've definitely passed the point of worrying about what we normally do,' he said dryly, 'so just talk. I want to know what happened.'

She paused. 'Mum found out that she was pregnant, and it was…difficult. For all of us. She was a single parent. My dad left when I was a baby so it was just her and us. And then Jamie.'

'So Jamie's dad isn't your father?' *Relationships*, he thought. *Always complicated.*

'No. And Jamie's father…well, he wasn't around either.' She didn't look at him. 'And then, neither was my mum. Five days after the birth she had a pulmonary embolism—a blood clot that lodged in her lung. Something to do with the birth and the hospital missed it.' She leaned her forehead against the window and stared down at the snow. 'She died when Jamie was just days old. And that was really…hard.' That single word encapsulated so much unspoken emotion.

He tried to imagine how that must have felt—to be fifteen and rushing home to care for a baby at a time when she was still a child herself. 'How the hell did you manage?'

'My grandparents moved in with us for a few years, and that was the worst time of all. When they first found out Mum was pregnant, they were horrified and they said so. Truthfully, they were vile to her.' Her composure slipped slightly, exposing a seam of anger. 'Then when she died they couldn't separate how they felt from the way they reacted to Jamie. They saw Jamie as the reason she was dead and it was just horrible. It was obvious that they just saw him as a mistake and a burden. That's why I snapped at you just now. That was exactly the word they used. "Sacrifice". They told us that Mum had ruined everyone's lives and if we kept Jamie we'd be throwing our lives away. They wanted us to put him up for adoption. They didn't want him—their own flesh and blood. Can you believe that?'

Lucas felt the ache in his temples. The pressure.

Yes, he could believe that.

'But you refused.'

'It was a hideous time. My sister and I decided to consult a lawyer and after a long, complicated battle which I don't intend to bore you with, we were given custody.'

'Long and complicated?' Another understatement, he thought, oddly disturbed by the thought of two teenage girls taking on the world in order to keep their baby brother with them.

'We had to show we were able to care for him. Fortunately there was money from Mum's life insurance. My sister gave up her plans to go to college and instead became a teaching assistant at a school with a crèche.'

'And your grandparents?'

She rubbed her forehead with her fingers, her expression resigned. 'Let's just say it's a tense relationship. For Jamie's sake we wanted it to work out but life doesn't always happen the way you want it to.'

And didn't he know it. 'I had no idea you had such a complicated history. You never mentioned it.'

'Why would I mention it? My private life isn't exactly relevant to the practise of architecture.'

'And no doubt you're about to tell me that this man you met, who was probably the love of your life, dumped you because you had a baby to care for?'

'Actually *I* dumped *him*. He was putting so much pressure on me to lead my own life and didn't seem able to understand Jamie *is* my life. Not my whole life, obviously, but a huge part of it. As for Edward being the love of my life—' She broke off and shrugged. 'For a while I thought he was, but I was wrong. I could never love someone who had such a casual attitude towards responsibility.'

'What about since then? Are you telling me you haven't dated?'

'As I said, the only place I meet people is at work and I'd never date anyone from work.' Her smile was a rueful acknowledgement of the contradiction offered by their current position. 'Which leads me neatly back to the place we started. Lucas, you have to accept my resignation.'

'No.' He heard the ice in his own voice. 'That is not going to happen. And I can't believe you'd even suggest it.'

'We are not going to be able to work together after this.'

'Yes, we are.'

'I am not going to be able to face you on a Monday morning knowing that we…that you…you're my *boss*!'

'It was just one night, Emma. Just one night.'

'You don't have to repeat yourself. Nor do you have to panic. I don't want a relationship any more than you do.'

The fact that she read him so well should have reassured him, but it didn't. 'If you don't want a relationship then I don't understand the problem. We carry on as before. Nothing has changed.'

'Except that I've seen you naked and you've seen me naked. I just think that working with you is going to be *so* embarrassing.' Pink-faced, she wrapped her arms around herself and he found himself watching every movement she made, aware of her in a way he'd never been before. He'd worked with her for two years but he'd never really seen her.

Or maybe he hadn't allowed himself to see her.

'Then get over it. And get over it fast because I'm afraid I'm going to ask something more of you. I want you to delay the start of your holiday until at least Tuesday.'

'What?' Appalled, she stared at him. 'No way! You can't do that. I promised Jamie I'd be home. This is my holiday.'

'You can still have your holiday, it will just start a few days later.'

'But why? It's not as if you need me. You're not even in the office for the next week or so. You're in Zubran.'

'I need you with me.' He'd made the decision when he'd woken and realised what lay ahead of him. And that had been another decision that hadn't been easy to make. For personal reasons, it would have been best to send her away. For professional reasons, he needed her there.

Her mouth fell open in shock. 'You want me to go with you to *Zubran*? The desert?'

'Desert and coast. Palm trees. Sand. *Sun.* All those rare things you are unlikely to find here in a typical British winter. Or a typical British summer if it comes to that. No more shivering. Just for a couple of days.' He hadn't expected her to argue because Emma never ar-

gued with him. Usually she anticipated what he needed
and provided it with smooth efficiency. 'And although
you'll be working for most of the time, there should also
be some downtime when you can chill by the pool.' *But
not with me.* 'And do some reading or something. While
I work.'

'Would you mind not emphasising the whole "one-
off" thing all the time. I get it, OK? You don't have to
attach a caveat to everything you say. It's very demean-
ing. As if you think I've suddenly turned into a creepy
stalker.'

'I was just trying to tell you that as well as work, you
should be able to have some time for relaxation.' Even
as he said it, he wondered if she even knew the meaning
of the word. It sounded as if her life had been one long
slog since her early teens. 'The meeting is tomorrow and
the launch party is on Sunday night. In between I have to
fit in media interviews. I want you to coordinate those.'

'I know about the meeting. That's why I drove here
with those papers that need your signature. And I know
about the party—I've been talking to Avery Scott about
nothing but that party for the past six months. I can re-
cite the guest list. I can itemize the menu.'

'Which is precisely why I need you there.'

'You want me at the *party*?' She looked puzzled and
then surprised. 'I assumed you meant that you wanted
me to deal with the media and attend the meeting.'

'That too. I had an email from the Ferrara Group this
morning. They want to talk about another possible development on Sicily. They've found a piece of land that
interests them in a different part of the island and want
to talk through ideas.'

'Yes, I get all that—' her head throbbed at the thought

of yet more work '—but why would you want me at the party? It's a social event.'

'It isn't a social event for me; it's an opportunity to showcase our work, talk to prospective clients and answer questions about the hotel structure and design. Attending alone isn't an option.'

'You were taking Tara.'

'Tara and I are finished.'

'Oh—I'm sorry.'

And that, he thought, encapsulated the difference between them because he wasn't sorry. He wasn't sorry at all. He ended relationships frequently and not once had he cared enough to be sorry.

But judging from her expression she was sorry enough for both of them, concern evident in her gaze. 'Were you in love with her?'

'No.' He didn't soften his answer. 'And she wasn't in love with me. I pick women who aren't interested in love because that is something I can't offer.'

'Presumably you must have liked *something* about her, but I must admit you don't look broken-hearted.'

'I don't have a heart, Emma. I'm sure you've heard that about me.'

'You're doing it again—delivering warnings, as if I need to be constantly reminded that last night was just one night. I'm going to have a T-shirt printed "I know it was just one night". That would cause a stir in the office.' She smiled and that smile made him catch his breath. Once again he was reminded that, although she looked delicate, she was never anything but robust.

'I apologise,' he murmured. 'I won't mention it again.'

'Good, because I can assure you that I don't want this to be more than one night any more than you do. I just want to get back to how things were before. I was just checking that you weren't upset about the whole Tara thing.'

'I'm not upset.' Nor was he used to people caring whether he was upset. He didn't tell her about the text he'd received from Tara, apologising, begging him to take her to the party. He didn't tell her that after last night he wouldn't have taken Tara if she were the last woman on earth. He didn't tell her that in all the relationships he'd had, he'd never once been upset when they'd ended.

He didn't tell her that there was something missing in him.

'She'll be disappointed not to have the opportunity to talk to all those famous people.' In that one simple sentence she summed up Tara's driving ambition. 'But I still don't see why you need me. We both know that in a room of glamorous women you'll be alone for all of five seconds.'

'I won't be alone. You'll be there.'

She shot him a look. 'Please don't ask me to do this. Not just because of the whole sex thing, but because my family is expecting me home. Angie has plans for tonight and Jamie needs me.'

'I need you.' It didn't occur to him to compromise because when it came to work he never did. He did what was best for the business. 'You drove here through a snowstorm last night to deliver me the papers I need so don't tell me you don't care about things being done well, because I know you do. It's the reason you're still working for me after two years.'

'So you're willing to take advantage of my work ethic? That isn't fair. Jamie has his school nativity play on Wednesday. Nothing is going to stop me going.'

'Fine. I'll fly you home on Monday in the jet, but

you'll be exhausted because the party won't finish until the early hours.'

'Have you considered that this might backfire on you? The only party I've been to in the last few years is when our neighbours invite us in for drinks on Christmas Eve. To even call it a party is probably being over-generous. I'm not really a party person.'

'That doesn't matter.'

'*I will embarrass you!* I can look nice, but not glamorous.'

He thought about the way she'd looked lying on the rug, her hair gleaming in the red glow from the fire, and knew she was wrong, but he didn't want to say that to her because he knew he shouldn't even be thinking it. 'I'm not asking you to dance or win a fashion contest, I'm asking you to stand by my side as another representative of Jackson and Partners. It's networking. For me the party is as much business as the meeting scheduled to take place before it. You talk to many of these people on a daily basis. People speak to you before they speak to me. It's good for you to put faces to names and good for other people to know you. For many people you're their first contact with my company.'

Torn by conflicting responsibilities, she gave him an exasperated look. 'I can't believe you're asking me to do this. It's unreasonable.'

Lucas didn't relent. He told himself that if she was angry towards him that was good. Hopefully that anger would supplant other, far more dangerous, feelings and the truth was he did need her there. 'I've never claimed to be reasonable.'

'You're supposed to be embarrassed. You're ruthless, self-centred and uncaring.'

'Yes.' He didn't waste time apologising for it, nor did

he tell her anything about the events that had made him that way.

She sighed. 'I don't know anything about Zubran. I can barely put it on a map.'

'What do you want to know? It's a Sultanate. A peaceful, progressive country, mostly due to the influence of the Crown Prince. Mal is super-bright and very charismatic. Women love him and so will you, so you can relax.'

'Mal?'

'Short for Malik.'

'You're on intimate terms with a Crown Prince?'

'We were at college together. He'll be at the party, but you already know that because you've seen the guest list.'

'All the more reason why I'm the wrong person to take! I don't know any of these people and I will have no idea what to say to them. Please tell me he has a really friendly wife.'

'Not yet, and that is a very sore subject so I advise you not to mention it.'

'Why is it a sore subject? He's divorced? He wants a wife and he can't find someone to marry him?'

'He's rich, so it goes without saying that there are plenty of contenders. There was someone, but—' Lucas broke off, knowing that there was no one less qualified to comment on relationships than him. 'Never mind. Let's just say that for Mal duty comes before personal choice. It comes with the territory, I believe.'

'So he won't marry for love?' Her innocent question would have made him smile had the circumstances been different.

'No. Which will probably ensure the success of the union.'

She tilted her head as she studied him. 'When I get my

T-shirt made, I'm getting you a matching one that says "Don't tell me you love me" on it. I can tell you now that I won't be any use at this party, not just because I'm not glamorous but because I know nothing about the politics of Zubran. What if I say the wrong thing?'

Every other woman he knew would have died before admitting to feeling out of their depth socially.

'You won't say the wrong thing. And if you do—' he shrugged, fighting the desire to take her straight back to bed and lose himself again in her soft warmth '—I know him well enough to have you bailed from a jail cell.'

Her shoulders slumped in a gesture of defeat. 'I'll have to call my sister.' Her expression suggested that wasn't something she relished. 'Angie has Jamie all week and she relies on me at weekends so that she can go out. She'll be really annoyed if I tell her I can't make it.'

'And yet you're the one who slogs all week to provide the money for the family—' He caught her frown and bit off the rest of the sentence. What did he know about a functioning family? Absolutely nothing so he wasn't in a position to offer advice or opinion. 'Tell her you'll be back for Wednesday with a big fat bonus. The truth is you wouldn't have been driving there today, anyway. The roads around the castle are impassable and we are always low priority for the snowplough and the gritting lorries.'

'Can't you get them cleared?' Her innocent faith in the breadth of his power and influence almost made him smile.

'I can have the estate cleared, but there are five miles of country lanes between us and the main road. I can work miracles, but local government bureaucracy requires more than that.'

'So if we're snowed in, how do you propose getting us to Zubran?'

'We're flying. We'll take the helicopter to the airport and then the private jet.' Relying on a well developed instinct that told him exactly when to push and when to retreat, Lucas strode towards the stairs without giving her the opportunity to argue further. 'Call your sister and then meet me downstairs in the kitchen. I'll make us breakfast.'

'Fine, I'll ring,' she muttered, 'but she's going to kill me. As long as you don't mind having that on your conscience.'

Lucas chose not to remind her that he didn't have a conscience.

It was a difficult phone call, not least because for the first time in her life she wasn't being honest with her sister.

'You stayed overnight with your boss? Are you *crazy*? Haven't you listened to a single word I've said to you over the years?' Angela's tone was sharp and Emma felt colour flood into her cheeks as she contemplated her sister's reaction if she were to find out the truth.

'I didn't have any choice. Have you looked out of the window? It's like the Arctic. The roads here are impassable.' There was no point in trying to explain that she'd been worried about her boss. That concern and care had kept her here long after she should have left. There was no way Angela would understand that. Nor was she going to understand the next part of the conversation. Bracing herself, Emma tightened her grip on the phone. 'Angie, do you remember the project I told you about? The Zubran Ferrara Resort that is opening next week?'

'Of course. It's all over the news. They're calling it an iconic structure and your boss is apparently a progressive genius much loved by eco nuts everywhere. They're missing out the fact that he cares more about buildings than people. Remember that, Emma.' Her sister's tone was sharp. 'The man is a heartless womanizer, incapable of sustaining a relationship.'

Not incapable. Unwilling. He'd been hurt so badly he didn't want to risk it again.

And he was obviously concerned that she was about to declare undying love. That she might start spinning one night into a lifetime.

Her sister was still talking. 'So what time do you think you'll be home?'

'That's why I'm phoning—' Emma closed her eyes and blurted it out. 'I have to fly out with him to Zubran, just for a few days,' she added quickly, 'and I'll be back for Jamie's play. I'm sorry. I know the timing is bad and there are things you're supposed to go to, but I'll make it up to you.' She was prepared for it and when it came it was spectacular.

'No! You can't do this to me! I have the staff party tonight!'

'I know, and I've already thought of that. I'm going to phone Claire and ask if she'll come and sit with Jamie so that you can go out. Why not? She was my best friend at school and she loves Jamie and he loves her.' Emma's heart was pounding. She hated fighting with her sister. Hated it. 'I'm sorry, Angie, I know it's really inconvenient but it's just a few days. Lucas needs me.'

'Before last night you were coming home for the whole week. And now, suddenly, he needs you? Just what form is this "need" taking? What the hell do you think you're doing, Emma?'

'My job. I'm doing my job.'

'Really? You're sure this is just about work?'

'Of course.' She couldn't allow herself to think it

could be anything else. 'I know what you're thinking, and you're wrong.'

'Lucas Jackson is rich, good-looking and single. Are you seriously telling me you haven't ever looked at him like *that*?'

'He's my boss.' And he hadn't always been single, had he? There had been a woman who had meant something to him and they'd had a child together. A child they'd lost. His aversion to commitment wasn't the attitude of a mindless playboy, but a man who had shut himself off from emotion. Realising that her sister was waiting for her response, Emma forced herself to stop speculating. He'd made it clear that he didn't want to talk about it, so that was the end of that. 'Stop worrying about me. I'm sorry about the weekend, but it can't be helped.'

'No, of course it can't. You absolutely have to go to this urgent and very glamorous party while I'm stuck with Jamie.'

'Don't say that!' This time it was Emma who raised her voice. 'Do *not* say that you're "stuck with him". He might hear you and it would upset him so much. I know you don't mean that.'

'Maybe I do mean that. It's all right for you—you're living this amazing life in London and I'm stuck at home with a child who isn't even mine.'

Used to her sister's outbursts, Emma took a deep breath and tried again to work out if there was any way she could have Jamie living with her in London. The economics just didn't work. Her job paid well but it was demanding and required her to spend long hours at the office. And on top of that she wouldn't have wanted Jamie living in her area.

'We'll talk about this when I'm home. And I'll get

Claire to take him so that you can go to your party to-night. And please, Angie, just go and give him a hug.'

'He's going through a horrible phase at the moment. I don't feel like hugging him.'

Emma bit back a response that she knew wouldn't be helpful in the long run. Angie loved Jamie, she knew she did, but her sister bitterly resented the impact that taking care of their brother had had on their lives. Swiftly she changed the subject. 'Have you picked out a dress for your party tonight?'

'I'm wearing the red one from last Christmas.' Angela sounded marginally less angry and Emma relaxed slightly.

'The one with the lace? You look lovely in that. I hope you meet someone gorgeous.'

'And even if I did, we both know he'd run a mile once he discovered that I come with a permanently attached nine-year-old brother,' Angela snapped. 'And talking of which, I have to go and make him breakfast. And on that subject, thanks for starting a routine of making pancakes on Saturdays because now I'm going to be glued to the stove for hours.'

'It doesn't take hours, and it's fun. We make them together. Jamie makes the mixture, I cook them.'

'He makes a mess when he cooks. It doubles the work. And talking of work, I'd better go and break the news that the good sister isn't coming home.'

'I'm not the good sister.' Emma thought that if Angela had seen what she'd been up to on the rug the night before, she definitely wouldn't have used that term. 'You're good too. It's just that you're tired and disappointed that I won't be able to take up the reins for a few days and that's understandable.'

'Stop being so bloody reasonable.'

Emma bit her lip. 'I'll be back on Tuesday. Have fun at the party tonight.'

There was a long pause and then Angela sighed. 'I'm sorry,' she mumbled. 'I'm a horrible bitch.'

Yes, Emma thought, you sometimes are. 'It's the end of term and you're just tired. And I promise that once I'm home you can just put your feet up and have some time to yourself.'

'So what are you wearing to this fancy party?'

'I've no idea. I suppose I'll have to buy something.'

'Just tell me you're not having dreams of being Cinderella.'

Emma looked around the turret bedroom, with its four-poster bed and velvet drapes. Then she looked at the rug in front of the log fire where, for a few special hours, she'd felt like the most irresistible, desirable woman on the planet. No one's sister, no one's PA and no one's stand-in mother. A woman. She closed her eyes and pushed the thought away. 'Can I speak to Jamie?'

'He's in the shower. He's going to Sam's to play this morning. I guessed it would take you a while to get home and I didn't want him standing by the window watching for you all morning and nagging me. From the sound of it it's just as well I made that decision.'

Emma felt a stab of guilt but at the same time she was relieved Jamie wasn't there to hear Angela's tirade. 'Tell him I love him and I'll call him again later.'

'If you're not too distracted by partying. Do I need to remind you that office romances never cause anything but trouble?'

'No, you don't need to remind me of that.'

'If you lose your job—'

'I won't lose my job.' Emma ended the call, depressed by the encounter. She knew what was behind it. She un-

derstood why Angela behaved the way she did and she
didn't blame her for that, given everything that had happened in their family, but it was still hard to deal with.

She couldn't think of anything worse than losing the
job she had with Lucas but nor could she imagine anything more uncomfortable than spending the next few
days in his company after what had happened.

What she really needed was space to sort her head out.

She needed to persuade him to let her go. How was
she going to do that? What was the one thing that would
make Lucas Jackson send a woman as far away from him
as possible? The answer came to her almost immediately
and Emma gave a tiny smile. Yes, she thought. *That*.

CHAPTER SIX

EMMA went in search of Lucas, trying to shake off the guilt that shadowed almost every conversation with her sister. She found him downstairs in a kitchen that looked like something that would have featured in a magazine shoot for a perfect country home. In fact the whole place would make the most incredible family home, she thought, as she looked around her. It should have been filled with happy children and noisy dogs.

Had he originally bought it for that purpose?

Her mind buzzed with questions but they were all too personal and she was trying to make their relationship less personal, so she didn't voice them. And anyway, she knew he wouldn't have answered them. That one devastating revelation of the night before had been dragged from him purely because she'd held precious evidence in her hand.

As she walked into the room he glanced towards her and she saw in an instant that everything about his body language was guarded.

Exploiting that, she leaned against the doorframe and gave him a soppy look. 'While I was upstairs I was thinking a lot about last night.' Watching, she saw the tension ripple through him like a current ready to repel intruders.

'What about last night?'

'I know you don't want to hear this but—I think I love you, Lucas.' She blurted the words out, wondering if she'd injected just a little too much Scarlet O'Hara into her tone. 'Completely, totally, with my whole heart. For ever. I was saving myself for my perfect man and now I realise that man is you.' Intercepting his appalled glance she almost laughed. 'I know you don't want to hear it. It's *awful* that I feel this way and the truth is that I feel more strongly about you with every minute that passes. I don't know what to do! The longer I stay here, the more in love with you I am. Goodness knows what I'll be like by Tuesday. I suspect I won't be able to get through an hour without hugging and kissing you at every opportunity. I may even have to burst into a really important meeting just to get my Lucas fix. I'm so glad you're taking me with you.'

His eyes narrowed to two dangerous slits and then the tension left him. 'Nice try, but I still want you with me in Zubran.'

'But I *love* you. Madly. Passionately.'

'It doesn't matter how much you "love me",' he drawled. 'I won't be sending you home until the job is done.'

Emma slumped onto the nearest chair. 'You know you're unreasonable, don't you?'

'Demanding, yes. Unreasonable, no.'

Demanding.

He'd been demanding when he'd virtually dropped her onto the rug and stripped her naked.

He'd been demanding when he'd helped himself to her body.

She shivered and tried desperately hard not to think about that. 'Do you realise that when a woman says "I love you" you go white and then look as if you're about to go for dental surgery? Apart from hearing that the Dow-Jones has plunged a million points, I'm guessing that the worst words you can hear are "I love you" so I'm going to be saying it every five minutes until I drive you so mad you'll leave me at home.'

'You have a warped sense of humour.' The sleeves of his sweater were pushed back and her gaze lingered on those strong arms, remembering the way he'd held her as the passion had ripped through both of them.

Emma squeezed her eyes shut.

This was impossible. Totally impossible.

'Coffee?'

She opened her eyes and stared into his. Blue now, but they'd appeared almost black last night in the firelight as he'd kissed her. 'Thanks.' Taking the mug from him she wondered whether she was going to be thinking about sex every second of every day for the rest of her life.

'So what did your sister say?'

'Oh, she was totally thrilled that I won't be able to make it home for the holiday—' Emma sipped her coffee, still feeling a bit sick at the thought of the conversation. 'She said something along the lines of, "Super, I didn't really want to go out and have fun anyway, so you just have a great time and don't worry about me".'

A wry smile touched his mouth. 'So she didn't take it well then.'

Emma tried not to look at that mouth. 'No. But I've messed up her weekend so I don't really blame her. She relies on me to take over from Friday night.'

'So she heaped on the guilt and you took it. Surely there are other options. Other relatives? Babysitters?'

'No relatives, just us. And we've never really used babysitters. I only see Jamie at weekends so I don't want to arrive home only to go out again.'

'Are those your words or hers?'

Emma put her mug down slowly, thinking that he was remarkably astute for someone who claimed not to care about people. 'Hers. But I think she's right.' Angie had Jamie all week. It would have felt wrong to go home and then announce she was going out on a Saturday night, wouldn't it? 'She was supposed to be going to a party tonight so I've texted my friend to see if she can look after Jamie but it's not something I've done before and it does make me feel bad.'

'So during the week you run around after me and at weekends you run around after Jamie and your sister. What about your own needs?'

Emma stared at him. 'I love my family.' Truthfully she didn't feel comfortable talking about her sister. The whole conversation was still too raw and her guilt too fresh and it felt disloyal to talk about her family to someone who couldn't possibly understand. She knew he was judging Angie and she didn't want that because she knew the whole thing had been harder for her sister than it had been for her.

'Does your sister always make you feel guilty?'

'It isn't her fault. Family stuff is always complicated—you know how that is.' It was a casual comment. The sort of comment that might invite an understanding laugh from another person. But not him. And her own smile faded because she realised she had no idea whether this man even had a family. She knew so little about him. Just that he'd had a daughter. The photo had been of two people—a little girl and her daddy. No third person. Which didn't mean anything, of course, because the third person could easily have been behind the camera, but she found herself wondering who had taken the picture. Someone he loved? A passing stranger?

Suddenly cold, Emma stood up and walked towards the big range cooker that dominated the kitchen. If she'd been asked to design her perfect kitchen, this would have been it. Perhaps she would have added some soft touches, some cut flowers in the bright blue jug that sat on the windowsill, and a stack of shiny fresh fruit to the large bowl that graced the centre of that table, but they were just small things. She could imagine Jamie doing his homework on the scrubbed kitchen table while she rolled out pastry and made a pie for supper. She could imagine lighting candles for a romantic dinner.

She could imagine Lucas, dark and dangerous, sprawled in a chair while he told her about his day.

'Do you like it? My kitchen?' His tone was rough and she glanced up at him, shaken by her own thoughts.

'Just planning what I'll do when I move in.' Walking back to the table, she shifted the conversation away from the dangerous topic of family and onto something lighter. 'Add a few feminine touches here and there—flowers, china covered in pink hearts. And of course I'll tell you I love you every other minute until you get used to it.' The coffee was delicious. And strong. As she sat down, she felt the caffeine kick her brain into gear. 'So do you always look like you're about to have root canal work when someone says "I love you"?'

'I've no idea. No one has said it to me before.'

'What, never?' Genuinely shocked, Emma thumped her coffee down on the table. 'All the women you've been out with and not one of them has ever said it? Why?'

'Because I would have dumped them instantly. I don't pick the "I love you" type.'

So what about his daughter? *Had she not come from love?* The questions rolled around in her head but she stayed silent and sipped her coffee, grateful for the warmth and the fact that sliding her hands around the mug gave her something to do apart from try desperately hard not to look at him. She wasn't used to having indecent thoughts about her boss.

Emma lowered the mug slowly, knowing that she wasn't being entirely honest with herself.

Was she really going to pretend that she hadn't always found him attractive? Because that wouldn't be true, would it? Right from the beginning she'd found him scarily attractive, but the fact that she worked for him had put him off-limits. That and the fact that not once in the two years she'd worked for him had he given the slightest hint that the attraction might be mutual.

But that had all changed, hadn't it? And it was the shift to the personal that made it so awkward to be around him. Maybe it would have been different had there been other people here, but alone it felt—intimate. And yet they were still strangers. Intimate strangers.

She couldn't undo what had been done. She knew things now that she hadn't known before and there was no way of unknowing them. She knew he'd had a daughter and that he'd loved her. She knew he blamed himself. *She knew he was hurting.*

He said that he didn't have a heart but she knew that wasn't true. He had a heart, but that heart had been badly damaged. He was obviously suffering deeply but even without hearing the details, she was sure that he was wrong in his belief that he was somehow responsible for his daughter's death. That couldn't be the case.

'Emma?'

She gave a start. 'Sorry?'

'I asked if you were hungry.' Apparently suffering none of her emotional agonies, he pulled open the door of a large modern fridge and she found herself staring at his shoulders, watching the flex of male muscle under the black sweater. His body was strong and athletic and she felt the heat spread through her body, the flare of attraction so fierce that she almost caught her breath.

'Hungry would be an understatement,' she murmured. 'I'm starving. Right now I could eat ten camels. Which I suppose I might have to if you insist on making me go with you to Zubran.'

'I was thinking of omelette.' He turned his head and their eyes met. Tension throbbed between them, a living breathing force, and she stood up on legs that shook and threatened to let her down.

'I love omelette. Where will I find a bowl?'

'You think I need your help to cook a few eggs?'

'Sorry. Instinct.' She sat down again, relieved to take the weight off legs that seemed to have forgotten their purpose. 'I usually do the cooking when I'm home. I'm teaching Jamie to cook—it's one of the things we do together. Every Saturday we make pancakes for breakfast, it gives us time to talk. And then we pick a different dish. Last week we did pizza. Today we were going to make Christmas cake—' She knew she was talking too much but she couldn't help it. She talked to fill the silence because otherwise she found it too disturbing. 'Of course, because of you, we won't be making Christmas cake but you don't need to feel guilty about that.'

'I won't.' He pulled a box of eggs out of the fridge while she watched.

He'd showered but he hadn't shaved and his jaw was darkened by stubble that made him look more bandit than businessman. She remembered the roughness of it against her skin, the heat of his mouth, the touch of his fingers—

She remembered all of it.

She closed her eyes. This was not working. Forget

love—all she wanted was to be able to be in the same room as him and not feel this almost unbearable sizzle. She wanted to be able to listen to what he was saying without thinking of everything else that he could do with his mouth.

She wanted to be able to look at him without thinking of sex.

She wasn't sure whether the fact that he clearly wasn't suffering the same degree of torment made it worse or better.

Better, she told herself firmly. Definitely better. At least one of them was still sane.

And then she caught his eye briefly, caught a glimpse of darkness and heat, and knew that she was wrong. He was feeling everything she was feeling. He was fighting everything she was fighting.

The knowledge made her limbs shake and she clutched her mug, her heart banging against her ribs. 'So tell me about this place. It's not somewhere I would have expected you to own. You're all about glass and cutting-edge design and this must have been built by Henry the Eighth.' She was chattering frantically to cover up the way she was feeling but of course he knew exactly what was going on in her head.

And he wasn't going to do anything about it.

His self-discipline in all things was legendary.

Except for last night.

Last night, he'd lost control.

But there was no sign of that now as he glanced at the walls of the kitchen. 'Slightly earlier than Henry the Eighth, with later additions. And it's true that if I'm de-signing a new building then I like to make use of modern techniques and materials, but that doesn't mean I don't love old buildings. The history of this place is fascinat-

ing. And I don't own it by myself.' He broke eggs into
a bowl and whisked them expertly. 'When it came onto
the market, Mal, Cristiano and I bought it. It's owned by
a company we set up together.'

'Mal, the Prince? And Cristiano Ferrara who owns
the hotel group?'

'That's right.' He poured eggs into the skillet and they
sizzled in the heat. 'The plan is that once I've finished
the restoration, we turn it into an exclusive hotel that will
probably be rented as a whole. We're planning to hold
traditional British house parties.'

'I love that idea.' She'd known he had powerful friends
but it wasn't until today that she'd realised just how powerful. 'I didn't even know this sort of place ever came up
for sale. How did you find out about it?'

He tilted the pan. 'I'd had my eye on it for a while.'

'Who owned it before? It must have been awful to
have to sell something like this.'

The change in him was visible and immediate. That
beautiful mouth hardened into a thin, dangerous line
that made her immediately conscious that she'd somehow said the wrong thing.

'It was built by a wealthy merchant in the thirteen-
hundreds,' he said evenly, 'and stayed in the family until
the last member gambled away all his money.'

'Gambled? Horses?'

'Much more twenty-first century than horses.' Lucas
tilted the pan slightly. 'Online poker.'

'Oh. How awful.' She glanced round the kitchen and
tried to imagine owning something like this and then losing it. 'Imagine losing something that had been in your
family for centuries. Poor man.'

'That "poor man" was a selfish, miserable excuse for a
human being who took great pleasure in using his wealth

and status to bully others, so don't waste your pity on him because he certainly doesn't deserve it. More coffee?'

Emma was so astonished she couldn't answer. It was the first time she'd ever heard him make an emotional comment about a business deal. 'You work with plenty of wealthy, selfish human beings. Who was this guy?'

Lucas slid the omelette onto her plate, his expression blank. 'He was my father. You didn't give me an answer about the coffee so I'll just top it up anyway, shall I?'

Had he really just said what she'd thought he said? 'Your *father*?'

'That's right. My mother was his archivist. She left university and found her dream job here, working with the collection that had been pretty much neglected. She worked here for fifteen years and they had an affair. But he wanted to marry someone with the right heritage and apparently that wasn't my mother—' his tone was flat '—so she lost a job that she adored, her home and the man she loved. Not that she should have worried too much about the last bit. I think that could have been considered her lucky break, but obviously that's just my personal opinion. Unfortunately, she didn't see it that way.'

It was the most he'd ever told her about himself. The first really personal exchange they'd had. 'So she basically had an affair with the boss.' Emma felt her mouth dry and he looked at her with that keen, perceptive gaze she found so unsettling.

'If you're making the connection you appear to be making then I can assure you there are no similarities at all. This was a lengthy relationship which was supposedly based on love and trust—' his tone was threaded with cynicism '—whereas—'

'You don't need to finish that sentence.' She interrupted him hastily. 'We've been over this a thousand times already. I know what last night was.'

'Do you?' He was unnervingly direct and she knew that there was no way she could confess that she couldn't stop thinking about it. Still less could she admit that it wasn't just the sex she was thinking about; it was *him*. The more she discovered about him, the more her vision of him shifted. He was no longer her cold, detached boss. He was a man with a past.

'I love my job. I'd never do anything to jeopardize that. To be honest I can't *afford* to let anything jeopardize that. And I'm not in a position to have a relationship with anyone right now. There isn't room in my life. And then there's the fact that you're far too bitter and twisted for me.'

He frowned slightly, those dark brows pulled together in silent contemplation as if he wanted to say something else. And she didn't want him to say it. She wanted him to stop talking because every time he spoke he revealed something else and the more he revealed the more personal it became.

'So your mum discovered that she was pregnant, and then what?' Colour touched her cheeks as she remembered a small detail from the night before. The man had been half out of his mind with drink and grief, but he hadn't forgotten the condom, as if some part of him was programmed to remember. And she was relieved about that, of course, because the situation was already complicated enough without adding to it, but still, it made her wonder.

'He duly announced he was getting married to another woman. Perhaps if she hadn't made that fatal mistake, he might have let her stay. He was perfectly happy to have a lover on the scene, but a child would have made the whole thing vastly inconvenient and not at all British, so that changed things.' The words flowed from him and it was so unusual to hear him talk like this that she sat still and just listened. She wondered if he even realised how much he was telling her.

'So your mother resigned?'

'No. My mother never would have resigned so he had to find another way of getting rid of her.' He sat down across from her and picked up his fork. 'He accused her of theft. So not only did he humiliate her and ruin her chances of getting another job, but he made her hate him. And it made her hate me too, because I was inadvertently the reason for all that.'

The lump in her throat came from nowhere. 'Couldn't she have taken him to court or something? Got some help?'

'I don't know what went through her head. Maybe she did talk to a lawyer. I don't know, but certainly nothing came of it—' he sliced his omelette in two '—all I know is that it was a struggle. We lived in the smallest room you have ever seen. It had just one window and it never let in enough light.' He frowned. 'I couldn't work out why anyone would have designed a window that didn't do the job it was intended to do. That was when I started to dream about buildings. Buildings with space that let in the light. I drew myself a house and promised myself that one day I was going to build it and live in it.'

It was easy to imagine him as the child, drawing his dream. Especially when you saw the man he'd become. 'Did he never acknowledge you?'

'No. And the irony was, he never had any more children. I was his only child. Now isn't that poetic justice? He wanted a family. The tragedy was that he actually had one, but he never acknowledged it. You're not eating. Is there something wrong with your omelette?'

She'd been so lost in his story she hadn't taken a single mouthful of her food. 'Did you meet him?'

'When she found out that he had no living heir, my mother was determined that I should have the recognition that she felt was my right.' His mouth twisted. 'Or maybe she was hoping that he'd take me on so that she could have her life back.'

'You went to see him?'

'Yes, but not because I wanted him to suddenly play "Dad". I wanted to give him a piece of my mind. And his response was that it didn't matter what she did, he would never give me Chigworth Castle. I was thirteen years old and so angry with him that I punched him, then I told him he didn't need to give it to me because I was going to just take it from him when I was ready. It gave him quite a laugh, this skinny kid without a penny to his name trying to give him a black eye and then threatening to take his castle.' He gave a cool smile. 'He wasn't laughing on the day I took ownership. Cristiano Ferrara fronted the deal so he had no idea who was buying it until it was sold. Not that it would have made any difference. He'd spent all his money so he wasn't in a position to negotiate or withdraw. But I wouldn't have put it past him to burn the place to the ground rather than stop me owning it.'

There was a dull ache behind her ribs. 'When was this?'

'Eight years ago. I was twenty-six, my career was on the rise and I'd landed a few huge commissions that proved to be life-changing.'

'The art gallery in Rome.'

He lifted an eyebrow. 'You've been reading my biography?'

'I work for you,' she reminded him. 'I send your biography to the media and prospective clients on a daily basis.' And with that single unthinking sentence she reminded him of the true nature of their relationship. The atmosphere shifted instantly.

'Of course you do,' he said smoothly, 'and that is why I want you with me in Zubran. Because you know all these things.' Once again he was cool and distant as he pulled out his phone and checked an email. 'I've been waiting to hear from Dan.'

Dan was his pilot and Emma often spoke to him about Lucas's travel arrangements. 'Is the airport even open?'

'Yes. They've cleared the runway and there is no more snow forecast so we shouldn't have any trouble with our flight.' He scrolled down, checking his other emails. 'The helicopter will pick us up from here in an hour. I assume you have your passport with you?'

The shift from personal to professional was startling but she went along with it. What was surprising was not that he'd suddenly stopped telling her about his past, but that he'd ever told her in the first place. He'd given her another glimpse of a private, secret part of himself. And she was gradually building up a picture of a very different man from the one the public saw.

She knew so much more about him than she had yesterday. And she suspected he would rather that wasn't the case.

She was going to forget it, she vowed, and just get on with the job. That would be best for everyone.

'I have my passport, of course.' There had been many occasions when she'd flown with him on short business trips to Europe and a few times to the US. She'd enjoyed the variety and as long as the trip hadn't eaten into her precious weekends, she'd never objected. 'The one thing I don't have is clothes. And I assume there isn't time for me to go home and pack.'

'No. We have to leave immediately and anyway, the roads are impassable. You're fine for the journey.' His eyes lingered on her sweater then lifted to her face. 'You can travel in what you're wearing and you can go shopping tomorrow before the meeting.'

'I have to wait until tomorrow?'

'Seven-hour flight, four-hour time difference—' he shrugged '—it will be evening when we arrive and you're already exhausted which is hardly surprising given the amount of sleep you didn't get last night.'

Presumably she wasn't supposed to react to that. Presumably she was expected to treat what had happened with the same matter of fact casualness as he did.

So that was what she did. 'Is there somewhere to shop close by?'

'Avery will be able to advise you on the best place.'

'Avery owns her own highly successful company.' Emma thought about the pictures she'd seen of the glamorous businesswoman. 'She's very nice and we've bonded over your guest list, but I suspect she and I may have a very different idea of what constitutes the "best" place.' It was all too easy to imagine how her sister would react if she blew a sizeable chunk of her precious salary on a dress she'd probably only ever be able to wear once in her life.

'I'm paying,' Lucas drawled, 'so the budget is irrelevant.'

'You most certainly are not paying.' Emma shot to her feet, deeply offended that he could even think she would agree to that. 'Just in case you hadn't already noticed, I am *not* Tara.'

'Let me stop you there before you embarrass yourself,' he interjected softly, leaning back in his chair and stretching out his legs, as supremely relaxed as she was ridiculously tense. 'I am offering to buy you clothes because you don't have any with you and because I'm asking you to dress for an event you're required to attend in your role as my PA, *not* because we had sex. I am in no way being contradictory. I am completely clear about the nature of our relationship, Emma. It's professional.'

And for a moment she'd forgotten that. And he knew she'd forgotten it. Feeling intensely foolish, Emma sat down again. And this was the problem, she thought helplessly. For her, the personal and the professional were now well and truly mixed up. It was impossible to separate them. When he'd mentioned buying her clothes, she'd assumed it was personal. 'Well, thanks for clearing that up, but I don't need you to buy me clothes for work either. I can buy my own clothes.'

He watched her steadily, a cynical gleam in his blue eyes as he acknowledged her tension and the reason for it. And along with the cynicism there was a tiredness that came, not from lack of sleep but from life. 'Right now, I think whether or not I buy you a dress is the least of our problems, don't you?'

He thought she couldn't do this.

Determined to prove him wrong, Emma lifted her chin and stood up. 'I don't have any problems. Do you?'

Zubran was an oil-rich state on the Persian Gulf. She'd expected sand. What she hadn't expected was the fascinating mix of red-gold sand dunes, mountains and stunning coastline that she saw from the air as they came in to land. The scenery provided a welcome distraction from dwelling on the change in her relationship with Lucas.

And really, there was nothing to think about.

She worked for him. If she wanted to carry on working for him, she had to pull herself together.

It helped that, from the moment they'd boarded the company jet, he'd been very much his old self. As focused as ever, he'd worked for the entire flight, pausing only to drink one cup of strong black coffee while, seated across from him on one of the ridiculously luxurious deep leather seats, Emma fretted and worried.

It was just a couple of days, she told herself. A couple of days during which she had to behave in a professional way and switch off any other thoughts. After that, once they were back in the office, everything would be easier.

'Fasten your seat belt,' he murmured, 'we're landing.'

She wondered how he knew that, given that he hadn't even looked up from his work. 'I know. I've been looking at the scenery. I expected desert.'

'Zubran is famous for its coastline. The country has a long seafaring heritage and the diving here is incredible which is why I incorporated an underwater theme in the design of the hotel.'

Emma watched as a graceful catamaran danced over the waves beneath them as they came in to land. 'How far is the hotel from the airport?'

'Half an hour along the coast. The Ferraras never build hotels in cities. They're all about fresh air and healthy living.' Finally he glanced up, but only to exchange a few words with the flight attendants who had found themselves seriously underutilized on this particular flight.

As soon as they landed, he was out of his seat, impatient to get on. 'Let's go and see if my hotel is still standing.'

The short walk from the aircraft to the sleek limousine waiting for them on the tarmac was enough to tell her that a shopping trip needed to be high on her list of priorities. The sweater that had provided woefully inadequate protection against a British winter now felt as thick and heavy as a fur coat. She was grateful for the fierce air conditioning that turned the interior of the car into the equivalent of a mobile fridge as they sped along a straight road that led from the city up the coast. Rising to her left were steep sand dunes, turning from gold to red under the warm glow of the late afternoon sun, and to her right were the warm waters of the Indian Ocean, sparkling like a thousand tiny jewels thrown onto a carpet of blue velvet.

The change in climate felt surreal after the howling winds and thick snow of England.

Knowing that the moment she stepped out of the car she was going to melt, Emma glanced at her watch. 'What time do the shops close? I need to buy something to wear that isn't made of wool.'

'You don't have time to shop tonight. I've asked Avery to put something in your room for this evening and she's going to take you shopping in the morning. After the meeting you should have time for a short rest.'

'A rest? Am I three years old?'

'No, but tomorrow is going to be a long night.'

'I don't need a rest to prepare for that. I will run on adrenaline.' Emma felt a tiny thrill of excitement. Was it a bit sad, she wondered, to be this excited about a party that was supposed to be business? She was supposed to be saying to herself, *What a bore, working when I'm supposed to be on holiday.* Instead she was thinking, *Yay, a party.* She was feminine enough to enjoy being given the opportunity to dress up and mingle with adults. And anyway, this wasn't any party. It was *the* party. People had been virtually clawing each other out of the way to get on the guest list.

Lost in thought, she hadn't even noticed that they were no longer on the main road until she looked up and there, ahead of her, rising up as if from the sea itself, was a beautiful glass structure in the shape of a shell. Of course she'd seen both the plans and the model, but nothing prepared her for the real thing.

'Oh.'

'All that hard work and your only response is "oh"? Let's hope my audience tomorrow night are a little more enthusiastic.' Smiling faintly, Lucas unclipped his seat belt as the car pulled up outside the main entrance.

Emma was so busy staring she stumbled as she left the car. 'I said "oh" because I was lost for words, not because I wasn't enthusiastic, not that I think for a moment my approval means anything to someone like you.'

'Perhaps it does.' He spoke softly and she turned her head to look at him, her heart beating hard. Warmth engulfed her and she repeated the word in her head like a mantra—*professional, professional.*

'In that case you should know that I think it's stunning. Beautiful and very clever. It must be hard designing something that works for this climate.'

'Despite the fact we're on the edge of the desert, it can become surprisingly chilly at night, although not as chilly as a castle in snowy Oxfordshire.' A frown on his face, he removed his gaze from her mouth. 'Air circulation and humidity was a challenge, as was the soil type but in the end it's all come together.'

The heat was starting to make her feel strange and she didn't know whether it was from the ferocious desert sun or the heat that came from being close to Lucas.

They reached the entrance and were greeted by a beautiful girl dressed in a smart uniform.

'Mr Jackson. Welcome! I hope your journey was comfortable.' She shook hands and then glanced at Emma, clearly expecting to see Tara. A consummate professional, her smile didn't slip. 'Welcome to the Zubran Ferrara Spa Resort. I'm Aliana, Head of Guest Relations. I hope your stay is comfortable, but if there is anything at all you need then do please ask.'

And judging from the woman's expression, nothing was off-limits, Emma thought, feeling a rush of jealousy that she knew was totally inappropriate.

'This is Emma,' Lucas said calmly. 'Emma is my PA.'

'Of course.' Despite the smooth response it was obvious that the girl considered 'PA' to be a euphemism for a very different role. 'If you follow me, we have your suite ready. And Mr Ferrara asked me to pass on a message when you checked in.'

'Message?'

The woman cleared her throat. 'The message was, "Tell him he's in the Presidential Suite and if it leaks I'm never working with him again." His words,' she said hastily. 'I'm just the messenger. I'm absolutely sure that nothing you designed would ever leak, Mr Jackson.'

Lucas simply laughed and Emma was about to ask why there would be any concern about the Presidential Suite leaking when a pair of glass doors in front of them opened with a smooth hiss and they walked down a gentle slope and into the most breathtakingly beautiful room she'd ever seen.

'We're under the water. Oh my—' she gasped as a shoal of brightly coloured fish swam right in front of her, darting through softly floating fronds of seaweed. 'It's amazing. Like being inside an aquarium.' For some reason she hadn't noticed this on the model. Or maybe she had, but just hadn't registered that it would be under the water. She was always so busy, she realised, she never really had a chance to appreciate the scope of his genius. It was truly imaginative. And restful.

'It's not entirely under the water. Just this room.' Frowning, Lucas turned to the woman. 'I told Cristiano to use the suite.'

'Mr Ferrara is here with his whole family, including his young daughters,' the woman said. 'His security team decided that the Coral Suite is more suitable for small children because it's possible to close off the pool. And you are, after all, the guest of honour. This amazing, iconic hotel is your brainchild.' She looked suitably star-struck but if Lucas even noticed, there was no sign of it.

'Right.' He put his briefcase down on the table. 'And when is the Prince arriving?'

'His Royal Highness sends his apologies. He intended to join you for dinner tonight but instead he finds him-self tied up with a delegation from Al Rafid. He looks forward to joining you at the party. As you know, every royal and celebrity in the world has been holding their breath hoping for a ticket.' Smiling, she handed him a slender object that looked like a remote control. 'The technology in the hotel is quite staggering but I suppose I don't need to give you a lesson on that, given that you were involved in all stages of the planning. It's all voice controlled.'

Voice controlled?

Emma had been so busy gawping that she was barely listening. She'd never been anywhere so luxurious. The use of glass made it feel as if they were actually on the water, part of the sea rather than the land. And it had been furnished to reflect the same sea, soft leather sofas designed for lounging, the floor covered in rugs in marine shades of blue and turquoise.

As the woman left them alone, she glanced around her. 'Voice controlled? So exactly which part of it is voice controlled?'

Lucas was prowling around the suite, checking various details. 'Everything. The lights. The blinds on the windows. The sound system. You can operate it all without once moving from the bed.'

His choice of words made her flush but fortunately he wasn't looking at her.

'So if I say music—' She stopped, enchanted as the smooth notes of Chopin flowed through the room. 'Oh that is *so* cool.'

Lucas observed her delight with a lifted eyebrow. 'That is just the default track. List the track you want and it will play it. And you adjust the volume by saying "volume up" and "volume down". I wish I could install something similar in my clients,' he drawled. 'And now you need to get dressed. I'm taking you to dinner.'

It was the last thing she'd expected him to say.

Ever since she'd woken this morning he'd been careful to keep his distance. He'd warned her off. Apart from that one unguarded confession in the kitchen, their relationship had reverted back to employer and employee. During the journey he'd been cold and more than a little intimidating.

But now he wanted to take her to dinner, in this beautifully romantic place where the sun was just setting?

She should say no. Her heart raced away in a frantic rhythm. 'I don't have anything to wear.'

His eyes were on his phone as he checked his emails. 'Avery has just sent a message to confirm that she arranged for a selection of clothes to be delivered to your room. She'll pick you up at ten tomorrow to shop for something to wear at the party.'

'But—'

'Whatever she's picked out should hopefully be enough to get you through until the morning.'

But Emma wasn't thinking about the dress. She was thinking about having dinner with him. She was wondering why he'd changed his mind. 'Lucas—' Her voice was croaky. 'Is this a good idea? Do you really want to have dinner?'

'Of course.' He didn't glance up from his emails. 'The restaurant is the most complex part of this structure. I want to see whether the end result gives the dining experience that I hoped for when I designed it.'

Dining experience?

Emma stood still, horrified to realise how close she'd come to making a total fool of herself yet again. Once again, her brain had twisted his words. A week ago if he'd mentioned dinner she would have assumed it was all about business. Now, she was imagining soft words and the promise of something more, whereas the reality was that when he'd asked her to have dinner with him it hadn't been a romantic proposition, but a practical one. It wasn't that he wanted to have dinner with *her*. It was that he wanted to have dinner in the restaurant he'd designed, and she was supposed to accompany him.

She breathed deeply, hating the fact that she felt disappointed. And as for the hollow feeling inside her—well, she hated that too.

Registering her prolonged silence, he finally glanced up. 'Is something wrong?'

'Nothing. I'll just go and change.'

Enough, she thought as she walked quickly into the second bedroom.

Enough.

How much clearer could he make it? Where was her pride and her common sense? From now on she was going to think of him as her boss and nothing else. That way, she not only got to keep her job, she got to keep her sanity.

CHAPTER SEVEN

THE situation was a thousand times more delicate to handle than he'd anticipated. He'd seen her face when he'd invited her to dinner and knew instantly that he'd made a major miscalculation. She'd wanted dinner to be something else. Despite all his warnings, she'd hoped. And he, who shattered women's hopes on a regular basis without thought or care, had found it hard to shatter hers. But shatter them he had and she'd slipped quietly away to the second bedroom with her dignity intact and had been there ever since.

Cursing softly, Lucas dragged his hand over the back of his neck and wondered if she'd been crying. The thought disturbed him far more than he would have expected.

He checked his watch again. Should he knock on the door and check on her? Avery Scott was nothing if not ruthlessly efficient so he doubted that the problem was with the clothes. Something she'd provided was bound to fit, surely? So what was taking her so long?

Reluctant to become embroiled in an emotional conversation that could only make the situation between them even worse, he decided to give her another few minutes.

Restless, he paced through to the living room and

switched on the news headlines. If nothing else it would provide him with dinner conversation.

'I'm ready.' Her voice came from behind him, crisp and businesslike and he turned, relieved that she sounded like the Emma he knew but then he saw her and realised that this woman was nothing like that Emma.

His instruction to Avery had been to provide clothes. He hadn't bothered to spell out the fact that those clothes should be practical rather than seductive. He'd seen dinner as an opportunity to talk business, agree the schedule of media interviews and all the other details they had to discuss and had assumed she'd dress accordingly. He'd expected a sober, sensible outfit in muted colours. Instead, he was greeted by a tempting swirl of vivid scarlet that was neither muted nor sober.

The dress flowed rather than clung, the cut and quality of the fabric skimming her curves. Curves that he remembered with disturbing clarity. Curves that sent him from a state of relative calm to one of intense arousal.

Knowing that he was in trouble, Lucas breathed deeply. 'I'm sorry. I hadn't realised she'd pick something so—' he fished for the right word '—red. You must be furious.' *He* was furious. And he wondered for a moment whether Avery had done it on purpose. It wouldn't have been the first time she'd tried to match him up with someone.

'You don't like it?'

'It's not exactly…practical.'

'Well, we're just sitting eating dinner, so how practical does it have to be?' Apparently oblivious to his struggle, Emma stroked her hands over her hips. 'It's not at all what I would have chosen, which is half the fun if I'm honest. It was clever of her to find something at short notice. I have no idea how she knew my size—'

Her eyes narrowed as she looked at him. 'Ah. You must have told her.' And if she were embarrassed about that, then there was no sign of it.

Lucas ground his teeth. Wasn't she supposed to be blushing and shy or something? Instead she seemed aware of her femininity in a way she hadn't been only days earlier. Or maybe he was the one who was suddenly aware of it. Watching her hands stroke her hips made him think of the way she'd touched him and suddenly he wanted to get her out of the damn dress and into the silk sheets of his bed. But if there was anything more dangerous than sleeping with this woman once it would be sleeping with her twice.

'If you don't feel comfortable wearing that to dinner then I can ask the hotel to send something else.'

'What would be the point of that? And I don't want to risk offending Avery when I'm finally about to meet her in person. I know I've only ever spoken to her on the phone but we get on really well.' She closed her hand around a slim purse. 'It's just a dress, Lucas. I hardly think a dress is going to bother you if it doesn't bother me.'

It bothered him.

It seriously bothered him but he couldn't tell her that without taking the conversation into areas he was determined to avoid. Given that fact, he had no choice but to accept the fact that the red dress was her chosen outfit for the evening.

The tension in him mounted. 'If you're too tired to join me for dinner I quite understand.'

'Tired? Don't be silly. I can't wait to see the restaurant. I remember it on the model and the plans and I'm so excited. I can't remember when I last went out to dinner. I mean, I know this is work,' she added, throwing his own rule right back at him, 'but I'm ridiculously excited to eat something I haven't had to cook myself.' Her enthusiasm was genuine and charming but he didn't want to be charmed. The feeling unsettled him in a way that was new to him.

Deciding that keeping his hands off her might well turn out to be the biggest challenge of his life, Lucas gestured to the door of the suite. 'In that case we should go. We have a table reserved. Can you even walk in those shoes?' They were clearly designed for sex, not walking. Before last night he would never have been able to imagine Emma in shoes like that, but now they formed an erotic addition to those incredible legs.

'Of course I can. I've been practising in my room. That's why I was late. Watch me.' Grinning, she walked up to him, a look of triumph on her face. 'See? I don't even wobble. It's all to do with putting your weight on the right part of your foot.'

She was different, he thought. Her skin glowed, her eyes shone, she *sparkled*.

And then she lost her balance on those heels and tumbled against him. With lightning reflexes, Lucas caught her. His hands closed over her shoulders, his fingers biting into warm flesh. Just that simple touch took him back to the night before and suddenly he wanted all of it again. Her lips, her warmth, *her incredible body*.

His mouth was dangerously close to hers and he was dangerously close to doing something about that. Furious with himself for being so weak-willed, he gave a growl of frustration and was about to pull away when she calmly detached herself.

'Oops. Sorry about that. Clearly your first assessment was right. I need more practice in the shoes.' Not looking at him, she tightened her grip on her purse. 'Shall we go? We don't want to be late.' And, with that, she walked towards the door, the wicked red dress swirling around her gorgeous legs.

Dropping two phones into her bag, Avery Scott kicked off her shoes and curled up on the soft sofa in the private dressing room of the exclusive boutique. 'You'll have to excuse me, but I've done enough of these parties to know that I'll have blisters by ten o'clock if I don't rest now. This is my last chance to sit down so I'm taking it. So—spill. While we're waiting for them to bring clothes, tell me all.'

'Do you seriously have time for this?' Trying to ease the pain in her feet, Emma flopped down next to her, thinking how nice it was to have female company. Her life was so frantic she'd let her friendships slip. Apart from the occasional exchange at the water cooler, she rarely chatted with anyone. 'Those shoes were gorgeous but it was a bit like walking round with my feet in the jaws of a crocodile. It's really kind of you to help me shop, but don't you have a million other things you should be doing before tonight?'

'I employ good people and I delegate. Now forget the shoes and tell me how that red dress looked.'

'It looked great. Too great. Lucas acted as if I'd chosen it on purpose to try and seduce him, which was pretty unfair given that I had nothing to do with it.'

'So did you? Seduce him, I mean.'

'No, of course not.'

'Ah.' Avery's beautiful eyes sparkled. 'Want to talk about it?'

'No. Let's just say that tonight I'm wearing a grey sack.' She was joking about it, but inside it didn't feel funny. It felt hopeless. It didn't matter what she did, things between them were never going to be the same again. They couldn't undo what they'd done. 'I work for him and I really need the job and now I've…I've messed it up.'

'How have you messed it up?'

Emma rubbed her fingers over her aching head. 'It's not really something I should even be talking about. Just make sure I pick out a boring dress so that I blend into the background tonight.'

Avery shuddered. 'I've never intentionally picked a "boring dress" in my life. I'm not sure I could even if I tried and I don't intend to try. Tell me what is going on.'

Emma was surprised by how badly she wanted to confide. 'You don't need to hear my problems.'

'Yes, I do. I'm fantastic with other people's problems. It's just my own I can't solve. And you're not the first woman to sleep with her boss.'

Emma gave a groan but didn't bother denying it. 'It's such a cliché.' And before she could stop herself she was blurting it all out. Everything. From the loneliness of living alone in London in the week, to the row with her sister and sex on the rug. The only thing she didn't mention was Lucas's daughter or the fact that his father had never acknowledged him.

That information was private. His secret, not hers to tell.

'Wow.' Effortlessly elegant, Avery uncurled her legs and sat up. 'You've led this life driven by duty and responsibility and then suddenly on one snowy night it's all blown apart. That's *so* romantic.'

'It's not romantic. It's embarrassing and inconvenient. And my life hasn't been driven by duty.' Emma shifted uncomfortably. 'It isn't like that. I adore Jamie.'

'I never said you didn't adore him, but that doesn't

change the fact you've always put him first. And you're so different from Lucas's usual type of woman.'

'What do you mean by that?'

'You're the home and hearth type that Lucas usually avoids like a non-alcoholic cocktail.' She gave a slow smile. 'And you spent the night together. How interesting.'

'It's not interesting. In fact I think it's fair to say he was appalled. He thought it meant I would automatically fall in love with him.'

'Whereas you were already in love with him.'

'No, absolutely not! I don't love him.'

'Probably why you slept with him,' Avery said helpfully, ignoring Emma's denial. 'Let's just hope he doesn't figure that one out. So—you've freaked him out. Lucas Jackson is Mr Cool so I'm looking forward to meeting the freaked-out version.'

'He is *so* freaked out he spent all yesterday making sure I knew it was never going to happen again. And he was really angry about the whole thing.'

'Definitely freaked out,' Avery murmured, 'which would explain his reaction to the red dress.'

'No, that was just because he thought it was too frivolous for work.'

'You think so?' Avery gave a cat-like smile and pulled her phone out of her purse as it rang. 'Excuse me for one moment while I get this—'

While Avery solved some problem that involved lighting and fireworks, Emma brooded on the grim reality of her situation. She wasn't in love with him. It would be madness to fall in love with a man who would never love her back. Even greater madness to be in love with her *boss*.

After his initial response to the dress, Lucas had returned to his detached, slightly intimidating self. Their evening had been starchy and formal. Their whole relationship had changed. They couldn't go backwards and it seemed they couldn't go forwards either.

'Right—where were we? Ah, the dress—' Avery came off the phone and looked at her. 'You were saying that he found it incredibly sexy.'

'I didn't say that. I said he was angry.'

'Presumably because he found you attractive and didn't want to.'

'I've no idea. I work for him and I want to carry on working for him. But I have to stop feeling this way.'

Avery shrugged. 'A man like Lucas Jackson comes along once in a lifetime. My advice? Take the sex and get a different job. Problem solved.'

Emma gaped at her. 'I could never pick sex over job security. You don't understand—'

'I'm the child of a single mother. A strong single mother, so believe me I do understand about the importance of job security. And I'm not really suggesting that you throw in a job just for sex, but it seems to me that this isn't the job for you anyway. You need to find something closer to home so that you can have a life. Maybe this is the trigger you need to make you do that. You've had far too much responsibility and not enough fun but we're going to fix that.'

A job closer to home? 'Even if I were prepared to look for another job it wouldn't make a difference. He isn't interested in a relationship. And I made a total fool of myself last night because when he invited me to dinner, just for a moment I thought he meant *dinner*, if you know what I mean.' She thumped her forehead with her fist and Avery looked amused.

'Yes, I know exactly what you mean. So the first thing

you have to do is find out whether or not Lucas is interested. Wear a really knockout dress tonight.'

'He'll think I'm trying to seduce him.'

'Not if you don't try to seduce him. Wear the dress but be businesslike.' Avery narrowed her eyes. 'If you dance, you dance with other people. If you talk, you talk to other people. Any connection with him should be brief and businesslike. If he really doesn't want you then he'll be fine with that. If he does—well, we'll see.'

'No, we won't see! He's my boss. He pays well and he's a good employer.'

'I pay well and I'm a good employer. You could always work for me and I don't care where you're based as long as the work gets done. Now let's get started on these clothes.'

Unable to summon up any enthusiasm, Emma slipped off her shoes. 'I thought after his reaction to the red, we'd better go for something a bit more muted. Maybe beige?'

'Sure. Let's just put you in a canvas sack and have done with it, shall we?' Avery shuddered. 'Emma, you are *never* wearing beige again. Your beige days are totally behind you. I've earmarked a nice boring navy dress for you to wear in your meetings this afternoon because it will make the contrast all the more startling when you dress up tonight, but your days of dressing like a nun are over. They're fetching me a selection of dresses and while we're waiting you can tell me something about Lucas, apart from the fact he rocked your world. What's going on behind that handsome face?'

'He's a clever man. Very talented. I'm really lucky to work for him.'

'I love a bit of moody, cerebral introspection as much as the next girl, but that isn't exactly what I was asking. I want to know why the man has never settled down. You do realise that of all the women he's ever been with, his longest relationship is with you?'

'I'm not a relationship. I'm his PA.'

'And before you he was getting through a PA every six weeks. But you've stayed the course. That has got to mean something.'

'It means I need the job too badly to resign.'

'Or that you've become important to him.'

Her heart skipped. 'Only in the sense that I make his work life run smoothly.'

'Really? So why did he bring you here?'

'Because he and Tara broke up and he needed someone with him.'

Avery gave a womanly smile. 'And you don't think Lucas Jackson has a million replacements waiting in the wings? Come on, Emma. He wanted *you*. And I'm so pleased he finally dumped that awful Tara.' She poured two glasses of water and handed one to Emma. 'Tara got horribly drunk at one of my parties a year ago and we had to tactfully remove her before she stripped on the dance floor. I've been wishing her bad karma ever since.' She frowned as the personal shopper in the exclusive store arrived with a selection of clothes. Within seconds she'd dismissed them all. 'I saw this bright blue dress at one of the shows in fashion week that would be perfect.' She named the designer and described it and the girl hurried off while Emma looked on in amazement.

'Do you know every dress in every designer's collection?'

'No. Only the ones that catch my eye. The others I forget—' Avery drank the water and looked longingly at the bowl of fresh dates that had been put on the table. 'I am starving, but if I eat that I'll never get into my dress for tonight. Ah—' She sprang to her feet as the girl returned carrying a sheath of midnight-blue silk. Avery took the dress from her with a crow of triumph. '*This* is the one. I would have bought it myself if I hadn't already picked one out for the party. It's going to look perfect on you.'

'How much is it?'

Avery rolled her eyes. 'Who cares? Just try it on. Every woman should own at least one dress like this. It is going to turn you from a sensible, professional woman into a wanton sex goddess.'

'Firstly, Lucas wants sensible and professional and secondly I'm not remotely wanton sex goddess material.'

'You will be by the time I've finished. Now shut up and try the dress, Emma. You're old before your time and we're going to fix that.' Avery thrust it at her and waved away the saleswoman with a winning smile. 'We're fine here. Thanks. But some more water would be great. That's another thing I have to do before a big party. Hydrate. Go and change, and while you're undressing tell me how you concentrate while you're working with Lucas. I'd be lying on his desk panting hopefully every morning saying "Take me, take me".'

Giggling, Emma slipped behind the curtain and slid her skirt off. 'You wouldn't really. He's horribly moody in the mornings. I try not to speak to him before he's had at least two cups of coffee.'

'I'm good with moody men. Are you dressed yet?'

'Nearly.' Surprised by how much chatting to Avery had lightened her mood, Emma slid the dress over her head. 'I think it might be a bit tight.'

The curtain was whisked back and Avery stared at her. 'Oh Lucas, Lucas,' she purred, 'you are in *so* much trouble. I almost feel sorry for you.'

Emma gave a nervous laugh. 'You don't think it's too tight?'

'That's not tight. It's called a perfect fit. Have you even looked in the mirror?'

'Not yet, but—'

'Then look.' Avery spun her round and Emma stared at her reflection.

'Oh my God.'

'Yes. My thoughts exactly. And the back of it is—'

'Non-existent.' Emma felt a lurch of excitement and terror. 'I don't look like me.'

'Yes, you do. But it's you as you've never seen yourself before.' Eyes narrowed, Avery reached forward and twisted Emma's hair into a loose knot. 'Hair up, hair down… Up, I think. Then he'll fantasize about letting it down over your beautiful, bare back.'

'I don't want him to fantasize about me! We're trying to get things back to normal, not make them worse! Avery, you have to stop this.' And she had to stop it too. She had to stop thinking about that night. She had to stop thinking of him as anything other than her boss. She had to—

Her eyes met Avery's in the mirror.

'The man is delicious and it's time he got together with someone decent instead of choosing shallow, brainless women who are only interested in his money and contacts. I'm going to arrange for you to have hair and make-up in your suite—' Avery whipped her phone out and sent a string of emails. 'Do you own any diamonds?'

'Of course not. Nor do I go anywhere that I could wear any.'

'Well, tonight you are. That dress needs diamonds,' Avery murmured without looking up. 'I'm going to arrange for one of the jewellery companies to loan you something for the evening. Smile—' She snapped a photograph with her phone and then proceeded to email it to someone. 'They will be able to decide what will look best with that colour and neckline.'

'OK, stop! Now you're going over the top.' Emma backed away. 'Tonight is about work. I'm supposed to be mingling and networking, not parading around in diamonds.'

'I've never understood why a woman can't look her best while she's mingling and networking,' Avery murmured. 'I suspect Lucas Jackson hasn't been so interested in a woman for a long time—maybe never. We should make the most of that.'

Emma found herself trapped. She couldn't tell Avery that the only reason Lucas had slept with her was to get through a truly terrible night. So now Avery had totally the wrong impression and this whole situation was spiralling horribly out of control and all she could do was mutter a lame, 'He's not interested.'

'He's interested. He noticed the red dress. Men only notice what a woman is wearing when it makes them think of sex.'

'Avery!'

'What?' She looked up from her phone. 'You are very, very pretty. You deserve diamonds.'

'I do not want to be wearing anything valuable. What if someone steals it from around my neck?'

'Do you want an estimate of the combined wealth of the people attending tonight?'

'No. I assume that the Crown Prince alone is worth a fortune. I wonder why he isn't married?'

Avery's smile faded and her pretty face lost some of its colour. 'Because, like you, he puts duty before his personal needs. Only in his case he intends to marry the boring virgin princess his father has picked out for him. I don't know who I feel more sorry for.'

'How do you know that?' Emma stared at her. 'Oh! You and he—'

'Yes. But not for a while.' Avery gave a bright smile. 'Our Sultan-to-be needs a well behaved obedient bride prepared to honour and obey and, as you've probably guessed, I am *so* not that person. Even if I could occasionally obey, which is a major struggle if I'm honest, I totally bombed out at the word "virgin".'

Emma wasn't fooled by the light tone. 'You're in love with him.'

'God, no,' Avery answered just a little too quickly. 'I'd never be stupid enough to love a man who doesn't like me to argue with him. I'd never be so stupid as to love a man, full stop. Now what are we going to do about shoes for you?'

Emma looked at her closely but Avery was back to normal again as she made arrangements for the dress to be delivered to the hotel.

'I'm worried this outfit is over the top. I'm his PA. I work for him and I want to continue working for him. This whole thing is so complicated.'

'Welcome to the real world. Love *is* complicated. Why do you think I'm so careful to avoid it? Nothing can ruin a perfectly planned and ordered life like love.'

'I'm not in love.' Horrified and defensive, Emma removed the dress carefully. 'Absolutely not.'

'So here's a little tip from an expert—' Avery's tone was conversational as she helped Emma out of the dress. 'If you don't want people to know you're in love, be careful not to let your face light up like a halogen light bulb when his name is mentioned. I'll deal with this while you get dressed—no, not the skirt you arrived in. Try this blue linen. It's cool and professional. Perfect for meetings.'

It was just physical attraction, Emma told herself as she slid into the blue dress. She *liked* him, of course she did, but she wasn't in love.

'How is the dress? Businesslike?'

'It's perfect. What about you? Has there been some-one else since the Prince? You must meet gorgeous men all the time.'

'I do. Unfortunately I have a congenital urge to want what I can't have.' For a fleeting moment Avery's eyes were sad and then she shrugged. 'Are you ready?'

'But if you have feelings for him then this whole party must be hell for you, because the Prince is going to be here,' Emma said slowly as the implications sank in. 'Why didn't you turn it down?'

'Pride.' Avery gave a lopsided smile. 'If I turned it down, people would think I was broken-hearted and I don't want him to have that power over me. I intend to go out there and show that his careless, heartless attitude hasn't made a dent in me.'

But Emma could see that it had. A big dent. 'You must feel terrible.'

Avery gave a careless shrug. 'Nothing that a pair of killer heels won't cure. That and the money they'll be transferring into my account when I've given them a party that no one is going to forget. This is business, Emma. I never feel terrible when I'm parting the rich from their money.'

Emma felt a flash of admiration. 'You make me feel guilty for moaning. If you can go out there and pretend you're not bothered so will I. Just share the secret of how you do it.'

'Look fabulous,' Avery said simply. 'Show him what an excellent time you are having without him. And if it gets too much just text me and I'll meet you in the Ladies. We can both cry in the toilet.'

Seriously distracted, Lucas tried to concentrate as Cristiano Ferrara outlined his objectives for the proposed development in Sicily. Across from him sat Emma, making notes in her usual efficient manner. Her hair was twisted into a severe, businesslike style and today she'd chosen to wear sober navy. A perfect choice. He'd insisted that their relationship remained professional and she was following that instruction with the same efficiency with which she followed every other instruction.

Everything should have felt fine.

It didn't.

In the past he'd always managed to compartmentalize his life and Emma fell into the category marked 'work', but suddenly the edges of those compartments had broken down. Instead of focusing on the business, he found himself focusing on *her*. He noticed things he hadn't noticed before, like the way she listened attentively to everything that was being said. She never missed a thing, which was what made her so good at her job. He was used to mixing with women who continually monitored their appearance and the effect they were having on the men around them. Emma did neither. If she was even aware of how she looked, she gave no sign of it.

He, however, was all too aware of it.

Never before had he had trouble forgetting a woman but he was finding it impossible to forget his one night with her. And it wasn't just the physical, he thought. It was so much more than that. The fact that she'd stayed when she could have left. The fact that she'd refused to leave him even though she had responsibilities elsewhere. The way she'd tidied up all the evidence of the party so that he wouldn't be upset. *The way she'd covered him with a blanket.*

He wasn't used to being on the receiving end of anyone's warmth or compassion. He'd made his own way in the world, nurtured himself and provided his own comfort.

And now…

Just one night, he thought savagely. It had been just one night and he hadn't been able to concentrate since. His body was in an almost permanent state of sexual arousal and as for his mind…

'We'll do a site appraisal,' he said, realising that his friend was waiting for a response, 'and then come back to you with an outline design that incorporates the features you just described.' It had been a mistake to bring her to Zubran. He'd thought he would be able to continue as if nothing had happened, but that was proving more of a challenge than he'd anticipated.

Across the table, Cristiano raised an eyebrow in expectation. 'Any initial ideas? Concepts? Normally, you're already sketching by this point in our discussions.'

Normally, his brain wasn't full of inappropriate thoughts. 'You want me to build in the shadow of the largest active volcano in Europe. We'll have to analyse the soil and consider the possible effects of volcanic activity. It isn't an ordinary project by any means. Naturally we'll address the usual issues of sustainability but air quality might have a negative impact on photovoltaic systems so we'll need to be creative in our design.' They talked at length about the Ferrara vision for the hotel while Emma continued to make notes.

Lucas knew that whatever emails needed to be sent would already be winging their way through cyberspace.

She was as ruthlessly efficient as he was. Nothing went undone. Nothing was forgotten.

'Fly over soon.' Cristiano's tone was conversational. 'Why not spend a few days with us? Mix business with pleasure. I'll take you to see the site and you can get a better feel for the area.'

Mix business with pleasure.

He'd already done that, Lucas thought, with devastating consequences. He'd thought it would be easy to put that one night behind him, the way he'd put other nights behind him in the past. But this time was different.

'Emma will put a time in the diary.'

Immediately she lifted her eyes and smiled acknowledgement, but the smile was for Cristiano, not him, and Lucas felt a flash of anger because she hadn't looked at him once during the meeting. Nor had she looked at him when she'd returned from her shopping trip with Avery. The fact that his reaction was illogical made no difference to the degree of his response. Nor did the fact that Cristiano was a happily married man and that Emma's smile had been friendly rather than flirtatious. There was nothing to explain the sudden surge of jealousy. It was a primitive response, entirely out of character for him and inappropriate given that the focus was an employee.

As they closed the meeting, Emma walked round the table to Cristiano and Lucas could hear her asking after his wife and children. He clenched his jaw as the Sicilian businessman withdrew his phone and showed Emma a series of photographs.

It was typical of Emma to know everything about everyone, he thought. It was what made her such an excellent PA. Nothing escaped her. She forgot nothing. She knew names, faces—hell, she knew whole family trees.

Angry with himself, Lucas rose to his feet. 'If we're

finished then we need to move on.' He shot Cristiano a pointed look. 'You and I have a string of media interviews to get through today.'

Work, he thought. The answer was to bury himself in work as he'd always done in the past and hope that the dress Emma had chosen to wear tonight was less provocative than last night's choice.

He could only hope that her sudden interest in navy would extend to evening wear.

CHAPTER EIGHT

EMMA stayed in her room until the last minute, rehearsing her expression in the mirror. Cool. Composed. Not bothered.

True to her word, Avery had arranged for both a hairdresser and a make-up artist to come to the suite so she'd been pampered and spoiled while Lucas had been tied up giving interviews to the media. She hoped that his mood would have improved. During the meeting he'd looked ready to explode.

A brisk knock on the door made her jump. 'Emma?' Lucas's voice came through the door. 'A security team has just delivered a necklace for you. Are you ready?'

Yes, she was ready. Or as ready as she'd ever be.

Pride, she reminded herself, thinking of Avery.

Breathing deeply, she opened the door. The white dinner jacket was a shock. She'd expected black and the dramatic contrast between the white and that raven hair made her hold her breath and not release it for a long moment. He was effortlessly elegant, everything masculine and altogether unobtainable. Despite all her best intentions, her stomach tied itself in a knot and of course he had to see her reaction because he was a man who saw everything. To calm herself, she focused her attention on the box in his hand. 'I hope it's nothing over the top.

Avery arranged it. She thought the dress needed something.'

His gaze scanned her in a single sure sweep. No doubt
he'd done the same to countless women far more beautiful than her but still she couldn't look away from him,
this man who had been told he was nothing and had made
himself something.

She'd expected at least a polite smile, but he wasn't
smiling. Instead his expression was deadly serious and
when he lifted those dangerous blue eyes to hers she felt
suddenly dizzy.

The situation called for a light, jokey response but
there was nothing like that in her head so Emma simply held out her hand for the dark blue velvet box. 'Can
I see?'

When he didn't hand it over, she reached and took the
box from him, knowing that if she wanted to keep her
job she had to prove to him that she could do this. That
she could be every bit as detached as he was.

He probably thought she was dressing for him.

She had to prove she was dressing for herself.

'I feel uncomfortable wearing anything valuable.' She
discovered it was possible to speak as long as the subject wasn't personal. Flipping open the box, she gave a
gasp. 'Oh it's gorgeous.' It was a sapphire pendant and
her heart gave a little skip as she imagined how it might
have felt to be given such a gift by a man who loved her.

Killing those thoughts fast, she was about to lift it
from the case when Lucas did it for her.

'Turn around,' he said roughly and she turned without thinking and then heard his sharply indrawn breath
and remembered that the dress swooped low on her back.

Would he say something?

There was a pause. A moment when she held her

breath and willed that admirable restraint of his to splinter. She closed her eyes and waited, wanting desperately for him to just grasp her and take control as he had that night in the turret bedroom. She wanted all of that urgency, all of that wild passion, and then felt guilty because she knew that urgency and passion had been fed by raw emotion and a situation so painful that no one would want to repeat it.

And then she did feel his hands on her skin, cool and steady as he fastened the necklace. The touch was minimal, but even that was enough to set her alight. Even with her back to him the attraction was so fierce that it took her breath away and she was relieved he couldn't see her face because she was sure everything she felt would be visible. No make-up, however clever, could conceal feelings so powerful. And now she had to pretend that their relationship hadn't changed even though it had changed beyond recognition.

'The meeting seemed to go well.' She couldn't say any of the things she wanted to say so she talked about work. 'It's the first time I've met Cristiano in person, although I've talked to him on the phone a lot. He's not as scary as his reputation.'

'He liked you.' There was an edge to his tone that she didn't understand and she picked up her wrap and then turned, smiling, making sure that nothing of what she was feeling inside showed on the outside.

'I'm ready if you are.'

From the moment they set foot out of the hotel it was clear that this was going to be a party like no other. Flames shot into the air from torches, and what appeared to be a million tiny lights lit the paths that wound through the grounds towards a spectacular marquee large enough to accommodate hundreds of people. Emma felt a rush

of excitement because she'd never, ever in her life been
to an event like this one.

'It's incredible,' she breathed and Lucas glanced down
at her, registering her delight with a frown that made her
wonder what she'd done to annoy him.

'Avery Scott is very good at her job.'

'Good? I'm not good, I'm brilliant.' A sultry female
voice came from behind them and Emma watched as
Lucas's mouth curved into a smile. And that smile made
Emma catch her breath. To describe him as handsome
would be to do him an injustice, she thought, watching
as a passing waitress dressed as a mermaid slid a tall,
slender-stemmed glass into his hand.

'Avery—' he leaned forward and kissed the cool
blonde on both cheeks '—you've surpassed yourself.
It's spectacular. Thank you.'

'My pleasure. May you both have an absolutely brilliant and unforgettable time and don't forget to tell your
friends, as long as they're rich and can afford me.' Avery
extracted herself from Lucas without smudging her lipstick and winked at Emma. 'I am *loving* that dress.
Lucas, what do you think? Am I a genius or am I just
incredibly good at what I do?'

Lucas gave her a speculative look. 'Be careful.'

Avery chose to ignore the warning. 'She is nothing
like your usual type. Hang onto her.' She gave him a
friendly punch on the arm and Lucas gave a slight frown.

'She's the best PA I've ever had so I certainly intend to.'

Avery was scanning the crowd, looking for problems.
'That wasn't what I meant, and you know it, you utterly
infuriating man. Now go and enjoy the party.'

'Emma doesn't like parties.'

'Emma doesn't go to parties,' Avery said gently,

'which isn't the same thing at all. She's going to totally love this one because I organised it and it's going to be perfect.'

Emma never found out how Lucas would have responded to that because at that moment there was a clacking sound in the sky and Lucas glanced over his shoulder towards the beach where a helicopter was landing. 'Looks as if the Prince has arrived.'

The change in Avery was instantaneous. All the fizz and bubble went out of her, like a glass of champagne that had been left sitting overnight on a table. 'If you'll excuse me, duty calls. I expect I'll see you both later. Have fun.' Without looking in the direction of the helicopter, she walked away on heels that should have made it impossible to balance. Emma, who could guess how bad she was probably feeling, wondered if she should follow.

'She and Mal have history,' Lucas drawled, 'but don't mention it now because here he comes and it isn't a good idea to talk about Mal's past relationships. Unless Cristiano and I are teasing him in private, of course. Smile. He's royalty.'

The next few minutes were a blur of introductions.

Emma found the Prince seriously intimidating. Surrounded by heavyweight security, he dominated his surroundings, which probably wasn't surprising given his status. What was surprising was the fact that he didn't dominate Lucas. The two men stood side by side, equal in height, stature but also achievement.

They talked easily, as old friends and peers, and as she listened, Emma realised that it was Lucas she was listening to, not the Prince. It was Lucas she was looking at. She hungered to feel that beautiful mouth on hers, to feel those hands on her, to dig her fingers into the luxuriant blue-black hair.

In despair, she looked away. *She was completely obsessed about a man she couldn't have.*

Was this how Avery felt all the time?

Emma sneaked a glance at the Prince, still in conversation with Lucas, and wondered if the feeling was one-sided. Was Avery also in love with a man who couldn't love her back? There was no sign of an inner struggle on that bronzed, handsome face. No hint that tonight might be as difficult for him as it was for her.

And then she saw the moment the Prince picked out Avery in the crowd and saw him go utterly still as the woman who loved him so deeply turned her head to look at him. Their eyes met and held.

Knowing that she was witnessing a private moment that shouldn't be witnessed, Emma turned away quickly feeling a flash of deep empathy with the other woman. And also for Mal because in her own small way she understood about responsibility and duty.

And then she felt guilty even thinking that because although it was true that she had a responsibility towards Jamie, he was also her brother and she adored him.

And if she had put her own life on hold, that was her fault, wasn't it? Not Jamie's. He'd never asked her to do that.

But Angie had. *I've had him all week and now he's yours.*

Emma frowned as she realised how much she'd allowed her sister's attitude to affect her. How much she'd tried to compensate for Angie's lack of warmth towards their brother. Angie expected her to take responsibility at weekends and Emma had gone along with that because she adored spending time with Jamie and because—she breathed deeply—and because she was afraid to stand up to her sister.

Jamie wouldn't care if she occasionally booked a babysitter and went out. But Angie would. Angie would ladle on the guilt.

She straightened her shoulders.

That had to change. And she had to be the one to change it.

She was standing here now, wearing a dress that made her feel incredible, because someone else had pressured her into it but she realised that she could have done this by herself if she'd made the effort. Not the party and the illustrious company—of course not that—but dressing up and meeting new people. She could have done more of that. She *would* do more of that. This holiday, she was going to sit her sister down and tell her that things needed to change for all of them.

And then Lucas drew her to his side and the next moment he was introducing her to someone and she was smiling, and talking, and making bright conversation even though the only coherent thought her brain could produce was *I want him.* They mingled, met what felt like a million people and Emma kept smiling until she felt her face would crack, until her cheek muscles were tired and her head throbbed with the effort of making polite conversation. She shook so many hands and kissed so many cheeks that faces and greetings blurred.

It seemed that everyone wanted a piece of him and she noticed people bunching close by, all waiting for the chance to talk to Lucas Jackson.

And then finally they moved towards the marquee, the magnificent tent lined in swathes of midnight-blue silk, studded with glittering jewels that shone like a million tiny stars in a night sky and the music slid into her and suddenly she wanted to dance and dance. She wanted to make up for all the times in her life she hadn't danced and she turned to Lucas, eyes glowing.

'Is it allowed? Can we?'

He narrowed his eyes as if he sensed the change in her but didn't quite understand it. 'It's allowed, but I don't dance.'

Emma was about to argue and persuade him when he turned to speak to yet another acquaintance—*did he know everyone?*—and she reminded herself that she could dance without him. That dancing without him might actually be a good thing. She was allowed to dance and have fun and the music was fast and infectious so she just walked away from him and onto the dance floor feeling ridiculously free. She never did this, did she? She so rarely did something just for her, because she wanted to. Sex, she thought as she closed her eyes and let the music take her. That was something she'd done just because she'd wanted to. Because it had felt right at the time, just as this did.

And now she danced because she couldn't *not* dance with the music washing over her and the smiles of the people around her. And she was smiling too as she raised her arms like everyone else and threw her head back and let her body move to the rhythm.

'Good to see you letting your hair down.' It was Carlo, the Ferraras' cool, enigmatic lawyer who she'd been introduced to at the meeting earlier in the day.

And she danced and worked hard to have fun, ignoring the small nagging part of her that wanted to be dancing with Lucas.

Dancing was personal.

It was a good job he'd refused her.

* * *

He'd brought this on himself.

He was the one who had insisted she join him at the party. He was the one who had sent her off shopping to buy something suitable so he had no one to blame but himself if she returned with a dress that made him think nothing but indecent thoughts.

He'd refused to dance with her because he knew it would make a difficult situation even more difficult and the result of that was that she'd danced anyway, and now she was with Carlo, the Ferraras' smooth-talking, handsome lawyer and it required a superhuman effort not to stride through the crowd of dancers and drag her away from him.

Did it make it better or worse that she wasn't even looking at him?

Better, he decided and then thought that no, actually, it probably made it worse.

He told himself that she was just dancing, as were about a hundred other people around her, but then the music slowed and she slid into Carlo's arms, the change in the tempo of the music immediately altering the atmosphere. The dancing shifted from impersonal to personal. Lucas watched through narrowed eyes as Carlo's hand curved into the centre of Emma's back. That smooth, bare back that had been distracting him all evening.

Lucas had a sudden image of firelight on soft skin and suddenly he was striding across the dance floor, through entwined couples, until he reached his target. If he'd been asked to explain his behaviour he couldn't have done so. Never before had he cared enough to extract a woman from the arms of another man but he did it now without pause or hesitation.

'My dance.' It was a command, not a question and Carlo acknowledged that with the lift of an eyebrow, but he clearly saw something in Lucas's face because he reluctantly released Emma.

'Perhaps I'll see you later,' he murmured and Lucas felt his mood grow darker by the minute.

'She'll be busy later. But thank you for looking after her while I was busy with clients.'

Emma's eyes widened and she opened her mouth to speak, but Lucas slid his arms around her and moulded her against him before she could object. For a moment she stood stiff and he thought she might push him away. Then she sank against him and he held her the way Carlo had held her, except that this was an entirely different intimacy because their bodies already knew each other. That recognition was there and with it the memories and he felt the shiver pass through her and into him. It was no longer just a dance.

They were surrounded by people and yet they might as well have been alone for all the difference it made to the attraction.

As Carlo strolled away from them, Emma looked up at him. 'You were rude.'

'You asked me to dance.'

'That was earlier. And you said no.'

'So? I changed my mind.'

'In the middle of a dance? You couldn't have waited?'

No, he couldn't have waited and the knowledge unsettled him because impulse and urgency had no place in his life and he didn't want to feel this way. *Never had felt this way before.* 'He was behaving in an inappropriate manner.'

'We were just dancing. What's inappropriate about that?'

The image of Carlo's hand on her bare back was burned into his brain. 'For someone who supposedly loathes parties you appear to be having an incredible time.'

'I *am* having an incredible time. And I never said I loathed parties. Just that I never have the chance to go to any. I'm making the most of it and enjoying myself. I would have thought you'd be pleased.'

'Why would I be pleased?'

She sighed. 'Not *pleased* perhaps, but I didn't think—' She hesitated, staring at his shirt and not his face. 'I thought this was what you wanted. I didn't really think you'd care what I did in my own time.'

It was a reasonable, logical comment but nothing about the way he felt was reasonable or logical.

Aware that people were watching them curiously, Lucas closed his hand around her wrist. 'Let's get out of here.'

She didn't argue and he felt her pulse flutter against his fingers as he strode off the dance floor virtually towing her behind him.

'Could you slow down? I'm still an amateur at walking in heels.' She tugged at her wrist but he didn't let her go until they were out of the crowd and back outside under the starry sky.

Then he released her and she stared at him, confused by what was going on and he had no answer for her unspoken question because he was confused too. And he wasn't used to feeling confused. *He was never confused.*

'Do you think it's unprofessional of me to dance? Is that what's wrong?' She spoke slowly, clearly ticking off possible explanations in her head. 'I did ask you and I thought as we'd done the meeting and greeting it would be—'

'It wasn't unprofessional.'

'Then—'

'Just drop it, Emma.'

'How can I drop it? You've dragged me off the dance floor so I've obviously upset you in some way. You have been glaring at me since you gave me that necklace. And in the meeting this afternoon you were glowering.' Her fingers fiddled with the jewel at her throat. 'I understand that you regret what happened the other night, but as far as I'm concerned it's in the past. Honestly, you don't have to worry. It's true that I wasn't sure I'd be able to get back to how we were, but I've discovered that I can. I know I can.'

Then she was doing better than he was because he didn't know that at all. 'So were you dancing with Carlo because you wanted to or because you wanted to prove to me that what we shared hasn't affected our relationship?'

'Does it even matter?' She looked back towards the tent, leaving him with only a glimpse of her profile and the curve of her dark eyelashes.

'You should be careful around Carlo.'

'Oh for goodness' sake, Lucas—he's the Ferraras' lawyer. I've spoken to him a few times on the phone when he's called the office and he is a really nice guy.'

'Based on what evidence? Because he's good-looking? Because he's charming? You're not exactly an experienced judge given the number of relationships you've had in your life.'

This time she looked at him with eyes that questioned his sanity. 'Carlo grew up with the Ferrara brothers. They are lifelong friends, so presumably they see admirable qualities in him. I suppose the way we feel about people is coloured by our own experience. Perhaps you're too harsh a judge and no one would blame you for that given your background.'

'Perhaps you're naïve.'

'I was dancing with him, not proclaiming undying love. Don't you think you might be overreacting?'

Overreacting? Lucas dragged his hand over the back of his neck. 'Maybe I can read his mind better than you can. He's a red-blooded male.'

'Even if you're right about that, why would it matter to you? You've made it clear that you want our relationship to stay professional and nothing else so actually it's irrelevant. You don't have to watch out for me. That isn't your role.' She paused as a couple walked past them, arm in arm, and then lowered her voice. 'We agreed not to talk about this and we certainly shouldn't be talking about it here.'

'Good point. So let's go somewhere we won't be disturbed.' Knowing that he was acting irrationally, Lucas closed his hand around her wrist again and drew her along the path towards the hotel, walking so fast she almost stumbled.

'For goodness' sake, Lucas, you can't just leave! There are people hovering waiting to talk to you.'

'I don't care.'

'You are not making this easy.'

'I don't care about that either.'

'Where are we going?'

'Somewhere private. Somewhere we can talk without an audience.'

She'd never seen him like this before. They were at a side entrance to the hotel and, barely pausing, Lucas swiped a card through a scanner and the doors opened.

And Emma saw immediately that they were back in the Presidential Suite but this time via a private entrance that led straight onto the beach.

The doors purred closed behind them and she waited

for him to release her but instead he kept his fingers locked firmly around her wrist as he strode into the living room.

She wondered if she ought to point out that he was breaking his own rule. 'Lucas, we really ought to—'

'Maybe you'll push him too far, have you thought of that?' His tone was raw and savage. 'Maybe he seems like a decent human being until circumstances turn him into something else.'

Emma blinked, confused, and then realised that he was no longer talking about Carlo, he was talking about himself. About what had happened between them two nights before and her breathing jammed because she'd been trying so hard *not* to think about it. 'Lucas—'

'And when that happens, maybe you won't spot the signals, because you didn't spot them with me, did you? You didn't know when to back off. You could have left. You should have left. But you didn't. And then—you couldn't stop me, could you?' His tone was thickened and the breath caught in her throat because she could see that he was on the edge and she'd had no idea that his feelings were so intense. *She'd thought it was just her.*

'I could have stopped you. But I didn't want to.'

'Why? Because you're such a giving person you were willing to sleep with me to help me out?'

'No. Because I find you incredibly sexy and always have. Yes, I could have left, but I didn't want to. I *chose* not to. I could have stopped you but I chose not to do that either. And I'm glad I didn't because what we shared was special to me. Not just special—' she paused, wondering how honest to be '—it was the most exciting, erotic experience of my life. I don't regret it. I would do exactly the same again.'

'Would you?' His eyes met hers and suddenly it was hard to breathe.

'Yes.'

There was a brief pause and then they moved towards each other at the same time. Her arms were round his neck, his hands in her hair, their mouths hungry for each other as they kissed.

His mouth on hers, Lucas groaned deep in his throat. 'I promised myself that I wasn't going to do this again.'

'Then I'm so glad you're breaking your promise.'

He lifted his head but his hand remained locked in her hair as if he couldn't quite bring himself to let her go. 'It's wrong of me. Selfish.'

'No—' Standing on tiptoe and lifting her face to his, she breathed the word against his lips. 'It can't be selfish if I want it too, and I do want it, Lucas. I want *you*.' Bold now, she traced his lips with her tongue and he gave up the fight, cupped her face and kissed her back, taking everything she was offering and demanding more. And the kiss was everything she remembered. He kissed with skill and assurance but this time she was determined that he should know this was her choice. That *he* was her choice. So she placed her hand in the centre of his chest and pushed him off balance. He fell back onto the bed and before he had a chance to recover Emma straddled him, pinning his arms above his head, smiling at his stunned expression.

'Forty-eight hours ago you were a blushing, shy, inexperienced woman.'

'So? I have a lot of time to make up for. Now be quiet and kiss me the way you kissed me the other night—' She brushed her mouth over his and he captured her face in her hands before sliding his hands down her bare back.

'The dress is beautiful but it has to come off.'

Smiling, she released his hands and sat up, carefully drawing the dress over her head. 'Seems a shame to take it off.'

'It's not a shame from where I'm lying.'

The dress slid in a slippery heap to the floor and suddenly she was back in his arms and his mouth was hungry on hers. Her hands tore at his clothes, impatiently stripping away jacket and shirt until he was naked too, until there was nothing between them except feelings and the truth. His eyes were fierce but she knew hers would be too because she wanted this every bit as much as he did. Perhaps she'd always wanted it, from the moment she'd walked into his office on that first day and seen him lounging behind his desk, remote and untouchable.

This time it was slow, where last time it had been fast. Everything stretched out, the intensity of it as agonizing as the anticipation.

Her mouth roamed over him and she heard his breathing change and felt powerful and desirable as she discovered how her touch affected him, how the stroke of her hands could drive him wild, how the flick of her tongue had him reaching for her. And he let her explore, until finally he could stand it no longer and closed his hands over her hips, shifting her above him in a sure movement that brought her into contact with the heat of his arousal.

Emma held her breath as she took him into her, felt the power and the fullness and then there was nothing but the rhythm and the incredible need that consumed both of them as they surrendered to it. Still holding her, he drove himself deep and she groaned his name against his lips, holding back the words that she so desperately wanted to say, knowing that honesty would ruin the moment. None of that mattered. Nothing mattered. Not the future nor the past, just the present and she gave in to that

and allowed it to take her until they hit the same peak.
They kissed their way through it, sharing all of it until
she thought she'd die from the pleasure.

Lucas lay still, holding her, wondering why he had no
desire to just get up and leave as he usually did.

'What was her name?' Her voice was soft in the darkness and what surprised him wasn't the question, which
he understood immediately, but the fact that he wanted
to answer.

'Elizabeth. I named her after my father's mother. Her
great-grandmother. I liked to think that had she still been
alive perhaps she would have done the decent thing and
recognised her granddaughter. Either way, I wanted
Elizabeth to know who she was and be proud of it.'

'I like that. He refused to acknowledge you but you
created the link anyway.' Her arms tightened around him
as she showed her approval. 'It's a pretty name.' There
was a moment's silence and then she held him tighter.
'I know you don't want to talk about your daughter, but
whatever happened I know it wasn't your fault. You are
so wrong to blame yourself.'

'You're making that judgement without knowing the
facts.'

'I may not know the facts, but I know *you*. I know it
wasn't your fault. I know you would have done whatever
could have been done.'

Lucas stared into the darkness. 'Your faith in me is
touching but misplaced. I was a lousy father, Emma.'

'That isn't true. And I should know because I had one.
Or rather, I didn't have one. The man who fathered me
wasn't interested in that role. He walked out after my sister was born. He came back soon after and my mother
once told me that the reason she had me was to try and

bring them closer together. How she could ever have thought a man who had never wanted one child would have been suddenly happy to have a second, I have no idea. He walked out for the final time while Mum was in the hospital with me. I've never even met him.'

Suddenly he understood more clearly why she would have avoided relationships. She had no reason to trust men. And she shouldn't be trusting *him*. Knowing that this was going to end badly, he tightened his grip on her. 'That must have been tough.'

'It was, but tougher for my mum and my sister. My sister especially because she always felt that for him to walk out there must have been something lacking in her. Which was wrong, of course. There was something lacking in him, but that isn't true of you so don't ever tell me again that you were a bad father.'

'I didn't leave, but I might as well have done.' And suddenly, wrapped in her warmth, the words that had been jammed inside him for years flowed. 'It was snowing. Exactly like the other night. I'd been working long hours, trying to juggle several big projects. Because I often worked late and Elizabeth would be asleep by the time I arrived home, I was the one who got her up in the morning. We had breakfast together. That was our time together and it was always just the two of us because Vicky never emerged before eleven. That morning we had breakfast as usual. Nothing was different. You have no idea how many times I have gone over and over it in my mind, trying to work out if I missed something, but I don't remember anything out of the ordinary. I made her toast. And I cut her toast into the shape of a house because I always did that.'

'She must have loved that.'

'She did. She always ate the chimney first. I kissed her goodbye and promised her I'd take her to the park in the morning. Then I dropped her at school.' Remembering it was agonizing, the desire to put the clock back and do things differently almost overpowering. 'I left a note for Vicky telling her I'd be home before she had to leave for the party.'

'You weren't going to the party with her?'

'I wasn't interested in spending an evening at a party where I knew no one. I wanted to be with my daughter. I was planning to leave the office at five to give me plenty of time to get home. Just before I left I had a phone call from Elizabeth's teacher, wondering how she was. Apparently she'd started feeling ill at school and they'd rung Vicky.' He paused to breathe. 'When I rang Vicky and asked her what the doctor had said she told me she hadn't been able to get an appointment so she'd just put Elizabeth to bed and let her sleep. At that point I knew. Don't ask me how, but I just knew it was serious. All I wanted to do was get home but the snow had made the roads almost impassable. Just like the other night.'

'It must have been terrible for you. I can imagine how helpless you must have felt.'

'I cannot tell you how bad that journey was, crawling through the snow, knowing that my daughter was sick. I rang Vicky again to tell her to take her to the Emergency Department but she told me I was overreacting and anyway she was just leaving for the party. We had a row. I told her she couldn't leave and she told me that if I'd been home on time it wouldn't have been an issue. She could have arrived at the party any time, but she wasn't going to let something as insignificant as a sick child ruin her social life.' The bitterness still flowed but it was weaker now, diluted by time. 'She left Elizabeth alone with an inexperienced babysitter. Call it instinct, but I called an ambulance and it arrived at the same time as I did. The moment I walked through the door I knew how sick she was. She was screaming. The screaming was terrible—' He stopped because thinking about it was just too painful. 'I saw that she had a rash. The paramedics were wonderful and they gave her antibiotics but it was too little too late. It was meningitis. The very worst type, with complications, and she went downhill so quickly it was shocking.'

'That's terrible. Truly awful.' Her arms tightened around him. 'But I don't see how, even in your darkest moments, you could blame yourself for any of that.'

'You want me to list the ways?' *There were so many.* 'If I hadn't gone to work that morning, if I'd chosen to take her to the doctor instead of leaving it to Vicky, if I'd left work earlier—she'd still be alive.'

'You don't know that.'

'But I don't *not* know it either, and living with that is hell.'

'When you left for work did you realise how ill she was?'

'Of course not. There were no signs she was ill at all.'

'Precisely. You didn't know. You had no way of knowing. Nor did you know that your wife wouldn't pay attention to the signs.'

'I should have known. She was always very clear about her priorities. Vicky never wanted Elizabeth any more than my mother had wanted me and she never made any secret of the fact that having a baby wasn't going to affect her life.' He turned his head to look at her, her features just visible in the semi-darkness. 'Now you're shocked.'

'Not shocked. Sad for Elizabeth. Sad for Vicky, I suppose, for never knowing how wonderful it is to love someone other than yourself.' She slid her hand over his chest. 'And sad for you, because you tried to be a family and it went badly wrong. But that wasn't your fault, Lucas.'

'I made her pregnant. That was my fault. I trusted her to show some responsibility towards our daughter that day and she didn't. I should have known she wouldn't. That was my fault too.'

'Your fault that another person put her own needs before that of a poorly child? I don't think so.'

'I knew what she was like.'

'You said you trusted her to show responsibility towards your daughter, which proves to me you still had faith in her. She let you down and that's terrible but it doesn't make it your fault.'

'Even if you're right, it doesn't make it better. My head is permanently filled with what-ifs. You name it, I thought it. I still think it. In the end none of it matters. All that matters is that I let my daughter down. I wasn't able to help her or protect her and she deserved so much better.'

'You're so wrong about that.' Her voice rang with sincerity, but her words of comfort slid off his skin like raindrops off a window, unable to penetrate the thick wall of guilt that had locked him in for years.

'I appreciate what you're trying to do, but you're the one who is wrong. You don't know what you're talking about.'

'Yes, I do. You're forgetting I saw the photograph. I saw a little girl with her arms around her daddy—a daddy she clearly adored. She didn't want or deserve better. She had everything she wanted and needed. You didn't let her down, Lucas.'

'If I'd been there she'd still be alive. Maybe I wasn't looking closely enough when we ate breakfast together.

Maybe I missed something a better father would have noticed.'

'You were having breakfast with your daughter. I can tell you that from a child's point of view it doesn't get much better than that. You have to forgive yourself, Lucas. You have to accept that you did everything that could have been done. You have to accept that you were a good father but that even the best father can't protect a child from everything. Sometimes bad stuff happens and it's rubbish, but it's no one's fault and we have to stumble on the best we can until we start to function again.'

'I function. I've built a highly successful business.'

'But you don't have a family.'

'I don't want a family.' He'd made that decision in the weeks that had followed that terrible night. 'I tried. I failed. I don't want any of that. I certainly don't want the responsibility of a child.'

There was a long silence and then she pressed her lips to his shoulder. 'It must be terrifying, to have had that only to lose it. You *dare* not love because you loved so deeply and so fiercely and you lost.'

He grasped her hand and kissed her palm, breathing in the scent of her. 'I don't want to hurt you. I don't want you feeling anything for me.'

'What if it's too late? What if I tell you I already feel something?'

'I'd tell you it's the sex that makes you feel that way.'

'Really? I wouldn't know because it isn't something I do very often.'

'Which makes it even more likely that what you're feeling is linked with the physical intimacy.'

'Or that what I feel is genuine. I have felt something for you for ages. Probably the reason I put up with your unreasonable demands in the office.' She took a deep breath and Lucas closed his eyes, willing her not to say what he guessed she was about to say.

'Emma, please don't—'

'Please don't say I love you? The trouble is, I do. I love you, Lucas.' She said it softly and then again, more firmly. 'I love you. And I'm not saying it because I want you to say it back or anything like that, but I want you to know how I feel. I know you don't like people saying it.'

So this was how it felt. 'No one has ever said it to me before.'

'What, *never*? What about Vicky?'

The mention of Vicky was enough to bring him to his senses. 'Vicky never loved me. She loved the idea of the two of us together. She loved the fact I had influential friends. And I didn't love her either.'

'Because you shut that side of yourself off when you were a child.' Her arms tightened around him. 'You are loved, Lucas, and you can love back.'

'Is that what you're waiting for? Because if so, you're wasting your time.' His voice rough, he cupped her face in his hands and looked down at her, refusing to be anything but honest. 'I can't say I love you. And I won't make you false promises. For me it's just sex and I'll move on because I always move on. It's the only way that works for me.' He was brutal because he had to be and he braced himself for her reaction. At the very least she'd walk away from him and sleep in the second bedroom.

But she did neither of those things.

Instead she kissed him again. 'Then we'd better make the most of tonight.'

Lucas was wide awake when he heard the knock on the door of the suite. He turned to look at Emma but she was still fast asleep so he rose quietly from the bed and pulled on a pair of jeans and a T-shirt before walking through the living room and opening the door.

It was Cristiano, and he was carrying his youngest daughter, Ella.

'Sorry to disturb you so early,' he said smoothly, 'but we have a family crisis. Our eldest, Chiara, has slipped and banged her head. Laurel and I are about to take her to hospital but we need someone to watch Ella for a few hours.'

Lucas stared at his friend's child. Saw smiles and innocence. His pulse suddenly sprinted. 'The hotel has an excellent nanny service. I'll get you the number.'

'Laurel won't entertain leaving her with someone we don't know. And neither would I.'

'Then ask a friend.'

'That's what I'm doing.' Cristiano's gaze didn't shift from his. 'I'm asking you.'

Lucas discovered that his mouth was so dry it was almost impossible to speak. 'You need to leave her with someone who can be trusted.'

'Which is why I knocked on your door, my friend.' Still holding his daughter, Cristiano put his hand on Lucas's shoulder. 'Laurel and I couldn't think of anyone we trust more than you. Will you take her? It will just be for a few hours.'

It was the ultimate vote of confidence but never had anyone's confidence seemed so misplaced. He was the wrong person for this task.

Lucas looked at the little girl in his friend's arms, stared into dark curious eyes identical to Cristiano's. He knew her, of course, and she knew him. He'd been at her christening, at her first birthday party and endless other Ferrara events. He'd watched her grow from babe to toddler to little girl, but always from a safe distance and never from a position of responsibility.

'No. I can't—' But before the sentence was complete he found himself with his arms full of the little girl and she was so light, so fragile that he tightened his grip instantly in case he dropped her. Panic threatened to choke him because he knew with an absolute certainty that he couldn't do this. He didn't trust himself. His arms shook but the result of that weakness was that Ella simply wrapped her little arms around his neck, her soft curls brushing against his cheek.

'Fish! I want to see the fish—' She beamed past him towards the glass wall of the living room that formed a private aquarium, oblivious to the fact that right at that moment he was drowning in his own inadequacy.

Lucas was afraid to move in case he did something to damage this perfect human being, but she tugged at his shoulder insistently until he had no choice but to give in to her demands. Enchanted, she flattened her little hand on the glass, her fingers spread out like a starfish as she tried to 'touch' what she was seeing. So absorbed was she that she didn't even look round when her father spoke.

'*Grazie mille.* I will see you later and we're so grateful.'

Lucas turned his head, about to say that he couldn't do this, that he didn't *want* to do this, but Cristiano had already left and he was on his own with the child.

Emma stood in the bedroom, holding her breath as she listened through the door. She'd known the knock was coming and it had taken all her willpower to pretend to be asleep. Her feelings were a jumbled mess. The happiness and elation of their night together was mixed in with the utter misery of knowing that he didn't share her feelings. She knew she had a difficult decision facing her, but right now she concentrated on him. How would he cope?

She'd heard the agony in his voice as he'd spoken to his friend. She'd felt his pain and now she had a lump in her throat because she knew how hard this was for him. Her instinct was to rush out there and give him support, but Cristiano had made her promise not to do that because it would make it too easy for Lucas to hand over responsibility. They'd agreed that this strategy was worth a try so she stood still and listened as Ella chatted away to him, pointing out all the different fish. And she understood now what Cristiano had meant when he had told her quietly that if any child could give Lucas his confidence back it was little Ella. She was outgoing and confident, fascinated by the world around her and not at all shy or intimidated by Lucas. Another child might have been asking for her daddy, but not this one. In different circumstances Emma would have smiled because the little girl had so much of her father in her. No doubt she would one day be running the business Cristiano and his brother had turned into a global corporation, but for now she was taking charge of Lucas, telling him what she wanted to play with and exactly what he needed to do to make that happen.

'I brought my colouring pens. We can draw the fish. And I want you to draw me a playhouse for my garden at home. Daddy says you draw buildings so you'd be the best person to do that.'

'I don't think—'

'I forgot to say please,' Ella muttered, contrite. 'Please. Please.'

'Well…all right. We'll design your playhouse together.'

'Can we have a fish tank in it? That way I can charge people to come and look at them.'

Emma smothered a smile, wondering if commercial vision was welded into the Ferrara DNA.

She wanted to see Lucas's expression but she didn't want to intrude on what was undoubtedly an important moment for him. The question was, would Ella's trust be enough to restore Lucas's belief in himself?

To prevent herself from walking out there to see what was happening, she went to the bathroom and locked herself in and spent the next hour relaxing in the bath, ready to leap out of the water if Lucas called.

But he didn't call. And when she'd dried her hair and dressed she just couldn't hide away any longer and walked into the living room to find both of them eating bowls of ice cream ordered from room service. Scattered on the floor next to them were several large pieces of paper covered in pencil drawings.

Emma raised her eyebrows. 'This looks fun.'

'We're playing tea parties. Lucas let me order from room service.' Ella pushed a spoon towards her doll as she pretended to 'feed' her. 'Guess what? Lucas has designed me a playhouse. I helped.'

Lucas, Lucas, Lucas. Every other word was Lucas.

Emma knelt down on the floor next to the little girl and looked more closely at the drawings. Like most architects, Lucas usually used computer software for his plans. In this case he'd used a ruler and pencil but the drawing was no less detailed for the lack of technology or the unusual nature of the 'building'. Emma caught his eye and he gave a faint smile as he read her mind.

'North elevation,' he said quietly. 'I didn't see any reason not to do it properly. It's a relief to know I can still use a pencil.'

A lump grew in her throat. This was a man who had designed some of the most iconic structures of recent years and there was something endearing about the attention he'd given to this project. Just one glance told her that Ella Ferrara was going to have the most beautiful playhouse any child had ever had.

Ella finished her ice cream and sprawled on her stomach, absorbed by the project they were creating together, oblivious to the significance of the encounter. 'Can I colour it in?'

'Colour away.' Lucas handed her the coloured pens and she took them and stared hard at the drawing.

'Lucas, can it have a chimney?'

He studied the drawing. 'Now why didn't I think of that? A chimney would be perfect. Where do you think it should go?'

'Here.' She stabbed her finger into the paper and Lucas handed her the pencil.

'Good decision. Draw it on. And any time you want to join my company just let me know.'

'You two have certainly been busy.' Smiling, Emma sat down next to them and helped herself to ice cream. 'Healthy breakfast, Lucas.'

'One bowl of ice cream isn't going to hurt her. We've ordered toast if you'd rather wait for that. You might want to move that chimney to the right a bit, Ella—'

Watching the little girl carefully drawing a chimney onto the plans while Lucas helped her, Emma wondered if he even realised how natural he was with the child and how much time had passed while the two of them had been designing their playhouse. At some point over the last few hours he'd forgotten the weight of responsibility and focused instead on just occupying her. And whatever he believed about himself, Emma saw the care he showed. It was evident in everything. From his infinite patience with the little girl, to the way he listened carefully to her every request.

When room service arrived with an order of hot toast, it was Lucas who spread the butter and then deftly cut windows and a door before presenting it to the little girl.

Watching, Emma wondered if he even realised what he'd just done.

'Oh!' Ella's face brightened as she stared at the plate. 'A toast house. With a chimney. I want my toast like this always and for ever. You have to teach my dad.'

Lucas stared at the plate, his breathing shallow.

Staring at the intimidating set of his features, Ella's smile faltered. 'I forgot the please again,' she said in a small voice. 'You're angry because I forgot the please.'

He squatted down to her level and smiled at her. 'I'm not angry. And I'm glad you like the toast.'

'It's the best thing ever.' Ella hesitated and then reached out and picked up the chimney. 'I'm eating the chimney first. Then I'm going to eat the door.'

Over the top of her head, Lucas's eyes met Emma's briefly and then he turned his attention back to the child. 'Ella, this is my friend Emma and you're going to play with her for a while because I have to—'

'You can't leave.' Ella slipped her hand into his. 'Our house isn't finished. If you're hungry, you can share my toast.' Carefully, she selected a window and slid it into Lucas's mouth.

'Ella—'

'More?'

'No.' His voice was hoarse. 'No more.'

'You forgot to say thank you.' Ella gave him a sympathetic look. 'Don't worry. Remembering is hard, isn't it?'

Lucas breathed deeply. 'Yes. Remembering is hard.'

'I'll help you if you help me.' Ella crawled onto his lap with the rest of her toast. 'I like staying with you. It's fun and you don't tell me off when I forget to say please. Can we do this again?'

Emma discovered that she was holding her breath. Perhaps it was too much. Perhaps it just wasn't going to—

'Yes—' Lucas rescued the plate before the buttered toast landed on his lap '—we can do this again. I'm going to be coming to Sicily soon to discuss a new hotel with your daddy. If you like, I could build that playhouse for you.'

'Perfect.' Ella beamed and flung her arms around his neck and Emma turned away quickly, tidying up some crayons to hide the tears on her face.

He'd made her a toast house, the way he used to with his daughter. And now he was promising to help her build the playhouse. That was progress, surely?

It was too soon to be sure, but she was confident that Cristiano's idea had been a good one. He'd trusted his friend with his most precious possession and that trust would hopefully propel Lucas forward a few steps.

And she had to move forward too. She had to stop avoiding things that she found difficult and face them.

She had to have an honest conversation with her sister.

Knowing that it was time to leave, she made her excuses and left the two of them together while she returned to her own bedroom to pack, breaking off only to send an email.

'This came for you.' Lucas stood in the doorway, an envelope in his hand and his eyes on the suitcase. 'You're still planning on leaving today?'

'I want to spend time with Jamie. Has Ella gone?'

'Cristiano just picked her up.' His eyes were still on the suitcase. 'Apparently Chiara is doing fine.'

Emma kept her eyes down, afraid of revealing that there had never been anything wrong with the eldest Ferrara daughter. They'd all agreed that only the threat of an emergency would have induced Lucas to look after the little girl and it had been worth the deception.

His hand covered hers as she pushed a pair of shoes into the case. 'If I asked you to stay another day, would you?' His tone was raw and her heart pounded.

'Is some aspect of my work unfinished?'

'This isn't about work. The work is done. If you stayed it would be about the two of us.'

Emma closed her eyes because it was so, so tempting. It would have been so easy to stay. So easy to fool herself that if she stayed his feelings might change. But she wasn't going to do that to herself. Or to him.

Reluctantly, she extracted her hand from his, horrified by how difficult it felt to do that. 'I have to go, Lucas.'

'One more day.'

'I can't.'

There was a long, tense silence and then he stepped back, his eyes guarded. 'Right. Good decision. I'll see you back in the office after Christmas. Aren't you going to open the letter?'

'It's not for me.' She folded the last of her clothes into the case she'd bought at the mall. 'It's for you. You should open it. It will save me the bother of putting it in another envelope.' From behind her she could hear the sound of the envelope being torn open. And then there was silence.

'Your letter of resignation.' His voice was flat and devoid of expression. 'I thought we'd dealt with this once. You agreed there was no need for you to leave.'

'There was no need to leave when we'd had one night

of sex.' Emma closed the case and lifted it off the bed and onto the floor. 'There is every reason to leave now I know I'm in love with you.'

He stilled. 'About that—'

'If you're going to tell me that I don't know my own mind, then let me stop you right there.' She let go of the case and straightened. 'I've told you about my father, but I've never told you about my mother.'

'Your mother?'

'She had a real talent for falling in love with men who couldn't love her back. Instead of walking away, somehow she always managed to convince herself that if she stuck at it, they'd come round. She did it with my father, even after he walked out leaving her to cope with a baby on her own. And then she did the same thing with her boss.' She saw understanding dawn in his eyes and nodded. 'That's right. Jamie is the result of an affair that my mother had with her boss. She fell in love with him. Unfortunately he didn't feel the same way about her but instead of leaving, she stayed. And the longer she stayed, the more she hoped.' And, for the first time, she'd been given a glimpse of just how hard it had probably been for her mother. And how easy it would be to take strands of hope and spin them into something substantial and meaningful.

'Emma—'

'No, don't say a word. You have no idea how much I want to pretend to myself that I can carry on working for you and that the way I feel won't be a problem. But I know it will be a problem. I'll have to see you every day, but not tell you how I feel. I'll have to take phone calls from the women you see and keep smiling while I do it, and I can't do that, Lucas.' She had to force the words out. 'I won't live my life hoping that one day I'm going to wake up and find my dream has become reality. I won't do that to myself.'

He watched her for a long moment and then paced across the elegant bedroom and stared out across the private swimming pool.

She waited for him to say what he was thinking and, as the silence stretched, so a tiny flicker of hope bloomed somewhere deep inside her. Even without her permission, it bloomed. And this was how it started, she thought. If she stayed, it would be like this. In every word and action, she'd be searching for a different meaning. Hoping, just as she was hoping now.

He drew back his shoulders, those strong, muscular shoulders that she now knew so well.

'You have a notice period.' His voice was businesslike. 'It won't be easy to replace you.'

And, just like that, hope died. The pain was sharp, like falling onto broken glass. She wondered if her mother had felt like that every day and, if so, how she had managed to get back up and keep going back for more.

'There's no need to worry about replacing me. I've already done it. Fiona Hawkings is currently working for John in Accounts and she's just what you need. Efficient, competent and not remotely interested in anything except a professional relationship. She was going to cover for me during my holiday so she's already fully briefed and if she has a problem then she has my number.'

Lucas's expression didn't change. 'You already had someone lined up?'

'If I'd been knocked over by a bus, someone needed to know how to run your office. So you're sorted. No need to worry.'

'And what about you? Is it wise to give up your job without another one to go to?'

No. But it was wiser than staying because every day she stayed would make it harder to leave. 'I'll be fine. I'm good at what I do. I'm going to find a job nearer to home and try and get some sort of balance in my life. I certainly don't have that at the moment. I want to spend time with Jamie, not just at weekends, but during the week too. I want to be able to go out in the evening occasionally without feeling guilty because I'm only at home for forty-eight hours.' She gave a half smile. 'I want to go dancing.' She said the words even though right now she didn't feel as if she'd ever be able to dance again.

'Will your sister approve?'

'Probably not.' And telling her was something she was dreading. 'That's something I need to deal with, I know I do. I've been avoiding it because it felt difficult.'

'Talking of avoiding things because they feel difficult—' his voice was harsh '—was it your idea to give Ella to me to look after?'

She shook her head. 'Cristiano's. You think you've never been loved, Lucas, but you're so wrong. Maybe your family didn't love you but you have friends who love you. Cristiano and Laurel, Mal—' she blushed '—I mean the Crown Prince. They all love you like a brother. And Ella, of course—' she managed a light smile '—she adores you.'

His gaze didn't shift from her face. 'And you.'

'Yes, me. But I don't love you as a brother.' Trying not to think about that, she picked up her case. 'I'm not using the jet. I'm not working for you any more so it seemed like a liberty.'

'For heaven's sake, Emma, use the jet.' He sounded irritable and angry but she knew it was just because she'd shaken up his routine. Lucas Jackson liked his life to run smoothly and her leaving was threatening that. He was worried that his business would suffer.

'Goodbye Lucas. Be kind to Fiona. And to yourself.' And without looking back, she walked towards the door.

'I'll hold the job open until the end of the month. Just in case your sister has a meltdown.'

'You don't need to do that. When I explain, she'll understand.'

CHAPTER NINE

'You resigned? Oh my God, are you *mad*?'

'I'm not mad. It was a well thought out decision.' The only decision she could have made and she clung to that belief as her sister's censorship and judgement eroded her self-confidence like acid rain. 'Don't worry, Angie. I'll find another job. And please calm down or you'll worry Jamie.'

'Worry Jamie? What about me? Don't you think I'm worried? I don't earn enough to support us all, Emma. I already have enough responsibility.'

'I don't expect you to support us all and I intend to take on more of the responsibility.' Emma forced herself to stay calm. 'I've told you—I'll find another job. I've already started to look and I've called a few people I know.'

'Why didn't you do that before you resigned? I mean why the sudden hurry? What happened?' Her sister paced the tiny kitchen and then suddenly stopped and turned, eyes riveted to Emma's face. 'Oh no—' Her voice dropped to a whisper. 'You slept with him, didn't you? You slept with your boss. *That's* what happened.'

Hearing her sister reduce her feelings to no more than a sordid encounter upset her more than she would have imagined possible. Suddenly she wished she had a different relationship with her sister. One in which she could confide and express her real feelings. She thought about the lovely chat she'd had with Avery and wished it could have been that way with her sister. The irony was that she'd been more open and honest with Lucas than she was with Angie. 'I'll get another job. That's all you need to know.'

Angie didn't appear to be listening. 'Knowing what happened to Mum, you slept with your boss?'

'I am *not* Mum. This is different.'

'How is it different?' Angie started clattering around the kitchen, crashing mugs together as she unloaded the dishwasher. 'Don't tell me, you love him and you think if you resign you can have a relationship. You think he'll suddenly waltz up here and ask you to marry him, is that it? Oh God, you're *exactly* like her. Delusional! A total dreamer.'

Emma was shaking. 'I am none of those things and that isn't what I'm thinking. I'm *nothing* like Mum and I don't want to talk about it any more because you just don't listen.' She couldn't even allow herself to think how her life was going to be without Lucas. It had only been a day and already she was aching.

But her sister seemed oblivious to her feelings. 'You had an amazing job and you've thrown it all away for nothing.' Another clatter of plates. 'You seem to have forgotten your responsibility towards Jamie. Lucas Jackson is not the settling-down type, Emma. Anyone can see that.'

'And I don't blame him for that, given his experience of family.' Struggling with her own feelings, unable to cope with her sister's too, Emma lost it. 'And you are supposed to be *my* family. You are supposed to love me and care about me. Instead all you do is yell at me and blame me and think about yourself.'

Angie looked taken aback. 'I do love you! That's why I'm so upset that you've done this.'

'No. You're upset that I've "done this" because you're worried about the impact it's going to have on *your* life.' Emma wrapped her arms around herself. 'You don't care about my life. You don't care that I'm in love with Lucas or that I'm hurting or that the thought of a life without him is breaking my heart. You don't care about any of that.'

'You're in love with him? You really are?' Angie looked so appalled that Emma closed her eyes.

'Yes, but if you're worried I'm going to be like Mum then don't be. I know he doesn't love me back so I'm not going to be hanging around waiting for that to happen. He can't love because he's hurting so badly—'

Angie looked baffled. 'How is *he* hurting?'

'Never mind. It doesn't matter. I shouldn't have said anything—' Her voice broke and she turned away but the next moment Angie had dumped the plates and suddenly she had her arms around Emma and they were hugging in a way they'd never hugged before.

'I'm sorry. I didn't know you were in love with him. I would have done anything for that not to happen. I saw how badly that affected Mum.' Angie was crying too and hugging her so tightly that Emma could hardly breathe. 'I'm sorry you're so hurt. I *do* care. You have no idea. It's just that I promised Mum I'd look after you and Jamie and not let anything happen to you and I feel like I've failed because you've gone and done *exactly* what she did. I never, ever wanted you to be hurt in this way. I did everything I could to protect you from it.'

'This is life, Angie, and you can't stop life happening. And you haven't failed. You held it all together and you gave up so much so that we could be a family, I'm not surprised you feel resentful about that sometimes. You wouldn't be human if you didn't.' Sniffing, Emma pulled away even though it felt surprisingly good to be held. 'But that is going to change. I'm going to find a job closer to home so that I can take care of Jamie and you can go to college.'

'I couldn't do that.'

'Why not?'

'Because I'm the head of the family.'

Emma shook her head, realising for the first time just how much responsibility their mother had loaded onto her elder sister. 'No. You've allowed me to do a job I love. Now it's your turn. Life doesn't have to be a self-sacrifice, Angie. Maybe it isn't possible to have it all, but we can do better than this.'

Jamie came running into the room and stopped dead when he saw them, the excitement in his face replaced by anxiety. 'What's the matter? What's wrong? Why are you both crying?'

'Nothing.' Angie pulled away, smiling. 'We're just hugging. Sisters hug. Anything wrong with that?'

'No.' Jamie looked at them curiously and Emma wrapped him in her arms, grateful for her family and trying to ignore the horrible, hollow ache in her gut.

'It's so good to be home. I missed you.' Determined not to mope, she released him. She had to pull herself together because the last thing she wanted was for Jamie to guess how bad she was feeling. 'Sorry it took me so long to get here.'

'It doesn't matter. I was at Sam's and that was really cool because he has a new puppy. And I played with the Lego Lucas sent. I can't wait to show you.'

Frowning, Emma released him. 'Lego?'

'The Star Wars ship. It arrived the day you flew to…
to…that place.'

'Zubran. Lucas sent you Lego? But how did he even
know it's your favourite?' And then she remembered that
she'd mentioned it. Just once. The morning after they'd—
She swallowed. 'Was there a note with it?'

Jamie poured cereal into a bowl, oblivious of the significance of the gift. 'Yes, but it was short. It just said he
was sorry he had to borrow you or something and that
the Lego would keep me busy until you came home. Can
I have sugar on my cereal?'

'No.' Both girls spoke simultaneously and Emma felt
her heart pound.

'That was a thoughtful, generous thing to do.'

Angie shot her a warning look. 'And that's all it was.
A thoughtful and generous gesture. And quite right too.
Don't go getting any ideas. Don't read anything into it.
You are *not* going down that route. Remember?'

But over the next few days, Emma discovered just how
hard it was to kill hope. Every time the phone rang, her
heart jumped. Every time someone knocked on the door,
she held her breath. But it was never Lucas and the disappointment was like a physical blow. The effort of keeping
a smile on her face exhausted her. Inside she felt hollow
and miserable and it must have showed because Angie
started to fuss over her in a way she'd never fussed before. Or maybe it was just that their relationship had
changed. Certainly they were talking more and Emma
had even persuaded her sister to pick up a prospectus
from the local college.

Two days later she had a call from Cristiano Ferrara,
offering her a job.

'I heard that you resigned,' he said, his Sicilian accent more pronounced over the phone, 'and I didn't want you to be snapped up by anyone else. You can work from home or we'll find you an office, whichever you prefer. I don't care where you are as long as you work for me. Our business is growing and it would be useful to have someone based in the UK.'

Emma listened as he outlined terms that were ridiculously generous and all the time he was speaking she just wanted to ask about Lucas. She wanted to know if he was all right. If he was working too hard. If he'd changed since he'd looked after little Ella.

But she didn't, because she knew she had no right to know the answer to any of those questions.

And she accepted the job without hesitation, ignoring that tiny part of her that said she was only doing it because it meant retaining a tiny link with Lucas. That wasn't it. What person in their right mind would turn down the chance to work for the Ferrara Group? Especially at the terms he was offering.

They agreed to sort out details in the New Year and Emma came off the phone wondering why she couldn't feel more elated.

Angie squealed with excitement when she told her and Jamie was delighted that she wasn't going to be away so much.

Emma couldn't even bring herself to think about working for someone who wasn't Lucas.

A few days after the madness of Christmas, she was standing in Jamie's bedroom, staring at the Star Wars Lego and wondering again why Lucas had sent it, when the doorbell rang.

Jamie and Emma had gone to scour the sales for bargains and she was alone in the house so she had no choice but to answer the door herself.

Lucas stood there holding a handful of crumpled papers, his Lamborghini attracting a crowd of awed teenagers in the street outside. 'Can I come in?'

Emma looked at him stupidly, resisting the temptation to fling herself at him like a puppy greeting its owner. *So* handsome, she thought, as she looked at that dark hair brushing the collar of the black cashmere coat. Handsome and guarded. 'I thought you were in Zubran.'

'Not any more. Are you going to let me in or slam the door in my face?'

Her heart skidded in her chest. She told herself firmly that what he was going to say wasn't going to be what she wanted him to say. It would be something to do with work. Something she'd forgotten to hand over to Fiona. 'You can come in, but I can't vouch for the safety of your car if you leave it there.'

'I don't care about my car.' Without waiting for her to move aside, he stepped past her and the brush of his body against hers caused them both to tense.

They created it between them, she thought. The electricity.

His eyes narrowed. 'You've lost weight.'

Emma thought of Avery and lifted her chin. *Pride.* No way was she going to let him know how bad she felt. 'No, I haven't,' she lied, 'it's just what I'm wearing. What's that in your hand? If it's a contract, forget it. I'm already working for someone else.'

'I know. Cristiano. Good. I'm glad that's sorted out.'

Emma closed the front door, thinking that the narrow hallway of their home wasn't the best place to be trapped with a man of his physique. She wanted to keep her distance, but there wasn't enough room to keep her distance when he dominated the limited space. 'You told him to employ me?'

'I can't tell Cristiano Ferrara who to employ. I merely told him you were available. He's a bright guy. I knew it would be a matter of hours before he offered you a job.' There was something different about him. Something in his eyes. A new energy and she felt relieved to see it because she'd been so worried about him.

'You're not here to ask me to work for you again?'

'No. I don't want you working for me again. Fiona is working out nicely. You were right about her. She's great.'

'Oh. Right. Well, that's—' her ego absorbed the blow '—good. That's really good.'

'Yes, it is good, because you have this thing about not having a relationship with your boss,' he said softly, 'so I don't want to be your boss any more.'

Emma felt strangely dizzy.

She was doing it again, she thought. Imagining things she shouldn't be imagining. Dreaming dreams she shouldn't be dreaming.

'Why don't you want to be my boss any more?'

'You're a bright girl. I would have thought it was obvious.'

Emma lifted her hand to her throat, too scared to speak.

He raised an eyebrow. 'Aren't you going to say something?' The corners of his mouth—*that beautiful sexy mouth*—flickered. 'I've never known you short of words before.'

'If you don't want me to work for you then…those papers in your hand aren't a contract?'

'No.' He handed them to her and she smoothed them with shaking hands and saw that she was holding a picture of a house, obviously drawn by a child but surprisingly detailed.

'Oh. Did Ella do this?'

'No. I did it.' His voice was rough. 'I was six years old and living in one small room with a woman who didn't want me.'

Emma looked at him, the breath jammed in her throat. His mother. He was talking about his mother. 'You drew it?'

'Living in that small room with just one tiny window felt wrong to me. To block it out I dreamed of the house I wanted to live in. I promised myself that one day I'd build it and to make sure I never forgot, I drew it. You're holding that drawing.'

'You kept it.'

'Yes. Because I never wanted to forget where I came from.'

The lump stung her throat as she thought of the little boy dreaming of his escape. 'Why are you showing me this?'

'Because it's time to build that house. I've built structures for many people, but never a home for myself because home meant family and I've always shied away from that for all the reasons you already know. Even when I married Vicky I didn't build this home. She chose an expensive house in an expensive road and I paid for it. But now I'm ready to build something special. And what I want to know is—' he hesitated, his gaze fixed on her face '—will you live in it with me?'

The papers slid from her fingers onto the floor. 'Me?'

'Yes, because a house is just a building. It's the people in it that make it a home and that's what I want. A proper home.' Stooping, he recovered the drawings. 'It doesn't have to be exactly like this. You can help me improve it.

And Jamie had better have some input as he'll be living in it too. And I thought we could build a separate house for your sister in the grounds, so that she can have her own life but still be part of ours if she wants that.'

'Part of ours?' If she'd been scared before, she was terrified now. Terrified that what she was imagining wasn't what he was asking. That his intentions might not match her hopes. That she might fall as her mother had fallen, and then stumble to her feet only to fall again. 'I don't understand what you're asking. I don't understand what you're telling me.'

He put the drawings on the hall table. 'I'm asking you to marry me. I'm asking you to live with me so that we can be a family. I'm telling you that I love you.'

Emma closed her eyes, unable to believe what he was saying. 'You can't love. It's the one thing you can't do. You don't *want* to do it.'

'I've discovered I was wrong about that. Apparently I can love.' He cupped her face in his hands and lowered his mouth to hers, kissing her gently. 'I love *you*. And I want to be with you, always. I can build you a house, Emma, I'm good at that part. But you have to help me make it a home. That's the bit I'm no good at. But you are. I've never met anyone like you before. You're fiercely loyal and determined. That night in the snow—I sent you away, but you wouldn't leave.'

'How could I leave you? I was so worried about you.'

'I was unforgivably rude to you.'

'Not rude. Just hurting.' She touched his face with her fingers, still unable to believe that he'd actually said he loved her. 'I stayed because I wanted to.'

'And last year—' he breathed deeply '—you stayed then too.'

'I only put a blanket over you, I didn't know what else to do.'

'And you locked the door and made sure no one saw me like that. And then brought me strong coffee all morning and fielded my calls, without ever putting pressure on me to tell you what was wrong.'

'I suppose I knew you wouldn't want to talk about it. And now I know, I'm not surprised you were drunk—' she slid her arms around his waist '—you suffered a terrible loss.'

'Yes. And that doesn't go away,' he said quietly, 'but spending time with you made me look at it differently. And look at myself differently. And then you and Cristiano cooked up that plan for me to have Ella.'

'It was Cristiano's idea. I was worried it might have been too much but he was determined to do something. He just made me promise not to come out of the bedroom and take over.'

His eyes gleamed. 'So you left me to struggle.'

'No, I left you to cope. And I hoped that once you realised you were coping, you'd start to regain your confidence. And you did.'

'Yes,' he said slowly, 'I did.'

'You've never even told me what happened to Vicky. Were you divorced?'

'We were never married. The moment I found out she was pregnant, I wanted her to marry me, but she wouldn't make that commitment. She thought it would make her less marketable. She didn't want to be seen as a "mother". The only thing that was keeping us together was Elizabeth and after she died, we went our separate ways. Last thing I heard Vicky was in Australia but we don't keep in touch.'

'I'm sorry.'

'Don't be. It was never a relationship. That was the problem. And I told myself I didn't want to even try it again. That night in the castle—it was so hard to tell you I wanted to keep it professional.' He lowered his mouth to hers and kissed her slowly and deliberately, until she gave a low moan and pressed against him.

'I really believed that was what you wanted. Then I started to wonder. Your reaction over the red dress—I thought you were just angry but Avery thought it was something different.'

He smiled against her lips. 'Avery is too astute for her own good.'

'I like her *so* much. She was the one who persuaded me to just dress up and have a good time. So that's what I did. I really didn't think anything would happen. And then you were so angry that I danced with Carlo—'

'Jealous—' Lucas groaned '—and *not* proud of it. But it was seeing you with him that made me realise that I didn't want to keep things professional. I'd never felt that way before.'

'I hadn't either. I'd always promised myself that I'd never fall for my boss and I really tried to stick to that, but I decided that night that I just wanted to spend whatever time I could with you. That I'd rather find another job if I had to.'

'I can't believe you sacrificed so much to support your family.' He gathered her close. 'When I think of the number of times I kept you working late at the office, not knowing that you were going home alone to a rented room.'

'I liked working late. Probably because I loved being with you.'

'I was a nightmare boss.'

'No! That isn't true. You were an excellent boss.'

'You slog your guts out during the week to earn money for your family and then you rush back here at weekends so that you can take care of them, not because you have to but because you want to. I've never seen that commitment in anyone. To be honest I didn't even believe it existed. You're so special.'

'I'm not special,' she stammered, 'I'm boringly ordinary. There are loads of people like me around.'

'Not true. And anyway, the only person I'm interested in is you. And because I'm horribly selfish I want you all to myself. I want you with a piece of paper binding you to me and I want you wearing my ring on your finger so that if I drive you mad you won't walk out.'

'I'd never walk out!' Emma was shocked that he'd even suggest it and then remembered that he'd never had any stability in his life, ever, and that realisation made her hug him all the more tightly because she was determined to change all that. 'You're so incredibly talented and clever and you've built so many things, but you've never had foundations of your own. You don't have to worry about me leaving. I'd never leave. I love you so much.'

'I know. And I'm so lucky that you love me. You are the most loyal, loving person I've ever met.' He buried his fingers in her hair and kissed her again. 'You've stuck with your sister and brother, no matter what. You took a job that paid well so that you could support them even though it meant living away from them. I've never met anyone as unselfish as you.'

'I wasn't that unselfish,' Emma murmured, leaning her head against his chest. 'I loved my job. Or at least, I loved being with you every day. Seeing you. I've missed you so badly it's been agony although very good for the figure.'

'You can still be with me every day, only you won't be working with me.' He stroked her hair. 'You haven't answered my question.'

'Question?'

'I asked you to marry me. It would be nice to have an answer.'

Emma felt as if she were walking on air. 'I thought the answer was obvious. I've already told you I love you. The answer is yes, of course. A huge yes. A massive yes.'

He slid his hand into his pocket and pulled out a box. Flipping open the lid, he removed a flawless diamond ring. 'Just so that you can't change your mind, I bought you this.'

Emma gaped. 'It's…huge.'

'I want other men to be able to see from a distance that you're mine.'

She gave a choked laugh as he slid it onto her finger. 'They can probably see it from Zubran. It's—' she felt overwhelmed, not just by the ring but by the sentiment behind it '—it's beautiful, Lucas but I think I'm too scared to wear anything this valuable. I'll need a bodyguard.'

'You have me.' Lucas lifted her hand to his lips and kissed it. 'And I'm going to build you a house that will keep you and the ring safe, but in the meantime how would you feel about taking the whole family to Sicily for a holiday?'

'Sicily?'

'I owe a certain little girl a playhouse. It's a small price to pay for what she did for me,' he said in a husky voice and Emma blinked back the tears that clouded her vision.

'I think a holiday in Sicily sounds perfect.'

* * * * *

TO CLAIM HIS HEIR
BY CHRISTMAS

VICTORIA PARKER

Victoria Parker's first love was a dashing heroic fox named Robin Hood. Then came the powerful, suave Mr Darcy, Lady Chatterley's rugged Lover – the list goes on. Thinking she must be an unfaithful sort of girl, but ever the optimist, she relentlessly pursued her Mr Literary Right, eventually found him lying between the cool crisp sheets of a Mills & Boon and her obsession was born.

If only real life was just as easy...

Alas, against the advice of her beloved English teacher to cultivate her writer's muse, she chased the corporate dream and acquired various uninspiring job-titles and a flesh-and-blood hero before she surrendered to that persistent voice and penned her first Mills & Boon romance. Turns out creating havoc for feisty heroines and devilish heroes truly is the best job in the world.

Victoria now lives out her own happy-ever-after in the north-east of England, with her alpha exec and their two children – a masterly charmer in the making and, apparently, the next Disney Princess. Believing sleep is highly overrated, she often writes until three a.m., ignores the housework (much to her husband's dismay) and still loves nothing more than getting cosy with a romance novel. In her spare time she enjoys dabbling with interior design, discovering far-flung destinations and getting into mischief with her rather wonderful extended family.

CHAPTER ONE

HE WAS GOING to propose. Any minute now.

It was every little girl's dream. A handsome man, one of the most beautiful she'd ever seen, sat opposite her at an intimate table for two, with a velvet box nestled in his inside pocket. Aristocracy, no less. The suave Savile Row sophisticate who was Viscount Augustus. The man who'd set the scene so superbly.

Dimly lit chandeliers cast a seductive romantic ambience throughout the room of the critically acclaimed restaurant, where Michelin chefs were famous for creating masterpieces of haute cuisine. Open fires crackled and crystal tinkled as exorbitantly priced champagne flowed, poured into flutes in an amber rush of opulent effervescence. And beyond the wide plate-glass windows lay the majestic vista of the Tarentaise Valley—Savoie, bathing in the rose-pink wash of dusk, its white-capped mountains towering from the earth like watchful sentinels over the exclusive lavish ski resort of Pur Luxe.

Stunning. Awe-inspiring. The stage was set.

All that was left were the words.

And Princess Luciana Valentia Thyssen Verbault was paralysed with dread.

Please, God, please get me out of this somehow...

There is no way out, Luce. Not only do you have a duty to your people but a deal is a deal. And you made one with the devil himself.

Lord, she hated her father right now. *'Go to the Alps,'* he'd said. *'Take a few days to think things over, get your head together.'*

Luciana had taken in his seemingly sincere autocratic face, paler since she'd last seen him as his health continued to deteriorate, and thought, yes, a few days to ponder. After all, she'd thought, she had years before her coronation, plenty of room to breathe, to barter for more time. But, as the saying went: Men plan. Fates laugh.

King Henri of Arunthia was being pushed by his doctors to retire. So she'd come to inhale the invigorating crisp air, to infuse her mind with solace. Reassess. Come up with a strategy where matrimony wouldn't equate to losing the only person she lived for. What her father *hadn't* said was that he was dropping her smack-bang in the midst of her worst nightmare by sending Augustus to seal the deal.

She supposed she should have seen it coming. Avoiding the Viscount via any means possible since her return home from China three weeks ago obviously hadn't worked a jot. All she'd done was delay the inevitable.

You can run but you can't hide. Wasn't that what they said?

Truth was, for so long she'd been living on borrowed time, wishing with all her heart that time would miraculously stand still. But time, as she'd soon realised, waited for no man. Let alone a woman as desperate as she was to avoid the ticking clock.

Now she would pay the ultimate price for bartering with her father five too short years ago. Five years of living a normal existence, well hidden in her sanctuary near Hong Kong. Five years of latitude and liberty in exchange for total compliance—starting now.

'Luciana? Is the *filet* not to your liking, *querida*?'

Her eyelashes fluttered as she fought the urge to squeeze them shut. Pretend she was anywhere but here. *Querida...* Lord, she wished he wouldn't call her that. Wished too that she could extinguish the heat banked in his blue eyes. Hadn't he had enough carnal relations for one afternoon? She almost asked him. If he'd enjoyed the brunette in his suite. The one who'd answered his door half naked and ravaged. But the truth was she couldn't care less. It was the endearments she loathed. They hinted at affection and love and there would be none in this marriage. On either side.

He was playing a part, though, wasn't he? She wondered, then, if he was going to get down on one knee. While she sincerely hoped not, he was a virtuoso at playing the press and they'd want the fairy story.

Fairy story. Yeah, right. A fool's dream. Like so many others that taunted her day and night.

'It's wonderful, thank you,' she said, attempting another small mouthful even as her stomach roiled.

It could be the best *filet mignon* in the world and it would still taste like black ash. Though no one would ever know it. Trained by the best, she was the perfect picture of elegant refinement. Graceful to a fault.

'Good. I want tonight to be perfect,' he said softly. Slick and skilful.

Luciana whipped out the serene smile she'd perfected since the cradle—not too bright or flashy, nor too dull. *Just perfect*, as her mother would say. Neglecting to add the tiny detail that it would strip her throat raw every time she faked it.

'I want tonight to be perfect.'

Guilt trickled through the turbulent maelstrom of emotions warring for dominance in her chest. He was trying, wasn't he?

Of course he is—he wants a throne of his own. Of course he's pulling out every weapon in his cultivated arsenal.

Still, it wasn't his fault that the 'arranged marriage' part of her conditioning hadn't quite taken root. It wasn't his fault that she dreamed of another. It wasn't his fault that she had a taste for dark and dangerous.

Yes, and look what trouble that landed you in. Surely you've learned your lesson by now?

And Augustus was good-looking. Very handsome, in fact. Sandy blond hair artfully shorn and midnight-blue eyes. He had women after him in their droves. Yet he was her duty—tall and fair. The man she'd been ordered to wed. And from there to his bed.

A phantom knife sliced through her stomach and instinctively she bowed forward to ease the lancing pain… Then she forced her poise to kick in, reached gingerly for her glass and poured the amber liquid down her throat. Maybe if she got tipsy enough she'd have enough anaesthetic on board to say yes without shattering into a million pieces.

Flute back to the table, Luciana picked up her fork to push the tenderised beef around her gold-rimmed plate on the off-chance that he'd reach for her hand again. Once this evening was more than enough.

Would she ever get used to his touch? It was nothing like when *he'd* touched her. Nothing like the wickedly high jolt of electricity that had surged through her veins, or the blaze of her blood creating a raging inferno inside her.

Stop! For the love of God, Luciana, stop.

Problem was, as always, she found it impossible to halt the flow. The fiery rush of memories. Memories of a man who'd given her a gift to last a lifetime.

Pain and secrecy thumped inside her ribs like a dark heart. Because no one could know. No one could ever, *ever* know.

Princesses of the realm, first in line to the throne, were *not* meant to disgrace themselves by breaking free of their dutiful chains. Not meant to alter their appearance beyond recognition to avoid the paparazzi and go to rock concerts in Zurich dressed like a hippy, doling out false names. Not meant to fall in love…no, *lust* at first sight and have wild, passionate love affairs. They especially weren't supposed to have them with Arunthia's enemy. Not that she'd known exactly who he was when they'd met.

Such an ironic twist of fate. One she would have reduced to a dream if she didn't hold and squeeze and hug and kiss the living proof of her reckless walk on the wild side every single day. Yet, despite it all—despite knowing she'd given her innocence to a treacherous, dangerous man—she could never, *would* never regret it. Because her first and only lover had given her a gift that was the single most brilliant, bright spark of joy in her world…her son.

Discreetly she sneaked a peek at the mobile phone hidden in her lap to see if Natanael's goodnight text had come through. Nothing. She stifled the melancholy of missing him by picturing him playing happily with her sister Claudia and baby Isabelle, while Lucas watched on adoringly, protectively. Possessively.

At times it physically hurt to look at them. The perfect family. So deeply, devotedly in love. Their beautiful marriage was eons away from the unions she was used to. Luciana hadn't known such a thing existed. She would do anything for that. Pay any price.

Envy, thick and poignant, pierced her chest with a sweet, sharp ache and she cursed herself for feeling that way. Wanting what she couldn't have. Plunging lower than the black trench of despair she'd dug beneath her own feet. On the verge of letting loose the scream that was irrevocably bottled up inside her.

Come on, Luce. You know happiness isn't written in the cards for a royal firstborn. Only duty.

Luciana tried to swallow and block the lash of repercussions her trip down the aisle would provoke before anguish swept her mind away on a tide of insanity.

Stop this! You're protecting him—just as you've always done.

But how was she ever going to leave her heart? The person she needed in order to breathe, as if he were the very air itself? Her gorgeous little boy.

Claudia had sworn she'd save him from the oppressive walls of Arunthe Palace, love him as Luciana did until she could figure out a way for them to be together always. As Queen she'd have more power. She would think of something. She *had* to.

In the meantime Luciana would always be near—but what about his tub time, and the way he liked to be tucked tight and snug into bed? Luciana wanted to run his bath with his favourite bubbles that made his tender skin smell sweet. And what about when he called for her in the night when he was having bad dreams? *She* wanted to hold him when he was scared.

The thought of him asking for her and her not being there... It tormented her mind. How she was going to explain it all to him she had no idea. And how was she going to leave Natanael behind if this man dragged her to his family estate in Northern Arunthia?

So tell him. Tell him. He might understand. Support you. Help you.

This man? No. No, she didn't trust him not to betray her confidence. Didn't trust anyone.

You made a deal, Luciana. Now you pay.

Ah, yes, a deal made in naïve, youthful folly. In desperation such as she'd never known. A pact etched in her mind like an effigy on a tombstone. A shiver ghosted over her as she was haunted by the past...

'Please...please, Father. I can't do it. I can't get rid of him.' She knew he was small, so small inside her, but she couldn't take him away, she couldn't give him up. She couldn't.

'Luciana, you are not married. You will bring disgrace on us all. You are the heiress to the throne and the father of the child you carry is an enemy of this nation. Do you

forget his assassination attempt? On me? He is a traitor to the crown.'

'Yes, but I didn't know who he was. I—'

'If this man ever discovered your child's existence he could use him as a pawn to gain power over us. He could take Arunthia. And do you honestly want his Satan of an uncle getting his hands on your son? We have avoided war for sixty years—do you want your people to live in tyranny as those in Galancia do?'

'No, no. But...no one need ever know. I could go away for a while. Please, I'm begging you. Pleading with you... Let me keep him.'

The King's deep sigh filled the oppressive air stifling his office and she teetered on the precipice of throwing her pride to the gale and plunging to her knees.

Then he said, 'Five years, Luciana. Five years of free-dom. That is all I will give you. But the world must never know he is yours because Thane must never, ever find him. You will never be able to claim him as your son and heir. Do you understand me?'

'Yes. Yes, I understand,' she said—wild, frenzied, frantic. Unthinking of the consequences of what she was agreeing to. So desperate she would have sold her soul in that moment.

'You will be hidden well in the Far East, and in five years you will return to take the throne and do your duty. You will marry, Luciana, am I clear?'

'Yes—yes, I swear it. I'll do whatever you want. Just let me have him.'

His steely eyes were clouded with disappointment and grief and sorrow. That gaze was telling her she would rue this day, this bargain.

Luciana ignored it. As long as her son got to take his first breath, got to walk upon the earth and live life to the full, without the constraints of duty like a noose around his neck, she would make a deal with the devil himself. And so she did.

* * *

Augustus's voice shattered her bleak reflection and she tuned back in to the chatter that fluttered around them in a hushed din.

All she had to do was remember that her happiness came second to Natanael's safety. And she *would* keep him safe if it was the last thing she did.

'Luciana? Would you like coffee and dessert or…?'

Or…? Lord, not now. Not when she was falling apart at the seams. She wasn't ready to hear those words. Not yet. *Not ever.*

She felt powerless. Completely out of control. Like a puppet on a string.

The room began to spin.

'Yes, thank you, that would be wonderful,' she said, her voice thankfully calm and emotion-free as she plastered a cringe-worthy beatific smile on her face.

Coffee. Crème brulée. That would buy her another twenty minutes, surely.

Panic fisted her heart as the tick of the clock pounded in her ears. Tick-tock. Tick-tock.

The walls loomed, closing in around her, crushing her lungs.

Calm down, Luce. What are you going to do—hyperventilate and pass out? Make a total fool of yourself?

She needed air. She couldn't breathe.

'I'm sorry—please excuse me. I think I need…' To go out on the balcony? No, no, no, he'd follow her and drop to one knee, she knew. 'To visit the restroom. I'll only be a few minutes.'

After all that she realised he wasn't listening. Someone on the other side of the room had caught his eye, and Luciana frowned as his lightly tanned face stained a ghastly shade of grey.

'Augustus? Are you all right? Did you hear what I said?'

Slowly he shook his head. 'I do not believe it. Luciana,

you will never guess who is dining in this very room. I had no idea. Your father will be most displeased. I am so sorry...'

He was *sorry*? Ah, wonderful. One of his women, no doubt. The buxom brunette from earlier, come to ruin his perfect proposal? She didn't want to know. It was her parents' marriage all over again. No doubt she'd be faced with his mistresses most mornings too.

Well, that's better than you warming his bed, isn't it?

Anything was better than that.

'Don't worry about it, Augustus. Your secret is safe with me.' Her father wouldn't care less who the man whored with. There was more likelihood of mutual backslapping. 'I'll be back soon.'

Ignoring her, on he went. 'Of all the places in all the world...'

Luciana bit into her bottom lip, stifling the impulse to run like a world class sprinter. Praying for this evening to be over. Praying someone would rescue her from this nightmare. Before the truth escaped on the scream that was building gradually, inexorably, and she single-handedly destroyed the very life she was trying to protect.

'Of all the places in all the world... What an unpleasant surprise.'

His cousin, Seve, who was seated to his right at the oval dining table, leaned his upper body sideways in an effort to be discreet.

'I can see the sweat beading on his upper lip from here. It's your old pal from that exclusive rich joint you were sent to in Zurich. Viscount Augustus.'

Prince Thane of Galancia deflected the gut-punch the word *Zurich* evoked and sneered. 'He was no *pal* of mine.'

For the one disastrous university term Thane had attended after his father's death the Viscount had caused him no end of trouble—which he'd soon discovered was a horrendously bad idea—and subsequently shaken in his shoes every time he looked Thane's way. Which had pleased Thane no end. It meant he'd generally kept a vast distance.

He couldn't abide the man. Augustus was a wolf in sheep's clothing. Polished until every inch of him gleamed, he was a silver-tongued bureaucrat with sly eyes and a treacherous mind.

Seve smirked as if Thane had said the words out loud and he'd found it highly amusing. 'What's more, he's dining with none other than Princess Luciana of Arunthia. One of Henri's stuck-up brood.'

Thane resisted the urge to growl. 'Then they belong together.' A match made in heaven. 'How do you know it's definitely her? Last I heard, she lived abroad.'

He couldn't remember the last time he'd seen a photograph of *any* of them. Recent intel was off his radar, since he had zero interest in becoming embroiled with his uncle's ongoing bitter feud with the house of Verbault. He'd made that mistake ten years ago, in his father's day. Had the scars and the bitter aftertaste to prove it. Nowadays every time he thought of that varmint Henri a seizure of antagonistic emotion diseased his mind, so the less he heard or saw of the entire family the better. Besides, his every waking moment was spent deflecting blows from the latest fiasco in Galancia.

'I *know* because the two of them having fun on the slopes made the French headlines this morning. Rumour has it she's newly returned from Hong Kong, due to take the crown any day.'

Thane would have predicted a snowball in hell before he felt envy for a Verbault, but right then envy was definitely the evil he was up against. He wanted *his* crown. Taken from the hands of his uncle and placed in his own, where it should be. Before the man caused his people further damage. Four years... It seemed eons away, and his patience was wearing perilously thin.

He thrust his fingers through his hair and tucked some of the long, wayward strands behind his ear. 'It isn't hard to work out what Augustus wants. The vapid Viscount has always been an ambitious sleaze with illusions of grandeur.'

Seve chuckled darkly. 'Very true. Although I will say that marriage to her will be no chore for him. Look at her. By God, she's absolutely stunning.'

Thane couldn't care less if she was Cleopatra. She was still a Verbault. Granted, he refused to get snarled up in that age-old vendetta again, but he wasn't ignorant or blind to the reasoning for it. Verbault greed had once crippled a vulnerable Galancia, and rebuilding its former glory was an ongoing battle. Forgiveness would never be proffered. So the day he aligned with one of them would be the day he rode bareback with the Four Horsemen of the Apocalypse.

Seve, meanwhile, was still staring her way. Smitten. Practically drooling. 'I don't think I've ever seen a more beautiful woman in my life.'

'That's saying something, considering how many you've bedded,' Thane incised sardonically.

His cousin, his second in command, his best friend—the only person he would ever trust—shrugged his wide shoulders. 'Wouldn't do you any harm to get laid either, cousin. Come on—I didn't drag you here just to hurtle down the black slopes all day.'

He knew fine well what Seve had dragged him here for. All work and no play made Thane a dull, arrogant ass, apparently—and for a minute or three he had considered it. But when the redhead sitting to his right had appeared from nowhere he'd turned to stone. Unable even to contemplate getting close to another woman. In fact, if she touched his arm one more time...

Dios, didn't she know he was dangerous? That his blood ran black and his heart was dead? That he was more powerful and more feared than any other man in Europe? Surely his scars were enough to give her a clue?

Maybe he should give the mindless female a lesson in Princes of Galancia. Top of the list: do not touch.

He *hated* being touched. Didn't want anyone close to him. Ever again. While getting beaten to a pulp couldn't possibly hurt him any longer, it was the softer stuff that was more dangerous. One taste and he might very well crave it. Long for more of it. Glut himself on it. Live for it. Every touch. Every caress. Every kiss. Until it was taken away, as it inevitably would be. Leaving him empty. Aching. *Feeling.* Weak. And the dark Prince of Galancia could not afford to be weak. Not again. When he was weak he took his eye off the ball and everything went to hell.

Thane reached for his tumbler of rare single malt, his hand stalling in mid-air as an army of ants marched across his nape. Instinct born from a childhood in the barracks made him turn to peer over his right shoulder. Past the garish pine trees smothered in red ribbons and gold baubles, declaring the onslaught of the festive season. *How quaint. How pointless.*

Ah, yes, there was Augustus. Averting his gaze like an errant schoolboy. No woman with him—not that Thane could see.

But what he *did* see was a striking, statuesque blonde walking in the direction of the hallway that led to the restrooms. No. Not blonde at all. Her rich, decadent shower of loose tousled waves reminded him of a dark bronze. Like new-fallen acorns.

Now, *she* was beautiful. And that thought was so incredulous, so foreign, that he felt a tingle of something suspiciously close to shock.

His avid gaze locked on its target, his usual two-second scan turning into a drawn-out visual seduction, and he trailed his eyes over the low scooped neck of the black sheath that hugged her feminine curves. Lingered on the lapels of her long white dress coat, frisking and teasing all that flawless golden flesh.

A faint frown creased her brow and Thane narrowed his

eyes as she raised one hand and rubbed over the seam of her lips with the pad of her thumb.

A pleasurable shiver of recognition rippled over his skin and his entire body prickled with an unfathomable heat.

Ana used to do that. Stroke her mouth that way. When he'd asked her why, she'd said it likely came from sucking her thumb when she was a little girl. Thane had smiled and cracked some joke about her still liking things in her mouth, and she'd proceeded to prove him right. Many times over...

The brazen fires of lust swirled through his groin, and when the woman inhaled deeply—the action pushing those full, high breasts of surreal temptation to swell against the thin silk of her dress—ferocious heat speared through his veins until he flushed from top to toe.

It couldn't be. Could it? His Ana? Here in the Alps? No, surely not. Ana's hair was sable-black. Her body far more slender.

Look at me, he ordered. *Turn around*, he demanded. *Now.*

And she did. Or rather she spared a glance across the room in his direction, then wrestled with her poise, giving her head a little shake.

Thane's hands balled in frustration. But he kept watching as she reached the slightly secluded archway leading to the restrooms. Alone, doubtless believing she was unseen, she tipped her head back, glancing skyward as if praying to God, and graced him with the elegant curve of her smooth throat.

Another flashback hit with crystalline precision—*his* woman, arching off the bed, back bowed as she seized in rapture beneath him, inarticulate cries pouring from her swollen ruby-red mouth. And for the first time in his life— or maybe the second—his insides started to shake. *Shake.*

Dios, was his mind playing tricks on him? *Months* he had searched for her. For that trail of sable hair, that mesmerising beauty mark above her full lips, those clothes that harked of dark blood, a roaming gypsy. No stone had been unturned in Zurich, since that was where they had met, where she had *claimed* to live. Torturous years of not knowing whether she was dead or alive. Living with the grief. The ferocious anger and self-hate that choked him at the notion that he might not have protected her. That she could have been taken from him because of who he was.

He blinked and she was gone. Disappeared once again. And before he knew it he'd shoved his chair backwards with an emphatic scrape.

'Thane?'

'Restroom,' he said, and followed the dark blonde, his heart stampeding through his chest.

Thane thrust the double doors wide, then took a sharp right down the first corridor—and came to a dead end. A swift turn about and he flung open the double doors to the wraparound balcony. Empty.

Impatience thrummed inside him. The notion of being thwarted tore at his guts. He closed the doors with a quick click, turned and—

Slam.

'Ooof.' He ran straight into another body so hard and fast he had to grab hold of her upper arms to stop her from careening backwards and crashing to the floor.

'I…I'm sorry. I wasn't looking where I was going. Please…'

Just the sound of her voice washed clean rain over him. She was breathless, winded, clutching his lapels as if he was her life raft in the darkest, most turbulent storm.

'Please. I need to…'

That soft, husky whimper flung him back in time, sent electricity sizzling over every inch of his skin. And the way she'd jolted—he would hazard a guess she'd felt it too.

Stumbling back a step, she jacked up her chin and their gazes caught, clashed…

Madre de Dios!

'Ana?'

Brandy-gold eyes flared up at him as bee-stung lips

parted with a gasp. And for the endless moments they stared at one another she seemed to pelt through a tumult of emotions. He could virtually see them flicker over her exquisite face. Fancied each one mirrored his own. She was astounded. Bewildered. Likely in denial. Half convinced she was hallucinating. And all the while Thane drank her in as if he'd been dying of thirst and his pulse-rate tripled to create a sonic boom in his ears.

He wanted to take her in his arms. Bury his fingers into the luxurious fall of her hair. Hold her tightly to him. Despite the internal screech of warning not to touch, not become ensnared in her again.

Thane swallowed around the emotional grenade lodged in his throat. 'Ana, where have you been? I looked for you. What happened? I…'

Unable to wait a second longer, he reached out—but she staggered back another step; her brow pinched with pain.

'No. No! Don't touch me. I'm sorry. You must be mistaking me for someone else. I…'

That pain morphed into something like fear and punched him in the gut.

'Please excuse me,' she said, and she made to duck past him.

His confusion made his cat-like reflexes take a second too long to kick in.

'Ana? What are you talking about?'

Why was she scared of him? He didn't like it. Not one bit. Everyone else? Yes. Her? No.

A man emerged from around the corner and when Thane recognised Augustus he almost swung his fist in the other man's face. Though at the last second he thought better of it. His word, he'd been told, was vehement enough. Consequently he opened his mouth to deliver a curt command but the Viscount beat him to the punch.

'Luciana? Are you all right, *querida*?'

Luciana? Hold on a minute… *Querida*?

What the *hell* was going on?

'Luciana? Is this man bothering you?'

Thane whipped around to face him. 'Back off, Augustus,' he ground out, jabbing his finger at the other man while he tried to think around the incessant clatter in his brain. 'And while you are doing that, if you know what is good for you, turn around and *walk away.*'

Augustus paled beneath his tanned skin, nodded and went to do just that. But not before he motioned to Ana with a jerk of his chin. Or was it Luciana? *Dios*, Thane felt as if his head was splitting in two.

'Why are you beckoning her? How do you know each other?' Thane asked, darkly incredulous.

Augustus straightened to his full height. Thane would give the man points for the gutsy move if he still weren't several inches shorter than him and trying on a smug smirk for size. But what really set Thane's teeth on edge was the way the disturbingly dashing Viscount—who was as suave and golden as Thane was dark and untamed—practically stripped the sheath from Ana's body with his lustful covetous gaze. It made a growl threaten to tear up his throat. He felt as if he could grow fangs.

'Luciana is to be my fiancée, Prince Thane. So I would appreciate it if you...'

The rest of his words were swept away on a tide of realisation and a watery rush sped through his ears, drowning out sound.

'*Fiancée*?' he repeated, black venom oozing from his tone. Because that meant... That meant...

With predator-like grace he pivoted to look back at the woman who had bewitched him so long ago. Invaded his every salacious dream for five years.

Eyes closed, she tucked her lips into her mouth and bit down hard enough to bruise.

'Do I take it I am in the company of Princess Luciana of *Arunthia*?' His voice seethed with distaste, so cold and hard he imagined it could shatter every windowpane within a ten miles radius. '*Am I?*'

His increase in volume snapped her awake and she elevated her chin, stood tall and regal, while she ruthlessly shuttered her expression.

'You certainly are, Prince Thane of *Galancia*,' she said, in a sexy, sassy voice that sent a dark erotic wave of heat rushing down his spine.

Ah, this was his Ana, all right. She looked more fearsome than Augustus could any day of the week, and Thane had the absurd desire to kiss that mulish line right off her lush, sulky mouth. Even *knowing* who she was. A Verbault. Henri's daughter. And didn't *that* fill him with no small amount of self-disgust? This had to be the universe's idea of a sick joke.

Thane crossed his arms over his wide chest and arched one livid brow as they faced off in the hallway.

'Did you know who I was back then?'

Had she known and set out to destroy him by luring him in? Because the Arunthian hussy had almost managed it. Almost driven him to the brink of insanity in the aftermath of her disappearance.

If he'd blinked he would have missed it. The way her smooth throat convulsed. The way she shot a quick glance in Augustus's direction as if to check he was still there. He was. Unfortunately. Soaking up every word.

'I'm afraid I have no idea what you're talking about. I've never met you before in my life. Now, if you gentlemen will excuse me, I suddenly find I'm very tired.'

Stupefied, he rocked back on his heels as she blew past them like a hurricane, leaving her signature trail of destruction in her wake.

A flash fire started in the pit of his gut and his mood took a deadly turn. The voracious heat was exploding to sear through his veins, to fire his blood as pure, undiluted anger blazed through his system.

Had she *actually* denied knowing him? *Him*? Prince Thane of Galancia? Had she *actually* walked away from him? *Again*?

A haze of inky darkness clouded his vision, his mind.

Ah, Princess. Big mistake. *Huge*. Massive, grave error of judgement.

He wanted answers. *Now*. Wanted to know if she'd known his true identity all along. If she'd been toying with him. Why she'd vanished in the middle of the night after she'd promised she would stay. Why she'd plunged him into the pit of Hades for months on end—something he would make her pay dearly for. But most of all he wanted her away from this sleaze-bag. Thane may no longer want to bed her, but he'd be damned if he stood by while Augustus took what was his.

Fact was he wanted her full attention. And, by God, he would get it.

This was not happening. This was just *not* happening.

Luciana shoved her clothes into her suitcase with one hand while she grappled with a cordless phone in the other.

Lord, she was shaking so hard she was likely calling Venezuela. One touch from that man and it was as if she'd been dormant in some cryonic stasis for five years and he'd plugged her into the national grid. Twenty minutes later her body was still burning; incinerator-hot, making her feel like a living, breathing flame.

Dangerous. That was what he was.

Worse still, when she'd literally crashed into him for a split second she'd thought she was dreaming again. That she'd conjured up his memory to save her from the nightmare her return had condemned her to. So often she slept with him in her bed, his fingers a ghost-like touch drifting over her body. Caressing, devouring with a fervour she longed for. And during that breathless moment in that hallway suddenly, shockingly, she'd wanted to cry. Weep in sheer relief that he was here. Holding her once more. Wrapping her in his ferocious unyielding strength.

That body… Such inordinate power that he vibrated with it. She'd met some powerful men in her time but Thane… No comparison. None. His every touch was a jolting shock-wave of acute pleasure and pain. And it had been so long since she'd been touched. She'd almost begged him to crush her against his hard, muscular chest for one blissful second, just so she could live in the illusion that he was here and she was safe.

But that was all it was—a fantasy. A fallacy. She would never be safe in Thane's arms.

So why did a part of her still crave him? Even knowing what and who he was?

Luciana moaned out loud. Her father was right—she was an absolute disgrace.

She'd do well to remember that invariably her dreams turned dark and his hands turned malicious and she woke in a cold, clammy and anguished sweat. That in actuality he was the most lethal, autocratic man in Europe, who co-ruled his country and his people with a merciless iron fist.

And that look in his glorious dark eyes when he'd gazed at her… As if she was his entire world… A lie. Her cruel imagination. If she needed proof to substantiate that theory all she had to do was recall his blistering disgust and anger as he'd ground out her title. Realised her true identity.

His granite-like countenance hadn't broken her heart. Certainly not. The man was rumoured to be a mercenary, for pity's sake.

Imagine that man getting hold of your son and using him as a pawn in his power-play?

Over her dead body.

That hypothesis was akin to someone upending a bucket of cold water over her head and she calmed enough to hit the right keys.

'I need a car outside in five minutes and a private jet waiting at the Altiport to take me to Arunthia. Can you do that?'

'Yes, *madame*.'

'Thank you.'

Depressing the call button, she flipped the lid of her case and yanked the zipper all the way around.

She had to get home. Get Natanael out of the country until she was sure Thane wouldn't come after her. The savage vehemence pouring off him as she'd left had scarred her for eternity. That was *not* a man you messed with.

The tap on her door flung her heart into overdrive and she crept up to the door to peek into the security viewer.

Shoulders slumping, she unlatched the lock and allowed the porter in to collect her bag. 'Thank you. I'll meet you downstairs.' Luciana pulled a two-hundred-euro note from her jacket pocket and conjured up a sweet smile. Feminine wiles and all that.

'The back door, okay?'

His boyish grin told her she was in the clear and she grabbed her handbag and scarpered from the room.

Down in the private elevator she went. Out through the back exit and into a frosty evening that nipped her cheeks.

The door of the limousine was an open invitation and Luciana sank into the plush leather, not wasting one vital moment. 'Can you take me to the Altiport, please? Fast as you can.'

The door slammed shut with a heavy clunk.

The locks clicked into place.

'Sure thing, lady.'

Lady? Frowning, she glanced up into the rearview mirror to see a peculiar pair of deep-set titanium-grey eyes staring back at her.

Luciana's blood curdled in her veins.

Then that voice—as brutal and vicious as the thrash of a whip—sliced through the leather-scented cabin, its deadly effect severing her air supply.

'We meet again, *Princess* of Arunthia.'

Vaulting backwards in her seat, she crushed herself into the corner and scoured the dim recesses of the car, her heart thudding a panicked tempo.

Black sapphire eyes glittering as starkly as the stars in the Courchevel sky, he raised one devilish dark brow and said, scathingly, 'Did you really think I would allow you to turn your back on me a second time, Luciana? Disappear into the night once more? How very foolish of you.'

Dressed from head to foot in a bespoke black Italian suit, he lounged like an insolent predator—a sleek panther perusing his kill.

'Well, let us get one thing perfectly clear right now. *This* time you will *not* walk away from *me*.'

CHAPTER TWO

SHE COULDN'T MOVE. Not one muscle.

'This time you *will* not *walk away from* me.'

What did he mean by that? Did she have to wait until *he* walked away from *her*? How long was that going to take? An hour? A day?

If she didn't start breathing she'd never find out.

Luciana yanked her focus dead ahead in order to stitch up the tattered remnants of her composure. She couldn't do that and look at him at the same time. It was futile. The mere sight of him, dangerous and dominating, skewed her equilibrium and turned her brain to mush.

The privacy glass rose up before her, sending her heart slamming around her ribcage. For a second she toyed with the idea of launching herself from the car, but then remembered the locks had snapped into place. A moment later the limousine began to rock down the steep incline from the lodge and the risk of hyperventilating became a distinct possibility.

Breathe, Luce, for heaven's sake breathe. He probably just wants to talk on the way to the Altiport.

Why, oh, why hadn't she looked at which car she was getting into? She was supposed to be avoiding trouble. Being good. The refined, beyond reproach, virtuous Queen she was born to be. She could already hear her mother... *So reckless, Luciana. So unthinking.*

She let loose a shaky exhalation, then took a deep lungful

of air. And another. Then seriously wished she hadn't. His audacious dark bergamot and amber scent wrapped around her senses like a narcotic, intensely potent and drugging as it swirled up into her brain, making her vision blur. Her entire body wept with want.

How did he still do this to her? After all this time? *How*? It was as if he engulfed her in his power, lured her in with his black magic. Well, any more of his lethal brand of masculinity and she'd be done for.

Clearing her throat, she straightened in her seat. With far more sangfroid and bravado than she felt, she said, 'Why am I here? What *exactly* is it you want from me?'

Seconds ticked by and he didn't so much as murmur. Merely allowed the atmosphere to stretch taut. And, since she was hanging on to the very last fraying threads of her control, it didn't take her long to snap.

Up came her head—*big* mistake as she realised too late it was exactly what he'd been waiting for, what he wanted: her full attention, total control over this…whatever *this* was. His gaze crashed into hers. Unerringly. Mercilessly.

Oh, Lord.

Overwhelming anguish held her in stasis as her every thought fled and she allowed her treacherous heart to devour the dark beauty that was Prince Thane.

Devastating—that was what he was. Bewitching her with that breathtaking aura of danger. Those high, wide slashing cheekbones and obsidian eyes framed with thick decadent inky lashes. That chiselled jaw that was smothered in a seriously sexy short beard. On anyone else it would be labelled designer stubble. But this was Thane and he wasn't vain in the least. Or he hadn't been. In truth, she'd been amazed at just how clueless to his gorgeous looks he was.

His hair was longer, she noticed. *Dishevelled* was a ridiculously romantic word for the mussed-up glossy black hair that fell in a tumble to flick his shoulders, one side swept back and tucked behind his ear. Unkempt, maybe.

Hideously long… But she kind of liked it. Craved to run her fingers through it. Had to fist her hands to stop herself from doing just that.

The dim interior lighting camouflaged his facial scars but she remembered every one. The slash in his top lip, just shy of the full cupid's bow. The second, enhancing the sensuous, kissable divot in his chin. Another slicing into the outer corner of his left eyebrow.

Her throat grew tight, swelling in sadness and hurt for him. Just as it had five years ago. Not that he'd ever talked to her about them. The one time she'd asked he'd shut down so hard it had taken her sitting astride his lap wearing nothing but lace panties to tease him out of it.

Ah, Luce, don't remember. Don't.

His tongue sneaked out and he briefly licked his lips, but otherwise he remained still, watching…waiting…his sensationally dynamic body vibrating with dark power. And she clutched her handbag tighter still, fingers burying into the leather—

Whether it was the feel of her phone poking through the side of her bag or the sudden realisation that the car was at a standstill she wasn't sure, but she crashed back to earth with a thud.

The car had actually stopped!

Luciana shuffled on her bottom to peek out of the window and saw the huge security gates of the lodge swing open in front of the car. Electronic operation. Unmanned. Drat.

Twisting the other way, she grasped the cushioned leather and peeked out of the back window, her eyes widening as she spied her bellboy, still at the top of the drive, waving for her attention, with her case in his hand.

Oh, my life!

Her speech faculties finally deigned to kick in. 'You have to turn around,' she said, with her best do-it-or-else regal intonation. 'You've left my case back there.'

And as soon as they pulled up back at the lodge she was making a run for it.

'Really?' he drawled, mock astonishment lifting his brows high above his vivid eyes. 'How unfortunate.'

Luciana narrowed her gaze on him. That was it? *Unfortunate?*

'Well? Aren't you going to go back for it?' she asked, her tone pitched to an ear-splitting squeak.

'And give you the opportunity to run again? I think not, *princesa*. Consider yourself under lock and key.'

The limo turned right onto the main road and picked up speed. But not nearly as fast as her temper.

Anger sparked. Revving up to be free of its leash. And she let it take hold. Uncoil deep inside her. Unravel at a breakneck pace. It was wonderful. Glorious. Just what she'd hankered for all day. *All day?* No. Since she'd stepped off the plane from Hong Kong, thoroughly powerless, with her façade firmly in place.

'Just *who* do you think you are? You can't just *take* me like this.'

Cool as you like, he simply said, 'Watch me.'

She sucked in air through her nose. 'Are you playing with me? You're taking me to the Altiport, right? I have a plane to catch.'

'We *are* going to the Altiport, *si*.'

'Good. That's good.'

Though he hadn't really said what was happening when they got there, had he?

Warily, she ventured, 'And you'll let me get on my own plane to Arunthia, yes?'

'No.'

Mouth falling agape, she coughed out an incredulous laugh. 'Are you *serious*?'

'Deadly,' he said, as sharp as a blade.

His eyes were as cold and hard as steel. Where once they'd been tender and warm. Had she known him at all?

she wondered, fighting a miserable flare of anguish. Even a little bit? Or had the last few years killed any ounce of decency and compassion he'd possessed?

Icy fingers of dread curled around her throat. 'So where *are* you taking me?'

'Galancia.'

The world tilted as if the car had skidded down an embankment with a five-score gradient and she went woozy. *Galancia?* No, no, *no!*

Luciana scoured his expression, desperate to find even a flicker of his dry humour, and came up blank. Galancia... She shuddered in her own skin.

'No way. You haven't got a hope in hell of getting me to that place. I have to go home.'

He pursed his lips and cocked his head in faux contemplation. 'Not today. Today you will go where I ordain.'

'But...but that's tantamount to abduction!'

'I suppose technically it is. Yet during the several minutes we've been in this car I haven't heard you call for assistance once.'

It didn't bode well that he was right. But, honest to God, the man was so distracting. Still, why *wasn't* she petrified out of her mind, screeching her head off?

'Give me a second and I'll scream blue murder. Though let's face it,' she said, gesturing to the luxurious car. 'There's no one to hear me, is there?'

'Not now, no. You are seven minutes too late, *princesa*. Though Seve may help you.'

'Who on earth is Seve?'

'The driver.'

She almost shuffled to the edge of the bench seat and raised her fist to knock on the glass partition. Almost. Frankly, she knew better.

'Friend?'

'Cousin,' he drawled, a flicker of a devilish smile playing about his mouth.

It was obscene how relieved she was to see that tiny flirtation with humour—that hint of the man she'd fallen for on a raucous, cluttered muddy field in Zurich. Particularly since it suggested he was enjoying her discomfort. What was all this? Payback for her walking away? Some kind of twisted revenge?

'You can't go about kidnapping people. It isn't civilised behaviour.'

Lord, she sounded like her mother. And, honestly, only a dimwit would put 'civilised' and 'Thane' in the same sentence. It had been his untamed earthy savagery that had attracted her in the first place. Obviously she had a screw loose.

Blasé, he gave her an insouciant shrug that said, *try and stop me*, and it made her anger boil into lava-hot fury until she felt like a mini-volcano on the verge of eruption. What *was* it about men trying to govern her life? She'd just escaped one control freak and run headlong into another.

Smouldering with resentment, she decided she wanted him to erupt too. It was as if he'd switched off his emotions. He was far too cool and collected over there. While she was sitting here losing it!

Look at him, she thought. Sitting at an angle, one leg bent and resting on the bench seat, he sprawled like a debauched lion, taking over half the enormous car—and *all* of the oxygen—in that outrageously expensive Italian suit. It *should* have oozed elegance and debonair refinement, but it made him look like pure wickedness and carnal sin.

And she detested him for making her hormones whisk themselves into a deranged frenzy over him. Wasn't she in enough of a mess?

Which reminded her... Woman on a mission, here. She wanted the playing field levelled.

'So the rumours are true, then?' she said, with as much chilly, haughty daring as she could muster.

Thane arched one arrogant brow. 'There are so many I'm at a loss as to which particular falsehood you refer to.'

'That your men steal women. That your father took your mother from her bed—stole her from her intended.' And by all accounts made her life a living hell in Galancia Castle. Rumour had it she'd thrown herself to her death to end the torment. Not that Luciana had ever believed that bit. No mother would do that to her son, surely?

Luciana waited him out. Expecting some kind of reaction. Something. *Anything.* What she got frustrated her even more. Nothing. Not even a flutter of his ridiculously gorgeous lashes.

'Ah, that one. Perfectly true. Indeed, we take what is rightfully ours.'

She was going to slap him in a second. 'And *where*, pray tell, do you get the idea that *I* am rightfully yours?'

Aha! As if she'd flipped a switch emotion stormed through his eyes. The dark variety. But right now she'd take what she could get.

'What is *rightfully* mine, Luciana, is an explanation. Answers.'

'That's all you want from me. An explanation?' It seemed a bit too easy to her, but she could answer fifty questions before they got anywhere near a plane. It was a thirty-minute drive at least. 'Fine,' she bit out. 'Ask away, Prince Thane. What do you want to know? Why I bolted in the dead of night?'

'Ah…' he said, with an affable lilt that belied the fury now emanating from him. 'So you *do* acknowledge that we have a history. Yet not thirty minutes ago you denied we'd ever met.'

Blast her runaway mouth. She should have known that would antagonise him.

'Yes, well, I don't want Augustus knowing about my personal life.'

'Worried, Luciana? That the prissy Viscount will not wish

to bed you or wed you any longer when he discovers you've been tarnished by our depraved association?'

She huffed. 'Hardly.' That would only be a *good* thing. And, absurd as it was, she suddenly had the strangest compulsion to thank her kidnapper for rescuing her from tonight's unpalatable proposal. Clearly she'd lost the plot.

As for his darkly intoned question—she'd lied through her teeth because all she cared about was making sure Augustus never put two and two together if he was ever faced with Natanael.

Natanael… *Oh, Lord.* She'd wanted to text him before he went to sleep. But it was far too risky to fish her phone from her handbag right now. The bag she clutched to her stomach like a lifeline. Thank goodness she'd carried it and not left it with her case.

More to the point, thank heavens she hadn't brought Nate to the Alps with her. The thought of Thane discovering him…carting him off to Galancia… No, that could never happen. *Never.* Thane was descended from a long line of militia. Royal males trained in guerrilla warfare. The best fighter pilots in the world. Some said all the boys were taken to the barracks to learn how to become soldiers at eight years old. The mere thought of Nate holding a weapon in four years' time made acid rise and coat her throat. Plus, she really had no idea what Thane was capable of. Considering abduction was his modus operandi for their reunion.

She shuddered where she sat, swelling until she felt she might burst with the need to protect Nate at all costs. She hadn't kept his identity a secret all this time to lose him now. Her little boy was having a long, happy and healthy life even if it killed her.

At this rate, Luce, it just might.

When she realised Thane was speaking again, she turned to face him and watched the soft skin around his eyes crinkle as he narrowed those black sapphire peepers on her.

'So you do not care? You do not care that your *fiancé* may no longer want you—?'

'He is *not* my fiancé.' Not yet anyway. And she'd rather bask in the fantasy of freedom a while longer, thank you very much.

'Now, are you *sure* about that, Luciana?' he jeered. 'Because he seemed to think you are. Or is your word now as empty as it was five years ago?'

She made a tiny choked squeak of affront. 'And what exactly do you mean by that?'

Brooding and fierce, he leaned forward, attacking her brain with another infusion of his darkly sensual scent. 'You made a promise to me. That you'd stay another week. That we would talk.'

She could virtually feel how tightly reined in he was, and Luciana delved into his turbulent stormy eyes because…was that *hurt* in his voice? Surely not. How could *she* possibly hurt this man? No. If anything she'd bruised his male ego. A man who wielded his kind of power likely wasn't accustomed to being deserted.

Though either way, to be fair, she *had* promised him she would stay. Hadn't she?

Yes. She had. They'd become hot and heavy so fast she'd wanted to tell him who she really was. Not to have lies whispering between the damp, tangled sheets. Because in her mind there'd been something so beautiful and pure about what they'd had together the dishonesty had shredded her heart.

She swallowed around the great lump in her throat. It was torture to remember. Utter torture. 'I did promise you—you're right. But that was before I found out who you were.'

With his bent elbow resting on the lip of the window, he curled his index finger over his mouth pensively and stared at her. 'So you didn't know who I was all along?'

Mouth arid, she licked over her lips. 'No, I didn't know who you were. Of course I didn't.'

'Are you telling me the truth? You swear it?'

'Yes.' Did he think she'd duped him? 'I couldn't have set up the way we met even if I tried, Thane. Don't you remem—?'

Slam! She locked the vault shut before all the memories it had taken her so long to ensnare were unleashed. Escaping to create havoc in her soul. Best to forget. For all their sakes.

'Let's just call it an ironic twist of fate,' she said, hearing the melancholy in her voice. 'We were young. Stupid. Reckless. I didn't know you at all. I'd fallen into bed with a stranger...' *And I awoke to a nightmare.* 'I found your papers, Thane.'

She'd never forget that moment as long as she lived. Standing in the dim light of their bathroom, feeling naked and exposed, his nationality papers for travel that she'd stumbled across quivering in her hand. The realisation she was sleeping with the enemy.

'And after three, almost four weeks,' he said fiercely, 'of our being inseparable, spending every waking and sleeping moment together, your first instinct was to run? With not *one* word? Do you have *any* idea...?'

Veering away from her, he clenched his jaw so tight she heard his molars groan in protest. And she swiftly reassessed the idea that she'd caused him pain by leaving the way she had.

Remorse gathered in the space behind her ribs and trickled down into her stomach to merge with the ever-present pool of guilt that swelled and churned with her secrets every minute of every day. The painful struggle between truth and darkness.

But, looking back, she remembered she'd been consumed with the need to flee.

First had come denial and bewilderment. She'd been unable to match the dark, dangerous, merciless Prince with the somewhat shy—at least around women—rock music lover who'd held her cherishingly tight through endless nights of bliss. Then terror had set in, leaving her panic-stricken, contemplating how he'd react when he discovered who she was. And heartache, knowing she had to leave before he found out. Knowing that while she toyed with the temptation of staying in touch, meeting up again, suddenly another hour was too much of a hazard, a risk, never mind some far-off midnight tryst.

So she'd run. Taken the good memories instead of tainting them with bitterness and regret. Run as fast as she could with her heart tearing apart.

Glancing out at the snow-capped peaks of the Tarentaise Valley, she took a deep breath and then exhaled, her warm breath painting a misty cloud upon the window. If he needed closure in order to forget and let her go, then so be it.

'I'm sorry I didn't let you know I was leaving. Write you a note or something. I didn't mean to hurt you that way. But it was over. We had an affair—that's all. There could never have been a future for us.'

Chills skittered over her skin and she crossed her arms over her chest, rubbing the gooseflesh from her shoulders. She was so lost in thought she didn't notice his hand reaching across the back of the bench seat until it was in her periphery and she flinched. Hard. Unsure what to expect from him.

'Are you afraid of me now?' he asked, his voice gruff as if she'd sanded the edge off his volatility.

Was she afraid of him? Genuinely?

No. Though she couldn't really understand why.

Because deep down you know he won't hurt you. Deep down you know the man who took your innocence with such gentle passionate persuasion would never physically hurt you in a million years.

But that didn't mean he couldn't emotionally destroy her. And Nate. *That* he was capable of.

So maybe she *did* fear him. Just not in the way he meant.

Luciana gave her head a little shake and he picked up a lock of her hair and rubbed the strands between his fingertips. 'I wouldn't have recognised you. How different you look this way.'

She had the ludicrous desire to ask him if he liked the way she looked. The real her. Or if he'd fallen for a black-haired hippy who didn't exist. But the reality was it was best she didn't know.

'It was a lifetime ago,' she said, immensely proud of her strong voice when she felt so weak when he was close. 'Forget the person I pretended to be in Zurich. I was just...' She had to swallow hard to push the words out. 'Acting out. Letting loose. Having a bit of fun.'

Such a lie. But maybe if he thought their wild, hedonistic fling meant nothing to her he'd hate her. Let her go...

Et voilà.

Easing back, he created a distance that felt as deep and wide as the Arunthian falls.

'Fun,' he repeated tonelessly. 'Well, that makes both of us.'

Her stomach plunged to the leather seat with a disheartened thump. Because it was just as she'd always suspected.

Stiffening her spine, she brushed her hair back from her face. 'There you go, then. There really is no point in dragging this out.'

He said nothing. Simply leaned back and glared at her with such intensity she felt transparent.

Jittery, she shifted in her seat and rammed her point home.

'Thane, you have to let me go back to Arunthia. To my family. They need me. I've got to get married soon. I—'

'No.'

'*No*? But haven't I given you an explanation? What more could you possibly want from me?'

'That is a very good question, *princesa*.'

And Luciana had the feeling she wasn't going to like the answer. Not one bit.

CHAPTER THREE

THANE IGNORED THE eyes that were boring into his skull and riffled through the mini-bar of the limousine for some hard liquor. She was turning him to drink already—he was insane even to contemplate what enticed his mind.

Snatching a miniature of bourbon, he unscrewed the lid, then tipped the contents onto his tongue and let the fiery liquid trickle down his throat in a heavenly slow burn.

From the corner of his eye he saw Luciana pick up a bottle of sparkling water and commanded himself not to look, to watch. To devour all that beautiful, riveting bone structure—her nose a delicate slope of pure femininity, pronounced razor-sharp cheekbones a supermodel would kill for—those intoxicating brandy-gold eyes and that glossy, over-full wanton mouth as she drank.

Dios, she made his flesh and blood blaze. And it had been so long since he'd felt anything that he was consumed. By want. By hate. It was a terrifically violent and lethal combination that was taking all of his will power to control.

While she speared darts of ire or disbelief in his direction, poised and elegant in her glamorous couture black and white ensemble, all *he* could think of was her pupils dilated, her hair tossed over his pillow in gloriously messy abandon, and raw, primal sheet-clawing passion.

But it was more than that, wasn't it? He'd thought his memories were long dead, murdered by the passage of time and the strife in Galancia, but since he'd touched her he'd started to remember.

Remember being held close against her bare skin, feeling truly wanted—a real man made from flesh and hot blood, willing to pay whatever price it took to sustain that feeling a while longer. And, while he wanted that back, he knew it was lost to him.

'Having a bit of fun. Letting loose.'

Any molecule of hope he'd harboured that she'd felt something for him disintegrated, and inside his chest that lump of stone where his heart should be cracked down the centre and crumbled to dust.

Good. He didn't want the weak and tender emotions involved in this. Never had to begin with. But the beguiling creature had lured him in. Lesson learned.

'Are you going to tell me what's going on in that head of yours?' she asked, before gnawing on her crimson bruised bottom lip.

'As soon as I figure it out, yes.' Because despite his misgivings, despite what she'd said, something…*something* told him she held the key to his fate. He couldn't explain it if he tried—just as he'd never been able to explain how he'd known she was in grave danger the day they'd met. How when their eyes had locked he'd known she belonged to him.

Ignorant of his internal debate, she heaved a great sigh at his cool reply. But it had taken him less than ten seconds to figure out the best way to play this game: total emotional lockdown. Which was no inconsiderable feat when that aloof haughtiness kept invading her body like some freakish poltergeist and he was overcome with the violent need to grab her and shake it loose. Then there was the way her mind clearly often wandered down a path that he suspected was paved with turmoil, because guilt would walk all over her face. It made him want to climb into her brain and seduce her secrets.

The bright lights of the Altiport runway came into view,

as did his sleek black private jet embellished with the Guerrero family crest—a large snake curling around the blade of
a sword—and she clutched her bag to her chest as if it held
the crown jewels. Which, he conceded, might be true. His
knowledge of women's paraphernalia was zilch.

'Thane, look. Be reasonable about this. I'm your enemy—
there isn't anything I could give you but trouble. For starters, the bellboy saw me drive away in your car. Does he
know who you are?'

He shrugged his wide shoulders. 'I imagine so. I believe
I am very difficult to miss.'

She rolled her eyes. 'Arrogance really should be your
middle name. My point is: come morning, Augustus will
know I'm with you. Then he'll call my father—because, let
me tell you, they are as thick as thieves. Soon after my father will be on the warpath. So you *have* to let me go home.
My family will worry if I just vanish into thin air.'

'Let them suffer,' he said. Just as *he'd* done. Trying to
fill the empty, aching void of losing her. Had she cared for
him? Obviously not.

She huffed in disgust. 'Well, how gallant of you. How
would *you* feel if someone you loved disappeared off the
face of the earth?'

His mouth shaped to tell her he knew exactly how it felt,
but first his pride stopped him, and then her words. *Love?*
This had nothing to do with love. He was a protective man
by nature, and naturally that extended to her. She'd been
his. Correction: she *was* his. Regardless of her true identity.
Moreover, he would kiss Arunthian soil before he admitted
any hint of vulnerability to *her*. To anyone. He'd been nine
years old when he'd last made that mistake—telling his father that enclosed spaces made him violently sick. Twenty-
four hours down an abandoned well had taught him much.

'Honestly, could you be a more heartless brute?'

It didn't escape him that he'd been called worse things in

his time—a murderer, a mercenary, a traitor—so why the devil it stung coming from her was a mystery.

'I'm sure I could if I put my mind to it,' he drawled darkly.

'But you're going to be a wanted man. Do you want to spend the rest of your days in a jail cell?'

Thane turned to face her and raised one mocking eyebrow. 'Your father would have to catch me first *princesa*—and, believe me, *that* is impossible.'

'It's not about catching *you*,' she said, pointing at his shirt before turning the same finger back on herself. 'He'll come for *me*. Do you want an Arunthian army on your doorstep?'

As if.

'They would never get through Galancian airspace. Do you forget who I am? Your security and your army are no match for mine.'

'You're probably right. But that's because we are peace-keepers. Not fighters. Our people don't live in fear of an iron-fisted rule. We are rich in life and happiness and that is more important to us.'

Thane scoffed. Did she think he didn't want those things for his own people? What did she think he fought for? The good of his health? But the topic did bring him full circle to his hellishly risky concept. She could, in effect, help him gain a better life for them. Relax that iron-fisted rule she'd just accused him of by placing his crown in his hands.

Dios, it was mad even to think any union could possibly work, but the notion spun his brain into a frenzied furore. Snagging on one name: Augustus.

He was the biggest unknown in all of this. What the hell was a woman like Luciana doing with a scumbag like him? He was missing something vital here, and he did not appreciate having only half the intel on a situation.

During the twenty minutes he'd waited for her to emerge from the lodge he'd accessed every file he could uncover.

Princess Luciana Valentia Thyssen Verbault. Born and raised in Arunthia. Schooled at Eton and Cambridge, England. No record of her time in Zurich. No surprise there, since she'd been a carousing black-haired gypsy. Five years in China. Low-key. There was only the odd photograph during that time, either with a dark-haired friend and two small boys, or back home at a royal function—as if she'd returned to Arunthia for that purpose entirely, only to travel straight back to China. So what had been there to lure her back again and again? A job? Maybe. But why did his instincts tell him it was a man?

One thing was clear: unless he got a better picture of her life his plans would be dead in the water before he'd even launched them off the jetty.

While all this circled around in his head like manic vultures, Luciana launched into another talkfest about Arunthia: how content the people were, how he could learn a thing or two. The bare-faced cheek of it! Her arms wafted in the air as she warmed to her subject. And, *Dios*, no matter what crap came out of her mouth, she was the picture of enthralling passionate beauty.

He'd adored that about her. How she could talk for hours. About nothing in particular. Silly, mundane things—music, movies and architecture. He'd revelled in that freedom from his responsibilities, the chance to forget the trouble at home for a while. Ironic that he'd chosen a Zurich festival, having been once before in his uni days, to get away from it all and met a woman from his own sphere who'd been doing exactly the same thing.

An odd memory hit and a smile curved his lips. One she caught.

'What?'

'I was just thinking of the time we went to the cinema and were thrown out because you wouldn't stop talking.'

A lie.

'Talking? We didn't get thrown out because we were *talking*. We got evicted because we were…' Heat plumed in the rapidly shrinking confines of the car, driving a flush high across her cheekbones. 'Never mind.'

He felt so smug he could hear his own grin. 'Shall I finish that for you?'

'No, thank you. It's best if we don't go there, okay?'

She was right. He should be getting a handle on her relationship with the Viscount, not testing her memory. Not watching that beautiful blush frisk down her neck and caress her collarbone. Not inhaling her subtle vanilla and jasmine scent until his body prickled with heat and unleashed a firestorm of memories that turned him hard as steel.

Like the sensation of those plump lips softening beneath his as she'd surrendered to him. The way she'd felt when he'd thrust inside her virginal tight body. The way her legs had curled around his waist as he took her over and over. Lithe, svelte legs…glossed with skin that had felt like finely powdered icing sugar beneath his palms and tasted just as sweet. The softest, most exquisite texture he'd ever touched. Legs that were taunting him now because they were fuller. Lusher. Just like her breasts…

Thane shifted in his seat, the creak of leather sharpening his arousal as his body roared to life. Feral lust pushed incessantly against his zipper. Worse still, she exacerbated his darkly erotic state by squirming and lifting her hair from her nape as if she were over-hot. Well, that made two of them.

Depressing the window button, he let the cool air slither through the gap in a wispy sheet of fog and relished the odd snowflake that settled on the back of his hand.

Luciana's answer was to snatch a bar of chocolate from the mini-bar and have ravenous sex with every bite. He could virtually hear her silent moans.

'Hungry?' he asked, his voice as thick as his throat.

She licked the sweet treat from her lips with a sensual flick of her tongue. 'Erm…yes. Dinner was awful.'

He took the opening for what it was. Perfect for getting him back on track. 'The food or the company?'

Her gaze drifted to stare unseeingly out of the tinted window. The runway floodlights flickered over her at intervals, highlighting the honeycomb strands in her lavish hair and lending her skin an incandescent glow.

Ethereal was surely the only word to describe her in that moment. Seraphic. And his ardour dulled as he was struck with the feeling that he was too dark to touch her. That he would taint her somehow.

Right at this moment she was crushed up against the door, as far away from him as she could get, and Thane hardened his body, trying to expunge the terrible self-awareness, the stomach ache that whispered of rejection. Not once had she rebuffed their volatile passion. Not once. The reason for which he wanted to know. *Now.*

'You never answered my question,' he said, his tone darkly savage. 'Was it the food or the company that was so bad you could not eat?'

Her absurdly long, decadent eyelashes were downswept. 'Does it matter?' she asked softly.

Patience dwindling, he went in for the kill. Even though he was unsure if he could go through with this if she said yes.

Astounding and unthinkable as it was, if she did he'd rather put her on an Arunthian plane without another word. The 'why' of it wouldn't be difficult to find if he cared to revisit his boyhood, watch misery trickle down his mother's face as she pined for another. But delve into the past he would not. That long-ago place was a dark punishment he would never descend to again.

'Are you in love with Augustus, Luciana?'

She massaged her temple as if he were a headache she wished to rub away.

'I wasn't born to marry for love, Thane. I have no choice over the direction my life takes.' Her voice was tinged with bitterness and he felt a flicker of suspicion spark in his gut.

Frowning, he narrowed his eyes on her face, his guts twisting into a noxious tangle. 'Have you been in his bed?'

If he'd blinked he would have missed it. Her wince of distaste.

'That is none of your business.'

'Have you been in his bed, Luciana?' he asked again—harder, darker. Almost cutthroat.

'What difference does it make?'

'For hell's sake, just answer the question!'

Up came her arms with an exasperated toss. '*No!* Okay? I haven't been anywhere near his rotten bed. Would *you* want to?' She groaned aloud as if she wished the words back, and shoved another chunk of chocolate between her pink lips.

Thane felt a smile kick the corner of his mouth as relief doused over him like a warm shower of summer rain. That temper of hers still gave her a candid, somewhat strident bent.

'And you still intend to *marry* this man?' Even though the idea appalled her?

'Yes.'

He would have to be six feet under first.

Clearly Henri was pushing her into it. *That bastard.* He should have killed the man years ago, when he'd had the chance. Fury pummelled at him to think she was being forced to the altar as his mother had been. And Thane's every protective instinct kicked in—he wanted her kept far away from Henri and Augustus. Where neither of them could reach her.

'You will not touch him, *comprende*? Nor will you allow him to touch you.'

Not that he was giving her the chance to do either.

Huffing a little, she arched one fair brow. 'That's going to prove a bit difficult when we are married, Thane.'

'Which is precisely the reason you are not marrying him.'

His mind was set. Firstly, she had the rarity of blue blood, and a union with her would give him his crown. Four years early. His struggles to build a better life for his people would end. His uncle's dictatorship would cease as Thane took total control of the throne. Finally he could make amends.

And secondly—he easily silenced the impish taunt of his earlier words—there would be no riding bareback into hell as he aligned with the enemy. Because while she might be a Verbault at this moment, Thane would soon make her a Guerrero. Tomorrow seemed as good a day as any. Saving her from a fate worse than death—namely the vapid Viscount and her father's political clutches.

Win-win. Let it not be said that he wasn't knight in shining armour material.

A faint crease lined her forehead as she fingered back the curtain of her hair to glance at him warily. 'I…I'm not?'

This could go two ways, he decided. Either he'd be flooded with a profusion of gratitude or she'd fight him under the influence of some misplaced loyalty to her father. So it was a good job there wasn't a battle he couldn't win.

'No. Instead you are marrying me.'

CHAPTER FOUR

IN THE DISTANCE Luciana heard the driver's door open, then close with a deft clunk. Then came a cacophony of voices that fluttered around the car—the cadence low, masculine. And all the while she stared at Thane, who wore a mask of impermeable steel. Her mouth was working but no sound was emerging as she swung like a pendulum, lurching from fighting tears of frustration to biting back a laugh that was sure to lean over to the hysterical side—because the proposal she'd expected had finally come to pass. From the wrong man entirely.

Are you sure about that, Luce?

Yes, she was sure—of course she was sure.

And the worst thing about all of this…? For a split second all she'd seen was Thane and all she'd heard was 'marry' and 'me', and the little girl inside her who'd gorged on fairytales and dreams of love—the one who *hadn't* seen the darker side of marriage and was blissfully unaware of her duties—had felt her heart leap to her throat in utter joy.

Foolish little girl. Foolish heart.

Blame it on temple-pounding awkwardness, but the silence finally pressed a sound from her throat.

'Thane? Are you crazy?'

Crazy? He was insane. Mad as a hatter. Nutty as a goddamn fruitcake.

'Quite probably.'

There, you see—he's even admitted it.

'We're enemies, or have you conveniently forgotten that?'

Oh, she could just imagine Thane having a chinwag with her father. *Hey, do you remember me? The one who tried to assassinate you? Well, I want to marry your daughter.* Yeah, that would go down well. *Not.*

If he *had* attempted the assassination. But why would her father spout such a heinous lie? Truth was, she was drowning in reasons why she couldn't marry him. And that was without broaching the topic of Natanael.

'You and I are not enemies, Luciana.'

His eyes took on the lustrous glitter of the black sapphires they reminded her of and she shivered in response.

'Any chance of that ended when I took your innocence five years ago and made you mine. If your father and my uncle wish to prolong the feud that's up to them, but it has no bearing on our future.'

She shook her head in disbelief. Bad idea. Dizziness took the car, and her, for a little spin. 'How can you say that?'

'Easily. I am my own man, and I will not be dictated to by anyone or anything.'

A scoff burst past her lips. 'Bully for you. I, however, don't have a choice.'

'Which is precisely why I am giving you an alternative.'

So it would seem. The question was: why? He wanted her away from Augustus—that much was evident. Every time the other man's name was brought up he visibly fumed, until she half expected him to snort fire like some great mystical dragon. As if the thought of the other man touching her was abhorrent to him. But not because he loved her. No, no. His biting words from earlier were enough of a clue… *'We take what is rightfully ours. I made you mine…'*

So in effect she could be a Picasso he'd spotted at Christie's and fancied would look wonderful mounted above his machete rack. A beautiful possession.

Fire-tipped arrows pierced her chest and flamed up her throat.

'Well, thank you for the offer,' she said satirically. 'But I'm not keen on your alternative, Thane. For starters, it's simply another demand. And, let me tell you, they are certainly racking up this month.' Her insides were shaking so hard it made her voice quiver. 'And another thing: unfortunately for you, as far as courting rituals and practices go, abduction does *not* score points.'

He frowned deeply and looked at the magazine pouch. As if he was spectacularly disorientated and the answer to her meltdown lay between the covers of the latest gossip rag.

Idly scratching his sexy, stubbled jaw, he glanced back up. 'Courting?'

Luciana blinked. Out of that entire speech, 'courting' was what he'd picked up on? 'Yes, Thane. Dating, courting.'

Surely he couldn't still be as mystified about women as he'd been five years ago? He must have had a truckload since then; he was sex incarnate. Not that she cared what he did. Absolutely not.

'You would prefer this?' he asked, stunned but apparently game.

Luciana squeezed her eyes shut. Lord, this was utterly surreal.

'My father would never give his blessing in a billion years.' Hypothetically speaking, of course. Frankly, she had no idea why she was engaging in this conversation. It was all impossible.

'I care not,' he drawled, his arrogance and power so potent she could taste it. 'If the man wants a fight on his hands for you he can have it. Gladly. He obviously cares little for you to subject you to such a marriage.'

Luciana eased back, pulling her spine upright. She rewound that little speech of his and replayed it in her head. Then felt butterflies take flight in her chest—winged creatures flapping furiously against her ribcage. Had he just said he would fight for her? She was pretty sure he had. As well as intimating that he cared for her happiness. Sort of.

Her thumb found its way to her mouth and she nibbled on the soft pad.

This was the behaviour of a callous mercenary? *Really?* No, of course it wasn't—she must be missing something. He had to have an agenda. Other than his ridiculous chest-thumping caveman routine, that was.

Problem was, when he fixated on the way she sucked her thumb, with wicked heat smouldering in his dark eyes, she couldn't think what day it was—never mind decipher his ulterior motives.

Maybe he wants you for you. Maybe your father was wrong about him. Maybe his reputation isn't as bad as it seems.

Luciana shook her head vehemently. No. That would mean she'd run when she shouldn't have. Made a mistake. And she refused to believe that. After all, proof of his piti-less, ruthless nature wasn't hard to descry, was it? Look where she was, for heaven's sake—atop the highest asphalted runway in Europe, about to be manhandled onto a plane!

On the verge of a panic attack, or at the very least an undignified fainting spell, she yanked at the door handle and—*yes!*—it gave way under the pressure of her grip and she flung it wide.

A second later she launched herself from the car, almost breaking her neck as her heels hit a dusty sheet of new-fallen snow and she slipped…swayed…then skidded to a stop.

Adrenaline spiked her pulse and she glanced left and right, back and forth, wildly searching for a way out. Even as her legs turned to lead at the very thought.

Stupid legs. Stupid heart.

Inhaling swift and deep, she slowly refocused her vi-sion on the mountainous white peaks looming from all an-gles. Dangerous. Breathtaking. Much like the man who now strode around the back of the limousine, moving towards her with a warrior's effortless grace. And yet she felt every step like a seismic rumble.

Instinctively she staggered backwards and pushed out her hand in a stop sign. 'Don't come any closer!'

Snow drizzled from the sky in fat, puffy white flakes and swirled around his tall, commanding body in eddies and whirls as if drawn to his magnetism. The braver ones dared to touch, settle on his ebony hair, kiss his broad shoulders, tease the lapels of his jacket—only to be annihilated in an instant by his unfathomable heat.

Stupid snowflakes.

'Luciana. Don't fight me,' he cajoled, in that sinful voice that made her shudder.

Translation—*Roll over and take it. Be a good girl and do as you're told.*

Yeah, right.

His hands fisted before he stretched the kinks from his fingers and lifted them to spear into his hair; brushing the damp glossy strands back from his forehead, bringing his face into sharp relief.

Oh, Lord.

Her insides panged on a swift stab of anguish. Natanael… The resemblance was spooky. Surreal. Bittersweet and oddly wonderful at the same time.

Arms plunging to his sides, he tipped his head and gave her a crooked smile. 'We need to leave. Come with me.'

Fighting the sting at the back of her eyes, she wrapped her arms around herself, hugging her body. 'No. I can't go with you, Thane. I'm sorry. And I can't marry you. I have to take my throne in two months. I have responsibilities of my own.'

But more than that—much more—I have a son at home: one you can never find, because I'm frightened of what will become of him. I have to protect him. You keep confusing me and I can't trust my instincts with you.

Fact was, she had no idea who this man truly was.

So find out, Luce. Go with him. Find out.

It was a risk she couldn't possibly take. Something told her that if she left with him she'd never return home. Thane would never let her go. His formidable dominance would wrap her up tighter than any other person ever could. Including her father. Loath as she was to admit it, at least if she married Augustus Nate would be safe—and so would she. Her emotions would never engage with *him*.

All that swarthy, sexy maleness took on a blistering intensity as Thane dipped his chin and locked his fierce gaze on her.

'That throne will not be yours if you marry that man, Luciana. You know it. And maybe your responsibilities now lie with me.'

Temper igniting inside her, she balled her fists. 'No, they *really* don't.'

He hitched one shoulder, as if to say he wasn't going to argue about it, that she should just take his word and accept it. Talk about *déjà vu*. It was like standing in front of her father's desk, listening to the latest of his twenty commandments.

And that was it. It dawned on her that there was just no point in arguing. None.

From the corner of her eye she noticed a workman bundled in ski gear as he fought the elements, dragging safety cones across the asphalt, and knew exactly what she had to do.

Luciana took one last look at Thane's dark beauty and memorised every wicked, gorgeous inch of him. Then she hiked her chin and declared, 'I am *not* getting on that plane with you. Goodbye, Thane.'

Off she went, veering in the workman's direction, begging her feet not to slip. Cursing herself for not taking three extra minutes back at the lodge to change her clothes.

'Excuse me?' she called out. 'Hello? Helloooo…?'

His head came up, eyes latched onto her and he waved back.

Thank the heavens above.

Keep walking, Luce, just keep walking—

'Oh, no, you don't.'

An ironclad hand curled around her upper arm and next thing she knew she'd collided with Thane's hot, hard, magnificent body.

Fear and excitement shot through her in equal measure. Yet her protest went the way of her sanity when he pulled her impossibly closer, snaring her waist with one strong arm and stroking up her neck with his free hand, his fingers curling around her nape to cradle her head.

She'd have to be dead not to feel the unabashed sexual charge that sparked in the air. And, like a stick of dynamite, her insides detonated in an explosion of desire, sending an avalanche of wet heat thundering through her.

Quaking, she had to bite down hard on her lip to stifle a whimper. It didn't quite work. She let slip a hum-like cry.

Those dark, fathomless eyes locked onto her, pupils flaring as she swept her tongue across her bottom lip, and from nowhere a memory cracked through the brume of her mind…

Luciana was perched on a brick wall, waiting for him to lift her down, waiting for him to make his first move. Just…*waiting* for him. As if that was all she'd done all her life. 'Aren't you going to kiss me?' she'd asked, yearning for him to do just that.

When his expression had morphed into a giddy blend of enthusiasm and alarm she'd been flummoxed.

'Haven't you ever kissed a woman before?'

A blush so faint she'd nearly missed it had crept over the carved slash of his cheeks. A little embarrassed. A whole lot nervous.

She'd slid down the wall to puddle at his feet. 'Can I kiss you, then?' she'd asked, smoothing his frown away with her fingertips, tucking his hair behind his ears. 'Would that be okay?'

Ignoring the rhythmic tic in his jaw, she'd pushed up on her toes and pressed her lips to his. Warm. Soft. And as sensual and commanding as the man himself. Because as soon as she'd coaxed his mouth open with a flick of her tongue he'd taken over with an instinct as old as time and claimed her in a sweet, devouring…

Luciana blinked back to the here and now—to the snow whirling around them on the chorus of the breeze, the frozen wet droplets peppering her face. To Thane's dark eyes, deep and hungry and shot with shards of amber, the power of their sexual pull crippling in its intensity.

'My jet is the other way, angel,' he drawled, as if her defiance had not only been expected but he found her as cute as a button because of it.

The urge to kick him made her rapidly freezing feet twitch.

Angel… He'd never called her that before. He must have sharpened his sinful seduction skills over the past few years. It was crazy for her to wish he'd only ever been hers. Just as she'd only ever been his. Crazy. Men needed sex every day, didn't they? This man certainly had. Up close to him like this, it was easy to remember the long, sultry days and hot nights. Twisted sheets damp with sweat. Sticky skin and the musky scent of their passion lingering in the air as he was controlled by a dark atavistic need to mark her again and again. The slight soreness that only made them desperate for more. Insatiable. Never getting enough.

The base of her abdomen clenched; her core twisted with want.

Oh, this was bad. Really, *really* bad.

'Thane, let me go,' she demanded, cursing inwardly at the feathery panting that accompanied her words. 'I'm not joking. This is not funny. I'm not coming with you and you can't make me.'

His dark eyes glittered with challenge and her blood thrummed through her veins. She was scandalous—that was what she was.

'You and I both know I can and I will. So, are you going

to walk or will I have to carry you over my shoulder?' he asked, his rich velvet voice doing nothing to hide the steely threat of his words.

Problem was, her heavy breasts chose that exact moment to glory in being crushed against him, and when a fleck of snow landed on his nose she had the strangest impulse to lick it off.

'Thane...' Lord, was *that* her voice? That breathless, wanton plea?

'Luciana...' he drawled, in a tone that said *Please be reasonable about this.*

It inched her temper into the red zone.

'Don't fight this. Don't fight *me*. You don't want to go back there.'

'But I *do* want to go back, Thane.'

'No, angel. You don't.'

Argh!

'I'll scream and that man over there will come running. I guarantee it.'

His mouth tipped at the corner in a devilish smirk. 'Go ahead and I will smother that gorgeous mouth of yours.'

A gasp hit the back of her throat. 'You wouldn't dare.'

'Want to find out?' he growled.

Shameful excitement made her heart thump frenetically. 'No, I don't,' she said, though her voice sounded like a flagrant whimper to her. So she strove for forceful. 'Definitely not. Now, let go of me.'

He tutted and shook his head. 'Try again, Luciana. And if you say it like you mean it, I just might.'

Ooh, he'd asked for this.

Writhing in his hold, she pushed and shoved at his chest, drew in a lungful of air for the scream building in her throat...

And his mouth crashed over hers, taking his words from threat to carnal promise.

Oh, hell. Don't kiss him back. Don't you dare.

Within seconds he'd captured her in his invisible force field, energy swirling, flowing around them like a mini-cyclone, and her breath unwound on a blissful sigh.

He cradled her to him with one hand cupping her nape and the other splayed at the small of her back, hauling her up against his hard groin as he tilted his head and ravished her mouth as if he owned her body and soul.

Wicked was the flavour that flooded her mouth. So sinful and debauched he was. Bad to the bone. And when he stroked past her lips with a teasing flick and then a languorous lick of his tongue, that was it. She melted against him—all molten lava. Followed the sculpted line of his shoulders with her greedy hands up the column of his neck and slipped them beneath his ears, into his hair. Hair she fisted, making him growl long and low, the sound vibrating through her on a violent tremor.

The earth was moving, she was sure. Then she figured out why when he lifted her high and coaxed her legs around his waist. Luciana wrapped herself around him and hooked her ankles at the small of his back until there wasn't a sliver of air between them. He palmed the rounded swells of her bottom, squeezing her to him, and the erotic sensation of his thick hard erection nudging her lace panties made her sex throb and weep. He felt *shockingly* good and she whimpered, shivered.

Though that might also have been because she was wet, soaked to her skin. But he seemed to know what she needed, and when warmth suffused her and he sat down…*somewhere*…she straddled his muscular legs, cuddling closer to burrow into his heat.

Never leaving her mouth, he tore at her sodden coat, yanking it down her arms, and then his hot hands were back, sliding up her cool bare legs, pushing her dress up to ruck it around her thighs. And when those depraved fingers dug into the flesh of her bottom, pulling her panties indecently tight, the tug and rub of lace against her swollen folds made her cry out.

Survival instincts kicking in, she tore her lips free and dragged air into her lungs. Took a mind-numbing rush of his potent scent too. And that made her woozy. Impelled her to arch her back in a promiscuous plea for him to nuzzle her throat.

'Luciana…'

His lush, moist kisses fell on her skin like rain on drought-stricken ground and she soaked up every caress, thirsting for more. It had been so long since she'd been touched, since this man had touched her. So wonderful. Such naughty, amoral bliss.

'Thane…'

Dipping her head, she searched for his mouth and he dusted his lips over hers, teasing her cruelly. He tasted of pure virile masculinity, undiluted power. Passion and heat and lust and *Thane*.

Needing to touch, she ripped at the top buttons of his shirt, relishing his raspy curse and the sound of fabric tearing, and dived into the space she'd made, smoothing over his collarbone. Felt his heart beat a rapid staccato against her palm.

'Hot,' she whispered past his lips. 'So hot.'

His chest rumbled with a reply and yet she didn't hear a word, because a weird whooshing noise was blowing through her brain. Before she could grasp the why and the how, he scraped his stubble up the curve of her jaw in a sensual graze, making her tremble and rock her achingly heavy pelvis against him. Wanting his hardness inside her so, *so* badly.

When he let loose a feral moan from deep in his throat she did it again. And again. Her frenzied elation ratcheted up when his thumb slipped around her hip to find her sweet spot unerringly and apply just the right amount of pressure to take her to the edge of an almighty orgasm and hold her there.

'Thane, *please*.'

'*Dios*, Luciana… No bed in here, angel. But I want you to come for me. Hard. I want to hear you cry out my name like you used to.'

'Yes. *Yes*…'

Hold on.

Here? No bed *in here*?

He circled that tight knot of needy nerves and it took everything she had not to tumble into the abyss.

Her lashes were fluttering and her surroundings came to her in flashes. Cream leather seats. Small windows. Like a… like a private jet. And…were they moving?

Moving?

Luciana jerked backwards, dislodging his hand, blinking frantically, prising her eyes wide, her gaze darting here there and everywhere.

'What…? Where…? How…?'

She was the only one who was confused and disorientated, she noticed. Because the man whose lap she straddled simply sat there, his chest heaving from their passionate antics, cheeks streaked with colour, watching her with an insufferable blend of satisfaction and wariness.

Down she came, back to earth with shattering intensity. And how she didn't raise her hand and slap his face she'd never know.

'You…you *bastard*.'

Wrenching free, she tumbled backwards off his knee and landed in a messy, graceless heap. Still trembling from the erotic turbulence.

Thane lurched forward in a move to help.

'Don't you *dare* touch me.' Tears of frustration and anger pooled in her eyes.

Cautiously, he eased back into his chair, a deep V slashing the space between his brows. The look on her face must have said it all, she realised, since this was the first time he'd backed off at her word.

Somehow she clambered to her feet and stood tall before him, sweeping her palms down her black sheath, trying to cover as much of herself as she could before that horrid, vulnerable feeling of being exposed and raw threatened to strip her flesh from her bones.

Fury and self-disgust roiled inside her. Didn't diminish even when she saw a flicker of doubt and unease pass over his face. Though he soon banked it. It didn't matter. She would make him rue this day if it was the last thing she did.

'Luciana—'

'No. *Don't* speak to me.'

Spine pin-straight, she walked towards the other large leather recliner, trying to wrap her mind around her new predicament. What on earth was she going to do now? She—

A thought slammed into her, and she whirled back on a swirling spin of dizzying dread. 'My bag,' she said, unable to hide the panic in her voice. 'Where's my handbag?'

He was staring out of the small window, rubbing his mouth with the inside of his finger. 'Sit down, Luciana, we are about to take off.'

'No, dammit, I *won't*!'

Shucking off his wet jacket, he kept his eyes averted. 'Did you leave it in the car?'

Oh, God.

Her stomach pitched as the jet lifted off the runway, and she grabbed the back of the chair to keep from crumpling to the carpet.

'Go back down. Land this plane. Right now, Thane. I need my bag. My phone. I *need* my phone.'

How was she going to call Natanael? Keep in touch with home? Text Nate as she did every morning, noon and night?

Desperation made her beg the man she loathed with every ounce of her being. 'Thane, *please*, I need my phone.'

He didn't turn, still wouldn't look at her. Just inhaled deeply and closed his eyes for a beat. 'Where we are going no phone of yours will even work, Luciana. Sit down and leave it.'

She gritted her teeth, mightily glad for the return of that cool, dominant inflection because it evaporated the acidic splash behind her eyes. She would not break. Not in front of this man. Nor any other.

'I hate you right now,' she whispered vehemently. Though she suspected she hated herself even more.

One kiss. That was all it had taken to vanquish every thought from her mind.

Self-loathing slithered through her stomach to writhe like a nest of vipers and she curled into the deep bucket seat to ease the ache.

No phone. No way to call Nate. No chance of escape. And she was flying straight into enemy territory.

If she got through this in one piece and found her way home it would be a miracle.

CHAPTER FIVE

HE FELT LIKE the big bad wolf. In more ways than one. Furious self-censure and unparalleled carnal hunger took equal pleasure in tearing at his insides with razor-sharp claws until he wanted to growl.

The lust made his body thrum with pent-up energy, yet all he wanted to do was storm over there, pick her up and put her right back on his knee. Eradicate the pain in her eyes by wrapping her up in his arms and holding her tightly to him.

Dios, when tears had glistened in those big, beautiful eyes he'd felt as if a bullet had ripped clean through his chest. He'd been a little boy again, looking up at his mother, unsure what to do, how to take her heartache away. A heartache that once again he didn't truly understand. And that had made him feel lost. Racking his brains to think of some way to stem her misery. Because somehow his mother had always managed to quell his, take his pain away—back when his flesh could feel such a sensation, that was.

Rubbing over his jaw, he recalled how touching her had often worked—holding her cold, trembling hand or trying to wrap his small, thin arms around her shoulders to hug her, wishing he was bigger, stronger. Instinctively he'd reached for Luciana, but she didn't want his touch. While he'd always treasured hers. Touch was precious to him, he realised. Infinitely rare and beyond price, it was something he hadn't experienced or allowed himself to feel since he'd been seven years old. Until Luciana.

'I hate you...'

How her words tormented him. How her tears made him feel barbaric. As brutal as his father.

While he still owned what he'd had to do, he conceded his tactics might not have been the most honourable. Had he been wrong to take his chance? Hell, no. Not when the alternative was her marrying another man. A man she didn't even wish to marry! Still, luring her onto a flight using their chemistry, when she'd exploded like some hot, sensual, sultry bomb in his hands, and then almost initiating them into the ranks of the mile-high club wasn't exactly coaxing her towards a priest with a gentle hand, was it?

The memory of her furiously wild, uninhibited passion made him shift in his seat with restless virile power—as if his body had lain dormant for an age of cold bleak winters and she'd awoken the deep-seated animalistic lust inside him.

And right then the truth crashed down around him.

For the first time in years he was feeling, and he was chasing it with the urgency and fervour of a madman. He felt hungry, starved of affection, and suddenly he despised it. Didn't want her to have that kind of terrific power over him. He'd had more control when he'd been handed his first gun at twelve.

Lurching from his seat, he went to stalk to his office, where he could think straight, past the chair where she sat curled up, knees bent, hugging them to her chest, in a pose that struck him as a defensive ball—and he slammed to a stop.

Thumb-print-shaped blotches reddened her silky soft thighs, courtesy of his rough ardour, and her neck was scored pink from where he'd kissed her, dragged his unshaven jaw up her delicate throat. Ravaged. She looked ravaged.

Dios, had he hurt her?

He closed his eyes, his conscience riven by self-contempt. Maybe he didn't deserve to have her in his life again.

He could never be good inside, where it mattered. That had been twisted out of him as a boy. He was darkness and she was all golden light.

Good versus evil. Beautiful versus beastly. Flawless versus scarred.

Fatigue lent a beautiful fragility to her face. And when a shiver rustled over her honey-gold skin his guts twisted tight. She looked scared, miserable and *attacked*. So damn vulnerable.

Idiot he was—of course she'd be worried. While they'd spent one month in each other's arms there were years of animosity between their countries.

Opening one of the top cupboards, he pulled down some thick fluffy blankets and lowered into a crouch before her.

Her little bow-shaped mouth was mutinous in her heart shaped face. 'Get away from me, Thane.'

'Luciana,' he said, his voice rich and smooth, 'I am sorry I've upset you this badly.'

'*Upset* me?'

She flared up with spectacular force—his ferocious little lioness. He actually felt himself blanch when he saw her eyes, pools of brandy swimming in betrayal.

'Oh, just go away. I'm not speaking to you.'

'You just did,' he said lazily, trying to lighten the mood, get her to come round to him.

'Only because you're forcing me to. You are such a control freak. Do you get off on being Mr Big and Powerful? Taking away people's choices?'

That wasn't what he'd done. Was it…?

'No, what I was doing was preventing you from making a mistake. Giving you freedom from your father. You owe him nothing, angel. Soon you'll realise I've done you a great favour, and when you thank me I will not be so arrogant as to say *I told you so*.'

Moaning, as if his very existence was painful to her, she

squeezed her eyes shut and banged her head on the headrest. 'You're impossible. You really are.'

Gingerly, he covered her in layers of dove-grey cashmere and tucked the ends underneath her.

'What's this? A peace offering?' she jeered.

'No, a blanket,' he drawled as he slipped off her towering white glossy shoes. Unable to resist that ticklish spot, he ran his thumb over the sexy little nub of her anklebone.

She flinched and tucked her foot under the blanket, rebuffing him.

Thane sighed, stood tall, and shunted a hand through his hair. Back to that place where he was lost. Only knowing in that moment that making her smile at him was more important than anything else. And that thought was not only unnerving but also perilous and highly confusing.

His office silently chanted his name.

'I'll leave you for a while, then,' he said, stepping away.

Naturally that was when she started ranting all over him.

'How do you *do* this to me, Thane? How do you make me want you and hate you at the same time? I have no sense when it comes to you. None!'

One fat tear slipped down her cheek and his cold, stony heart cracked in two.

'Now look at the mess I'm in.'

The desolate anguish in her voice made him remember, and he couldn't just stand there paralysed. He had to do that in his own country, almost every damn day.

Ah, to hell with it.

Swooping in, he scooped her up...

'Hey!'

He turned and plonked them both back down in her seat, holding her close.

'I...I told you not to touch me again,' she choked out, trying to fight him and her tears at the same time. 'Honest to God, do you listen to one single, solitary thing I say?'

Palm to her cheek, he pushed at the side of her face to

nestle her into his neck. 'It may not seem so, but, yes. I just…
Let me hold you. Warm you up. Please? Just for a moment.
You're shivering.'

He tucked the blanket tightly around her, from her sexy
knees to the feminine slope of her nose, until she was swad-
dled, unable to move an inch.

'There you go. You look like a cute furry Egyptian
mummy, but that's better, *si*?'

If looks could kill, he'd be dead.

'It may be better if you remove that damp dress from
your skin,' he suggested.

It was shrinking by the second, he was sure. He was
also sure he wanted it off her, since he could easily conjure
up far more pleasurable ways to make his thoughtless arrogance up to her.

Hiking her chin up over the cashmere, she harrumphed at
him. '*As. If.* Now you're trying to get my clothes off? Forget
it, Romeo. This Juliet isn't falling for that.'

Thane frowned. 'They were enemies, weren't they?'

'Yeah… Ring any bells? And there was no happy ending for them either. She killed herself, so let that be a lesson to you.'

Spine rigid, he stiffened up…then slammed down the
memory before it invaded him and the blackness tainted
his soul. No, that would *never* happen with Luciana. She
was not his mother. He and Luciana had history. He'd made
her happy once and he would again. He was a man now—
stronger, more powerful—he would be enough this time.
Wouldn't he?

'Thane?' she squeaked. 'Can you let me breathe? You're
squashing me, here. Are you trying to suffocate me now?
First you abduct me and now you're squeezing me to death.
Frankly, I'm not too sure if you even *like* me, so why you'd
want to marry me is beyond my comprehension.'

'Ah, sorry, angel.'

He loosened his hold a touch and nuzzled a kiss into her

hair while he could—while she was wrapped up and couldn't protest or reject him.

'Of course I like you,' he said. 'I'll have you know I don't go around kissing just anyone.' Speaking of kissing… 'Did I hurt you earlier? Was I too rough?'

The luxurious spill of her hair tumbled over one shoulder, a shimmering flow of dark bronze that Thane swept back from her face tenderly.

Those absurdly long lashes fluttered, yet she prised her eyes wide, fighting it. Fighting *him*. It just made him want her all the more.

'Yes, you hurt me. Inside you hurt me. And I'll never forgive you for that stunt you just pulled.'

'Admittedly I didn't think it would backfire in such a spectacular fashion,' he drawled, trying his utmost to ease the tension he could feel coiling in her body. Her luscious, curvy weight was glorious, he decided. 'Would you consider that I thought your tongue down my throat meant yes?'

'No, I most certainly would not.'

The haughty lash of her riposte made him retaliate with his equally devilish mouth. 'What about the way you rode my lap?'

Her lips parted on a stunned smack. 'Lord, you really *are* wicked.' Punching at the blanket for some wriggle room, she shoved at his chest. 'Go away. Go and take your guilt elsewhere. I'm not pacifying it for you. You deserve it.'

'Who says I feel guilty?'

He did. Terribly. He might have wanted to lure and beguile her, but upset her this much? No. That was the last thing he'd wanted. It made him wonder if he was missing something vital. Surely being rescued from a repulsive royal marriage was something to celebrate, not to weep over.

'I can see it all over your face. And you *should* feel guilty too. I told you I was not getting on this plane, but did you listen? Of course you didn't. Then I begged you to go back for my bag, my phone…' Sighing heavily, she thumped her head back down on his shoulder. 'I hate you.'

'So you said. But, like *I* said, your cell phone would not have worked in Galancia. At least nowhere near the castle.'

Like Fort Knox with scrambling systems, its obscene opulence was locked up tight.

And right then, for the first time, he thought of his birthright and doubt slithered its sinuous way up his spine. Not only did he loathe the place but also his uncle… He didn't want his uncle anywhere near Luciana. Because as soon as his uncle set eyes on her he'd know Thane planned to overthrow him and doubtless stir up trouble.

To hell with that. He needed Luciana to say *I do* first. And to get her there he needed time. Time only for them. When he wasn't distracted by having to peer over his shoulder.

Glaring up at him with a fierceness that verged on the adorable, she mocked, 'My phone wouldn't work in the castle? Truth or lie?'

A laugh burst past his lips—one he hadn't heard in an age. For a woman who had been in Zurich to let loose and have *fun*, she remembered quite a bit. 'Truth. Swear it. Why do you want your phone so badly?'

She flung her now unencumbered arm out in front of them, exasperated, missing his face by an inch.

'Why do you think? My family will be beside themselves with worry by morning and it's heartless of you not to care.'

He *was* heartless. Completely heartless. Yet every time he thought of that single tear he didn't want to be. Not for her. And that was akin to tying a garrotte around his own neck. By opening up he would give her the power to destroy him again, and he couldn't go through that a second time. It would kill him. No, he had to keep his head straight and focus on his end goal. The crown.

But, unlike him, Luciana had a huge heart, and he didn't want her fretting about her family so he'd have to fix that too. He didn't want her mind on anything else but him.

'Are we talking about the same family who is pushing you into an arranged marriage that you don't want?' he asked.

'First off, what *you* have offered isn't much different.'

She had a point there. What could he give her in a marriage that Augustus couldn't? Just as he despised Henri for dragging her towards matrimony, he didn't intend to do that either.

Which begged the question—how was he going to entice her there?

'Maybe it isn't. But that man will never be in your bed as long as I live and breathe.'

'Neanderthal, much?'

He gave a breezy shrug. She could call him what she liked; it changed nothing.

'And, secondly, I'm not merely talking about my father. I'm talking about my sister, Claudia. She'll be frantic by morning.' A devious light flashed in her eyes. 'Speaking of Claudia... Oh, you don't want to meet *her* husband in a dark alley. In fact when he hears about this he'll make you wish you'd never been born.'

Thane lounged back with a lazy smile on his face. 'This would be Lucas Garcia? Once head of national security for Arunthia?'

'That's exactly who it is.'

'And you think *I* fear *him*?'

She scrunched up her nose. 'Yes, well, come to think of it that *is* a flawed strategy. The devil himself wouldn't scare *you*. But one day you're going to meet your nemesis, and I'd love to be there when you do.'

He had a feeling he already had. In this woman.

'If I have my way you *will* be there.'

'On this occasion I'm afraid you'll have to accept defeat. I'm not staying with you. I'll move heaven and earth to get home, and the sooner you realise that the better. You can't always have what you want, Thane.'

'Ah, Luciana. When there is a war to be fought I will always be the victor. Especially when I want the prize so very, very badly. And I want *you*, Luciana—very, *very* badly. So I will do whatever it takes to make you mine.'

Those smooth, satiny cheeks flooded with a warm sensual blush of pleasure even as she pursed her mouth in an expression that screamed cynicism.

'Whatever it takes, huh? I don't think personality transplants are available on this continent, Thane. And, believe me, it will take more than a dishonourable kidnapping rat to woo me down the aisle.'

At the blatant challenge he felt his blood heat and he arched one brow.

'Okay. So I haven't been the most noble of men today.'

'Ha!'

'I honestly didn't think it would upset you this much. I am struggling to understand why you want to go home so desperately when there is nothing for you there but a ball and chain and a vapid viscount.'

She shifted uneasily and pulled her lip into her moist mouth with a scrape of her teeth. Before he could discern if he was seeing guilt or not, she ground that curvy, firm bottom over his rapidly hardening groin and he had to grind his jaw to stop a feral moan escaping.

Unclamping his jaw took some effort. 'All that being said, perhaps a more subtle approach *would* have been better— but I cannot turn back time.'

'You could take me home,' she suggested hopefully.

Not if the survival of mankind depended on it.

'What about if I make a deal with you instead?'

That grabbed her attention, and she focused those incredible eyes back on him. Where he wanted them to stay.

'What kind of a deal?'

'You give me two days to…what did you call it? Court you? Date you? And if after those two days you still wish to return home I will take you myself. Escort you to your father's door and never darken it again.'

Not that it would come to that.

The knowledge that he was using military tactics to keep his princess in line did not impress his sense of fair play, but then again fair play had flown out of the window when he'd clapped eyes on her in the company of Augustus. She was his gorgeous little lioness. The answer to his royal prayers.

In his arms, he could feel the tension ooze from her body, and a corresponding flood of gratification unravelled the anxious knots in his mind.

'You mean it?'

Her brandy eyes melted to warm honey and flowed through his chest like blissful nectar, soothing his every raw nerve. He brushed the back of his index finger down her nose. Over her lips. Luscious lips that he glossed with the pad of his thumb, where they were still bruised from his kisses.

A new kind of tension sizzled in the air and a glow of unsatisfied desire filled the space between them—an invisible presence that moved over his skin, sliding over them both like a caress. A teasing, taunting, tempting caress.

And right *there* was the difference between him and Augustus. Bedevilled, off-the-charts sizzling chemistry. Black magic.

This. This was what he would play on.

Regardless of how he'd got her on this jet, he still made her weak with desire—and right now that was all he had to work with.

Rebelling against the inner voice warning him to stop, to keep his head this time and cajole her with a gentle hand, he brought his mouth to the edge of her ear and closed his teeth around her lobe.

Her breathless panting whispered over his neck and made his pulse thrash against his cuff. It was a low, husky carnal want that made him murmur, 'Absolutely I mean it. I swear it on my very life.'

Two days were all he needed to lure her over to the dark side.

'Let me show you the most beautiful place on earth.'

He knew the perfect spot for the ultimate seduction, where his Queen would surrender right into his waiting arms.

'What do say, angel?'

CHAPTER SIX

LUCIANA WAS IN the throes of a wonderful dream and she never wanted to wake up. Amazingly strong, muscular arms wrapped her in the warmth of their protection and the rhythmic sound of the ocean lapping over the shore lulled her mind into a tranquil peace she hadn't felt in aeons.

A muffled lyrical trill shattered the halcyon bliss and beckoned her to rouse.

Bright was the splash of daylight behind her eyelids. Soft and sensually luxurious was the satin beneath her tummy and her cheek. Sweet was the scent of buttery pastry…or possibly French toast.

The musical chime hushed to a harmonious end.

Luciana writhed on the deeply cushioned mattress and stretched the kinks from her body, then prised her eyes open once, twice—and bolted up on all fours.

'Where the—?'

Rocking back, she sat on her ankles, her heart thrashing a symphonic staccato as her gaze bounced around the gargantuan almond-white room.

Holy-moly…

Paradise. She was in an enormous satin-drenched bed in paradise. Not only that, it felt inordinately pure. Minimalistic, all in varying shades of white, it serenaded a desperate search for solace.

In front of her and behind were the only solid walls, and when she swung to her right Luciana gasped at the fifty-foot-wide unencumbered view of a beautiful azure sky and the glistening crystalline waters of the Med as it frolicked with champagne sands. It was as if the entire wall had been rolled back and hidden to one side.

A wide wooden deck ran from the room to the shoreline and she smiled when a small lizard scurried across the sun-drenched teak.

Flipping her gaze to the left, to the opposite open expanse, she was faced with a rugged slab of rock dyed a deep charcoal-grey by the waterfall that sluiced down from some great height she couldn't see, to rush and froth and pool, then run beneath this very room…out through the other side and down toward the beach. Under the deck, she'd guess.

Gripping the edge of the bed, she tipped over to look at the floor, her hair spilling around her face. *Oh, wow*. Glass. The entire floor was glass. And she watched a vivid kaleidoscope of teeny-tiny fish dip and swerve and play beneath her.

So beautiful.

Giddiness leapt inside her at the sheer awesome natural beauty of it all—stunning architecture and a visual feast for the senses had always fascinated her. Odd that Thane was probably the only man she'd ever told that too.

Speaking of Thane… She lurched back upright to sit on the bed. Where the heck was he? And her heart-rate did *not* shoot through the roof when she thought of his name. Absolutely not. She hated the man. Yes, she did.

That would be the Thane who'd appeared so desperate to carry her into the main house, since by the time they'd arrived her insides had been battered and bruised from pummelling emotions and she'd been shivering with exhaustion. The Thane who had lain her gently in his bed…and after that everything was a bit blurry. Oh, Lord. Was it too much to ask that she'd booted him out of the room and banished him to Hades? Of course it was.

But, in her defence, her barricades had been low. And the devil was a maestro at taking advantage of that.

Lingering anger had her fisting the sheets.

She might have agreed to this bargain—*ha!* Agreed? As if she'd had *any* choice. But he was in for a nasty shock—because she was only here to prove she'd be the wife from hell. She'd evict him from her mind for ever while she focused on her end-game. Getting home to Natanael, come hell or high water.

On the plus side, seeing the real dark Prince in action, embroiled in some villainous scheme, would be just the ticket to satisfy her conscience that she'd made the right choices for them all. To ameliorate the guilt that constantly ate at her insides because she was keeping her son's existence a secret.

Though, honestly, she was mad even to trust that he'd take her home in two days. But the alternative was hauling out the big guns—her father. Who would likely kick off a military invasion. And that was the last thing she wanted. Hence she'd surrendered to the dark Prince.

Certifiable? Probably.

The opening bars of muffled Mozart trilled through the room—*again!*—and Luciana vaulted off the bed, the bare pads of her feet hitting cool glass as she searched every table-top. Because that sounded suspiciously like her phone. Which made no sense considering he'd told her it wouldn't work anywhere near the castle. But maybe he'd changed his mind about taking her there, maybe they were miles away from the horrid place—

'Oh, good Lord. My bag!' She'd never been so darn happy in her life! She could *kiss* that horrible brute right now.

Snatching the black leather heap from the side table, she shoved her hand in, rummaging to the bottom.

'Don't ring off…don't stop. *Please* don't stop ringing.'

Shaking like a windswept leaf, she barely managed to hit 'accept' and mash it to her ear.

'H…Hello?'

'*Luciana?*' Claudia's voice was a sound for sore ears.
'Thank God—where are you?'

'I'm…'

Common sense smacked her upside the head. Where the
blazes was Thane? She didn't want him party to this conversation.

'Hold on a minute,' she whispered frantically as she
ducked and dived all over the room, opening and closing
doors, her heart slamming around her chest, feeling like an
extra out of a badly acted eighties cop show.

Aha! There he was. The fiend. In the distance, standing
on the beach, talking to a short dark-haired man. Throwing
a stick into the water, of all things.

Unleashing a pent-up breath, she slumped where she
stood. Looked pretty innocent to her. No dastardly guns
drawn or fisticuffs. *Yet.*

'Okay, I can talk. Is Nate all right?' she whispered, stepping back out of sight, hoping the walls didn't have ears. Or
maybe she was on camera. Her gaze darted around the four
upper corners of the room just in case.

'Of course he's all right. He's out with Lucas and Isabelle.
Now, for heaven's sake, where *are* you?'

Good question. She actually couldn't believe she was
about to say this. 'I'm in…Galancia.'

'*Galancia?*'

Claudia's holler had Luciana wrenching the phone from
her almost burst eardrum.

'Oh. my God. I thought Augustus had been smoking pot
or something.'

'The only thing Augustus gets high on is women.'

'*Eww.* He didn't? When you were *there*?'

'Sure he did.'

'You can't marry that man, Luce.'

Oh, great—Claudia sounded like Thane. Thane who
wanted her '*very, very badly*'.

Luciana rubbed the heel of her hand over her left breast.

Naïve fool that she was, she wanted to believe those three
little words. Words that whispered to a secret place inside
her. So it was fortunate that his mind-blowing pheromones
hadn't obliterated her every brain cell. Obviously he wanted
something from her—everyone always did. She just wasn't
sure what.

'Did Augustus tell Father?' she asked.

'No, not yet. Lucas made him keep his mouth shut until
we heard from you. Half of me wondered if you'd just ducked
out on Augustus, so we were giving you today to contact us
before raising the alarm. Especially with Dad the way he is.
Luce, what were you *thinking*, going there with that man?'

'I didn't have much choice.'

She stormed around the room, shaking the kinky mess
from her ratty locks. *Ugh*, she felt gross. And *that* was when
she spied her case on a pale ecru velvet chaise longue. *Her
case!*

Mid jiggy-dance, she froze as every ounce of blood
drained to her toes. Had he searched it? Hauling it from the
chaise, she plonked it on the end of the bed and fumbled
with the lock. The still locked lock. *Phew.*

Shoulders slumping, she tuned back in to Claudia's voice.

'What do you mean, you didn't have much choice? Did
he force you? Did he…*kidnap* you? *Did he*?'

Claudia's glorious indignation flew down the phone line,
and it was so good having someone in her corner. She took
a great gulp of air to rake him over the hot coals…

And her gaze crashed into the wide stretch of canvas over
the carved bedstead, making the words jam in her throat.

'Oh.'

'What do you mean "oh"? Luce, did you hear me?'

'Yes—yes, I heard you. Sorry, Claudia.'

'Did that Galancian brute *steal* you? *Did* he? That's it. I'm
sending Lucas over there right now. He'll raze that place to
the ground and get you out—'

'No.' What was she doing? *What are you doing, Luce...?*
'No, he didn't take me, Claudia. I...I agreed to come.'

'Mmm-hmm. You sure about that?'

'Yes. He...he asked me to stay with him a couple of days to...talk. Yes, to talk. Then he's bringing me home.'

'Mmm-hmm.'

'Honest.'

Claudia's voice softened. 'Luciana, darling, do you really know what you're doing?'

Lifting her hand, she pressed her fingers over her mouth, felt them tremble against her lips, unable to take her eyes off the picture in front of her.

'Not really. But now I'm here I need to know. I need to...' *Prove to myself I'm over him. Make sure I've done the right thing.*

'Okay, I hear you. Even the stuff you're not saying. The feelings that put that desolate look in your eyes...they haven't gone, huh?'

'No,' she whispered. *They scare me.* 'And that's ruinous, Claudia, because he's bad for me. He's dangerous. I'm reckless with him. He makes me want to be wicked. I spiral out of control. And I can't do that because I have to protect—'

'Luce. You know who you sound like, right? If there is one thing our father is good at it's the old brainwashing technique. Stop listening to his voice. It isn't wicked to want. Maybe...' She let loose a heavy sigh. 'Maybe these two days are exactly what you need. But that's all I can give you before I have to tell Father. Though with his weak heart I'd rather send Lucas in.'

'It'll be like the clash of the titans.'

'My money is on Lucas,' Claudia said, in the confident, proud way only a wife madly in love could.

And there was Luciana with her money on Thane. What that said about her she wouldn't like to guess.

'Just...call me whenever you can, okay?'

'Okay.' Luciana sneaked another peek outside, to check

he still loitered on the beach. 'What has Nate been doing?' she whispered achingly. She missed him so much.

'Playing with Isabelle, painting, making his list for Santa. You name it. He's as happy as a pig in muck. Don't worry. You weren't due back for a couple more days anyway. He's just munching his way through his advent calendar and waiting for his present from your trip since that's before the big day.'

Luciana smiled, glancing down at her case. The case Thane must have sent for. How *dared* he send her into another freefall when she'd just started detesting him?

'I have it for him. Will you tell him I'll text later and that I love him, Claudia? Please?'

'Of course I will. He knows you do. That little boy is rolling in love.'

But not the love of a daddy. Had she ever allowed herself to acknowledge that? No. Because she'd always thought that was something she couldn't give him.

Throat raw and swollen, her words hurt. 'I'll keep in touch, Claudia, I promise.'

'Be careful, Luce.'

At the dead tone Luciana tossed her phone to the bed and tilted her head, her hair sliding over her shoulder as she stared at the past.

Predator-like, stealthy footsteps sounded across the deck and her nefarious blood thrummed in exhilaration. Then his alluring scent hit her, courtesy of the ocean breeze: dark and divine and oh-so-drugging.

'*Buenos dias.*' Rich with heat and layered in sin, that voice curled around her body in a hot, hungry embrace, making her shiver with want.

Somehow he'd sucked all the oxygen from the vast expanse, so when she took a deep breath to peek at him and came up short the room did a crazy little spin. 'G…Good morning.'

A glorious full-bodied smile kicked his lips up and her

heart into gear. And—*oh, Lord*—that solitary dimple she adored so much…The iridescent lustre of happiness in his black sapphire eyes… As if seeing her here, in his home, was the best sight in the world.

All it took was one long look and the burning butterfly in her stomach fluttered its wings, enflaming her mind with reckless, shameless abandon. Didn't they always say the real enemy was within? Ah, yes… Her body—the traitor.

He carded his fingers through his tousled raven-black hair and she was inclined to think he'd spent the morning at a magazine photo shoot for sex incarnate.

Suave black suit trousers hugged his mighty fine muscular legs, and he'd paired them with a slim-fit crisp white open-collared shirt for a look that oozed sinful gravitas and delectable danger. But that wasn't the worst of it. *Nooo*, of course it wasn't. Because the universe had it in for her, remember? So of course the delicious brute was clean-shaven, and that sexy scarred divot in his chin begged to be licked and kissed as she stroked that smooth jaw.

Groaning inwardly, she crossed her arms and winced when she chafed her heavy, sensitive breasts. *Darn it*. The man knew it too. Cocking one dark brow as if he knew precisely what he did to her. The wretch.

'It was wonderful to wake up with you in my arms again, Luciana.'

Her stomach did a slow, languorous roll. 'Oh, really? Did you do that without permission too?'

Mock affront widened his deep, devastating eyes. 'Absolutely not. In fact I had every intention of sleeping elsewhere. But you refused to let me go.'

'I…I did?'

He nodded with deep satisfaction and tutted, as if she'd been very, *very* naughty. 'You were most displeased when I tried to move this morning.'

Heat exploded in her cheeks. 'Obviously I thought I was

in bed with someone else.' Surely that would set off his cave-man alarm bells and twitch his temper?

Except all he did was take a lethal step towards her. And another. Until she felt hunted, pursued, desired beyond measure.

'No, it was definitely *my* name you were calling in that sexy purr of yours.'

He spoke with a debauched rasp and frisked his prurient gaze down the length of her, snagging it on her chest. His gaze was covetous. Heated.

And *that* was when she realised she was wearing only her black lacy camisole and panties.

'Oh, Lord…'

She yanked a loose, rumpled almond sheet from the bed—the bed *they* had slept in—and hastily wrapped it around her, toga style.

'There is nothing I haven't seen before, Luciana,' he growled, his voice thick with lust as he stepped up close.

'Th…That's not the point.'

Up came his arm and he tucked a lock of hair behind her ear—his touch as light and feathery as dandelion fluff—then trailed one licentious fingertip down her throat…over her décolletage…whispering scandalous promises to her flesh.

'Nothing I haven't stroked or licked or sucked or kissed before either. And I cannot wait to do all of those things again.'

Her core twisted with want even as panic shot down her spine. Was he trying to seduce her? Oh, no. No way. He wasn't doing this to her again. She would *not* surrender a second time. Regardless of that dissolute brooding certainty.

'I'm not giving you the chance.'

'Is that right?' he drawled with a devilish smile, as if the mere suggestion that she could resist him was delightfully droll. *Horrid man.*

Luciana stumbled back a step and hauled the white shift

dress she'd taken to Courchevel to wear by the pool out of her case.

All fumbling arms, she wrestled herself into the dress and wriggled from the sheet, rambling to cover her discomfort. 'And, actually, there's plenty you haven't seen before. Twelve whole pounds of plenty. And despite what my mother says about curves being out of fashion, and how I'm not setting a very good example, I'm owning every one of them. Because one: I can't get shot of them, no matter how much I starve, and being hungry really is no picnic. And two: every single one of those pounds was worth the—'

'Worth the…?'

Closing her eyes for a beat, she realised everything was too raw, too close to the surface. She felt like a tiny volcano that could erupt at the wrong word or look and spew forth the burning destructive truth.

'Those…' She twizzled her index finger, making a little circle in the air. 'Round American chocolatey crunchy biscuits with cream in the middle. Can't remember what they're called off the top of my head.'

'Then when I meet *these*…' he twirled his finger too '…round American chocolatey crunchy biscuits with cream in the middle, I shall thank them personally. They look good on you.'

'They do?'

Aw, Luce, what did you ask him that for?

'Better than good.' He licked his lips, as if tasting her would be just as sweet and luscious. 'Fabulous.'

Yeah, right.

'Wow, considering how we ended up in bed the first time…' In short, she'd had to beguile him into undressing her—not exactly ladylike behaviour. 'Your repertoire for seduction skills really *has* come on.'

His smile was full of virile disrepute. 'You only have yourself to blame. I was inaugurated and taught by the best, after all.'

Imagine who'd been slain in his bed ever since he speared her with a warped arrow of pain and pique. 'Then clearly I created a monster.'

Laughter rumbled up from the depths of his chest. 'I think you did, angel.'

With that, he glanced up at the canvas stretched across the wall and his smile faltered.

'Right there. It's a good likeness—a stunning rendition. Don't you think?'

She had to swallow around the great lump in her throat. 'Yes, it is. It's…beautiful, Thane.'

Why? Why did he have a painting of their favourite spot in Zurich? Where they'd stayed. A dramatic panorama of the Rhine Falls. Luciana could virtually hear the roaring rush of water, feel the moist mist peppering her skin, see the craggy jutting rocks, the Prussian blue lakes.

'Do you remember the day we met?' he asked distractedly. He stared at the scene with a deep frown. As if it was the first time he'd allowed himself to really look at it.

To remember was to open a vault she'd bolted shut years ago. A perilous endeavour, just as dangerous as he was. But, as always, this man silenced the screams of her self-preservation.

'If you hadn't walked by that day…' Scary to think what might have happened.

'What were you doing there, Luciana?'

'Celebrating the end of finals.'

She'd caved in to temptation and jetted across Europe with some trusted friends from her politics class. And while her father had been under the illusion that she'd remain in London for another month, Luciana had gone incognito and ventured into her first foray into rebellion.

She'd been intoxicated by the heady taste of absolute freedom. One she'd failed to find at university, as she'd hoped. Eyes had still watched and reported back to her parents. Gossip had still fuelled the press. But in Zurich, for the first time in her life, she'd been a normal person. A woman the paparazzi wouldn't look at twice. Lost in the crowd and having the time of her life.

Until a two-hundred-pound strung-out Viking had cornered her behind a tour bus, the foul scent of beer leaching from his every pore, wanting some 'fun' of his own. And in those terrifying moments she'd cursed her naïve recklessness and prayed for someone to appear. For *this* man to appear.

It had been Thane who'd torn him off her and knocked him clean out with one punch. Thane, who'd locked onto her eyes and never let her go. Thane, who'd kept a careful distance as he'd walked her back to her apartment as if she were some fragile fawn.

The romantic little girl in her had called it serendipity. Thinking about it, dark and dangerous should have screamed at her to run, yet she'd been petrified that he'd leave. Take that awesome powerful protection with him. So she'd finagled him into having a coffee, then dinner, and drinks after that. And suddenly she'd been dependent, hooked on him like a drug, and all she'd craved was the next fix.

She'd been addicted to the intense highs. Though she'd do well to remember the aftermath. Horrendous heart-wrenching lows. Lost. Unfocused. She'd sworn she would never be dependent on another man.

Still… 'You saved me.'

'He is lucky to still walk the earth,' he said scathingly, in a fierce, low, dominant tone.

And she couldn't help it. She smiled wide—big and genuine and just for him. Because she'd been terrified and he'd been…*awesome.*

Eyes locked with his once more, she couldn't break free of his hold. They were drawn together like powerful magnets. As it had been from the start.

His initial confusion at their combustible attraction was unforgettable. As if he'd never known such passion and lust could exist. Endearing. Dazzling. He'd enslaved her in seconds.

Do you remember our first time? her heart whispered. *Yours? Mine? Teaching one another how to give pleasure and take? I remember every tender, evocative touch, every blissful second in your arms. The longing. The delirium as you drove deeper and deeper into my body until I felt indelibly marked. Branded. Claimed. Wanted. Desired.*

Yours.

Her heart ached, and Thane stared into her eyes as if the secrets of her soul were nothing more than words on a page.

Oh, Lord. She was in so much trouble here.

She was supposed to be reassuring herself that her secrets were better kept buried. Ensuring that Thane rued the day they'd ever met. Yet here she was, reminiscing about 'the good ol' times' and trying not to think of the damage they could do to the bed. They had busted a frame or two in their time...

What she *wasn't* supposed to be was more confused than ever. But within the space of ten minutes all her carefully erected defences were crumbling down around her, leaving her brain reduced to chaos and rubble.

And she hated it. Hated that the semblance of control she'd been hanging on to was as precarious as her future.

Luciana had to remember who he was and how exactly she came to be standing in his bedroom. Instead of musing that underneath, where it counted the most, he might still be the man she'd fallen for. And if that was true they were all in a bigger mess than she'd ever imagined. A wealth of pain at her hands. Because she was a mother and if her son could have a father who was a good man, hell would freeze before she kept them apart any longer.

Insides shaking, she tore her gaze from his. And as soon as that powerful connection was severed the fog began to clear.

Remember who he is, how you got here. How he once

tried to assassinate your father. Don't forget that you're enemies.

She had to stop listening to the longing of her heart. Get through the next two days unscathed, then run as fast as she could. Before she started doubting her own mind and cracked under the pressure. Told him the one secret that would change their lives for ever. The one secret she would never be able to take back.

CHAPTER SEVEN

DESPITE THE CLOAK of aloofness that suddenly settled over her, Thane had an incredibly light, airy feeling. Much like the five-foot dazzling iridescent aqua dolphin balloon he'd once bought Luciana. She'd adored the garish spectacle and, seeing that same gorgeous smile on her face moments ago—the one that made his heart kind of...*stop*—he'd known he'd played the perfect pitch by bringing her here.

She'd visibly relaxed since speaking to her sister—he'd heard her softly spoken goodbye and made a mental score to thank Seve for unearthing her case and bag pronto. By dusk today she would fall into his arms like a sweet ripe apple tumbling from a tree.

Already she was unravelling more by the second—nothing like the Princess who'd slid so gracefully into his car only yesterday. Rumpled. Tousled. Looking sublimely natural and sexed-up. No show or lipstick or pristine dress, she was sexier than anything he'd ever seen or, he suspected, would ever see in his lifetime.

He growled inwardly. Wanting her under him. Beneath him. Surrendering to him. Insane, she made him insane with want. But, as much as he knew she desired him with equal wanton abandon, something held her back, so he refused to rush this or lose his head.

Velvety rich, the scent of coffee and pastries wafted on the sultry breeze, and when Luciana's stomach grumbled

Thane satisfied himself that he could at least pacify one of her cravings this morning.

'Breakfast,' he said. 'Then you can choose where you wish to go today. *Si?*'

Her head jerked up where she stood, hastily zipping up her case, and he was smacked with the suspicion that the contents were something she'd rather he didn't see. Not that it mattered. By the time he was finished her every secret would be unearthed.

'Wow, Thane. Colour me surprised—you're giving me a *choice*?'

For now. '*Si*, of course. The first of many. Come and sit with me—let me feed you.'

As if she were an antelope and he a great ferocious lion, she approached him warily. Such an astute character, she was. Then he heard a canine sniff from behind him and accepted that he wasn't the only predator in the vicinity.

'Ah,' she said. 'Now I get why you were throwing sticks. Why are they smacking their lips as if I'm on the menu? Good Lord, they're huge. What *are* they?'

Slipping his arm around her waist, he tugged her to him and murmured in her ear. 'Rhodesian Ridgebacks. Maybe they find you as delicious as I do. Must be all those round American chocolatey…'

With a long-suffering sigh, she rolled her eyes and pushed past him. 'Yes, yes—all right, Romeo.'

All that feisty sass made him grin as he pulled out a chair and watched her sashay into the padded wicker seat.

'Thank you.'

Bending at the waist, he pressed his lips to the graceful slope of her bare shoulder and murmured, 'Welcome…' relishing both the shimmy that danced down her body *and* the way he'd already stripped her of that haughty veil.

He sank into the chair adjacent to hers and strove for nonchalance. 'I take it you spoke to your sister?' That he was ignorant of the whole conversation sat in his guts like a rock.

The sun bathed her in a warm glow, picking out the honeycomb strands in her hair, and she swept a stray tendril back from her temple in a decidedly nervous gesture. 'Yes. I told her I was staying with you for a couple of days.'

Thane didn't bother arguing that point. *Yet.*

'So, thank you for…' She shook her head, sending that wayward lock tumbling back over her face. 'Why on earth I'm *thanking* you for returning my own property to me, when it was originally your fault I lost it, is beyond me—but I do appreciate you sending for it.'

'You are most welcome. See? I am not so bad after all.'

'Oh, you are *very* bad, Thane. Of that I am in no doubt.'

A dark laugh erupted from his chest. 'Fortunately for me you like me that way. It turns you on.'

A blush that spoke more of pique than passion flurried across her cheeks, but her scathing retort perished as his man at the house—Pietro—appeared and laid a mound of homemade madeleines, croissants and cream-filled pastries on the table before her.

That serene breeding of hers came rushing to the fore. 'Everything smells delicious—thank you so much. Did you make these?'

Pietro fastened his warm hazel gaze on her. 'My wife, Your Royal Highness. But she will only cook for our Prince.'

Thane's good mood disintegrated and he clenched his teeth. It didn't matter how many times he told the man to call him Thane, he still got *our Prince.* Respectful, yes, but it shafted him with guilt—because despite his title his hands were largely tied, and if he'd played things differently he'd be in the position to do a damn sight more for them.

Luciana arched one brow in his direction. 'Why only Thane?'

'Eat, Luciana,' he ordered, knowing what was coming.

He didn't want Pietro's gratitude. It was Thane's job to procure him a better life. He was the one to blame for the mess they were in. If he'd been stronger, hidden his true ambitions better, his father would have given him the throne upon his death. Instead of passing it over to the power-hungry, greedy lech that was Franco Guerrero.

Naturally Luciana didn't take a blind bit of notice—*Dios*, she was an obstinate little thing—and she blinked up at Pietro with those gorgeous brandy eyes no man could possibly resist. Not even happily married Pietro, with his six girls and loose tongue.

'He gives us a home, our own land. No one but the crown owns land on Galancia, but Thane gives us acres of his vineyards and my family make the best wines on the island. Then he makes sure my girls can travel north, go to school. He fixes everything.'

'Pietro…don't. Please.'

Every time he heard those words it just reminded him of the thousands of others he couldn't help. Though now he had Luciana all that would change, wouldn't it? *Dios*, he couldn't wait. His patience shredded more by the day.

Luciana, whose only focus was Pietro, said, 'Oh, he does?'

As if some mental explosion had occurred in that ingenious brain of hers, so many emotions flickered across her exquisite face that he was hard-pressed to pick out one.

'*Si,*' Pietro said avidly. 'The best man to walk the earth. And now *you* are here, and everything will be—'

Thane glanced up to silence him. He didn't want these two days to be mired with talk of his throne. But, fisting his hand beneath the table, he warred with an internal battle to be forthright. At least with himself. Truth was, he wanted Luciana to want him. To choose *him* over Augustus. Not to feel pushed or obligated in any way. And he refused to read too deeply into that.

'Now I'm here…?' Luciana prompted.

Pietro grinned. 'He will be happy at last. All will be well.'

Guilt blanched her flawless skin and she composed a

spurious smile that made Thane uneasy. Made him doubly sure he was missing something.

'You must meet my wife. I will never have peace if she does not speak to you.'

Thane almost groaned aloud. They would be here all day and Luciana would be subjected to God knows what.

'Pietro? I don't think we have time. Luciana wishes to explore—isn't that right, angel?'

The wide-eyed gleam she launched his way was anything but angelic. It was positively devious and it made his blood hum. She wanted to hear more, he realised.

'We have plenty of time...*darling*.' She emphasised that endearment—the very one that made his heart lurch—with a swift kick to his shin as she peered up at the other man all guile and innocence. 'I think that's a wonderful idea, Pietro. I would love to meet her.'

Relishing Thane's discomfort, she flashed her teeth at him, all saccharine sweetness. The dark look he volleyed back said she would pay highly for it. Later.

Then again, Pietro had wandered off—so why wait?

Easing forward in his seat, he slid wicked fingers over the delicate curve of her knee beneath the table, then made small teasing circles as they ascended higher and higher up her inner thigh.

The light flush that coloured her cheeks made a gradual descent across her chest, down over her breasts, and the glass of freshly squeezed orange juice in her fist rippled as she clamped her thighs together, imprisoning his hand.

'See that knife?' she whispered in a rush, motioning to the lethal blade on the table-top. 'I won't hesitate to chop those fingers off.'

'Ah, you won't do that, Luciana.'

'I wouldn't be so sure, if I were you. Don't underestimate me, Romeo.'

Flipping his hand, he forcibly nudged her legs apart. 'While I have no intention of underestimating you, I believe you'll soon see sense. Because what will I pleasure you with then?'

Her breathing became short and shallow, making her deep cleavage taunt him with a subtle quivering heave, and he had the sinful urge to ramp up her erotic want higher still. So he stroked one finger over the lace of her panties and ran his tongue along his bottom lip suggestively.

'Actually…who needs fingers? I can think of various other ways to torment you.'

And he would use every one to lure her in. No matter what it took, by the weekend both Luciana and the throne would be his.

She was going to murder him. Wrap her hands around his throat and send him to meet his maker—the devil himself. That was if she didn't choke on the uncut testosterone in the air first. Arrogant and downright debauched—that was what he was.

She couldn't move or whimper a sound, since Pietro was still fiddling with a coffee pot at the far end of the deck—and of course the shameless reprobate just *loved* that…the possibility of them getting caught likely got him off. It certainly didn't excite *her* blood. A woman of her gentility and refinement should be appalled at his sybaritic behaviour. And she was. Utterly.

Squirming, she tried to dislodge his hand and alleviate the dark pulse that throbbed in her pelvis. She wanted them back on topic. Wanted to hear every word that *wasn't* being said. It was that stuff that interested her—far more than his wandering lasciviousness.

Liar.

She felt like an insect that had inadvertently strayed into a spider's web, her every move ensuring greater entrapment, but right now she didn't care. Entangled as she was, there was far more going on here than met the eye.

Pietro vanished around the corner and she smacked Thane's arm away as she spun on him, eyes narrowed.

'Your uncle runs Galancia in a dictatorship, does he not? No government, no parliament to speak for the people, all the power coming from the man at the top. The state owns every acre of land, therefore every piece of brick and mortar too.'

That did it.

He flung himself back in his seat, taking his wicked fingers with him. It was if he'd found a state of mindless pleasure and was put out at her stopping his fun. *Tough.*

'I am sure you know he does, *princesa.*'

'So by giving Pietro his own land you're breaking your own rules?'

He picked up his espresso and downed the treble shot. 'They are not mine.'

'No? Are you saying you don't agree with them?'

His nonchalant shrug belied the curious tension in his menacingly hard frame. 'I don't think it's fair that the people can't reap the benefits of their hard work, that's all.'

Fair? 'You're indirectly hinting at a democracy, Thane.'

'I might be.'

Shock made her rock back in her seat. The dark, dangerous, autocratic Prince of Galancia wanted a *democracy*? While Arunthia had been a democratic state for years, it was the last thing she'd expected here.

'Is this what you're planning to do when you rule?'

'I might be.'

Good Lord. 'And so you take from the rich to give to the poor in the meantime?'

He scratched his jaw lazily. 'On occasion. Or I may just have paid Pietro's family for building this house.'

'How much? Thirty million?'

'I'll have you know it's the going rate.'

'Is it *really*?'

This was unbelievable. Staggering. She'd been absolutely right. She had no idea who he was. And nor did anyone else.

Including her father. Which wasn't surprising. Since Thane didn't have overall control he naturally wanted to keep his true agenda firmly under wraps.

'Still being a hero, then, Thane?' she asked softly.

Just as he'd been when he'd saved her from a fate worse than death in Zurich. Just as he'd been when he'd appeared once again out of nowhere in Courchevel. As if she'd conjured him up. Like some freak happenstance or serendipity.

An assassin? A mercenary? *This* man? She doubted that very much.

But, oh, no, he really didn't like being called a hero. The angry glitter in his eyes told her that. He was a testament to leashed power, Luciana decided. No need to shout when he could incite a quake with one look or a word. So intense. And he was heart-thumpingly gorgeous with it.

'Quiet, Luciana. Or I will silence that mouth for you. *Again*. And don't think I won't.'

His dominant power pushed at her, hot and hard, and she blushed like a teenager with a crush.

'Oh. I believe you. But this time I'm not giving you the chance.' That was what had got her into this mess to start with.

She might be here against her will, or rather she'd had little choice, but the sliver of pride she had left was a precious commodity she could ill afford to lose. So there was no way she was falling for that again. She knew better. Kiss her once and he'd had her on a plane. Kiss her twice and she'd find herself bound for Outer Mongolia, or flat on her back on her way to a priest. Though why the man wanted to marry her specifically she couldn't begin to fathom.

Why can't you just accept he wants you for you, Luce?

Because that would be plain stupid.

He arched one of those devilish brows. 'You know better than to challenge me, Luciana.'

The dark promise in those words made her shiver. And if his obsidian eyes had seemed compelling before, now they were like magnets, pulling on the iron in her blood, making it race around her body.

Lifting her tall glass, she splashed some orange juice down her parched throat, relishing the tangy sweetness that burst over her tongue, determined to wrestle back her poise. *Get back on topic, for heaven's sake.*

'Anyway,' she said. 'Why build a home here? Don't get me wrong—it's absolutely stunning—but why not live at Galancia Castle?'

His gaze drifted out to sea, but not before she saw the shadow of pain wash over him. 'I live there too. But my uncle and I are not the best of housemates. Even with thousands upon thousands of square feet and over two hundred walls.'

Seemed to her they were divided in more ways than one. Even as she struggled to take it all in she dug for more. 'I've heard it's one of the most opulent, palatial castles in the world.'

'It is the devil's lair.' A deep feminine voice sounded from beside her. 'Our Prince is better here. That place makes him dark and that man drains the life from him. Welcome… *welcome.*'

Thane shoved his hands through his raven hair, discomfort and agitation leaching from him.

Luciana yearned to straddle his lap, take away his pain just as she'd once done, but instead she jiggled her chair backwards to welcome Pietro's wife.

'Buenos dias,' she said, standing to accept a warm greeting and a kiss to both cheeks. The astounding affection filled her heart with elation and almost thrust her into a stupor.

Cupping her face, the petite brunette spitfire beamed. 'Good gracious, you are a real beauty. Little wonder he will not take—'

'Hanna,' Thane ground out in warning.

'Ah, hush. Let an old woman be happy.' She clapped her palm over her chest. 'This will be the best Christmas we have ever seen.'

It took all of Luciana's willpower to maintain her serenity. Never mind that the woman had just told the dark Prince to hush—why the blazes was she casting her festive aspirations on Luciana? Why should she think Luciana would be here for Christmas? Was Thane so darn confident he'd been shouting it from the rooftops?

Of all the arrogant, conceited...

It was on the tip of her tongue to tell every Galancian within hearing distance that she'd be long gone by then. But as if Thane sensed her freefall he picked up her hand, lifting it to his lips. Tenderly he kissed the sensitive pulse-point that pounded at her inner wrist as he locked those mesmerising eyes on hers.

His electric energy zeroed in on her. The panicked dizziness abated. All extraneous noise drained from her perception until there was only him. Until she plunged back to her seat in a dreamlike daze.

How do you do this to me?

And then there was this couple, welcoming her with open arms despite the inbred hatred between Arunthians and Galancians, behaving as if she were their saviour. It was surreal. But it was wonderful too.

Even his beasts gazed at her with loving amber-hued puppy-dog eyes, one of them even resting its slavering chin on her knee. Lord, she couldn't resist his dogs. Had to stroke the short, furry wheat-brown coat. Brush those velvety ears between her thumb and forefinger.

Natanael would adore you, she thought with a stab of anguish.

He would adore all of this. He had pined and pleaded for a four-legged friend and he loved people, being the centre of their world. She could just hear him chattering, see him frolicking on the beach, dwarfed by these huge hounds, building sandcastles with Thane, his—

Luciana closed her eyes and swallowed thickly around the fear clotting her throat. She didn't want to make the connection—didn't want to acknowledge who this man was to her son. Had to focus on escaping, protecting Nate...

But what if in reality it wasn't Thane he needed protecting *from*? What if Thane was the only person in the entire world who could truly protect *Nate*?

He wasn't the man she'd met in Zurich. He was harder. More ruthless. More determined. And yet he wasn't the monster people claimed him to be.

Head pounding, as if it had been jammed in a nutcracker and split open, she couldn't think. Couldn't breathe.

So she smiled and nodded in all the right places while the endless waters of the Med called to her, the sound of its gentle lap, its tranquil stillness, soothing the disharmony in her heart and mind. But she didn't need to be looking at the ocean to realise she was burying her head in the sand. *Again*. That was exactly what she'd done in Hong Kong. Her utmost to pretend that her time wasn't running out. And where had it got her? Into inevitable torment when faced with reality.

If she waded through the mess of enemy nations and her throne she was a mother. First and foremost. Yes, if Natanael came to light it would ruin her in the eyes of her people and her father would likely disown her. But so be it. The only reason she'd kept him quiet was to keep him safe.

She'd pleaded to have him. The fact that he was alive right now was why she lived with the pain. The fact that his beautiful face lit up her entire world was why she lived in the dark. But if there were no danger to him there would be no reason for his true identity not to be known. His happiness was the most important thing to her. And if her little boy could have a daddy who was a good man—who would love him and protect him above all else—then Nate deserved that and so did Thane.

As for her crown... Her father would have to bend his rules and laws. Allow Claudia to take the throne despite the fact that Lucas wasn't of blue blood. Or he'd have to get over the fact he'd washed his hands of Andalina years ago and command her return from New York. Granted, the thought of Andie being Queen was hellishly scary, but her father would have no choice. If she was ruined, the damage was already done.

For the first time in years Luciana had choices. She only had to use them wisely. Be absolutely sure she was doing the right thing by telling Thane the truth.

Hanna and Pietro bade them a fond goodbye, leaving them alone once more.

'I believe I promised you a date,' he drawled. 'Lunch at the southern reef? A horse-ride along the beach or up into the vineyards? It's beautiful up there. What's your pleasure, angel?'

You. Heaven help me…you.

The man being worshipped by the sun before her. She wanted him to be real. Wanted the portentous voice inside her to be quiet, cease whispering that she was sitting in an audience watching a play—a performance being acted to perfection just for her—while she was blind to the true intent of the show.

'What do you want, Luciana?' he asked huskily.

A proper family. A wonderful daddy for Natanael. Love.

But all she said was, 'All of the above.'

CHAPTER EIGHT

IN HINDSIGHT, A horse-ride probably wasn't the greatest of ideas, considering he'd almost choked on his own tongue when Luciana had poured that luscious body into some lightweight fawn jodhpurs and a figure-hugging cerise pink T-shirt—the outfit borrowed from one of Pietro's rake-thin girls. Talk about an exercise in torture.

He'd just put in the longest twenty-minute car-ride of his life. And now he cursed the *idiota* who had secreted the royal stables so far inland. He would fire the man if he didn't suspect it had been himself.

Arms folded across his wide chest, his foul temper exacerbated further still when every stable boy tripped over himself to attend her, but eventually she chose a deep chestnut thoroughbred named Galileo and Thane took his favourite black stallion, Malvado. The twinkle in Luciana's eyes told him she thought 'wicked' a very apt name for his beast of a mount. He didn't bother arguing. It was true that only Thane could dominate him.

Unsurprisingly, she rode like a pro and lured him into a race up into the vineyards, with the rich earth spraying in their wake, the fresh breeze whipping her bronze hair behind her and slapping her cheeks with colour.

Never had she looked more bewitching or more free. More real and more like his Ana.

Gradually she slowed to a trot, then an easy walk, and Thane pulled at the reins and drew up beside her.

'Good?' he asked.

'Yes. Wonderful.'

Those pink-smothered breasts rose and fell with her every soft pant and a huge smile curved her lips. Lips he wanted to make love to until her breath was ragged for *him*.

'I didn't expect it to be so gorgeous here. Warmer than home for December.'

Thane felt the muscle in his jaw spasm as he ground his teeth hard. Galancia would soon be her home, and the sooner she accepted that the better for his state of mind.

'Then again, you are closer to Africa here,' she went on. 'The air is hot and sultry. Everything just feels…'

'Relaxed? Calm?'

'Exactly. Maybe too calm—like the calm before a storm.'

A pensive crease lined her brow and she threaded the leather reins in between her long fingers, staring far into the distance as if she were a million miles away. Much as she'd done at breakfast. It vexed him because he was blind to the reason. He wanted her *here*. With him.

'Penny for them?'

She fobbed him off with a rueful smile. 'I doubt they're worth that much.'

Thane didn't believe her for a second, but let it go when she lifted in her saddle to twist and take in their surroundings. The endless rows of vines were heavy with juicy red grapes and lush dark green foliage.

'So these are your famous vineyards? Never tried the wine myself.'

'You should. In fact tonight I'll pour you a glass of one of the best wines in the world.'

She arched one brow at the vainglory lacing his words but he gave a nonchalant shrug. Why shouldn't he be proud of what they'd achieved? And moreover…

'The northern terrain is home to our much-lauded olive groves too. Far better than yours.'

'Now, now, Thane. Your head is getting a little *too* big over there.'

He grinned, amazed that they were joking about what had once been a life-threatening issue.

'Once upon a time we grew the best oranges too. Arunthian oranges are tasteless in comparison.'

She rolled her eyes. 'Of course they are.'

'I'm serious. Our crops were said to be the best in Europe. But your great-grandfather didn't like it that overseas trade demand was greater for ours, or that we made more money than he did. So he sent in men to disease our crops. Not one survived.'

Her head reared as if he'd slapped her. 'That's a lie! Nothing more than propaganda!'

'It is not. I swear it. In many ways we continue to suffer from that loss now.'

'But…but that's terrible.'

'*Si.* It is. Just one of the spats our countries—or should I say the houses of Verbault and Guerrero—have engaged in over the centuries.'

Her nose scrunched up as she grimaced. 'Hard to believe we were allies—sister islands at one time. I have heard some gruesome and horrific accounts…'

'And I bet we were always the villains.'

Thane didn't bother to wait for her to agree; they both knew he was right.

'I won't lie—I imagine we committed many an outrageous act not to be proud of, but most were in retaliation. If you care to go back far enough it all comes down to Arunthia's greed. Galancia has always been the richer in industry, and many an Arunthian leader has tried to take it by force. Almost succeeded two or three times too. But it just made us stronger. Hence we have an indomitable military presence. Now no one would dare to touch us.'

Those decadently long lashes swept downward, as if his words weighed heavily on her mind. 'I can see why you wish to be feared, in that case. To protect what you have. No matter what it takes.'

Thane narrowed his gaze on her, sure there was a deeper meaning to her hushed words—which had been spoken in a cracked parody of her usual tone. When she failed to elucidate he ploughed on, riding the imperative desire for her to know. Understand.

'We stop at nothing. Which has caused a whole new set of problems for us. Because to protect, to build an army, takes an obscene amount of money. More than you could ever imagine. So the crown hoards the land for revenue and taxes businesses until they can't breathe—until we've suffocated our own. All to make us indestructible. More powerful than any other. While our children need new schools and our hospitals are in dire need of repair.'

Sadness crept over her demeanour, making her eyes darken. 'That makes so much sense it's scary.'

'My uncle will never release those bonds on our people. Nor will he let the feud go—just like my father before him. His father before that. The hatred is inbred.'

'I know. My father is the same. But what I don't understand is why Franco Guerrero is in power and you're not. Why haven't you taken your throne?'

'Must we talk about this now, Luciana?'

'Yes, Thane, we must. You brought me here against my wishes. You talk about marrying me...which is ludicrous. We don't even know one another. And basically all you expect me to go on is rumours and secrets and lies. So here I am blindfolded, smack-bang in the midst of a labyrinth, not knowing which way to turn. Can't you see that?'

Disquiet hummed through his mind. He didn't particularly want her to know how dark he was inside, how deeply twisted by it all.

They'd reached a shaded wrought-iron arbour often used by his workers and Thane swung his right leg over the saddle and dropped onto uneven ground, determined to tread carefully over the minefield that was the past.

He was too close to success to risk everything now, by admitting he'd been a trigger away from assassinating her father. Especially when some days he regretted not doing so, since his people had ultimately paid the price. Other days he accepted it would have severed the very last thread of humanity he'd been clinging to at the time. And today, looking at the man's daughter—the woman he wanted as his wife, the woman who would give him his crown—he couldn't help but wonder if fate truly did move in mysterious ways.

Vigilance tautened his striking features, telling Luciana she was trying to open a conversational door best left shut. Then an artful devious light shone in his dark eyes and he stretched out his arms, gripped her waist and lifted her down, dragging her body against his.

The friction charged her pulse and set off a chain reaction she was powerless against. Inside her bra her breasts grew heavy, aching to be touched. Those burning butterflies went wild, flitting in and around her ribcage, and her panties suddenly felt too damp, too tight.

'Let's have lunch in the shade,' he murmured, his voice enriched with sin. 'It's stifling out here in the open.'

Translation: *I'll seduce you in the bushes until you forget your own name, never mind this discussion.*

Er...*no*. She thought not.

Though her resolve would be less painful to stick to if she stopped gawping at the man. Thane in a pair of tall sepia leather boots, black riding trousers and a skin-tight red polo shirt—collar flicked up to tease his hair and short sleeves lovingly caressing his sculpted biceps—was a head-rush all on its own.

So she made a clumsy job of sidestepping outside his magnetic force field.

Out came his arm, to snake around her waist, and she

dodged like the netball champion she'd once been and shook her head. 'Oh, no, you don't. I know full well what you're up to, Romeo, and you can forget it. *Talk.*'

Growling, he turned away. 'Fine.'

Then, just as she breathed a sigh of relief, he came at her from another angle, as if he'd played her with misdirection and now…*pounce*…stole a tummy-flipping, bone-liquefying kiss from her mouth. Only to grin with acute smugness and walk away.

Her hand shot out and she found Galileo, to steady herself, even as she bit her lip to stifle a gurgle of laughter. He was incorrigible. Couldn't stand being told no. Losing in any way. And, seriously, she shouldn't laugh—because the man was dangerous with it. Kidnapping, stealing kisses… He was off-the-charts unpredictable, and that scared her more than anything.

And it thrills you just as much.

Thane grabbed the lunch bag and Luciana rolled a blanket across the grass beneath the leafy trellised ceiling, where it was blissfully cooler. Then she sat cross-legged and unpacked a tapas feast of cold cut meats, cheeses and rosemary-scented bread.

Throat dry, she drank greedily from a bottle of sparkling water, trying not to splutter or drool as Thane dropped to the red chequered blanket and lounged back on his elbows in an insolent pose, crossing one ankle over the other. She had the shameless urge to climb over his lap, sit on those muscular thighs and feel all that latent erotic power beneath her. And—just her rotten luck—he caught her staring and fired her the most indecently hedonistic smile she'd ever seen.

Luciana deflected his corruption tactics with a haughty sniff. 'I'm waiting. So talk.'

'I have the strangest urge to take you over my knee.'

She harnessed the shiver that threatened to rattle her spine. 'And *I* have the strangest urge to get back on that horse and leave you to eat lunch by yourself.'

The brute actually grinned at that, then popped an olive in his mouth. Though when his humour faded, to be replaced by an aching torment, she almost let him off the hook, hating to see him in the throes of anguish. Oh, he banked it soon enough—but it was too late.

'When my father knew he was dying I had only just turned seventeen...' He paused, as if figuring out his next words. 'He ordered me to do a job, and at the very last moment I defied him. I thought I'd seen and felt his fury before then. I had seen nothing.' He shrugged blithely. 'I deserved every blow for going against him, and I could have lived with that, or anything else he doled out to me personally. What I hadn't expected was the depth of his wrath and the price my people would pay.'

Abruptly, he jerked upright and rested his forearm on one bended knee.

'When I failed him he decided I was too cocky, too young...too free-thinking to rule. Too liberal. I had shown my true colours. My father and my uncle are of the same ilk. Dictators. Born and bred militia. So my punishment was a stipulation that said I couldn't take power until I was thirty years old. Until I had learned my lesson.'

Outrage and the fiercest taste of bitter acrimony roiled in her stomach. To give his uncle time to work him over, no doubt. As if *anyone* could reshape Thane's mind. The very idea was ludicrous.

'I deserved every blow...'

The man didn't even flinch or care that he'd been beaten. No, all he cared about was that he'd failed his people.

'What made you break from the pack?' she asked, awed. 'Being of the same ilk and all.'

Luciana couldn't begin to comprehend the strength it would have taken to set himself apart from such men. The stories she'd heard—the ones she had nightmares about, imagining Natanael embroiled in them—brought her out in a cold sweat.

In one graceful movement he was up on his feet, leaning against an iron post, focused on the rolling hills.

'My mother, I think. It was her dream, and she used to talk about how her family would pray morning, noon and night for a better tomorrow. A tomorrow when the people could speak for themselves, have a say in how they lived. A day when they owned their own lands and could reap the benefits of what they sowed. When people's lives would be that much richer and more fulfilling if they were given the chance to aspire.'

Heaviness encroached on her chest at the grief painting his words blue. 'She sounds like she was a wonderful woman, Thane.'

Luciana knew he'd lost her young. And if the stories were true and his mother had been taken, stolen from her loved ones, his childhood must have been a war zone in more ways than one.

'A tortured soul is a more apt description.'

She could hear the dark resonance of his painful past echo through him, distorting his voice, and her eyes flared as he grabbed hold of a tangled vine from above and ripped it down, its thorns spearing into his palm. Within seconds blood dripped from his fist.

Luciana scrambled to her feet. 'Thane…?'

His eyes were the blackest she'd ever seen, and she realised he wasn't even aware he'd hurt himself. Panic punched her heart.

'Don't do that, *querido*. Look what you're doing. Thane? *Thane*!'

He blinked, over and over, refocusing on her. 'Sorry, angel, what is it?'

'G…Give me your hand.' She pulled a handkerchief from her pocket and wrapped the white cotton round his palm, biting her lip when deep red stained the cloth.

Thane searched her face with a confounded expression,

as if no one had ever cared enough before to stop him hurting. And that made her aching heart weep for him.

Pointing up to the small scar on his chin, she asked softly, 'Did that hurt when you did it?'

'I can't remember. I do not think so.'

Good Lord, his pain threshold had to be off the charts.

'When did you do it?'

'This one?'

Up came his hand and he rubbed over the thin white line with one fingertip.

A fresh stab of wretchedness almost struck her down. It was just like when Nate talked about falling out of the blossom tree at their apartment near Hong Kong. He would touch the scar on his arm when he recalled it. The likeness in mannerism was uncanny—and so bittersweet.

'I was twelve, I think. I'd dropped a thirty-five-millimetre and shattered the casing.' He smiled and shook his head ruefully. 'Let's just say I never once fumbled with the damn thing again.'

'Twelve? And he punished you? He beat you for...?' She swallowed thickly. 'How could he *do* that?'

He shrugged off her empathy. 'It's not an issue. I was born to rule, just as he was. Raised to defend, not to feel. A honed weapon. He did what he had to do. Probably what had been done to him. I accept that.'

'No. *No*, Thane. No child should have to accept that. Don't you *dare* accept that. He didn't have to be brutal or so cruel. Are you saying because you were raised like that you would do that to your children? Your son?'

Snatching his hand away, he stepped back as if she'd physically backhanded him. Anger, affront and hurt flooded the space between them. 'How could you think me capable of that, Luciana?'

Oh, God, she'd had nightmares about exactly that. As her father had filled her head with tales—and yes, okay, some facts too—she'd fought her own instincts. Scared witless, out of her mind. Missing him so badly she couldn't eat or sleep or breathe without hurting. So she'd written letters. What seemed like hundreds of letters. Only to burn them.

Tears splashed up behind her eyes. She couldn't stop them. And he didn't like it—not one bit.

Panic laced his voice. 'Luciana, what is wrong?'

'I'm sorry,' she whispered. 'I'm so sorry.'

His riveting handsome face creased with confusion. 'Why? Why are you sorry?'

Shaking her head, she forced a smile. She knew it wept with sorrow and dejection, so she made it brighter. Smoothed the damp hair from his brow.

'Do you feel *me* when I touch you?' she asked.

'You're about the only thing in the world I do feel, Luciana.'

Oh, God.

Out of control—as always with this man—she reached up in search of his mouth. Desperate to take his pain away. To take hers with it too. Because she now knew what she had to do and it would likely destroy them. Destroy this. Destroy any chance of happiness they would ever have.

As she lifted up on her tiptoes he surged downwards, closing the gap, pressing a frantic kiss to her lips.

She reached up and grabbed handfuls of his shirt, feeling the flex of his hard muscle beneath her fingertips. One kiss, she promised herself. Just one kiss so she could feel his lust and affection. Surely it would be enough to last? It would have to be enough.

Thane's fingers speared into the heavy fall of her hair, cradling her nape, his grip fierce and exquisitely firm, and with one long, languorous flick and thrust of his tongue into her mouth her knees buckled underneath her.

His cat-like reflexes kicked in and he dropped his hands to her waist to keep her upright.

'*Dios*, I crave you like a physical ache. Not here, though, angel. I can't lose it with you here,' he breathed in a rush of warm air over her cheek as he ran his nose up the side of hers and rested there for a gloriously intimate beat.

No. She couldn't possibly sleep with him. It would make everything a hundred times worse. And what was more…

'Thane, you have to stop calling me that, okay?' It tore off another piece of her heart every time he did.

'What…? Angel? Why? It's what you reminded me of last night in the limousine, with your hair this colour. Darkly spun gold. Seraphic. Beautiful. As *you* are, Luciana. Inside and out.'

'D…Don't put me on a pedestal, Thane. I'm no angel. Sooner or later I'll drop from a great height.'

And, like finely spun glass, she would shatter to the floor in a million pieces.

A rueful light flickered in his eyes as he hiked one broad shoulder. 'Then maybe we will be equal.'

Guilt. So much guilt it seemed to suffocate his soul.

'What your father did—giving control to your uncle—it's not your fault.'

Scepticism vied with his obvious desire to believe her.

'What job or mission did you refuse to do, anyway? What would anger him so much that he'd delay your taking the throne for so long?'

That had to have been ten years ago…

A shadow swarmed over his face and in that moment somehow she *knew.*

Foreboding crackled down her spine and she stumbled back a step. 'Go on. Say it.'

He shoved his hands through his wind-tousled raven-black hair and his chest swelled as he hauled in air. 'How did you know?'

'I wasn't sure until right this moment. But rumours have a way of reaching the right ears and poisoning minds.'

A muscle ticked in his jaw as he gave a short nod. 'I disobeyed a direct order and refused to kill your father.'

CHAPTER NINE

LUCIANA CURLED UP on a cushioned recliner on the beach and gazed up at the midnight sky, wishing on a billion twinkling diamond stars that Thane's business calls would take all night. But, as she already knew, burying her head in the sand would help no one—least of all herself.

The drive back down to the coast had been taut with tension, and by the time dinner had been served on the upper floor balcony Luciana had been strung so tightly she'd barely eaten one mouthful of the delicious seafood paella Hanna had slaved over. Which had only made her feel guiltier still. And she wouldn't have thought that was possible.

Closing her eyes, she recalled their brief conversation in the car.

'I didn't want to tell you,' he'd said. 'I thought you'd hold it against me.'

'I'm glad you told me. You saved his life in the end. It must have been a horrendously hard call for you. Thank you...'

Thane had saved her father's life. Paid an extortionate price for disobeying his tyrannical King. All for a man he hated. His enemy.

And how is he being repaid? His son is being kept from him. I didn't know. I didn't know any of this.

The guilt and pain tearing through her in one relentless lash after another wouldn't cease. Not for a second.

One day. She'd been here one day and the enormity of

what she'd discovered had her reeling. In truth, she wasn't sure she was taking it all in.

The rush of the ocean lapping over the shore was broken by the sound of bare feet padding down the deck, sending her heart trampolining to her throat and her stomach vaulting with a hectic tumble of dread and anticipation.

Thane straddled the recliner in front of her, one long-stemmed glass of ruby-red liquid in his large grip.

With a wriggle, she edged back to give his broad frame more room, and rested her head against the mocha cushion to drink him in.

He was breathtaking. His dark, fathomless eyes pulled at her like a hypnotic suggestion pressing against her mind. A constant murmur of want that was becoming impossible to ignore. But fight it she would.

'You are very quiet since we got back,' he said, his voice low and warm with concern.

'Just thinking.'

'No more thinking of the past tonight, hmm? Let's focus on the future. On us.'

She wasn't sanguine enough to believe there would be an 'us' come the dawn.

You don't know that for sure, Luce. He might listen to you. Try to understand.

It was a sliver of hope she clung to.

Raising her arm, she brushed his hair back from his gorgeous face and his decadent sable lashes fluttered as if weighted in bliss, as if he adored her touch. It broke her heart.

'Relax, Luciana. You seem brittle enough to shatter.'

Smooth as silk, his voice caressed her skin—a tangible touch of his magnetic heat and power that lulled her to calm.

'Here—take a taste.'

Glancing at the glass of red wine he'd promised earlier, she tried to swallow past her raw, swollen throat. Heavens, no. Thane was intoxicating enough. Half a glass and she'd be the centrefold in the tawdriest scenario her imagination could conjure up.

'I don't think that's such a good idea, Thane.'

Truly, she was way out of her depth, lying here as he towered above her, dominating her world. Thane on a sensual mission was a demonic tidal wave to be reckoned with. But she wasn't convinced sleeping with him would do either of them any favours in the long run.

Still, the yearning pushed at her soul. Stronger in force since the revelations of the afternoon. *'You're about the only thing in the world I do feel...'* That must be why he'd brought her here. Right? She made him feel and he was chasing it. Why else would he go to the lengths he had? And more than anything she wanted to bring him pleasure in any way she could.

Those devastating eyes fixed on her as he swirled the wine around the crystal, giving it air, then took a sip before dipping one of his sinfully adroit fingers into the ruby depths.

Memories of the debauched passion those hands could wreak made the briny ocean breeze stutter in her lungs and she panted out, 'Thane...I think maybe I should turn in for the night. I'm tired and I...'

I'm petrified I will give in, and it would be so reckless, so stupid, no matter how much we both want it.

She inhaled deeply, grappling for strength, only to be drugged by his dark, delicious scent. It infused her lust-addled mind and corrupted her veins. It blazed a firestorm through her midriff that eventually simmered low in her abdomen in a searing burn.

Venturing to eradicate that hot, dark pulse at her core, she squirmed to sit upright in the recliner. 'Thane...I should go to bed.'

By morning she'd have figured out what to do. What to say. How to explain.

'I—'

'Do you think I don't know what I do to you, Luciana? Do you think I can't hear and see your body crying out for mine? Stop fighting this, angel. It's inevitable.'

Claret drizzled down his finger in red droplets as he reached up and painted her lips with the lusty juice, let the rich flavour flow over her tongue, where it blossomed into an ecstasy of ripened grapes, aged wood and sunlight.

With a whimper she flicked her tongue over the very tip and sucked it into her mouth, loving the underlying saltiness and texture of his skin.

A feral groan ripped past his throat and he stared at her glistening lips, where her tongue swirled around his finger... Then he whipped it out, swooped down and captured her mouth in an erotic devouring kiss.

Push him away, Luce. Do it now...

Can't. Impossible.

Luciana laced her fingers through his hair, fisting tight so he couldn't escape, and slanted her mouth over his, licking between his lips, duelling with the sinful lash of his tongue in total surrender.

She'd missed this so much. Kissing. Being held close. The amazing feeling of intimacy with a man—*her* man. Being a sensual woman, someone who was desired. Cosseted. Craved with a burning urgency that rendered her almost weak. It was heady and powerful and she'd missed it.

The robust richness of the wine blended with the potent dominant piquancy that was uniquely Thane—something that exuded vice and sin and seduction—and annihilated her every thought until she was trapped, entangled in his wicked snare.

They tore apart to breathe and yet he never stopped the cherishing ardour, only brushed kisses along her jaw and down her neck in a slow, wet slide that made her shiver and arch in a sinuous serpentine wave beneath him. Begging for his touch. Which he gave by brushing his knuckles down over her breast, teasing her nipple into a stiff peak.

Her wanton moan rent the air, and in reward he rained kisses over her cleavage where it spilled over the top of her low-cut dress. She pressed him in close to her, never wanting to let him go.

'I want you writhing for me, Luciana.'

His hot breath gushed over her skin.

'I want to make love to you, feel you cling to me, hear you beg for release. And then I'll hold you and kiss you in the dark, watch you fall asleep. Only to wake you by sliding down your body and devouring you with my mouth.'

Her lower abdomen clenched and turned achingly heavy, dampening her panties with wet warmth. And she wrapped her legs around his waist to grind against his thick erection in a silent plea for him to do all of that and more.

Gyrating, he ground back against her with long, animalistic groans. 'Just…' He scraped his teeth over the throbbing vein in her neck. 'Just make me feel again, Luce. Please.'

Oh, God. *You're about the only thing in the world I do feel…*

The last wave of doubt drifted away as a tide of longing swept over her. To give him pleasure where she could. To take his pain away while he'd allow her to.

Cupping his jaw, she lifted his head to meet her gaze.

'I've missed you,' she whispered.

It was a shockingly dangerous thing to confess, because it left her so exposed and vulnerable. But in that moment the need for him to know how deeply she felt outweighed any sense of self-preservation she had left.

He eased back, his brow creased as he studied her face. 'Truth?'

'Absolute truth. I've missed you so much. So much I ached with it.'

Ah, Luce, you never had a hope of resisting him. Of keeping your heart locked away.

Farther back he moved, withdrawing from her, and her

stomach hollowed. Mind twisting, she wondered why he vibrated with rancour. And his touch…

He stroked up her thigh, burrowing beneath her floaty blush-pink sundress, his touch riding the line between pleasure and pain as if he were in the throes of anger. Suspecting she lied. His other hand roamed the curve of her waist, slid up to her midriff, where his thumb brushed the heavy underswell of her breast.

'You've missed me?' he said, flat and cool. 'Yet how many men have touched this body since I took it, Luciana? Since I made you mine?'

Staring into his turbulent eyes, she shook her head gently. 'Only you, Thane. There has only *ever* been you.'

Bizarre as it sounded, even to her own mind, she watched his barriers crumble and fall before her. Saw the floodgates to his emotions flung wide and time reversed. They stood still in the past. And there she was—his only focus, his entire world, the moon and the stars beyond. As if everything she'd convinced herself had been merely a dream was now a thrilling, breathtaking verity for her eyes only.

Her heart cracked wide open and she knew he could take it from where it lay, weak and defenceless outside her chest.

'Luciana, I…'

He cupped her face and she could feel his hands tremble as he rubbed his nose alongside hers, faltering, as if he feared what he truly wanted to say.

Instead he murmured against her lips, 'I…I need you.'

'Have me,' she choked out. 'Take me. However you want.'

One night was all they were likely to have and she would give him everything he desired. Everything in her power to give.

Tenderly he pressed his mouth to hers, then slanted his head and thrust his tongue into her mouth in a slow, languorous lick.

Luciana parried right back, glorying in his devout advance and retreat, the touch of his tongue against hers, as he took them both to passionate heights. And higher still into oblivion as he rucked her dress up and broke their lip-lock to tear it from her body. His hands were suddenly everywhere and nowhere. Big and clever, strong and capable hands. Leaving a trail of rapture in their wake.

She trembled all the while and let loose a pleading sob. 'Thane...I want you.'

'You have me, angel.'

'I want you naked. I want to feel you.'

He smiled wickedly as he stood tall, framed by the moon-lit ripple of the ocean like a bronzed demigod. 'You always did,' he said, his voice raspy with lust.

The back of her head dug into the cushion as she craned her neck to stare up at him. Unable and unwilling to look anywhere else as inch by delectable inch his burnished skin was revealed.

Thane grabbed the hem of his T-shirt and with a sleek twist of his mighty fine torso, ripped it up and over his head.

Luciana had to slick her dry lips at the sight of his arms stretched high, thick with muscle and threaded with veins. The sculpted perfection of his ripped chest, the ridges of his twelve-pack and the sweat-slicked super-sexy V of muscle on his pelvis. The arrow that teased and tormented its way down to the thick ridge that burst past the waistband of his low-slung board shorts.

She wanted them off too.

His long fingers went to the fastening and he cocked one brow, faltering—*no*, teasing, tormenting until her heart beat in her throat, thump-thump-thumping in excitement and exhilaration. Waiting. Wanting.

He unpopped the button. Excruciatingly slow.

Her impatience spiked. Two could play at that game.

She unclipped the front of her bra, but held it closed.

He growled.

She smiled.

And then he shoved the material down his densely corded legs.

Oh, wow.

Lord, she'd forgotten how big the man was. Thane— naked in all his rock-hard, battle-honed glory, frosted by moonlight—was a mind-bending orgasmic pleasure all on its own.

'You like, angel?'

'I absolutely *love*,' she breathed. 'Far more than any angel ever should.'

His dark eyes zeroed in on the lacy confection veiling her breasts, which were rising and falling under her laboured breathing, and he dropped back to the chair and unwrapped her as if she were a precious, delectable gift, slowly tugging the lace free. Then with splayed hands he smoothed down her midriff, watching, enraptured, as her flesh shimmied and pimpled in delight.

He'd always used to look at her that way. Fascinated. Glorying in what he could do to her. Just as his restraint had always evaporated when he reached the satin that shrouded the tight curve of her femininity, sending her torn panties somewhere over his left shoulder.

'This is better,' he rasped thickly, leaning down, closing in, teasing his tongue along her bottom lip. 'Much better.'

Possessive and heated and bruising in his intensity, he ravished her mouth, her throat, winding his way down to where he moulded her breast and thumbed her tight nipple. And when his tongue glossed over the plum-coloured peak her sex clenched around thin air, desperate for him to fill the aching void she'd languished in for years.

Arousal at fever-pitch, she hooked her legs around his back and ground against the erection that lay snug over her folds, the sinuous movement pulling a deep groan from his chest and making him suck harder, drawing the tight bud into his mouth. The responding tug in her core ripped an inarticulate cry from her throat.

'*Thane*...'

Feverish, she felt her pulse rocketing into the stratosphere and...*heck*, she was seconds away from hyperventilating. Had to remind herself to breathe.

'Patience, Luciana,' he growled, coercing her legs wide, lifting one up and over the chair-arm, then the other, until she was splayed for his depraved enjoyment.

'I'm going to kiss you until you can't breathe,' he said as he nuzzled down her stomach, grazing her skin with a day's growth of stubble and glancing up to meet her eyes through the sable fringe of his lashes. 'Lick you everywhere. Touch you everywhere. And you, Luciana, are going to lie there and *take it*.'

Oh, *yes*.

He crawled backwards, like the sleek, rapacious predator he was, dipping his head to drop a hot, open-mouthed kiss to each of her inner thighs. Luciana moaned and lifted her arms above her head to grip the top rail of the chair. Knowing he was about to blow her sky-high. Just the sight of his dark head bent, the feel of his hot breath teasing her throbbing sex, already pushed her to the brink.

'Oh, God, Thane. Come on—do it, *please*.'

She was sure he laughed. The callous brute. Though he did make up for it by parting her and raking over her folds, lavishing her with the velvet stroke of his hot tongue. He blew against her, then lashed his tongue once more.

'You're so aroused, angel. I forgot how sweet you taste— like honey. I could eat you alive, Luciana.'

She whimpered in shameless pleasure and thrust her hips in a rhythm that matched his tongue. He found her nub unerringly, sucking it into his mouth, and the cords of erotic tension inside her pulled tighter and tighter, until she was a boneless, quivering mass of desire.

'Thane. I can't...hold...on...'

She gasped for air. Then cried out when he pushed two thick fingers deep inside her saturated channel and stroked her to a splintering crescendo so magnificent her mind blanked with sensory overload.

Every muscle in her body stiffened and seized for one, two, three beats of her heart—then she exploded. Screamed as hot, hard sexual pleasure short-circuited her every nerve, shocking her into ecstasy so powerful she levitated off the lounger...suspended on an erotic plane, eyes locked on the midnight sky, the stars glittering above her...then literally slammed back to earth.

When she roused herself from delirium he was leaning above her and her heart fisted. She adored the way his damp hair hung around his face, making him look wicked. A perfect picture of debauchery.

He licked his lips and let rip a feral growl that seemed to come from the depths of his chest. 'I'm going to take you, Luciana. Fill you up. Pour myself into you. But I'll be damned if I'll do it on a beach. I want you in my bed.'

He lifted her up effortlessly and she wrapped her legs around his waist as he strode up the deck into his bedroom, kissing her all the while, never leaving her mouth even when they tumbled onto the bed, hands everywhere as they desperately tried to touch as much of each other as they could reach.

She tore her lips from his. 'Thane, please. Don't make me wait.'

Pushing his arms beneath her shoulders, he cupped her head in his hands, pinning her completely as he trapped her in his dark hypnotic gaze. 'You're mine, Luciana. You've always been mine.'

And then he pushed inside her in one long, deliciously hard thrust.

The stupendous clash of their cries filled the air, caromed off the walls.

Lord, the relief. The screaming, delirious relief and joy and rightness. The inordinate power they created was so all-consuming she slipped into that boneless delirious state once more.

Every one of her senses was as sharp as a pin and yet the moment was dreamlike. Even the erratic rhythm of his breathing seemed in perfect tandem to the thrash of her own heart.

Thane crushed her to him, cradling her, still embedded deep, his strong, muscular body shaking, his face buried in her neck. '*Dios*, Luciana. You feel so snug. So incredible...'

As if being inside her, reuniting their exquisite connection, had doused some of the urgency, deeper emotion now flooded the space between them, and Thane lifted his head and tenderly brushed her damp hair from her face, kissed her cheeks, her nose, her brow. So lovingly, so affectionately, that her heart splintered.

Too much, Luce, this is all too much. Back off or you won't survive this. Him.

No. She couldn't let go. Not yet.

His touch sculpted her behind, hooked around her thigh and urged it to curl over his hip as his pelvis locked with hers.

'That's it, angel, now let me watch you.'

He ground against her, watching, as if taking in every nuance of her feverish response, and when he hit her sweet spot she shivered and cried out, gripping his hair. He exploited it, rolling his hips, pushing his iron-hard length deep inside her, thrusting over and over until she was mindless, begging, delirious beneath him.

'Thane...'

Bliss opened up before her, fathoms deep, a chasm that would take her—body and soul. For one shimmering, breathless moment she teetered on the brink...and then she was falling, falling, tumbling, crashing as she hurtled towards ecstasy.

Thane picked up the pace, slamming into her, chasing his own nirvana, until he stiffened with a guttural cry of release, pouring himself inside her, racked with convulsions that left him weak and heavy in her arms. Trembling with

the aftershocks like tiny flashes of lightning as the storm
dissipated. And she loved it. Revelled in his weight, in his
ragged breath whispering over the sensitive skin beneath
her ear, his pounding heart against hers.

When lucidity fully returned she realised silent tears
were tracking down the sides of her face. She saw again
the Rhine Falls of Zurich—a stoic, bittersweet witness to
her fragile joy. Because it didn't matter how tightly Thane
wrapped her in his arms, as if she was all he'd ever wanted.
As if she truly were his angel and they basked in the heavens. Because come the dawn all hell would break loose.

Luciana wrapped herself in a robe—the black silk her only
armour and sat at the base of the bed, leaning against the
carved footboard, watching the morning sun dapple over
the hard contours of the man who lay sleeping, naked, on
his stomach.

He was a study in masculine perfection. So beautiful. His
face reminded her with exquisite poignancy of Natanael.
And for the first time she didn't look at him and feel fear
or trepidation or anger or dismay. She looked at him with
one crystal-clear thought. Or rather she allowed herself to.

This was the man who had given her the son she loved
so much. This was the man who'd helped to create a miracle
of joy and wonder and beauty.

This man was the father of her child. The very man she'd
fallen in love with so long ago. And she could not, *would*
not keep their son from that man a moment longer. No more
than she could keep Thane from Natanael.

And that man would not cast her out or take Nate from
her. He would protect them both always. Even through his
anger and rage. And, darn it, she would be strong through
this. As lion-hearted and courageous as he was.

Satin shifted across the sumptuous mattress as he
stretched and smouldered in all his abeyant heat. Her gaze

locked on the muscles in his back, on the flex and bunch of his ruthless power.

Luciana fisted the folds of the robe at her neck, ordering herself not to reach out. To touch. Become lost in him all over again.

He prised his eyes open and smiled sleepily at her. Lord, it *hurt*.

'Come back up here, Luce. Let me hold you.'

She inhaled a lungful of fortifying air.

Come on, you can do this.

'I…I can't, Thane. I have to go home today. I have to go back to Arunthia and I need you to take me—like you promised.'

He sat up in one lithe rippling movement, like a panther uncurling, and pushed his tousled air back from his forehead. 'No, Luciana, don't say that.' His husky, lethargic voice grew stronger, firmer. 'You belong here with me. There's no reason for you to go back.'

Luciana swallowed around the searing burn in her throat. 'But there is, Thane. Someone is there that I can't leave. *Ever.*'

His expression darkened and she felt a frisson of fear. Flinched when he suddenly ripped the sheet from his body, vaulted from the bed and shoved his legs into a pair of black silk lounge trousers.

Hands on his hips, he spun on her. 'You love this person?'

'Yes,' she said, her voice cracking under pressure. 'I love him more than life itself.'

His eyes grew furious, dark as rain-laden thunderclouds. And she knew it was only going to get worse. This, she realised, was merely the beginning. God help her.

'Who do you love?' he demanded.

You can do this, Luciana. For him—for Natanael. Thane will rip your heart from your chest but this is not about you. It is about the little boy you love and his father. You are doing it for them. They deserve this from you. Do it. Do it.

'Please don't hate me, Thane,' she whispered, begging him. 'I was only trying to do the right thing. I was scared. I only wanted him to be safe—'

His beauty took on a terrifying, dangerous edge. 'Who, Luciana?' He flung his arms wide. 'Who do you love?'

'Your son. *Our* son.'

CHAPTER TEN

THANE'S PULSE ROCKETED and the room took an untimely spin, making his breath whoosh past his lips in a sickening rush.

'You...you had my child? I have a son?'

He couldn't have heard her correctly, he assured himself. But her beautiful brandy eyes filled to the brim and one drop escaped, glistened as it fell. Shimmered over her pink-washed cheeks, along the side of her nose and down to the corner of her full mouth.

A mouth that whispered, 'Yes...'

Thane shook his head jerkily. No. He could *not* be hearing her right. He would know. If he had a son he would know. Yet her words wouldn't stop ricocheting around his mind.

'You were pregnant?'

'Yes.'

'How?' he asked stupidly, feeling adrift and as vulnerable as the boy he'd once been. Trembling inside, feeling weak. He loathed it.

Luciana blinked, her brow pinching, her voice so small she appeared just as lost as he. 'Do you mean which time? I was on contraceptives, so I don't know. There were...'

So many times? Yes, there had been.

And they had made a baby. Together. His child. His *son*.

Then—*then* it hit. Like a bullet ripping through his chest. And it tore his world apart.

He jabbed his fingers through his hair and fisted the silky

strands. 'How does no one know my son exists, Luciana? How do *I* not know my son exists?'

'I fought to have him. I went away to have him. I—'

Acid flushed through his stomach and surged up to his throat. 'Ah, so he is your dirty little secret? My son. With Galancian blue blood. The man who will take my throne. He is *your dirty little secret*?'

Affront clawed inside his chest with merciless razor-sharp talons and he slammed his hand over his bare ribs to rub, to try and ease the gashes of pain tearing through him.

With an unsteady hand she reached out imploringly. 'I made a pact to have him. To keep him. I went to Hong Kong, where we were safe…'

'*Safe?* You kept his identity secret to keep him safe? Safe from *who*?' he hollered.

He didn't understand this. Any of it.

A sob racked her frame and she covered her mouth with one hand, fingers quivering over her lips. Lips bruised red and swollen from his kisses.

Dios, he had just made love to a deceitful, dishonourable bitch. He had just been embedded inside a liar and a thief. The woman who had stolen his son. Who *did* such a thing?

She's an Arunthian, Thane, what did you expect?

His brain was working so fast his thoughts tripped over themselves before he could even process the last.

'No one ever asked? *Suspected*?' he asked, dark incredulity pouring from his tone.

Sitting at the base of the bed, she bent her knees and wrapped her arms around them, curling that incredible hateful body into a defensive ball.

'No. We had a nanny—Crista—who has a son of her own. Very few other staff. I wanted him to have a normal childhood. A free life without the constraints of the crown. Without being suffocated by duty—'

Thane flung his arms wide. 'Yet you take away his rights

as a born royal! Why didn't you tell me? Were you *ever* going to tell me I had a son?'

Dios, he had a son. Maybe if he kept repeating the words it would sink in.

'I tried. So many times. I wrote letters—so many. I burned them. We didn't really know each other, Thane—you didn't even know my true identity.'

With the tips of her fingers she rubbed the moisture from the tender skin beneath her eyes and took a deep breath.

'Our countries are enemies—you know this. Only yesterday you admitted you almost assassinated my father. He knew, Thane. He *knew* it was you. I was so scared. And the rumours, the horrors I'd heard of this place—they chilled me. Your childhood...' She rocked a little, as if the mere thought of his youth pained her. 'The fact that you're staunch militia...raised for war, for fighting. I couldn't bear the thought of him being raised like that. Getting hurt. I still can't.'

She looked up at him through the veil of her lashes, those huge eyes pleading. Thane had to stiffen himself against their power.

'Please try to understand. I didn't even know you and your uncle were divided. I just—'

'Stop. Just *stop*.'

He couldn't abide her voice any more. Because it was becoming increasingly clear that the person she'd been trying to protect their son from was *him*. The only woman he'd ever let past his shields, the only woman he'd wanted to live his life with, thought him so monstrous that she'd feared for their son's life. And that almost killed him right where he stood.

'I cannot bear to hear your excuses any longer. Where is he? *Where* is my son?'

'At...at home—'

He sliced her off with a razored slash of his hand through the air. 'No, Luciana. He is not at home. His home is here—with *me*.'

Unable even to look at her, he pulled on his T-shirt and

bounded out onto the deck. Oblivious to where he was going. Blind to what he was doing.

He felt vile. That ever-present blackness was rising like a demonic tide inside him, swirling like a toxic storm. He despised it. Despised *her* for causing it. Would do anything to stop feeling—*anything*. And she'd done that too. Torn down the walls that had barricaded his emotions, leaving him defenceless, only to stab him in the back.

He brought his hand up in front of his face, watched his flesh tremble and gritted his teeth as he balled it savagely until his knuckles and wrist cracked and his strength began to return. Until his heart was black and his blood ran cold. Then he spun on his heels to stride across the patio.

'Thane, *wait*. Where are you going?'

That was one thing he *did* know.

'To get my son.'

A flash of memory arrowed through his mind and he crashed to a halt. Turned with lethal calm to see her climb from the bed and stand tall on those amazing legs—such works of art. He'd had them wrapped around his waist as he'd taken her against the shower wall, not two hours ago, and it sickened him.

'The photograph I saw. Of you pushing a young boy on a swing. In a park. When you were in China. He had ebony hair just like mine...'

Dios, he'd been staring at a picture of *his own son*.

She frowned and her flawless skin went impossibly paler. 'Photograph?'

'*Si*. I pulled files on you back in Courchevel. I saw him and I didn't even think he could be mine. Didn't even *think* you would be capable of such a heinous crime.'

His tone was getting louder and louder and he couldn't seem to stop it.

'I brought you here from the Alps—where you were... what? Vacationing? Having *fun*, were you, Luciana?' He felt as if the blood rushed downwards from his head and there was a roaring in his ears. '*Dios*, no! You were with that sleazy bastard Augustus. Does *he* know about my son?'

'No—no, Thane. He doesn't know. No one does.'

'*Si*. Well, this is fortunate for you both. Still, you didn't even tell me you'd left *my son* behind in Arunthia. I brought you here and you left him there in that...that *place*.'

He was drowning in an ocean of pain. Betrayal.

'I'm sorry but, Thane, I didn't know what to expect from you. You practically abducted me in broad daylight, for heaven's sake!'

What did *that* have to do with anything? Anyway... 'It's a damn good job I did. Otherwise my child would've been lost to me for eternity. Two days you've been here. Not once did you say a word.'

'I...I'm telling you now—'

'Ah, yes. So you are. Did I pass your rigorous testing, Luciana? Am I good enough to be in my son's life now? My son... *My son!* My own flesh and blood and he doesn't even know me.' Something was tearing apart in his chest. 'Well, he will soon enough.'

'You can't go and get him. How will you get past my father? I don't want any fighting or trouble, Thane.'

He jabbed a menacing finger in her direction. 'On *your* head be it.'

With that, he surged across the limestone patio, rubbing his face with his hands.

Within seconds Luciana had gripped his arm, was pulling him round to face her.

'No, Thane. Where my son is concerned you *will* listen to me.'

There was a fierce light in her eyes. As if she had some voracious maternal instinct.

Cynicism curled his lip. This woman? Who'd denied her son his father for more than four years? Thane's father had been a brutally fierce man, but when Thane had asked for him he'd come. Just as Thane should have been given the chance to be there for his son. But, no, he'd had that opportunity *stolen* from him.

'Do you honestly want your introduction to Natanael to be throwing punches or behind prison bars? He isn't like you, Thane. He's not big and tough, resilient and strong. He's small and kind and loving and beautiful, and he's only four years old. Please. Let me go and get him. Bring him here.'

Thane wrenched his arm out of her grasp. 'Let you go and not return? Disappear off the face of the earth? With my son? *Again?* I think not, Luciana. To suggest it just shows how much of a fool you think I am.'

'Then let me ask Lucas to bring him.'

'Lucas Garcia?' he said disgustedly. 'Are you mad?'

'Natanael loves him and Claudia—they're his family. He's with them right now.'

The sharp teeth of anger bit into his heart. '*I* am his family.'

Her eyes closed momentarily. Those long lashes were coated with crystals and it vexed him that he was still noticing such things about her. Vexed him beyond belief.

'Just…please let us make this as easy on Natanael as possible. I don't want him scared. Let him come here on your turf and meet you properly. Peacefully. *Please*, Thane.'

He hauled in air, trying to think through the clattering maelstrom. The last thing he wanted to do was frighten his son; the boy didn't even know him. But he didn't trust Luciana to come back. He didn't trust her at all. Never would again.

Furious that she'd pushed him into a corner, he bit out, 'I will give Lucas Garcia three hours. Then I will go for my son myself and to hell with your father. I will get past him if I have to crush Arunthe Palace into the ground.'

She curled her quivering hand around the base of her throat. 'They'll be here.'

When she glanced up at him, with those brandy tarns full of anguish, for a moment he felt himself falling under her spell. So bewitching. Making him blind to anything but her…

Not any longer.

Thane forced himself to deflect her considerable charms. She'd lured him in for the last time.

'They'd better be here,' he incised. 'I'll never forgive you for this, Luciana. Four years I have missed of him. And if you think I am missing one more day you are grossly mistaken. When he steps foot on Galancia he is here to stay—and so are you. You will not leave here. Neither of you will. We will marry without delay and he will be acknowledged if it is the last thing I do on this earth. And *that* I promise you.'

CHAPTER ELEVEN

LUCIANA STOOD IN front of the double porcelain basin in the sumptuous marble bathroom suite and flipped on the faucet. Cupping her hands beneath the flow, she watched the icy clear liquid pool and then splashed it over her face, dabbing the tender puffy skin beneath her eyes.

Keep it together, Luce. You'll get through this.

She plucked an oyster hand-towel from the rail and patted her face dry, daring to peek at her reflection in the mirror. Lord, she still looked ghastly. And the black jeggings and white shirt she'd chosen to wear didn't help a jot. Not that she cared for her appearance—she just didn't want Lucas to latch on to her wretched state or he wouldn't leave. Didn't want Natanael to pick up on her mood either. This would be hard enough on him as it was.

Insides shaking, she gingerly walked back through to the bedroom…and, darn it, just the sight of those rumpled sheets and the lingering scent of their passion brought the wave of misery rushing back—so tall and wide it flooded over her in a great gush and she couldn't stand up in it. Couldn't even seem to breathe through it.

Crumpling to the bed, she tried her damnedest not to break. Not to splinter apart. She had to stay strong, because the next few days would be hard enough. *Days?* Try weeks. Try a lifetime.

Her conversation with Lucas played back in her mind.

'Please, Lucas, you're the only person I trust to get past

my father and do as I ask. Thane knows. If you don't bring him I don't know what he'll do.'

Already he paced like a caged animal, face dark, implacable. Cold. And if his brutal, austere demeanour wasn't enough for her to know she'd destroyed any chance of happiness between them, his words tormented her heart and soul.

'I will never forgive you for this... We will marry without delay...'

Luciana was unsure what was worse. An emotion-free marriage in which her heart was safe. Or being married to the man who'd always owned her heart and yet hated her in return. And loathe her he did. She'd never forget the look on his face. Such disappointment. Such hatred.

But Nate will have his daddy and you won't have to leave him any time, any place, anywhere. You'll spend every day with him and see him grow into a great man and that will be enough.

Of course it would be enough. It was all she'd ever wanted since the day that little stick had turned blue.

Lucas had promised to be here on the hour—though he wasn't happy about it. His tone had suggested she'd gone stark raving mad. But luckily Claudia had smoothed the way. Thanks heavens for Claudia and her huge heart and quick mind.

Breathe, she told herself. In and out, slow and even as she made her way up four flights of stairs to the vestibule.

The future was staggeringly vague—and wasn't that the story of her life? No idea what tomorrow would bring, how they'd live in this strange place where they didn't know a soul. She was asking herself how they would fit in, how she'd explain to her father that she wasn't taking her crown, how her own people would react on discovering they'd no longer have a new queen in the spring.

Thane had said she'd never leave, but that had to be his anger talking—he couldn't possibly be serious. She'd have to go home before they wed...give a speech renouncing her

birthright. Then enter a marriage she couldn't bear to contemplate. And, *wow*, that seemed to be happening a lot lately.

All of it was churning in a relentless, nauseating roll.
Until she felt insecure. Vulnerable. Defenceless. And by the
time she stepped beneath the overhang of the palatial entryway, restless angst clutched her midsection, making her
bow forward so hard she faked tying the satin bows on her
pumps to cover it up.

*Come on, Luce, you can do this. It's just like being at
home, right? Serene smiles. Cool façade. Think…poise and
grace. By Christmas you'll be a carbon copy of the ice queen
that is your mother and in a barren, loveless marriage.*

Oh, God.

Luciana pinned her spine straight and stood on the top
step, squinting at the black dot swelling beneath the sun.
Plagued by the need for someone to take her hand, tell her
everything would be okay.

No, not someone. Not just anyone.

Chancing a look at Thane, she sneaked a peek towards
the base of the stairs where he stood—separated from her
by metres that felt more like a vast yawning chasm she had
no clue how to fill.

As if he could feel her eyes on him Thane turned his head
to catch her stare. His dark eyes were stormy and full of
condemnation as they snared hers in an unbreakable glare.

She wanted to battle it out with him, make him see her
side of things, but this wasn't the time or place. And deep
down she knew he'd never look at her in any other way. Certainly not the way he had last night. With need and adora-
tion and respect. Something close to joy.

Luciana sank her teeth into her bottom lip, unable to sever
the dark, hypnotic pull, and for a second—when the faintest crease lined his brow—she imagined those beautiful
obsidian eyes shimmered with striations of golden warmth.

Hope spun its crazy web inside her…

Then, with a curl of distaste at his mouth, he tore his

gaze from hers. And that web disintegrated into the pit of her stomach.

Deafening, the whoop-whoop of the helicopter grew louder and louder. Her hair whipped around her face and she focused on the only thing that truly mattered.

The colossal machine lowered into a lethal squat on the landing pad in the centre of Thane's huge circular driveway. And the need to run to Natanael—see him, hold him, touch him—had her bolting forward and hurtling down the steps.

At the bottom, Thane snagged her arm to pull her back.

'Wait,' he ordered fiercely.

'Let go of me, Thane.' She felt as if she was hanging by the slenderest of threads over a vast, dark churning abyss and at any moment now the line would snap.

'It is too dangerous—wait a moment.'

He stood with rigid tense-jawed focus, but when the black door swung wide, and Natanael emerged, for a split second he looked as if he'd seen a ghost.

Nathanael careened towards her at a speed of knots. And though he swam in her vision she could still see those gorgeous dimples in his smooth caramel cheeks, those deep expressive eyes so much like his father's.

His father—whose entire body had gone rigid, as though he was desperately fighting to maintain control.

Luciana threw hers to the winds and ran.

Thane had a curious feeling in his chest—as if someone had reached in and taken hold of his heart.

It was like looking at himself. Turning back the clock and gazing in the mirror to see himself as a small boy. And at that moment Thane vowed to do everything in his power to ensure his son would not suffer hurt or cry in pain. He swore it. Swore to move heaven and earth to prevent any of it.

He'd always been adroit at killing his emotions—with the exception of those evoked by Luciana—but he'd never felt anything close to this. Emotions…so many emotions flooding over him. All-powerful. All-consuming.

Natanael—meaning 'God has given'. He tried it out on his tongue for the first time, because maybe he hadn't truly believed it until now, and acknowledged how good it felt—how right.

Thane's fingers burned with the need to touch all that smooth skin, his silky hair—ebony, like Thane's own. But he didn't want to frighten him. The scars on his face were enough to scare anyone, let alone a child.

So instead he ground his feet into the gravel and soaked up every nuance as his son shouted in utter joy, with the biggest smile Thane had ever seen, when he spotted Luciana.

'Mamá!'

Luciana lowered herself into an elegant crouch to catch him and ended up on her bottom in the dirt, not caring about it one iota, hugging him with a glorious smile of her own, smoothing the thick glossy waves of his hair, kissing his brow, his soft cheek.

Never had he seen anything like it. Or maybe he had. Maybe the sight before him resurrected memories he'd rather keep buried six feet under.

Dios, his chest was imploding.

A sweet strum of a giggle flew past Natanael's perfect lips and Thane wondered what she was doing to make him laugh. Saw her fingers tickling his sides, realised he must like that, even though he was yelling, 'Stop! Stop!' And then she was wrapping him in her arms again, kissing him and touching him. All over.

And in that moment there was something so profoundly, exquisitely beautiful about her he felt the strangest sensation in his throat, behind his eyes. Like tiny hot needles pricking.

'Did you see? I was in the big black 'copter, Mamá!'

'I know, darling, and I'm so glad because it brought you to me.'

Darling. The endearment fisted Thane's heart.

'I've missed you so much. My goodness—I swear you've grown an inch.'

Natanael gazed up at her with a fierce male pride that punched Thane in the gut. He was a Guerrero through and through.

When his little mouth geared up for the next zealous outpouring, he stalled—his attention seemingly snagged on Thane.

His insides turned over and he wondered if this was what it felt like to be nervous.

Natanael gaped at him with steady unblinking eyes, scrutinising the scar on his chin as if he couldn't quite believe what he was seeing. Then he looked up at Luciana, and then back to Thane, his tiny mind processing.

It was utterly fascinating, Thane decided. And—for want of a better word—nerve-racking. *Dios*, he felt ill.

Then, as if Natanael had finally accepted Thane was real, he exclaimed, 'Wow! He looks like me. But a whole lot bigger. Do you fly?'

Huh?

'*Si*…actually, I do. I am a pilot and I have my own fighter jet.'

'I knew it,' said Natanael, unequivocally awed. 'You're one of the New Warriors. Did you just come down from InterGalactica?'

Thane blinked. 'Is this in Europe?'

'No, silly. It's in outer space.' With a smile and a nod he gave Thane a knowing look. Then he tried for a wink that scrunched up his entire face as he whispered, conspirator-like, 'You *know* it is.'

Luciana lightly cleared her throat. 'He's into…er…superheroes. Like Batman and Ironman…that kind of thing. And one of them looks uncannily like you. And him too.'

Thane supposed he could live with that. Although what would happen when Natanael asked him to actually fly? He was far too small to go in his military jet.

He hunkered down until they were at eye level and commanded himself to relax, to think of something to say.

'Actually, I *am* a warrior of a kind. I'm the Prince of Galancia and I live here, and I was hoping you would come and live with me too.'

It occurred to him that they'd have to have the 'I'm your daddy' conversation—but, frankly, that petrified him. Plus, he wasn't keen on Garcia being within hearing distance for that. Right now all he wanted was for his son to agree to stay.

Natanael huddled into Luciana, a spark of panic blanching his beautiful face, and Thane realised a second too late his mistake.

'Mamá too?'

He cursed inwardly. Of course he would panic. The love he could feel between them was palpable. 'Yes. Of course. Absolutely. Mamá too.'

Luciana nodded and achieved the perfect smile—though to Thane it verged on brittle, and made him ache even more.

Natanael peered around him, unconvinced. His nose was scrunched, as if he wasn't overly impressed with the tree-lined driveway or the kaleidoscope of manicured blooms flourishing in the borders. Granted, the mansion looked like a one-storey cottage from the top of the cliff. The towering five-floor vista from the beach was far more dramatic and arresting. Though perhaps not for a child.

Thane scratched his jaw. Stumped. Then intuitively he glanced at Luciana. Who, in turn, mouthed a word at him.

He frowned, striving to catch her meaning. What the hell was she saying? 'Dog?' he asked.

'Dog?' Natanael said, perking up. 'You have a dog? *Really?*'

Ah. This, Thane realised, was of great importance. '*Sí*. Lots of dogs. And horses too.'

'You have horses?' Dark eyes, the precise shade of Thane's own, grew huge and glittery with excitement.

He didn't seem afraid, so hesitantly Thane reached out

and touched the soft caramel skin of his cheek. The astonishing surge of connection rocked him to the core. Phenomenal. His little boy was the most miraculous thing he'd ever touched. Just like his mother, Thane thought, with a wrenching tug on his guts.

'Many, many horses. You can have your very own. But they don't live here… Yet,' he added hastily, thinking he could easily build a stable for a few. Dozen.

Natanael jumped up and down on the spot. 'I can have my own *horse*, Mamá! Can we go and see the dogs? Right now? Can we? *Can we?*'

Relief poured down Thane's spine. Victory. This was good. He could kiss Luciana for that dog hint. Though he quickly squashed the impulse.

'I think so. Thane, are they downstairs?'

As if she'd experienced the same kind of bone-melting sense of appeasement he just had, she made a clumsy effort at rising to her feet and Thane bolted forward, curled his fingers around her tight waist and lifted her upright.

Surprise widened her eyes. 'Oh. Thank you,' she whispered.

And when he saw her perfect white teeth bite into her bruised red bottom lip a surge of heat spiked his pulse. One he couldn't understand. Didn't want to feel.

Jerking his hands away, he stepped backwards and cleared his throat. 'Pietro will let them out. When I've had a word with Garcia I'll join you.'

With a strained smile she nodded, and glanced at Lucas Garcia herself.

Thane wasn't sure what he'd expected, but it was certainly not her embracing him like some long lost lover. He had to clench his fists to stop from tearing her off him.

'Thank you so much, Lucas,' she said softly, shakily. 'For everything.'

Garcia pulled back and shot her a meaningful look that

pricked Thane's nerves. 'Remember what I said, Luciana. Any time, night or day.'

Another of those frangible smiles, but she brightened it for Natanael and took his small hand in hers—as if she was physically unable to stop touching him. Thane felt an absurd pang of envy that filled him with self-disgust. Surely it wasn't healthy or natural to feel envious of his son? *Dios*, he truly was black inside.

Those clasped hands swayed back and forth as they waltzed into the house, then he turned back to Garcia.

Voice stony, he bit out, 'She will not be contacting you. Everything she needs is right here.'

As if in a standoff, they weighed one another up. One soldier to another.

Garcia's midnight-blue gaze hardened. 'You hurt either of them and I will come for you.'

Thane almost laughed. Almost. Instead he sneered at the other man. 'If you had any sense, Garcia, you'd never set foot on my island again. I've allowed you into restricted airspace to bring my son to me. Next time it will be denied.'

'Do you think that will stop me? I'll be honest, here— I'm not getting a very good vibe between you and Luciana, so I'm not entirely convinced that leaving them here is the right choice.'

'I care very little for what you think. My relationship with Luciana is none of your business.'

'*That* is where you are wrong. She is family, and I will not have her here against her wishes. Are you understanding me?'

Thane's mouth shaped to tell him she was emphatically *not* here against her wishes, but then he realised he'd given her little choice. *Dios*, he'd been so angry. Still was. Couldn't remember half of what he'd said to her.

Whether or not Garcia picked up on his inner turmoil Thane wasn't sure, but he abruptly let loose a sigh that marginally shrank his impressive shoulders.

'Look, I understand this must be a shock—difficult for you.'

Thane wanted to ask him how the hell *he* would know how it felt, but then he remembered the man had just had a child of his own.

'But know this: she has not had one moment of peace in the last five years. Knowing you were out there has tormented her. There is a reason they say ignorance is bliss. She's had to live with her decision for years. Do not forget we have been enemies for a long time, Guerrero. She begged. She bartered. She made a pact. Just to bring Natanael into the world. I know she wanted your son more than anything in this life.'

Begged? Bartered? Meaning Henri had wanted her to destroy their son? For the umpteenth time in history Thane wished he'd pulled that trigger. Vibrated with the urge to rain a hellish firestorm on the man's head. Crush him beneath his almighty foot.

Of one thing he was certain. He would do everything in his vast power to ensure Henri Verbault was erased permanently from his wife's life. And his son's too. Their relationship was officially at an end.

Dios, he was so vexed his insides shook. In fact blistering fury was all he could feel in every molecule of his body as it ran like red-hot lava through his veins. Anger towards every person who'd kept him from his son. He wanted to punish them all.

And that still included Luciana. Because she should have come to him five years ago. He would have protected her from the start.

Thane crossed his lethal arms over his wide chest. 'You love your daughter, don't you? How would you feel if she'd been kept from you for the first four years of her life?'

His voice was iron-hard but he was genuinely interested to hear this answer. What would a normal person feel right now? Should his insides be so black with hatred? Or was he truly twisted with darkness inside?

But then Garcia had to shock him by being brutally frank.

'Not just angry. Furious. Cheated. Betrayed. All of the things you are doubtless feeling. But if I looked at the bigger picture I would see that above all else Luciana put her son—*your* son—first, believing he was unsafe. I have no idea how much of your reputation is true, but one fifth of it would be enough to persuade me. She protected him as any mother would. And I could not hate her or blame her for that.'

On that note, he spun on his heels and strode back to the helicopter.

Thane watched the blades whip into a frenzy, slicing through the air. The vociferous clamour lent him a moment of mental peace. A chance to breathe without it physically hurting.

'I only wanted to keep him safe... We're enemies... I was scared...'

Then the sonorous roar receded and it all came rushing back in one titanic tsunami of agony—and he turned and ploughed his fist into the stone wall.

Dressed in Hawaiian-style shorts and a funky matching T-shirt, Natanael was a red blur, sprinting along the shoreline, dragging a long stick that drew a wavy line in the damp sand, while those great lumbering dogs pranced around him. Her little boy in seventh heaven was a glorious sight to see.

Slanting another glance over her right shoulder, she kept watch for Thane. The helicopter had soared into the sky over an hour ago and she felt flimsy and tenuous—like a kite that would blow away with one gust of wind.

Sloshing through the shallow waters, she slowed her step, 'Hey, Nate? Shall we build a sandcastle and wait for Thane?'

'Sure, Mamá.'

Together they scooped sand into a mound, and Luciana watched those sweet little hands pat-pat-pat their creation into shape. This was good. She had to keep busy. Too much time to think and regret and fret would drive her loopy.

'May I join in?'

She flinched at Thane's low, masculine tone and rocked back on her knees to peek up at him.

'Of course,' she said, her stomach hollowing at the pain that darkened his eyes. At the way he shunted frustrated fingers through the swarthy mess of his hair.

When his hands plunged to his sides her gaze snagged on his raw swollen knuckles and air hit the back of her throat.

'Thane?'

Lord, had he hit Lucas? Reaching up, she dusted over his torn skin.

'Did you fight?' she whispered.

'No.'

He snatched his hand away and she curled her fingers in her lap. He'd closed himself off to her. Emotionally. Physically.

Natanael—oblivious to it all—said, 'Sure, you can help. You can build the moat of the castle if you want. That's a *biiig* job.'

'I think you're right,' Thane said easily, sinking to his knees. 'Where do you think I should put it?'

'Right there.'

Nate pointed to a slope that was close to him, Luciana noticed. As if he wanted Thane closer, in his space.

That was a big enough clue for her and she shuffled backwards, giving them some room, some time together, while her heart lodged itself in her throat. It was like watching a fantasy she'd replayed in her mind, but reality was even more incredibly beautiful.

'Is your name really Thane? Like the warrior?'

Those broad shoulders seized up. 'Yes. But...'

Dark turbulent eyes darted her way in a silent plea that said he didn't want Natanael to call him Thane. Of course he didn't.

'Do you want to tell him now?' she whispered.

Incredible as it was, he blanched—as if drowning in pure fear. Almost as if he expected a rejection.

She couldn't abide it. This was her doing and she didn't want him hurting any more than he already was.

'Nate…' she began. 'You know how Auntie Claudia is Isabelle's *mamá* and Uncle Lucas is his *papá*?'

'Mmm-hmm.'

'Well…' She licked lips salty from the sea breeze. 'Thane is…your daddy. He's your papá.'

His dark head jerked up. *'Really?'*

'Yes.'

A huge smile stretched his face as he looked at Thane, then back to her. 'Oh, *wow*—my daddy is a New Warrior.'

'He is,' Luciana agreed, fighting tears. 'He saved me once. Many years ago.' Her throat felt thick, and it burned as if aflame. Stung so badly her words came out on a choked whisper. 'He's a real superhero.'

She could feel Thane's eyes searing into her cheek, but before either of them could exchange a glance or say a word Nate launched himself at Thane like a cannonball, almost knocking him over.

Luciana watched those big, strong, protective arms curl around their son, wrapping him in instantaneous instinctual love. And knew, no matter what the future held, she'd done the right thing.

So while she kissed goodbye to any chance of a loving marriage those glorious sounds of male bonding were sure to keep her warm at night. And as Nate tugged on Thane's hand, to coerce him down to the water's edge, half of her felt as if she'd lost her little boy. The other half reasoned that there had merely been a part of her son that was never hers to begin with. That part was solely for his daddy.

As for her and Thane… Some things were meant to be. And some things were not.

CHAPTER TWELVE

HIS SON NEVER stopped talking, Thane realised, not even to take a breath. And within three days he had the entire household wrapped around his tiny butterscotch pinkie finger.

He said, 'Christmas tree!' and Pietro was lugging ten-feet-tall firs into the main lounge, trailing dirt across the antique Persian rugs. The biggest monstrosity Thane had clapped eyes on was deftly smothered with garish ornaments and enough twinkling lights to illuminate the Taj Mahal.

To say Thane didn't 'do' Christmas was the understatement of the millennia, since it ordinarily tainted his mind with an abundance of achingly dark memories. But he couldn't seem to say no to Nate any more than anyone else could.

Luciana included.

Which was how now, fresh from his shower and dressed to kill in sharp business attire at the ridiculous hour of seven in the evening, he'd known where to find them. Known she'd be clearing the debris in the kitchen after baking Nate his favourite white chocolate cookies for supper while he happily munched and drank his milky way into bed.

Pandering to his every whim. As if she yearned to be needed. As if she had to keep busy or she'd shatter to smithereens. Not that her outward regal poise had faltered, but he didn't trust that cool façade of hers. It wasn't the real Luciana and it set his teeth on edge. Though he only had himself to blame. By creating this ever-widening gulf between them.

But, *Dios*, he'd felt so volatile after her revelation. Drowning in emotions he was ill-equipped to handle. So angry. Betrayed and devastated. So black inside he'd been petrified to go anywhere near her. Unsure whether he wanted to yell and vent or bury his pain inside her. Beg her to touch him, make him forget—which felt tantamount to an insult to his pride. So conflicted. Torn. His usual ruthless decisiveness obliterated until he felt weak. Less of a man. At the whim of dangerous emotions that no hardened commanding warrior should feel.

Every day he waged an internal war. Knowing that in many ways her arguments held weight. They'd been enemies for centuries. He *had* almost assassinated her father. And for the last three nights he'd been engaged in political warfare with his uncle, who was going to extreme lengths to keep Thane from his throne. Instigating trouble left and right. Leaving Thane uneasy, in no doubt that he needed to get Luciana down the aisle—preferably yesterday. Needed to claim his heir before Christmas. Ensure his absolute safety.

And if this was the way she'd felt years ago—afraid, panicked, verging on desperate to shield their son—Thane would have to be made out of stone not to understand her predicament. His uncle's reputation wasn't founded on fresh air, and nor was Thane's. He was lethal even in his sleep. So, prevaricating aside, could he honestly blame her or hate her for doing what any mother would? *No.*

But all the reasoning in the world wasn't eradicating the ache. Or helping him forget that he'd missed four years of his son. Lost the sound of his cry when he came into the world. Had Nate's first word robbed from his ears. Missed the amazing sight of his first step. And the thought that he couldn't get any of that back drenched his heart in sorrow. Coated his mind with resentment and fury.

It was taking everything he had to switch off, just so he could function like a rational member of society, wrestle for control where he could and pave the way for their future.

Leaning against the kitchen doorframe, he crossed his arms over his chest and did a swift recon of his flour-bombed kitchen. Only to be hit with bone-deep longing, wishing he was a part of the warmth that pervaded the room. But, no matter how much time he spent with Nate, at times like this he felt like an outsider looking in. Unable to breach the dense walls of their love. As if they were the family and he the dark intruder who didn't belong. Unworthy as he was. And envy was so thick and poignant it pervaded his chest, making it hard to breathe.

Then one look at Luciana and he was back to battling in the internal war. Distrusting her. Still wanting her.

Wrapped in a long, thick wheat-coloured cardigan, chocolate-brown leggings and socks that scrunched around her ankles, she looked so young, so adorable. So hatefully sexy. All that lavish honeycomb hair was pinned in a messy knot atop her head, the odd stray tendril curling, caressing her cheek, and when she lifted one hand to brush it away with her wrist she left a smear of creamy buttery sugar streaking her flawless skin.

He wanted to lick it off. Taste the honeyed sweetness of her skin. Let it saturate his tongue.

Damn him to Hades for allowing her to beguile him.

Nate's voice yanked Thane from his turmoil and he watched him swipe at his milk moustache with his Batman pyjama sleeve.

'Eight sleeps until Christmas, Mamá. What would you like from Santa?'

Luciana plopped down into the seat beside him and dabbed his mouth with a tissue. 'I want you to be happy. Are you happy here?'

So loving she was with him. Selfless. Protective. So much like his mother. And Thane realised then that never had he thought so much of his childhood since Luciana had stormed back into his life. Something else to mess with his head, shove him to the edge of sanity.

'Yep. I like living on the beach, and my new dogs, and my new daddy, and my room isn't great…it's *awesome*.'

That would be the room that now resembled outer space, with a galaxy of stars painted across the ceiling that shone in the dark.

'You won't fit into my new spaceship bed tonight, Mamá, so will you sleep with Daddy, like Auntie Claudia with Uncle Lucas?'

Luciana closed her eyes for a beat. 'Er…no, I don't think so, darling. Maybe I'll sleep in the suite next to yours, in case you need me.'

Aversion constricted his throat. Was that how it would be between them? Separate suites? Strangers who shared a house? A son? The thought made him cold to his bones.

'I'm a big boy now,' said Nate, all Guerrero fierce pride. 'You can go further down the hall with Daddy.'

Thane couldn't think of anything worse. Luciana lying beside him in that slippery, silky, lacy black camisole and shorts, that vanilla and jasmine scent taunting his senses. So close yet unable to touch. Bad, *bad* idea. He didn't trust himself not to reach for her when his defences were low. When his anger was asleep. When he craved oblivion from the pain.

Frankly, she didn't deserve to be used in such a way. Since he doubted she still shared their fatal attraction. Since she'd moved in with Nate and shrank from him the odd time he accidentally touched her. As if he were some dangerous predator who would maul her at any moment. And he could hardly blame her for that since it was exactly how he felt. Toxic. Lethal.

Luciana, who was clearly reading from the same map, said vaguely, 'We'll see.'

Nate gave an immense cat-like yawn, hair flopping over his brow, and Luciana stroked the ebony tufts back and smiled indulgently. 'Come on, sleepy-head. Time for bed.'

Heavy eyes blinked up at her. 'Can I have a carry?'

Thane pushed himself off the doorframe. 'I believe that is my job.'

Luciana glanced up and for a split second he was sure he saw pleasure light a fire in her brandy eyes, but then she trailed that gaze down over his attire and the flames flickered and died. He took a scissor-kick in his stomach and when he drew up close suffered another swift jab. She looked like an exhausted Botticelli angel—the violet smudges beneath her eyes a vivid contrast against her unusually pale skin.

And right then he realised they couldn't go on like this much longer. While he'd never wholly trust her again, completely forgive and forget, he had to try and move on—for all their sakes. He just wasn't sure where to start.

Nate found a burst of energy to bounce in his chair and raise his arms. 'Daddy! Will you give me a carry downstairs?'

'I certainly will.'

Down they went, Thane stealing a hug on the way, inhaling that glorious warm bathtime scent, loving those fragile arms wrapped around his shoulders trustingly, giving him a 'squeezy cuddle' right back. He'd been initiated into the realms of squeezy cuddles yesterday, and found they were strangely addictive displays of affection.

Luciana pulled back the star-encrusted navy bedcovers and Thane eased him down and kissed his brow, stroked the back of his finger down that cherubic cheek. 'Sleep well.'

'You too, Daddy.'

He walked to the door as Luciana fussed.

'Love you, tiger,' she said.

Nate mumbled sleepily, 'Love you too, Mamá.'

Thane leaned against the hallway wall outside his room, telling himself to leave now. Avoid confrontation. Any kind of temptation.

His traitorous feet didn't like that idea—suddenly had

a mind of their own, wanted to be with the woman that haunted his body and his mind.

Luciana pulled the door closed and warily met his gaze. *Dios*, she was so beautiful. Made his heart ache. And he couldn't fathom that any more than he could understand anything else he was feeling.

Nate's words from earlier penetrated his brain, and before he knew it he said, 'He expects to see a marriage like your sister's.'

Her eyes drifted downwards to where she scuffed the parquet with the toe of her fluffy sock.

'He does. But all marriages and families are different. He'll learn that too.' Her husky voice teemed with yearning. 'Claudia's marriage is…unique, I suppose. They love each other intensely. Talk constantly. Wouldn't dream of being in separate beds. They married for love, not because of duty or a child. Ours won't be that kind of marriage.'

He knew that, so why a dagger lanced through his heart was a mystery.

'I suppose ours will be more like my parents'. They always had separate beds. It didn't affect me…'

A small furrow lined her brow as she nibbled on the pad of her thumb.

He didn't believe her. Not one iota. Began to wonder if the revered Verbault union was more myth than fact and had affected her in ways he couldn't see. Throw in the longing in her voice and he was more certain than ever that their marriage would be a far cry from what she truly coveted. Which was why he didn't trust her not to run again.

'Where did you sleep last night, Thane?'

Wrapping her arms around her gorgeous curves, she frisked her gaze down his midnight Italian suit, his ice-blue shirt, and he'd swear a shiver rustled over her skin.

'Are you going there again?'

'*Si*. Galancia Castle,' he said easily, unsure why that

would sadden her, or wreak the anxiety he could see cloud-ing her brandy gaze.

He had to grind his jaw to stifle the explanation hovering on his tongue. He didn't want her knowing there was trouble afoot. Didn't want her worrying for their safety. He'd prove to her he could protect them if it was the last thing he did. She hadn't believed in him five years ago, so this time he'd move the planets out of alignment to ensure she did. And if that meant he was running on two hours of sleep, con-stantly looking over his shoulder in the hellhole that was his birthplace, so be it.

'Guards will be posted here, upstairs and down.'

'All right,' she said, her body deflating as she gazed down the hallway and out of the west-facing double doors, to-wards Arunthia, in a way that dropped an armoured tank on his chest.

Heart-wrenchingly familiar, it said she wanted to be a million miles away from here. From *him*. It said she wanted to be with her family, with people who truly loved her. Not a black hearted prince. It was a look he remembered well. The look of a woman imprisoned.

Dios, he couldn't bear it. Didn't know how to get rid of it. He'd never been able to with his mother, had he?

He pushed off the wall. Hardened his body into the emo-tionless indestructible weapon it had been honed to be. Fo-cused on what he could control with some semblance of rationality.

'Nate has asked to see Santa Claus and the Christmas fête is in Hourana this weekend. I was thinking we could all go as a family. For Nate.'

He knew that would sway her so he used it abominably. But they had to go out and paint a united front. Play happy families. Deflect his uncle's attempts at undermining him. Word of his impending marriage had spread like wildfire and his people were in a celebratory mood. It was the per-fect time to introduce them.

'For Nate. Right.'

She gave him a short nod and forced one of those serene smiles that sparked his temper. Made him want to shake it out of her.

'I'm sure he'd enjoy that.'

Another victory. But no relief in sight. 'Good. I'll see you in the morning.'

He stepped towards the staircase, stopping when her fingers tentatively touched his sleeve, sending a fresh arrow of heat through his veins.

'Thane? Please wait. Don't go yet. We need to talk. About when I can go back to Arunthia.'

Never.

'I need to leave now. Maybe we'll talk tomorrow.'

A soft sigh slipped past her lips. 'I can't marry you without tying up my life at home. I have my own responsibilities. And you said we'd talk about it yesterday, when you dropped the "we're getting married on Christmas Eve" bomb on me. As you were walking out of the door, I hasten to add.'

That spark of temper ignited in the pit of his stomach and raged through his body, firing his voice to a blazing pitch. '*Si*, well, you owe me four years, so I'm damn sure you can wait another day.'

Guilt thrashed him and he instantly wanted the words back. He was unsure why he'd said them with such a vicious lash of his tongue. Maybe because she'd called Arunthia home. Maybe because he knew she didn't want to marry him, only wanted to leave, no matter what excuse she gave herself. Henri was quite capable of tying up her life. She wanted her freedom. Something he could not, *would* not give her. His son was here to stay.

Moreover, the date was set, their marriage arranged. She would become his wife in less than a week. And if the thought that they had to perform for the crowds tomorrow wasn't enough to convince him to tame his tongue and start building bridges, the way she flinched as hurt darkened her beautiful eyes certainly was.

Luciana knew regret when she saw it. Though it still failed to lessen the strike of his words—each one like a knife-blow to her chest.

At the searing impact, his deep pained frown vanished behind her eyelids and the sound of his retreating footsteps gave way to the forlorn thunder of her heart.

Three days of this and she was ready to crack. Living on a knife-edge while a red river screamed through her blood, chanting for her to escape. Sleep was a fool's dream. One day blurred into the next. And stone-cold silences caromed off the oppressive walls until she felt a relentless ache of loneliness that refused to abate.

The only thing keeping her standing—Nate.

Luckily enough she knew the drill. Had seen it all before. And so, with the asset of royal breeding, she kept her head high and smiled on demand. Her mother would be so proud.

Why was he avoiding the subject of her going home? There was no way she could marry him without renouncing her throne. How would *that* look to her people? What was more, she at least wanted her sister at her wedding—but had he asked her who she would like there? No. She'd just been told when and where. Truth was, she couldn't understand the hurry. Why not springtime?

Ah, come off it, Luce, you're petrified. Scared stiff of committing to a loveless marriage. Where you'll be eternally powerless. Trapped by invisible shackles. His mistresses secreted behind closed doors...

Slumping against the wall, she slid to her bottom, bending her knees to hug them to her chest.

Stop. Just stop jumping to conclusions. Stop with the portentous predictions.

Problem was, three days of silence had slowly turned her mind inside out—and with it came unadulterated panic exacerbated by Thane's sporadic vanishing acts. Every day he spent with Natanael, every evening he disappeared until dawn, leaving her with enough bodyguards to secure Fort Knox. His cousin Seve being one of them.

Could the man scream, *I don't trust you not to steal my son* any louder?

She felt like a captive, with no way to escape. And, since he couldn't seem to tolerate the sight of her, was he getting comfort from elsewhere now? Was that where he was? Did she have the right to know who he was sleeping with?

Her mother would say not.

She'd always divined that her mother truly loved her father but it was disastrously one-sided. Luciana could have only been twelve or thirteen when she'd spied one of her father's mistresses slipping down the hall, seen her mother's tear-tracks when Luciana had sneaked in her bedroom to ask about her.

'We don't talk about such things. Go back to bed, Luciana.'

Considering how cold Luciana had felt in the last few days, Marysse Verbault deserved a gold medal for that cool façade she'd perfected. Imprisoned by duty. Funny thing was, Luciana could have put up with all of that from Augustus. But the thought of Thane being in another woman's bed…

Squeezing her eyes shut, she dropped her head to her knees and forced air into her lungs, past the heavy, tumultuous maelstrom that swirled like a thick brume. Tried to cling on to the rapidly fraying threads of hope that he'd come round. That they could somehow find each other again.

She shoved desperate thoughts into her brain to keep faith afloat. Telling herself he'd brought her here for a reason. That she was the only person he could feel. That the fact he wanted them to go out tomorrow as a family meant there was light at the end of the tunnel.

If only she could believe it.

CHAPTER THIRTEEN

WHETHER IT HAD been her midnight sniffle-fest to Claudia—who'd told her to stop being such a darn pessimist, painting her future blue when it was only early days, which Luciana conceded was a fair point—or whether it was Nate's hyper-chatty mood as they clambered out of the luxurious bulletproof Range Rover to behold an authentic winter wonderland, she wasn't sure. But for the first time in days her spirits had lifted and she was determined to make the most of their first family affair. To think positive *unpessimistic* thoughts and refrain from pondering on why Thane looked exhausted. What *exactly* he'd been doing all night.

No, she wasn't torturing herself with any of that. Nor was she allowing his invisible power storm to buffet her like a ship in a restless sea. And that ominous slinky dread coiling in the pit of her stomach, warning her that trouble was coming…? Not listening. Not today. Today she was channelling her inner cheeriness—Nate deserved nothing less.

The rich nutmeg and cinnamon scent of gingerbread wafted over her, courtesy of the warm breeze, and she inhaled deeply. 'Wow, that smell is amazing. It's the strangest thing—to be looking at Santa's grotto, surrounded by reindeer and heaps of snow, in twenty degrees—but I've got to admit what they've achieved is fantastic. It's Lapland!'

Slamming car doors, Thane murmured, 'It is…' in that distracted manner he'd worn for days, as if his mind was in constant turmoil.

Guilt and unease weaved in and around her ribcage, and for the thousandth time she wished he would speak to her. Let her past those impermeable steel barricades he'd erected so they could work through this.

'Would you like your bag?' he asked, his voice making a sudden shift to that deep drawl she loved so much, as if he'd just found something amusing. 'You have a tendency to leave them in vehicles and make me fetch them.'

The return of his humour—however slight—was so shocking, so wonderful, she smiled up at him, squinting against the burnt orange and red haze of the lowering sun. 'Yes, please. I would. And, just think…you don't have to send someone to France this time.'

'What a relief,' he said sardonically, even as he frowned. As if he was just as surprised at his quip as she was.

Her heart was buoyed up a little more and she wondered if their moods rubbed off on each other. Vowed to be extra chipper, just in case.

'Oh, actually,' she said, 'I think I'll leave my coat in there. I can't believe how warm it is.'

With a roll of her shoulders she shrugged off her long cream jacket and pushed it into Thane's waiting hand. When that hand didn't move a muscle she glanced up and caught his heated stare—which doused her in his particular brand of fire.

Another return. The first time in days that he'd paid her the slightest attention. And as that searing gaze trailed down her body, from the V-neck of her coffee and cream polka dot dress to her cinched waist, all the way down to the flared kick of the skirt, where the fabric kissed her skin just a peep above her knees, her heart floated higher still and beat an excitable thrum in her throat.

He lingered on her bare calves until she felt positively dizzy.

'You look…stunning, Luciana. Truly beautiful.'

That voice was husky. Intimate. All *Thane*. And wanton

heat surged upwards into her cheeks as her stomach imploded with shameful want.

She dug her cream kitten heels into the asphalt to curb her squirm. 'Thank you. You don't look too bad yourself.'

Understatement. Right there.

Suave and sinfully hot, that commanding body was sheathed in one of his *de rigueur* custom-made Italian suits. The biscuit hue was striking against his olive skin as was the torso-hugging crisp, white open-collared shirt he wore beneath. In short, he oozed gravitas from his every debauched pore, and the brooding expression on his face made him look as dangerous and piratical as ever.

Those dark eyes fixed on her mouth as she slicked her glossy lips with a flick of her tongue. 'Luciana...' he murmured. 'I...'

And when they flicked back up to meet hers a meteor shower of dazzling sensation exploded inside her pelvis.

Oh, Lord, he still wanted her. She knew it. Also knew he was fighting it. Fighting it with all his might. As if his anger lingered and he wanted to hate her but couldn't persuade his body to obey.

'You were going to say...?' she prompted.

His throat undulated on a hard swallow. 'Only that I'd like us to try and be a family today.'

She wanted to ask why. For whose benefit. But caught herself in the nick of time, annoyed at her suspicious mind. Who cared why? He wanted to try and that was okay with her. An enormous step in the right direction.

'I would too,' she said softly. 'And maybe later we could talk?'

The sooner they discussed her going home and their marriage the better for all of them. They couldn't go on like this.

Thane gave her an enigmatic smile that failed miserably to instil her with any kind of confidence. But before she could pin him down Nate burst between them, bouncing on his loafered feet like a coiled spring.

'There's Santa's house! And look over there! A big sleigh! Can we ride in it? *Can we?* Oh… Is that the Three Kings? They look *scary*.' Of course he looked up to his big warrior. 'I don't want to see them, Daddy.'

Luciana watched those wide shoulders relax, watched bad-boy, dominant Thane disintegrate like milk-sodden cereal in the face of all that cherubic idolisation.

'I'll take you to meet them and show you there is nothing to be afraid of—okay?'

Nate didn't look convinced, but climbed up Thane like a monkey all the same. 'Okay. I'm ready.'

'Are *you* ready, Luciana?' Thane asked.

To spend an evening being a family? Something she'd always dreamed of?

'I'm definitely ready.'

Ten minutes. That was all it took to sense that Nate's insuperable case of hero-worship for his father was nothing in comparison to that of Thane's people.

The intense magnetism he exuded grew in strength the further they walked, until he was an imposing impression of vibrant and unrelenting power. But those waves of energy flowed with a palpable warmth that was positively endearing. And for the first time she didn't see a ruthless soldier, born to fight, she saw a prince of the realm born to be King.

It was such a thrilling sight she couldn't calm the flurry of burning butterflies inside her, their tiny gossamer wings stroking her heart with pride and her stomach with want.

The town was utterly delightful. Stone façades with deep wooden lintels and picturesque fairytale windows lined the intricate alleyways, and there was a lovely blend of quaint bespoke shops and chocolate box family homes. A few were a little shabby, and there was a subtle cloud of poverty in the air, but it wasn't so obvious as it had been in the outskirts they'd driven through to get here.

As Thane had told her, his uncle's tyrannical rein choked his people. The fact that they were still so pleasant and joyful was humbling. In truth, she still found it amazing they were so accepting of *her*. The enemy in their midst.

By the time they reached the main square night had fallen, and the colossal fir tree taking centre-stage near the clock tower burst into a dazzling display of a million twinkling stars of light.

Nate gasped in delight, cheering along with the flock of festive gatherers, and Thane laced his warm fingers through hers with a gorgeous half-smile that sent a shower of unadulterated happiness raining over her. It was one of those moments in time she wished she could freeze-frame, because it held the promise of unaccountable tomorrows. Of what might be.

He was trying so hard tonight. And she was determined not to suspect that his efforts were merely for the cameras. The cameras that now flashed around them in a dazzling firework display.

Squeezing his hand, she relished the spark of their fiery magical connection and tugged him towards a carpet of colour: rows of stalls that were a complete festive indulgence. Jingle-bell-shaped cookies. Apples dunked in glossy red candy and Swiss white chocolate. Unique crafts and *objets d'art*. Handmade jewellery and amazing tree decorations—intricate blown glass figurines, hand-carved wooden rocking horses and baubles etched with snowflakes.

Thane bought half of that stall, since Luciana and Nate oohed and ahhed over it all.

The yummy, nutty smell of roast chestnuts and frangipane Stollen floated in the air and lured them to the food tent, where Thane and Nate indulged in pancakes drizzled with chocolate sauce. Luciana chose the Galancian version of mulled wine, its scent heady and seductive, and by the time she cradled her third cup she felt half sloshed.

'Thane, is this stuff strong?'

'A little.' He narrowed those black sapphire eyes on her.
'Do you drink often?'

'Nope.'

'Okay, no more for you.'

His hand a claw on the rim of her cup, he tried to wrangle
it from her death grip. Then he pursed his lips to stem the
laughter that glittered in his gaze.

'Let go, Luce.'

Luciana peeked up at him through the veil of her lashes,
feeling naughty and reckless and so happy that he was smiling again. 'Make me.'

He growled—the sound dangerously feral. 'Are you
drunk?'

'Don't be daft. Of course not.'

The tent made her a liar by taking her for a spin.

'Good, because we are going ice skating.'

Oh, heck.

'Fancy a coffee?'

For four minutes Nate was like Bambi on ice—all legs and
flailing arms. Not that he was discouraged by smacking off
the hard surface every five seconds. Guerreros were made of
stronger stuff than that. He just picked himself up, wobbled
a little, and off he went again.

As for Luciana, she was all style and grace—but the
Galancian mulled wine had put her in a fun-loving, giggly
mood that was so infectious it obliterated the darkness that
had been festering inside him.

'Daddy, watch *me*.'

Nate perfected a double twirl and Luciana clapped, sending a battalion of bystanders cheering along with her.

Daddy. Why he'd chosen that over Papá was a mystery,
but Thane liked it. Every time he heard it his heart did a
funny little clench.

Nate suddenly faltered and Thane skated over, scooped
him up by the waist and lifted him high into the air like an

aeroplane. His huge grin as he squealed in delight etched itself into Thane's memory, his heart.

Time slowed.

Snow drifted lazily from the canopy ceiling as they spun round and round.

Nate screeched his name and whooped with joy. And realisation hit him with the ferocity of a thunderbolt.

He wouldn't even be a daddy at all if it weren't for Luciana, would he? She'd gambled with her reputation, risked bringing disgrace upon her house, her country, overturned the colossal expectations of a royal firstborn heir and fought to have his son out of wedlock. Without her courage Thane wouldn't have this moment. This perfectly wonderful moment in time.

No matter where he'd been for the last four years, no matter what he'd missed, without Luciana he wouldn't be gazing into eyes so like his own. Wouldn't have this precious fragile body to hold, to cuddle or to spin in the air. Wouldn't be able to incite the adorable innocent smile that never failed to lift his soul. Without Luciana he wouldn't have this moment or one hundred more just like it. The opportunity to have a million more after it.

And then came a crack of lightning, incinerating the remnants of his anger, leaving him awash with need. The need to wrap Luciana in his arms and thank her from the bottom of his black heart. Come to think of it, the fact she'd wanted Thane's son so badly at *all* astounded him.

When Nate was safely perched on his blades and had tootled off, Thane instinctively swivelled to find her—and somehow, like a whirl of fate, she crashed into his arms, her gorgeous curvy body plastered flush against his.

'Oops,' she said breathlessly. 'I nearly went over. Are you okay?'

Why? he wanted to ask. *Why did you want my son so badly?* The son of her enemy. That had to mean something. Right?

'Thane?' Affectionate concern etched her brow as she stroked his jaw, rubbed her thumb over his cheek. 'What's wrong? Why are you looking at me like that?'

He speared his fingers into the fall of her hair and dived into her eyes. 'Thank you.'

'For what?' she whispered.

'For fighting for him. Making sure he took his first breath. For telling me now, for trusting me now, so I can have him in my life.'

Tears brimmed in her eyes. 'Oh, Thane, I'm so sorry you've missed so much. If I could turn back the clock I would do it in a heartbeat.'

He believed her. He did.

'I can tell you everything,' she promised in a frantic whisper.

'I'd like that.'

'Every last detail. Show you a million photographs so you can see it all...'

'Shh.' He pressed his index finger to her mouth, then dragged it downwards, curling her plump lower lip, coaxing her to open for him as that ever-present magnetic pull—the one he'd been battling for days, the one he was powerless against—drew them together. And when their lips touched that blistering crackle of electricity jolted through his body, sizzled over his skin, fired heat through his veins. Stronger than ever before.

Luciana made a sound that came perilously close to a whimper and Thane let loose a soft growl as they shared one pent-up breath. Then he slanted his head to find the perfect slick fit, desperate to taste, luxuriating in heady relief, because she still wanted him after he'd put her through hell.

Her hands clutched at his broad shoulders, followed the column of his neck, and slid under his ears into his hair as her tongue skated against his. Thane's danced right back, and the slip and slide of their lips took them higher and higher.

The seductive pull of her mouth was a pure exhilaration he never wanted to end.

Dios, he'd missed her. Missed this.

The rapid flash of cameras lit the air around the vast indoor rink, but it was the joyful chorus of spectators chanting their names that brought him back to earth with a thud.

Ending their kiss, he pulled back a touch and pressed his lips to the corner of her lush mouth, the high curve of her cheekbone, inhaling the rich jasmine and vanilla scent from the decadent tumble of her hair.

'Oh, Lord. We're making out in public,' she said, a smile in her husky voice as she buried her hot face in his neck.

'Want to make out at home instead?' he rasped, curving his hands around her sculpted waist to steady her and pull her tightly against him. *Bad* idea, when the crush of her heavy breasts took his arousal up another notch.

Her wanton sigh of 'Yes...' was a stream of warm air over the skin beneath his ear, coercing a shudder to rip up his spine, and when she lifted her face he grinned at her bright pink cheeks.

If the crowds hadn't adored her before they were soon smitten when she spun to face them and dipped into a beautiful little curtsey, stealing the heart of every Galancian in the room. She was going to be a fabulous queen—he knew it.

As if the crowd had picked up his thoughts they began repeating a mantra: 'Queen Luciana of Galancia!'

Her dark blonde brows nigh on hit her hairline. 'They're a bit premature, aren't they? How bizarre. I'm years away from *that*. And you know what's stranger still? I know you'd gladly take your throne now, but I don't feel anywhere near ready.'

The ice shifted beneath his feet, tilting his world on its axis. 'Of course you are ready—you were born ready.'

'You sound like my father,' she grumbled. 'I may have been raised to be Queen, but I would never have chosen it for myself.'

Dios, he hadn't thought for one minute she would be averse. 'But you were about to take power...'

'Not through choice. I was being pushed early because my father is— Thane?' Her palms splayed down his chest, settled over his pecs. 'Why have you tensed up?'

Rolling his neck to slacken his body, he cursed inwardly at the idea that he was about to give her yet another reason to leave. Not to desire their marriage.

She narrowed her eyes in suspicion. 'Why do I get the feeling I've just stumbled on a landmine that's about to blow up in my face? What's going on, Thane?'

'We'll talk later.'

'Ah, no. You're not fobbing me off this time. I'm missing something here, and you're going to tell me *right now*.'

'Luce, I...' He cleared his throat. 'I will take my crown after we marry next weekend.'

She jerked backwards, her footing skewed, and a sense of *déjà vu* rocked him—the jet back in Courchevel—as he instinctively reached out and snatched at thin air as she dodged him. The loss of her warmth froze the blood in his veins.

Skidding a little, she found her balance. 'Wh...What did you say?'

Something told him he was about to have another battle on his hands. He had to remind himself that he hadn't lost one yet.

'By marrying you, a blue blood heir. I can take my crown four years early.'

CHAPTER FOURTEEN

THE SMILE SHE'D been taught in the cradle carried her through fond farewells and the car-ride back to Thane's beachside mansion to tuck a happy, sleepy Nate into bed, even while her heart was tearing itself apart and her mind was working her into a pained frenzy, connecting the dots.

By the time she walked into the suite that had been her palatial prison for days the riotous flow of turbulent emotions was a swirling, churning, flaming volcano at critical mass. And she fanned the flames of that anger—because the alternative was crumbling, breaking, shattering and she steadfastly refused to be that woman. The very woman she'd found curled up against the wall last night in the hallway. Loneliness burrowing into her stomach. Fighting defeat. Almost broken. Allowing *him* to control her. All for what? Because she was desperate for the love of the dark Prince?

Clearly it wasn't him who was crazy. It was her. She should know better. Since when had love or romantic happiness ever entered the equation of her life? *Never.* From the day she'd been born she'd been a means to a crown.

Her hands shook as she gripped the bed-rail and lifted one foot like a flamingo to tug off one kitten heel, then switched legs to yank off the other. And when she spied Thane walking through her door, his dangerous stride a purposeful prowl, only to close it behind him and lean against it, crossing his arms over his shirt-clad chest, ready for battle, she *blew*.

She launched her shoe across the room to clatter off the

wall—and, *God*, that felt great!—then spun on him like a furious firestorm.

'You seduced me for your crown, didn't you? You played me from the start—abducted me from Courchevel, brought me here against my wishes—to get you your throne. *Didn't you*?'

'You could say that,' he hedged, his easy stance belying the tension emanating from his honed, dominant frame.

How she didn't go over there and slap his hideously handsome face, she'd never know.

'Makes perfect sense, really. Why else would you want me "very, *very* badly"?' she bit out, throwing his perfect passionate prose back in his face. 'Your scruples really are abhorrent—do you know that?'

Fool, she was. Total, utter fool. She'd known he had an agenda but, as always, self-preservation had taken a darn hike and cowered in the woods with this man.

There she'd been, protecting Nate from a power-play, and she'd walked headlong into the lion's den. Blind to the warning signs flashing in glaring pink neon, brighter than a Vegas strip. Hanna and Pietro going on as if she was their saviour, for starters...

He'd played her like a puppet on a string. And she'd followed his every beat.

She didn't miss the way he shifted slightly on his feet, thrust his despicable hands through his hateful hair.

'Luciana...angel...'

'Ah, no, Romeo. You can forget the charm. No longer required. You've got me right where you wanted me. *Bravo*, Thane. Really, you should be proud.'

Was that her voice? That fractured aria of sarcasm and bitterness—that portrayal of a heart betrayed?

He rubbed at his temple as if she was one of those Sudoku puzzles that twisted her brain into knots.

'I cannot see the problem, Luciana. You didn't wish to marry Augustus and so we would both benefit.'

Of *course* he couldn't see the problem. While he'd been polishing his crown she'd secretly been building castles in the sky. But that was *her* problem. Not his. One she'd simply have to accept. Because she'd given him the one guarantee that would get her down the aisle: Natanael. Not that she'd ever feel regret over that. Seeing them together made remorse utterly impossible.

Now all she had to do was face those portentous predictions she'd been battling for days. A loveless prison of an autocratic marriage would be her future if she wasn't careful.

With a shrug she tore off her coat and slung it to the bed. 'See, Thane? Right there. *You* decided we would both benefit. *You* made that choice for me. Much like the wedding you arranged yesterday, behind my back. Has it never occurred to you that I would like to be asked?'

Hopeless, pathetic romantic, she was.

'I told you the other day we were getting married.'

'Precisely. You *told* me.' But she hadn't argued the toss, had she? No,' she'd allowed him to control her. For the last time.

He hiked one devilish brow. 'So what is the problem?'

She shot him a glare which he impudently ignored.

Lord, he just didn't get it, did he? While she could feel the ropes of a noose tightening around her neck.

From the start it had been the same. No choices. No requests. Only kidnappings and kisses and demands. Either it was ingrained in him to dominate, literally stamped into his DNA, or he respected her so little he didn't value her opinion or her own wishes. Whichever the case might be, what kind of marriage would they have? A hell of a lot worse than her parents'—she knew that much.

Her lungs drew up tight, crowding her chest until she could barely breathe. She'd been under the command of a control freak all her life and suddenly she couldn't commit to a moment longer. Heaven help her, she would *not* live under another man's rule for eternity.

'The problem is,' she said, pleading with her strength not to fail her now, 'I would like some control over my life. To at least be involved in decisions. I would like a partnership, Thane. *Not* a dictatorship. You talk about giving your people a voice. Yet you silence mine. Don't you think that's hypocritical?'

'That is absurd, Luciana,' he said fiercely. 'You speak when you wish to and I listen.'

She groaned aloud. The man was delusional.

'Did you listen in Courchevel, when I told you I wasn't getting onto that plane? *No*. Did you listen when I told you I had to go home before we could get married? *No*.'

A frigid draught swept over her, pebbling her skin with goosebumps.

'*Home*?' he incised. 'Galancia is your home.'

It wasn't his words that bothered her—it was his granite-like tone. The one that said Arunthia was to be forgotten and she should accept that.

He'd have to bury her six feet under first.

She wrenched open the antique armoire and hauled out her suitcase.

'Luciana? What the hell are you doing?'

'What does it look like I'm doing, Thane?'

She was leaving this place. This island. As soon as the dawn broke. And *nothing* would stop her.

'I don't think—'

'Oh, Thane, right now I don't care what you think. And if I were you I would start listening to me. Because your days of controlling my life are *over*.'

Frustration mounting, his pulse spiked, making him feel light-headed as Luciana whirled around the room like a tornado, shoving clothes into the sinister suitcase that sprawled over her bed like a black stain on pure white satin.

'Would you like to tell me why you are packing?'

He had no idea why—she wasn't going anywhere.

Seeing her beautiful clothes and those delicate bottles of cream that made her radiant skin smell sweet being haphazardly tossed into that vile contraption made his fists clench into thwarted balls of menace.

'I would've thought that was obvious. I'm leaving. I need to go home for a few days. I need time. I need to sort out my responsibilities there. If you had stood still long enough this week we would've already had this discussion—but, no, you dictate and you command. And I've *had* it.'

Darkness fell over his eyes until he was blind to everything around him. She was not leaving him again. Nor was she stealing his son a second time.

'No, I am sorry, Luciana, but you are not going anywhere. And *that* is final.'

His conscience was screaming at him to stop. To think about what he was doing. Saying. But if he let her go she wouldn't come back. He knew it. Just as she hadn't five years ago.

Her heavy sigh infected the air. 'You need to trust me, Thane.'

'*Trust*?' The vicious swirling cyclone in his chest picked up pace and he whirled on her in a gust of fury. 'Trust the woman who disappeared in the night and never told me I had a son? Are you *serious*, Luciana?'

Those thick decadent eyelashes descended and her voice turned heartbreakingly weary. 'I know it's early days, but are you *never* going to forgive me? Are we ever going to get past this?'

The memory of earlier tonight, when he'd peered through a different lens…her frantic whisper that she would show him what he'd missed…doused the furious fire in his blood.

He thrust his fingers through his hair and exhaled heavily. 'I'm trying, here, Luce.'

Truth was, even before this evening he'd started to appreciate the turbulence she must have gone through. Which was why he didn't want her or Nate anywhere near Henri

Verbault—the man who'd almost cost him his son. Thane would never forgive him or trust him, and he was amazed Luciana could contemplate either. Obviously she was blind to the man's influence over her, so Thane would protect her from that too. By keeping her here with him.

'Just let your father deal with the Arunthian crown. He places it above your importance anyway. You don't need to go back and see your family ever again. You have Nate and I.'

Her hand plunged from where she'd pinched the bridge of her nose and her jaw dropped agape as she spluttered, 'Of *course* I need to see them. You can't expect me to give up my family. That's just *insane*... Whoa—hold on a minute. Did you expect me to get married next Saturday without my family there?'

'Basically? Yes. I do not want your father anywhere near my wedding.'

'And what about my sisters? My *sisters*, Thane! And, no matter what grudges you have against my King, he's still my father and he's sick. I don't know how long he has left and—'

That stopped him in his tracks. 'He is sick? I didn't know this.'

She flung her arms wide in an exasperated flourish. 'Why *would* you? Since you've never asked or cared to know about that part of my life. If you had you'd know why I was being pushed into taking *my* crown early.' Her smooth brow pleated and she shook her head. 'It's almost as if you haven't accepted who I really am. Do you still wish I was the nobody you met in Zurich, Thane? Have you even acknowledged that I'm a Verbault?'

He flinched. Actually flinched. And he wasn't sure who was more surprised.

'Oh, my God.' A humourless laugh burst from her mouth. 'Did you honestly believe giving me your name would erase my heritage? Stop me from being my father's daughter?

Even if I become Queen of Galancia I will still be a Verbault in *here.*'

With her fist she thumped her chest, and when her voice fractured he felt the fissure in his own heart.

'I'll still be the enemy. You are kidding yourself to think otherwise.'

Pivoting, she spun back to the dark wood armoire, yanked open another drawer and scooped up a mound of pretty, frilly, lacy garments to dump in her case.

Thane slumped against the wall, rubbing over his jaw, his mind going a mile a minute.

In a way she was right. He'd never truly acknowledged who she was: a sister, a daughter, a friend, even the heir to the Arunthian throne. Simply hadn't wanted to admit it to himself. Not because she was his enemy, but because he would have been slammed up against the naked truth—she had responsibilities of her own. To her family, her people. Responsibilities that could take her away from *him.*

So not once had he considered or asked if she wished to take her rightful place. Because he feared her answer. Was scared she'd choose her crown over his. Her family over him.

Self-loathing crawled through his veins. He was so selfish with her. Was it any wonder desperate panic loitered in her brandy-gold eyes—a silent scream that confessed she wanted to be away from here? From him. It cut his black twisted heart in two.

And the way she eluded his own gaze struck him. The night his mother had died Juana Guerrero hadn't been able to look at him either. Her every move premeditated, she'd known what she'd devised. Just as Luciana did. She'd move heaven and earth to leave him. Permanently.

Luciana was kidding herself if she believed otherwise. Why else pack her every solitary possession into that case? A case he hadn't failed to notice had been already half full of Nate's clothes when she'd opened it.

The walls began to loom from all sides and suddenly everything appeared malefic and pernicious. Even the black rails of the ironwork bedframe seemed to uncoil and distort and writhe in front of him. Every drawer she flung open clattered and squealed and rattled, as if it bore the menacing teeth of a monster.

'You are wasting your time, Luciana. There is no way for you to leave here.'

'I'll ring Lucas to come for me.'

His heartbeat raced, threatened to explode. 'I will deny him access to Galancian airspace.'

She froze in her frenetic rush, head jerking upright, eyes slamming into his. Even from the other side of the bed he could see her glorious, voluptuous frame vibrate with pique and pain.

'Are you serious?'

'Deadly.'

Up came her trembling hand, her fingers curling around the base of her throat. 'You can't do this, Thane. I am *not* your property. I am my own person. And you can't keep me here against my wishes. It isn't right. I've felt like a prisoner in this house for days.'

Her pitch escalated as her breathing turned choppy, raspy, and she clutched her chest as if struggling for air.

Every ounce of his blood drained to his toes and a cold sweat chased it. Bolting forward, he thrust out a pleading hand. 'Luciana, calm down.'

'No, you need to *hear* me this time. What I said before— it's right and you don't see it. You don't listen to me.' Her eyes pooled with moisture, making them overly bright. 'By controlling me you take away my choice. You silence my voice. My whole life I've had this gag around my mouth, and I can't *breathe* when I think I'll have a lifetime of that with you.'

Thane raked his hand around the back of his neck, tearing at the clammy skin. He did *not* silence her; he only wanted what was best for her. She hadn't wanted to marry

Augustus. He only wanted them here so he could keep them safe. Protect what was his. And yet his conscience argued vehemently. Because he *had* told her she was marrying him. And he knew precisely why—even if he wasn't eager to admit it.

She collapsed against the hardwood drawers as if she no longer had the energy to stand upright. 'For once, just *once*, I would love someone to ask me what I truly want. Everyone who is free in the world is asked that very question every day, I imagine, and I often wonder if they realise how precious it is. If they take it for granted. I want to yell and scream at them that they shouldn't. They should cherish it. I *envy* them, Thane. I envy their freedom of choice.'

It was like being tossed into the past, hearing his mother's wistful voice—the hopes of a woman trapped like a bird in a gilded cage. And suddenly he felt like the damnable hypocrite Luciana had claimed him to be. He refused to ignore the truth one second longer. The reason he had never given her a choice.

'What are you saying, Luce? You don't want to marry me?'

'No, Thane,' she said, shaking her head, her brow pinched. 'I don't.'

And when one single diamond teardrop slipped down her exquisite face he felt as if noxious venom infected his veins, surged through his body, making him destructive, malevolent, black. As if he contaminated her with his darkness.

What more proof did he need than the evil voice whispering in his mind to *make* her marry him? Force her by threats to take away her son. And that disgusted him. It made him sick to his stomach even to think of it. The idea he was turning into his father.

She smoothed her hand over her midriff, as if he made her ache inside, but her tone strengthened as if she was resolved. Her stance one of weary resignation. 'But I will marry you. For my son. He needs you and he loves you.'

Thane closed his eyes. Why didn't that make him happy? Why couldn't he be satisfied with that?

Verity hailed down on him in an icy blizzard, pummelling his flesh through to his bones. He longed for her to want only him. For Thane to be enough.

Idiot, he was. He'd done the one thing he'd sworn he'd never do. He'd let her creep past his defences. *Again*. And that petrified him—because he'd never be enough to make her happy. Just as he hadn't been enough for his mother. To make her want to stay. He was too much like the man he'd sworn he'd never be. Twisted, selfish, possessive, dark inside.

Look at her, his inner voice whispered.

She was so beautiful she made his breath catch, his heart stall in his chest. But that solitary tear-track that shimmied a pearlescent dew down her cheek said it all. It said that one day she would hate him for imprisoning her here. Despise him. It said that one day she might fly to her death with a euphoric look of peace on her face as she finally found freedom. From him. From her life here.

And he couldn't do that to his son. Take away the woman who loved him beyond Thane's wildest imagination.

He wanted Nate to be happy. Have the kind of childhood Thane had never had. Peaceful and joyous. Learn how to be a good man with a pure soul and to be able to love another with his whole heart. Surely that was the greatest gift he could give him? More than horses and dogs and spaceships and candy canes. And to be that person Nate needed Luciana. Not Thane.

Unchaining the doors to the cage, he threw them wide open, his throat so swollen and raw every syllable hurt. 'You are right, Luciana. Of course you are right. You need to go back.'

That glorious body slumped as she gave him a tight, grateful smile. 'We'll just be gone a couple of days. Back for this…this wedding on Christmas Eve—'

'No.' He cut her off with a shake of his head, commanding his tone not to falter, to stay strong. 'There is no need. No hurry. Spend Christmas with your family if you like.'

That had been his mother's worst time for missing her loved ones. Had once made blood trickle from her wrists as the depths of her depression found no bounds.

Unwanted, harrowing, his dark, tormented mind made one of those incongruous leaps, placing Luciana in that bloodbath...

Dios, maybe her leaving long-term was for the best after all. It would only be a matter of time before he destroyed her. He'd rather have her alive somewhere else in the world than dead by his side. And, while he truly believed Luciana had more strength than his mother had, Thane could easily kill her spirit—was already doing so—and that would be a great tragedy in itself.

He lavished himself with one last long look. At that incredible dark bronze tousled tumble of hair. The perfect feminine curves of her body. Those big, beautiful brandy-gold eyes now swimming in confusion.

'Well...if you're sure,' she said, relief blending seamlessly with her bewilderment. 'We could think about getting married in the New Year. But don't you want to spend Christmas with Nate? He'll miss you.'

'No,' he said, turning his back on her, unable to lie to her face as he strode to the door.

If he thought for one second that she might come back he would hold out hope. And it had almost killed him waiting night after night in Zurich, praying she'd walk through the door. A second serving of that persecution would ruin him.

Fingers curled around the door handle, he pushed his final retort past his lips. 'I won't force you into a marriage you don't want, Luciana. In the long run that will only harm Nate. I'll explain to everyone that things haven't worked out between us.'

'Wha…What do you mean? What about Nate? Your crown?'

'I'll find another way.'

There *was* no other way. But in that moment he realised he'd crawl through the dust of his heart to give her what she wanted, needed. He'd make up for the delay to his people somehow.

'As for Nate—we will arrange visits.' Though how he'd manage to say goodbye every time, he wasn't sure.

'Thane? Turn around—look at me, please.'

He couldn't. He'd change his mind.

'I'll arrange a jet for early morning. But I can't be here when you leave. I'll be at the castle. Business.'

The barracks was his destination, and he knew it. He needed to be out cold when she left. He didn't trust himself otherwise. And there was no better way to vanquish his emotions than via his father's legacy.

'Be careful, Luciana. Love my son for me.'

'Thane, *please* wait. Talk to me.'

The soft pad of her footsteps sounded behind him and he momentarily stalled as her sensual jasmine and vanilla scent curled around him in an evocative embrace, luring him back.

No. No more talking. He didn't want her to see what lay beneath. Something too dark to describe.

Thane hauled open the door before she could touch him and vaulted up the staircase to the foyer, where he snatched his keys from the side table and stormed into the night.

CHAPTER FIFTEEN

TWELVE HOURS LATER thousands of miles separated them, and not only was Luciana still reeling from their final showdown but the man refused to leave her be.

Blind to the lush Arunthian vista as the car snaked up the steep incline towards the palace, she saw only those intense obsidian eyes searching her face before he'd sped from her suite, as if he were committing her to memory, as if she were the brightest star in his universe—it was a devastating impression she couldn't erase.

Nor could she erase the questions trying to wade through her woollen, sleep-deprived brain—why was he suddenly willing to give up twenty-four-seven access to his son, delay taking his throne?

Because despite his inglorious method of coercing you into Galancia, his intentions were pure. His only thought was for his people, and he wouldn't force you down the aisle for anything.

And she couldn't have made her desires clearer, could she? *No.*

A fiery arrow of self-censure tore through her chest and she squeezed her eyes shut. *'No, Thane, I don't want to marry you.'* But in that moment—that gasping, suffocating moment—she truly hadn't. Had only envisaged a life of dictatorship, one-sided love and the misery of duty. Where she became a dark blonde replica of her mother.

And that had petrified her. Thrown her into a panic that

had whirled out of control. Muscles burning, aching to run and never, *ever* return. And the idea that she could consider, even for a millisecond, parting him from Nate again made shame crawl over every inch of her skin.

With a restless shake of her head she cuddled Nate to her side, forcing herself back to the present, and glanced up at the fairytale façade of Arunthe Palace—all cream stone walls and fanciful turrets with conical slate roofs— as the car rocked to a stop outside the grandiose scrolled iron gates.

And when the habitual dread *didn't* pervade her body, *didn't* line her soles with lead, suddenly, astoundingly, she watched a smile play at her mouth in the reflection of the window. Apparently battling with the dark Prince had given her the courage to face anything. Even her mother's disapproving glare and her father's steely, vexed countenance as he rehashed her latest escapades in reckless rebellion.

But, unlike five years ago, he would not make her feel guilty, dirty, shameful or unworthy—he no longer held that power over her. She *refused* to grant it to him. It was not wrong to want her son or to wish for the hedonistic passions of love. To reach beyond her expectations. Thane might fight dirty at times, but at least he fought. *Hard.* For what he believed in, what he desired above all else. Taking a leaf out of his book wouldn't hurt.

Thinking about it, right at this moment she'd never felt so strong in her life.

Claudia—tall and dark, striking and radiant—appeared at the arched entryway, shielding her eyes from the sun, and leather creaked as Nate bounced at the sight of her.

'Go inside with Auntie Claudia, darling. I'll just be a few minutes.'

'Okay, Mamá,' he said, darting from the car and bolting up the stone steps.

Luciana raised splayed fingers—*five minutes?*—and on her sister's nod, the door slammed shut.

The locks clicked into place and she depressed the internal speaker for the driver.

'Another limousine, another town. How are you, Seve?' She'd swear she'd seen more of this man in the last few days than Thane.

Down came the privacy screen on a soft whirr, until she stared into deep-set titanium eyes sparkling with amusement in the rearview mirror.

'You beat me to it. I'm impressed. What gave me away?'

'Let's just say I can feel his protection.'

All around her. Wrapping her in warmth when she was so cold inside, missing him already. Wondering what he was doing in that darkly disturbing castle, who he was with. Why her inner voice shrilled that he was with no one, had only his dark pain for company.

'How does it feel, driving a car embellished with the Arunthian royal crest?'

Seve grimaced, and she couldn't help but laugh a little.

'So…are you my new shadow?' she asked.

'I sure am. Until he's satisfied you're safe and that your father won't push you into anything you don't want.'

Wry was the smile that curved her lips. Leopards and their infallible spots. He couldn't quite let go. And the hell of it was she adored him for it. They might not share love, but he cared.

'What is he doing in that castle, Seve? Who is he with?'

Unease permeated the air-con cooled air and he rolled his brick-like shoulders.

'Please, Seve, he won't talk to me.'

Exhaling heavily, he met her gaze in the rearview mirror. 'If I know Thane he's into his third bottle of Scotch after a bout in the barracks while my dear old dad cracks open the champers, celebrating his continued reign.' Anger rode his tone hard. 'I don't know what infuriates me more.'

Luciana frowned deeply. 'Barracks? What would he be doing there? And, hold on a sec—your dear old dad?'

He arched one dark brow. 'Much like Thane, I lucked out in the father stakes. My dad is Franco Guerrero.'

'Oh, Lord.' It struck her then, with everything that had gone on last night, that she'd never given Thane's uncle a thought. 'By marrying me Thane would have overthrown him. I imagine he isn't best pleased about that.'

'Understatement of the millennia, Princess. He's been causing Thane trouble for days—ever since you dropped the Nate bomb on him.'

She groaned aloud. 'Dammit. *That's* why he's been going to the castle. Practically pushing me down the aisle. Why didn't he tell me? The insufferable man doesn't *talk*.'

But she knew the answer before Seve muttered it. He wouldn't have wanted her worrying. Had to be the hero, didn't he? While she was doing her usual—painting a prophesy of desolation in a gilded cage.

Why did she *do* that? Claudia was right—she was a darn pessimist. An optimist would believe fate had brought them together again, regardless of Thane's agenda, say they had a son and that in time love could grow. An idealist would reason that duty didn't necessarily bode a farewell to happiness. They were not her parents—they could strive to have both.

And the duty that put the fear of God up her didn't have to be a noose around her neck—it could be an adventure with Thane. The greatest adventure of all. She just had to fight for it. Make it happen. Be her own hero. And maybe Thane's too, for once. Give him the crown he so desperately wanted. Help him free his people from tyranny. Make his mother's dreams come true. The woman he couldn't even speak of without pain engulfing him with a tenebrous shroud.

'His mother...' she began warily. 'Does he ever talk about her?'

'Never. The world could end tomorrow and he'd die with those memories locked in his soul. She was a manic depressive, you know? She self-harmed and…' Seve blew out an anxiety-laden breath. 'That's why I hate him being in that mausoleum. Makes him blacker than night.'

Panic gripped her stomach at the thought of him hurting somewhere she couldn't reach. 'Listen, I need a couple of days here. So right now you're going to go back there, tell him I'm fine—perfectly safe—and get him out of that castle for me. Aren't you, Seve? Tell me. Give me the words.'

He gave her an incredulous look that said *hell, yeah*, which did a somewhat splendid job of easing the crush in her lungs.

'Good. Okay. And after that I need a favour. Or three…'

A few days later. Christmas Eve.

He had the hangover from hell. Why Seve had ordered him to haul his 'sorry ass' out of bed and get in the shower he'd never know. That Thane had actually obeyed the man was even more incongruous. All he'd wanted was to sleep through Christmas. After that he knew he'd be fine. Great. Wonderful.

His groan ricocheted off the onyx marble as he braced his hands, palms flat, against the shower wall and dipped his head beneath the deluge. The cold water was like shards of glass, biting into his scalp and skin. And this was *post* eight shots of espresso. Some big tough warrior he was. He was just glad Nate wasn't here to see his hero slide down the drain, and Luciana—

Ah, great. He'd just blown his 'I won't think of them for ten minutes' pact.

The floor did a funny tilt—his cue to jump ship— and he stepped onto the rug, wrapping a towel around his waist.

Spying a bottle of headache relief on the countertop, he

reached for it, his hand freezing in mid-air as a shard of light sliced through the dim haze.

'Turn the damn light off, Seve!' he hollered. Was he trying to split his head open?

'Not Seve,' said a delectable honey-drenched tone. 'And, no, I don't think I will.'

His heart stopped. His jaw dropped. And he stared at the door that was cracked ajar. Was he hearing her voice now? His mental state was seriously disturbing these days.

With a shake of his head that made him curse blue when his brains rattled, he turned back to the basin and picked up his razor.

'Are you going to be in there all day? I'm gathering dust, aging by the second, out here.'

Clatter went the blade into the porcelain sink.

He watched his hand move at a snail's pace towards the handle...fingers curling, gripping. Heart leaping, hoping, as he eased the door fully open.

Two steps forward and—*Dios*...

'Luciana?'

Hallucinating or not?

Perched on the vanilla-hued velvet chaise longue, one leg crossed over the other, she rested her elbow on her bent knee and propped her chin on her fist. But it wasn't the sight of that exquisite serene face that jolted his heart back to life, it was the seraphic vision she made dressed from head to foot in ivory-white.

The gown was pure Luciana. No fuss or bustles or froth. Simply elegance that sang a symphony of class. Straight, yet layered and sheer, with a sensual V neck and a pearl-encrusted band tucked beneath her breasts. Lace was an overlay that capped the graceful slope of her shoulders and scalloped around her upper arms in a short sleeve. And atop her head was a diamond halo from which a gossamer veil flowed and pooled all around her.

He rubbed his bare left pec with the ball of his hand

where he ached—God, did she make him ache—and those hot needles pricked the backs of his eyes.

'Luciana…' Her name was an incoherent prayer, falling from his lips. 'You look so beautiful. Like an angel.'

She gave him a rueful smile and spoke softly, 'I've told you before, Thane, I'm no angel.'

Whether it was because he felt utterly broken inside, or because the sight of her had turned the gloomy morning into pure sunshine he couldn't be sure, but his mouth opened and for the first time in his life he was powerless to stop what poured free.

'But you were *my* angel. And you never stopped being mine—not for one minute. Even when I was furious with you, you were still my only light in the dark. And no matter where you are in the world that will never change.'

Down came long lashes to fan over her flawless cheeks as she bit down on her lips. Lips she now covered with trembling fingers.

Panic punched him in the gut. 'Luce?' He took a tentative step closer, relieved when she breathed deeply, pulling herself up to sit tall and straight, with a gorgeous watery smile just for him.

'My sister,' she said, with an airy wave that belied that quivering hand, 'who is somewhere around here, tells me it's bad luck to see the groom before the wedding—but you know what I think?'

While Thane knew nothing about these things, the fact that she resembled a bride and spoke of weddings and grooms wasn't lost on him—but hope was a fragile beast he tethered. Because despite the agony of losing her he would not take her down the aisle without happiness in her heart.

Brushing his wet hair back from his face, he eased down onto the edge of the bed, never taking his eyes off her in case she disappeared. 'What do you think, Luce?'

'I think we make our own luck. I think fate offers us opportunity but *we* are the masters of our own destiny. I think

I've allowed people to control me for too long, and now I'm going to take my life and my happiness into my own hands. Are you ready, Thane?'

Happiness.

He was ready for anything as long as she didn't leave.

CHAPTER SIXTEEN

SHE WAS GOING to propose. Any minute now.

It wasn't every little girl's dream. But, when you'd been governed since the day you were born, being the commander of tomorrow was a unique dream all its own.

So here she was. Sitting opposite a handsome man—*the* most beautiful she'd ever seen. The dark, dangerous divinity that was Prince Thane of Galancia. And maybe she hadn't set the stage so superbly—no dimly lit chandeliers or intimate tables for two, but it was *their* scene, their intimate paradise—the place where she'd been reunited with the other half of her soul—and to her it was perfection. Beyond price.

So all that was left were the words.

And Princess Luciana Valentia Thyssen Verbault had to press her palm to her stomach, desperately trying to calm the swoop and swirl of anxious butterflies, their dance wild with exhilaration and anticipation, before she stood tall. Because she had the horrible feeling she might pass out. She'd felt less nervous renouncing her throne yesterday, before hordes of press. The news would be broadcast at twelve noon and by then—hopefully—she'd be this man's wife.

Sucking in a shaky breath, she rose to her feet and walked over to where he perched on the edge of the bed, his honed body glistening, those black sapphire eyes holding hers captive. And, despite the fact he looked like hell, the mere sight of him, in all his myriad beauties and unguarded mercies, still made her weak at the knees.

Down she went onto the floor before him. Never leaving his gaze, loving the way he opened his legs to let her in. The way he reached up hesitantly, fingers trembling, as he brushed a wayward curl from her temple.

'Luciana…' he murmured. 'I…' A faint crease lined his brow. 'What are you doing down there?'

'I'm doing this right. On one knee.'

'Doing what right?'

When light dawned, he shook his head vehemently.

'Like hell you are.'

He grasped her waist and lifted her up, plonking her astride his knee with a rustle of her skirts.

'You will not kneel before me. And isn't that *my* job?'

'Not when we're living in this splendid era called the twenty-first century, Thane.'

Not when she heard that hint of panic in his voice—the one that reminded her of the day on the beach with Nate. That fear of rejection. She could kick herself for not considering it before. That by taking away her choice he gave her no option to say no. To reject him. Lord, it was amazing what a mess two people could make in a few days.

Wriggling back, she tried to clamber off his lap. Thanks to Thane, she somehow ended up on the bed, where she hoisted up her skirts—slipping and sliding as tulle and chiffon met satin sheets. By the time she was on her knees again she felt like a triathlete after a three-day event. Likely resembled one too, with her tiara askew. But one look at the man of her dreams, wearing a towel that left *nothing* to the imagination, getting on his knees too, as if he needed them equal, and her every thought zeroed in on him. Only him.

'And why shouldn't I kneel before you?' she said. 'I respect you. I'm proud of you. For breaking free of your father's hold, for fighting for your people.'

She trailed her fingertips down the scimitar line of his jaw and stared into those beautiful dark fathomless eyes.

'You're going to be a powerful and noble King and I'll

be honoured to stand by your side. Our son needs a wonderful daddy too, and that man can only ever be you. And *I* need the man I love with my whole heart to be with me always. So…Thane Guerrero of Galancia…will you do me the great honour of becoming my husband?'

His throat was convulsing, and his magnificent chest shook as if he fought his emotions. Until one rogue teardrop finally spilled on his first spoken word.

'L…Love? You *love* me, Luciana?'

Holding his jaw in her hands, she leaned forward and kissed his tear away, breathing him in. 'Oh, I love you. I always have. Since the moment you knocked out a Viking in my honour.'

'Really?'

'*Really*, really. I just didn't believe in fairytales and happy-ever-afters. Didn't believe in happiness for myself at all. The right to dream beyond duty was drummed out of me when I was three feet tall. Duty was why I would marry—not for love. So, like a self-fulfilling prophecy, I ran years ago, when my heart screamed at me to stay and tell you who I was. I listened to my father and an age-old feud, ignoring my every instinct to come to you with our son. Duty would never bring happiness—my parents are proof of that—so when I discovered I was the key to your crown I ran scared again.'

She brushed his damp hair back from his temple, tucked one side behind his ear.

'But I think if we try we could have both. I promise I'm not running any longer. I'm here to stay—more than ready to be your Queen. Your wife and your lover too, if you want me. So what do you say?'

'Yes.'

Swooping in he came, and back down she went to the mattress, the heat of his body spilling over her.

'Yes. Yes, I'll marry you.' He wrapped her in his arms in a cherishing crush and breathed against her neck. 'I want it all too, Luciana. You'll always come first to me. *Always*. I love you so much. You've always owned my heart. Only you.'

A sigh feathered the aching wall of her throat and she closed her eyes as the last stain of doubt was erased. Replaced by the sweet sherbet-bright happiness that fizzled inside of her. If she'd heard him right, that was.

'I have?'

'Always,' he said, his lips moving over her skin.

For long moments they held on tight. Breathing. Loving. Calming. Trying to accept a dream beyond dreaming, a thing too precious ever to risk again. Then he was kissing her with exquisite annihilating tenderness and she was melting beneath his fervid ardour.

'Why else would I search for you for weeks, turn over every stone in Zurich looking for you, while my heart wouldn't beat and my lungs could barely breathe?'

She felt one fat tear trickle down the side of her face. 'Ah, Thane, why didn't you tell me?'

'I didn't want to give you that power over me again. Stupid to think I had any control over it at all. I even kidded myself I was only after my crown. That worked for...'

He hiked his shoulders and she felt the play of muscle against her palms.

'I don't know—maybe a day? I wish I'd told you that at the ice rink, instead of making it all about the throne. I was a coward.' Red scored his cheekbones. 'And now I'm rambling.'

She laughed at his newfound candour. 'No, you're not— you're talking, and I love it. It's wonderful. That's what I need.'

'To share. You told me. See? I do listen to you, Luciana, I just... At first I thought I was doing the right thing. And, *Dios*, I should have asked you to marry me, but I didn't want to hear your voice say no. I *was* silencing you, and that made me as bad as my father. Black. Twisted up inside. I kept having these visions of you hurting yourself, like my mother used to, and—'

'Hey, look at me. *Never* going to happen. She wasn't well, Thane. And that was your father's doing—it had nothing to do with you. You're nothing like him. You're a heroic man in *here*.' She placed her palm over his heart…a heart that thumped in tandem with hers. 'Will you tell me about her one day?'

Closing his eyes, he rested his brow against hers. 'One day soon. Just not today. Let me enjoy having you back in my arms.'

'Okay.' That was plenty good enough for her. 'Just promise me you'll keep talking. If you're hurting I need to know, so I can be there for you. In the silence I'd convinced myself we were doomed. When you don't share with me my mind runs wild. You were at the castle, trying to keep us safe, and I was picturing you with mistresses, you know?'

His eyes sprang open and his head reared back. '*Que*? You are *crazy*, Luce.'

'Yeah, well, one day I'll tell you about my childhood. Or, better yet, I'll sleep out one night and not bother telling you what I'm doing and who—'

'Like hell you will.'

'Need I say more?'

He growled. 'I didn't think of that. But I swear you'll see a snowball in hell before I ever take a mistress.' He brushed his lips over hers, back and forth. Teasing. Tormenting. 'Only you.'

Then he began to rain lush, moist kisses down her throat in a golden trail.

'I've been the only lover in your life, yes?'

Blood thrumming, she writhed against the satin sheets. 'Y…Yes, you know that.'

Nudging at the lace covering her breast, he swirled his hot breath over her skin as he murmured, 'And you are the only lover in mine. There has only been you and there will only ever be you.'

Blame it on the havoc being unleashed on her body, but it took her a second to catch on—and then she pushed at his shoulders to gauge his expression. 'You mean you haven't slept with anyone since *me*?'

Nonchalance made his shrug loose, as if he didn't see the big deal. 'No. It felt wrong. Like I was betraying my heart.'

'But…but you're a *man*.'

A laugh rumbled from the depths of his chest. 'I am *so* glad you've noticed that, angel.'

'And you're…*hot*.'

His eyes smouldered along with his smile as he towered above her, dominating her world, as always.

'I am *hot* for you right now,' he growled, with such sexual gravitas she shivered. 'Hot enough to show you exactly how much of a man I am.'

His sinful tongue licked across the seam of her lips in silent entreaty and she fisted his hair and surrendered, holding him to her as that black magic enthralled her.

It was the distant tinkle of glasses and music that pierced her lust fog.

'Oh, Lord, Thane, our guests! You have to get dressed. We're getting married on the beach in…' Lifting her head, she peeked at the bedside clock. 'Crikey—seven minutes.'

And she wouldn't like to guess what she looked like. Their wide eyes met and they both burst out laughing like lovestruck teenagers.

'Seriously, though, I was thinking this private ceremony could be for us. We'll have a big splash at the cathedral, before your coronation. It will give my father time to come round too. We need peace between our houses, Thane. I want us to end this feud. You and I. Together.'

'Whatever you want—whatever makes you happy. I can be nice to your father. For thirty seconds at least.'

'Make it sixty-nine and I'll pay you in kind.'

He growled like a virile feral wolf. 'I'm having you back in this bed within two hours.'

'Then move it.'

Tornado-style, they whirled around the room, yanking suit hangers and buttoning shirts and shoving feet into shoes. Before she knew it they were at the door.

'You look indecently gorgeous, Prince Thane. I adore you in this black Armani. All dissolute and wicked. How do *I* look?'

He pointed his index finger north. 'Your halo is wonky.'

Her smile exploded into laughter. 'You mean my tiara?'

'*Si*. Not that I care. To me you look perfect. A debauched angel.'

'And I bet you like that, huh?'

'Of course,' he drawled.

She was beaming—she knew it. 'Okay, Romeo, are you ready to marry your Juliet?'

'I am ready to marry *you*, Luciana. To finally make you mine.'

She laced her hand through his and he gripped it with warm fingers and devout love and the promise of unaccountable tomorrows.

'Then let's do it. Let's make our destiny our own.'

* * * * *

I'LL BE YOURS FOR CHRISTMAS

SAMANTHA HUNTER

Samantha Hunter lives in Syracuse, New York, where she writes full-time for Mills & Boon. When she's not plotting her next story, Sam likes to work in her garden, quilt, cook, read and spend time with her husband and their dogs. You can check out what's new, enter contests or drop her a note at her website, samanthahunter.com.

1

ABBY HARPER'S EYES clung to the man who stood not twenty feet away, dressed in an expensive silk suit that glided over his broad chest and muscled arms like water over rock.

Reece Winston.

She frowned, watching the restaurant hostess sidle up a little closer than necessary, making sure Reece had a clear view down the deep V of her low-cut blouse.

Abby couldn't blame her, not really, taking in the impressive figure Reece made as he turned, noticing the way the tailored pants clung to a perfect masculine ass that had her fingers itching to reach out for a squeeze.

She knew just how it would feel. She'd been there, done that.

Almost, anyway.

Once, a long, long time ago. How unfair—or pathetic—was it that she could remember the feel of one man's backside from eight years before?

To his credit, Reece barely seemed to notice the hostess, as he was deep in conversation with a small, hawkish man who stood beside him. Abby had heard Reece was home but hadn't seen him around, even though he lived next door.

That wasn't unusual. He'd come home a few times over the years since he'd left for life in Europe, but their paths had never intersected. She'd been off to school, or busy working at her parents' winery, and Reece had his life as a famous race car driver on the Formula One circuit. With the differences between their two lives, the half a mile between their homes might as well have been a thousand.

This was the first time she'd actually seen him anywhere but in a local newspaper or television sports report. Her heart beat a little too quickly for her liking. So she turned her attention away, though she wasn't really looking at the crowds milling around the Ithaca Commons, the artsy, outdoor shopping plaza in the heart of the small central New York city.

It was almost a month before Christmas, the Friday after Thanksgiving, which she had spent catching up on inventory. Abby and her friend Hannah were meeting here for lunch, something Abby had been looking forward to all week. Some downtime and a chance to forget about work for an hour or so.

Some light snow fell, blowing and circling around the booted feet of shoppers and local shopkeepers who were moving around the walkway. She hardly noticed. Her mind insisted on reminiscing about Reece.

She'd only kissed him once, on a crazy, wine-drenched evening one summer when he'd been home from college, the semester before he took off for Europe. They were both at the same lakeside party given by a mutual friend.

Even then, Reece ran with a crowd way out of Abby's league.

Abby had been seeing Josh Martin back then, a graduate student from Cornell Veterinary College who helped out at their vineyard, where they also hosted a small petting zoo with goats and sheep. Josh was a great guy. Cute.

Abby had been lying in wait by a dense hedgerow, intent on seducing her date. When she pulled the man she thought was Josh into the quiet, dark spot, she didn't give him a chance to say anything. She kissed him in clear invitation before he could say a word.

Abby discovered early on that she liked some kink with her sex, and Josh had a kind of quiet reserve that she took as a challenge. Sex outdoors at a party, with people right on the other side of the hedge, was an exciting thought for her, but she knew her mild-mannered date would have to be convinced.

She had pretty much made her way around second base heading for third when she told him how pleased she was with his sense of adventure and wondered what other experiments he might be up for.

Reece had chuckled softly and whispered in her ear that he would be happy to try anything she wanted to suggest.

She'd recognized his voice, and her mistake, immediately.

It had been *so* humiliating. Even now, her cheeks burned to think of it. She'd popped out from the hedges without even fixing her clothes, much to the amusement of some onlookers in the yard. Reece walked out, too, completely unapologetic with his shirt still unbuttoned, his eyes hot and the top button of his jeans undone. The button she had been undoing when he'd spoken up.

Worse, as furious as she was, she'd wanted to go back behind that hedge and finish what they'd started. Reece smiled and told her to lighten up, that he wouldn't have let it go too far. She imagined he and his buddies had a great laugh about it later.

Then he told her that Josh had received an emergency phone call and had to leave suddenly. Josh had asked Reece to find Abby and let her know. He'd started to say something else, but Abby had turned and left, and that was the last time she'd seen him, until now.

Reece had been her tormentor since childhood. The boy who always hid her lunchbox in the wrong locker, who tugged her pigtails and always, always rubbed it in that his parents' vineyards were bigger, more profitable and better than her family's smaller organic operation.

Though Reece teased her, he was never really mean. When she was fourteen, in fact, he defended her when another boy had been needlessly cruel about her braces, making her cry. Reece had almost punched the other boy, she remembered. Abby hated to admit it, but a secret, nasty little crush on him developed in that moment.

And he knew it.

And she knew that he knew, even when they both emerged back out from behind the hedge and he'd smiled at her so *knowingly*.

"Hey, earth to Abby?" The voice finally broke through as Hannah Morgan, her best friend since high school, returned to the table, sliding back into her seat.

Abby shook her head clear and blinked the past away.

"Sorry, lost in thought."

"Yeah, I saw Reece at the door. From the roses blooming in your cheeks, I assume you did, too."

Abby grunted. "It's just warm in here."

Hannah grinned widely. "Warmer since Reece walked in," she said without shame, watching him where he sat across the room from them. "I guess he's home because of what happened with his dad."

"I'm kind of surprised to see him, really. He had a bad crash last spring and has been recovering ever since—it was really serious," Abby said, shuddering as she remembered seeing the replay of the accident on the news. Reece had been on his way to superstardom, living a glamorous and high-profile life as a race car driver until the crash.

Hannah cocked an eyebrow. "I'd heard, but didn't realize you followed racing that closely."

"I just watch the news. And I might have read a few things online."

"Well, he looks healthy and hale to me," Hannah said with a playful leer.

Abby knew better than to look again, but did anyway, and sure enough, as soon as she peeked, Reece turned his head to look directly at her.

The shared look nearly sucked the breath out of her.

The years disappeared, and she was the crush-stricken teenager again. His eyes narrowed, and she knew that he recognized her, too, even though she was now twenty-five pounds lighter and her previously plain, boy-short brown hair was now long and layered, curling softly with honey-blond highlights, her one indulgence.

"Why does he have to be so *hot?*" Abby mumbled,

deeply annoyed and digging in to the beautiful salad that a server set before her moments ago. Shoving a forkful of spinach and various greens, fresh pears, walnuts and blue cheese into her mouth, she barely tasted it. Reece's fault.

"Hey, I think he's coming over," Hannah whispered across the table, looking up with a big smile as Reece approached them.

"What?" Abby sputtered, swallowing a mouthful of greens, promptly choking on her food as she saw Hannah was right. Abby coughed, reaching for her water, but suddenly strong hands had her from behind, spanning her rib cage and pulling her back against a rock-solid chest.

"I'm okay, I'm okay!" she insisted. She could sense the heat from his hands on her skin in spite of the sweater she wore over her blouse. His hold released, and she took a few breaths, composing herself.

"Abby?" he said in a voice that was deeper than she remembered, his breath just brushing the back of her neck.

She didn't turn around, not yet. Picking up her water, she took a sip, using the moment to focus. Then, smoothing the front of her sweater, she faced him with a bright smile.

"Reece. How nice to see you," she said, and was yet again flung back to those hedges as his gray eyes sparkled with warm recognition. He was remembering it, too, she could tell. Damn it. "Thanks for the first aid, but I really was okay," she said.

"Glad to help," he said. "So, Abby Harper, all grown

up. No more pigtails or braces," he said with a smile and a wink.

Her cheeks heated and she wanted to kick Hannah for grinning so broadly.

"I'm sorry to hear about your father. I hope he's doing well," Abby said, meaning it, determined to act like an adult.

She noticed a network of thin scars, recently healed, that ran along the side of his neck, and what looked like another behind his ear. "And you, too," she continued. "That was an awful accident they showed on the news. I'm so glad you're up and around. You look great," she said, proud of herself for sounding so mature, like an old friend who was happy to see him again.

Reece's expression became more serious. She thought he looked bigger now, more muscular than she remembered. She assumed that all race drivers kept to a rigorous fitness regimen and needed to be physically fit to withstand the physical and mental pressures of racing, but…wow.

Those beautiful, thick-lashed eyes were the same, as were the sharp cheekbones and full lips. She'd always loved how his pin-straight, raven-black hair had fallen in his eyes, a little long in the front, but now he kept it cropped short, which only accented his features all the more.

"Thank you. Dad's recovering well. Doctors are very optimistic."

He obviously didn't want to discuss his own near miss, and she couldn't say she blamed him. Regardless of his celebrity status, it couldn't be fun to have your private life and health problems made into entertainment news.

Abby nodded. "Is he still at the hospital? I imagine he'd probably be happy to be back to work when he can."

Reece frowned. "Actually, he won't. The surgery was remarkably fast—they can do amazing things these days. He and Mom were only home for a few days, but they're down with Ben now, in South Carolina. The doctors advised it, so that he'd be in an easier climate, closer to hospitals. They'll live with Ben and his family for a while, which will make it easier on Mom. Then they plan to find a new place down there."

"Oh," she said, her reaction part surprise and part regret. She liked the Winstons and would have liked to have seen them before they left. They'd been good neighbors. "Who's taking over the vineyards? You?"

It was what she'd done when her parents retired. They were off catching up on all of the travel they had put off all those years. Abby was happy for them and she loved the updates they sent her and posted on their Facebook pages. Her parents—world adventurers.

"Not exactly," Reece said, looking cautious. "We've decided selling is the best option. I'm taking care of the details, though, and I have some buyers interested, but—"

"You're selling?" she interrupted, in shock.

"Yes, I'm afraid so."

"But, I thought…now that you're not racing…"

Her misstep was reflected in the tightening of his expression.

"I want to be back to racing next year," he said shortly.

"As soon as possible, really. So there's no choice but to sell. Which reminds me," he said, glancing over at his table, "I have to get back to my meeting. I just wanted to say hello."

"Oh," was all Abby managed to say.

Reece's expression shifted from cool to friendly again. Maybe a little too smoothly, in Abby's estimation.

"It's good to see you, though. Maybe we'll get a chance to have a drink together over the holiday, catch up on old times. I should be home for the month, to see the sale through and finish things up here," he said.

"Yeah, sure," she responded, but he'd already turned to walk away. This time, she did notice a slight hitch in his gait and wondered about his injuries. Things might be happening behind the scenes that the public didn't know about...still, she'd thought from what had been reported in the news and online that he was out of the sport.

"Wow, I can't believe he's selling," Abby said again, her mind returning to that bombshell. There were some new start-ups along the lake, and some of the vineyards had closed over the years, but Maple Hills and Winston Vineyards were the two oldest in the area. "All the news said he was out of racing. His accident left him with injuries that simply won't allow him back in."

"He seems to think differently," Hannah said absently.

Abby watched Reece sit down at his table and then turned to see Hannah worriedly chewing her lip.

"What?"

"I hope he hasn't been talking with the Keller Corp.

rep. The same guy who bought out Stevens and Harvest vineyards last year."

Abby put her fork back down, her hands turning cold.

"No."

"It's a possibility."

"He…can't. He can't sell to them. It would ruin Maple Hills!" As if selling wasn't bad enough, selling to Keller would be a disaster.

Keller was a housing developer that had been buying up lakeside property and building cookie-cutter housing developments that ruined the area's natural appeal. They didn't care about the watershed or about the long tradition of wineries in the area. They didn't care about anything, except for making money.

The runoff from pavement, lawn chemicals and the potential for septic leaks and so forth, would be awful for her business, ruining her land. Not to mention scarring the beautiful view of the lake.

"Every wedding couple we book wants to be married out on the vineyard, with the view of the lake. We'd lose them all if the backdrop is a bunch of prefab houses," she said, shaking her head.

Even in the economic hard times, people still got married, and these days many of them decided to do so locally to save money. Her wedding bookings were up considerably, and that helped when wine sales were down. In fact, she was preparing for a wedding reception that was scheduled for two days before Christmas. Weddings and other special events had become a big part of her bottom line.

Harvey Winston, Reece's father, hadn't been an

organic farmer, not strictly, but he used the least harmful methods available and made sure to observe a buffer between her grapes and his. And all of the vineyards worked to maintain the beauty of the landscape, as it was to their collective advantage.

No way would Keller Corp. care. In fact, if they drove her out, they would buy up her family business, as well.

"He can't do it, Hannah."

"Well, he can, sadly. And probably will if he wants to sell fast and for a good price," Hannah said flatly, making Abby sit back in her chair, utterly losing her appetite altogether.

"There has to be some other way. I should talk to him, maybe we can work something out."

"I'm sorry, hon, but I do your accounting, and there is no way you can afford to buy him out. Speaking as your friend, without Sarah, you already have more than you can manage alone. Maybe if you hire someone…" Hannah said sympathetically.

"I planned to, in the summer. I don't have time for interviews now. But if he sells, none of it will matter."

Sarah had been her manager and her second-in-command. She'd known the winery and their vineyards inside out, had been with them since her parents ran the place, but finally had also decided to retire a few months before. It had been tough finding a suitable replacement. Abby had been running in circles handling everything.

"What are you thinking?" she asked Hannah, who had that look that told Abby her friend was clearly cooking up something as she smiled mysteriously.

"Well, he was awfully eager to get his hands on you—no way were you choking badly enough for him to jump in and Heimlich you."

"What are you saying?"

"I'm saying you two always had some chemistry, always had a little push and pull between you. Maybe that's something you could use to your advantage."

"You're deluded."

"You know it's true. You said yourself that he was a great kisser and you wish that snafu behind the hedgerow had gone further. So…"

"No fair. I said that when I was really drunk."

"And we know alcohol is like truth serum for you. But why not give it a try?"

"Are you seriously suggesting I sleep with Reece in order to get him to change his mind about selling?"

"I wouldn't put it that way. Just…strike up your old friendship, flirt a little, see if you can make him more sympathetic to your cause. Or at the very least, keep your enemies closer so you know what's going on. He seemed interested in meeting up for a drink, and well, it can't hurt, right?"

Abby narrowed her eyes. "I don't believe I've seen this side of your personality. Very *Desperate Housewives*. But it's not for me. Besides, that incident behind the bushes was a mistake. Before that, the only chemistry we had was him tormenting me since second grade."

"Boys always punch girls in the arm when they like them."

"You've been watching *Brady Bunch* repeats again, haven't you?" Abby accused, and both of them collapsed in laughter for a moment, before Abby sighed, sobering again.

"I'm afraid we'll have to come up with some other plan."

"Maybe it's for the best," Hannah suggested. "I know the developments suck, but you haven't had a vacation in almost two years, and have you even been out on a date in that time?"

"One," Abby challenged.

Though that hadn't been so much of a date as a disaster.

"All you do is work. Your parents never meant for you to have no life when they turned the place over. Maybe if you sold it, you could—"

Abby looked at her in horror. "How can you even say that? My parents risked everything, worked their entire lives to make this business a success, and at a time when organic farming had hardly been heard of, let alone been popular. How can I just sell out on them?"

Hannah shrugged. "It's worth thinking about, from a practical perspective, hon. Things change. Sometimes you have to change with them."

Abby knew she had been working too hard, almost constantly since Sarah retired, and Hannah was right on one score—as her parents' only child, they were delighted to give her the business, but they were also huge believers in balance. They would be the first ones to tell her to ease up—yet they would also never sell to somebody like Keller, Abby knew that in her heart of hearts.

There had to be some way she could talk to Reece, find an alternative or get him to change his mind. Short of sleeping with him, not that the idea didn't have some appeal. He was gorgeous, undeniably.

"I guess I could at least talk to him," she said lamely, watching Reece deep in conversation with his business associate over big sandwiches. Thinking about those strong hands on her rib cage and the hot kisses they had shared, she wondered if Hannah wasn't on to something.

Maybe her friend was right. Why not? They were old friends—sort of—but they were both grown up now. She hadn't had so much as a kiss good-night in months. She knew for a fact that kissing Reece wouldn't be any sacrifice at all, and if it would get him to listen to her…

All of her appetites kicked back in, and with a dash of hope she dug back into her salad.

Hannah's lips twitched and she had a self-satisfied look. "You're thinking about it, aren't you?"

Abby couldn't resist a smile. "Hey, you're the one who wants me to go out on a date. Besides, it's not like I would let it go too far," she said, echoing Reece's words from so long ago. "I wouldn't trade sex for him selling the place to me or anything tawdry like that, but as you said, maybe just some flirting, spending time together, might help him see my side of things a little better."

"Exactly. Just be careful. Remember from eleventh-grade chemistry what happens when you put two volatile substances together," Hannah warned, but her eyes were twinkling with mischief.

"Maybe," Abby said, but her mind was racing ahead, intrigued by the idea of flirting with Reece. "But what a way to go."

REECE WAS HAVING a hard time focusing, and it had nothing to do with the injuries he'd sustained nine months before and everything to do with the unbelievably sexy woman sitting across the room. He could hardly believe that was Abby Harper.

Seeing her had been the first pleasant surprise he'd had since coming back to help with his family's affairs. Life had been one long string of disasters for the past year. First, two members of his racing team had to be replaced at the start of the season, after which they'd lost a major sponsor, and then he'd had his accident at the end of March, right when he'd been about to turn a major corner in his career.

Everyone told him he was lucky to be alive and in one piece, walking and talking again, and he supposed that was true. He'd been in a coma for three days, followed by six months of language and physical therapy after he had emerged from the coma, his head injury leaving him with a broken memory and speech problems. He'd overcome it all. Mostly.

Some of the guys he'd known hadn't made it through crashes that left them with lesser injuries, but there were a lot of days when Reece didn't feel all that lucky, especially since they told him there would be no more racing, not until a neurologist cleared him. Then his dad had a major heart attack. It had been one thing after another, and Reece found his time split between his recovery and wanting to get back to racing and having to help out his family. They'd been there for him, and there was no way he'd leave them in the lurch now, but it sure didn't make things easier. His life was an ocean away.

For months his mom and dad had been traveling back

and forth to Europe, where Reece lived just outside of Paris. It was too much strain for them to try to run the winery and travel so often, and his father's illness was proof of that. He felt responsible, and although they'd bent over backward to tell him it wasn't his fault, guilt demanded he stay here and help in any way he could.

He'd been here, in central New York State, for a few weeks, though he had spent most of the time at the hospital, in hotels and then getting his parents to his brother's home down South. He couldn't help the feeling that his real life was passing him by. He could only be absent from racing for so long. There were always new guys coming up, ready to take his place, and sponsors had short memories. Few drivers came back after a crash like his; hell, few survived.

But Reece wasn't ready to retire yet. He just had to sell the winery, to do the best he could by his parents and get back to France ASAP. At thirty-one, he didn't have too many years left to get back into the game.

Though some guys raced into their forties, it was getting to be less and less the case, so he needed to still show he could do the job. The doctors were apprehensive, but he planned to prove them wrong. He'd come this far, he was going the rest of the way.

He thought again of Abby's shocked face when he'd said he was going to sell the winery. His parents weren't thrilled, either, but they'd long ago accepted that both of their boys had other lives now. Still, Reece was bothered by the clear disapproval in Abby's gorgeous brown eyes when he'd made the announcement.

"So, I can bring the Keller representative by tomorrow, if you like," Charles said.

Charles Tyler was one of the premiere real estate agents in the area, and he was also a shark—if anyone could sell the place for the best price, it would be him.

"They'd be a last resort. I thought I made that clear."

Charles sighed, smiling slightly at the pretty server who delivered their lunch. "Well, if you want it sold for the asking price and fast, they are the best bet. They'll jump at a property as large as yours."

Reece frowned. They'd also tear down the renovated farmhouse he grew up in, and they'd flatten the vine-yards, rows of Riesling, Chardonnay and Pinot Noir grapes, paving them over with cul-de-sacs and drive-ways. He'd been away, but he kept in touch, and he'd seen the changes along the lake since he'd come back, few of them good.

"Some of those vines have been around longer than my parents have been alive, planted by my grandfather," Reece murmured, not realizing he'd said it out loud.

"Well, you might be able to sell to another winery, but it won't go for nearly as much, not in this economic climate," Charles said with a sigh, no doubt disappointed that sentimentality could get in the way of a larger com-mission for him. "And it could take quite a bit longer."

Reece nodded, thinking. "Keep Keller on the line, but let's not move too fast. If they want it now, they'll want it a month from now, but let's see what comes up in the meanwhile," he said, his eyes drifting back to Abby.

"Who's the girl?" Charles asked, following Reece's gaze.

"Abby Harper. An old friend, her family owns the winery next to ours, Maple Hills."

"More than a friend?" Charles asked.

"No. Just a girl I knew in high school," Reece said.

"Any chance she might be interested in selling, as well? I could get you a sweet deal if you two went in on a sale together—that could significantly up the price Keller would offer."

"I doubt she would ever sell, and definitely not to Keller," Reece said.

"They're not the devil," Charles said dryly. "They just build developments, nice ones, which tend to fill up very quickly."

"I know what they do," Reece said absently, his attention still on Abby.

Charles picked up the check and changed the subject, droning on about local real estate markets or some other big sale he had just completed, all of which Reece tuned out.

Abby was in close conversation with her friend, whom he only vaguely remembered from school. He and Abby hadn't really belonged to the same crowd, even though they grew up next door to each other and shared a common interest between their families.

Her folks were always a little different than everyone else on the lake—more iconoclastic, with their organic methods and sustainable farming beliefs, the petting zoo and homespun lifestyle. Those things were all the rage now, of course. Maple Hills could ask twice for a bottle of wine what other noncertified organic vineyards could.

While they were still primarily a small family business, Maple Hills had broadened its distribution and marketing quite successfully in recent years, so his father said. Probably Abby's doing. She had a good head for business and was growing it well.

She'd taken a lot of ribbing in school—she and her parents being called hippies and so forth—and quite a bit of that had been from him. He hadn't meant any of it, not in a mean-spirited way, but even then, Abby had been fun to tease. He could never resist.

Her cheeks turned pink if he even looked at her, and he's always thought it was cute. He'd never suspected she would be as hot and as daring as he had discovered that night at the lake party.

It was the last time he'd seen her until now. Though he'd kissed plenty of women in between—including a few A-list celebrities—the memory of Abby Harper pressed up against him and kissing him for all she was worth, her hands everywhere, was as clear to him as if it had happened five minutes ago.

He'd wanted to drag her back behind the hedge that night, and he'd regretted making light of it afterward. She'd bolted before he could ask her out. On a date. So they could do it right.

He wanted to make up for what he'd been too much of an immature idiot to do in high school. He'd always liked her, but when he was young, he was too worried about what his friends would think. Typical teenage boy stuff.

A few years later, on that night by the lake, he didn't care what anyone thought, but Abby was clearly not interested as soon as she found out whom she'd been feeling up behind the bushes.

He'd known, in some corner of his mind, that she hadn't been in real danger of choking at her table earlier, but seeing her had somehow led to the immediate need to touch her. He'd become semihard from the way her pretty backside pressed against him when he'd been trying to help her, his wrists just brushing the undersides of her full breasts when he'd wrapped his arms around her.

Sad, when emergency Heimlich was your excuse to get close to a woman, but Reece hadn't had sex since before his accident and, apparently, his body was more than ready for some action. Despite lingering effects from his injuries, that part of his nervous system seemed to be in fine working order.

What if he decided to pursue that drink with Abby and see if they could pick up where they'd left off by the bushes? She hadn't been interested back then, but he could swear he'd felt her respond to his touch today, and not just in a panic about choking.

It was fun to think about, and it might be worth seeing the look on her face if he asked. He couldn't resist the idea of teasing Abby, even now, though the way he wanted to tease her had taken on a whole new dimension.

He chuckled to himself, feeling better than he had in weeks.

"Something funny about that?" Charles asked, obviously peeved, either because he knew Reece wasn't listening, or because Reece had just laughed at something he shouldn't have.

"Oh, no, sorry. I was just thinking about something else," he said vaguely.

"Okay, well, I'll start pushing the property and see what we can do to hold Keller off for a while, but unless you want to wait longer, they may be the best deal in town," Charles repeated.

"I'll talk to them, but I just want to see what other offers we get. I'll be living at the house, so you can get me there. You have my numbers," Reece said.

"I'll do my best." Charles stood and shook Reece's hand firmly, an action that sent a buzz of numbness rushing up his arm, making him wince and reminding him all of the problems from his accident that still remained.

The short-lived nerve reaction ticked off a bit of desperation, nearly making him tell Charles to sell to Keller now. Reece had to get back to Europe, had to get better and had to race again. It was the only life he knew or wanted.

But Charles was on his way out, and Reece took a breath, calming down. It would be okay. He'd healed faster than anyone thought he would, and he'd be on the track again before next summer. Still, the sooner he could conclude his business here, the better, he thought with a small pang of regret as he took one more glimpse of Abby before leaving the café.

2

THE NEXT DAY, ABBY was busy from the moment she woke up, barely able to keep up with everything she had to get done, even though it was a weekend. Weekends—Saturdays, anyway—were busier than weekdays for her, and today was no exception.

She'd waited all morning only to be stood up by an electrician who was supposed to show up during the week, but had rescheduled and then stood her up again. Some overhead lights kept flickering intermittently in the main room of the winery, and she needed it fixed yesterday.

Today they'd had three tastings and tours offered at ten o'clock, noon and two, and in between that she was fielding online orders, wedding prep and Christmas decorating that should have been done two weeks ago. The guests were fewer than they had been over the summer, or on holidays like Valentine's Day, when they did their wine-and-chocolate parties. Still, they'd had a respectable showing for each tour.

Right now she was in the middle of the last tasting, and while she was exhausted, her mind running in a million directions, she focused on smiling, explaining the type and origin of each wine and its story.

All of their wines had stories, background about how old the vines were, where they came from, who planted them and anything fun or anecdotal that happened while the wine was being made. It personalized the experience and made people aware that the wine they sipped wasn't just any generic wine, but a drink with a specific history, made by real people.

"This peppery Baco Noir," she said, finishing her presentation, "is called 'Just the Beginning' and it is one of our classic vintages. One summer night almost forty years ago, two lovers walked over the fields behind us, and the man asked the woman he was with to marry him. They didn't have enough money for rings, but he handed her a small plant, the beginning of the Baco vines from which these grapes still grow. Those people were my parents and, yes, eventually he did buy her a ring," Abby said warmly, smiling as she did every time she told the story.

A chorus of appreciative comments and chuckles about the ring followed. She discussed nuances, taught newcomers the basics of wine tasting and then moved to the desk where people purchased their wine and other goodies from the small gift display.

It was a good day, and she'd enjoyed her guests. By six, though, she was ready for bed. Her other employees were gone for the day, and they rarely had guests staying in their few upstairs rooms, used mostly for wedding parties in the winter. So, she closed up shop and thought of what needed to be done next.

She did need to get the trees decorated—three gor-

geous Fraser firs that graced the tasting room, the entry
to the winery and the first floor of the main house. Her
home, a private residence, was built off the central rooms
where they hosted tastings, receptions and sold their
wines. In the back of the property, above the vineyards,
were the animal barns and the building where they made
and stored the wines. Their specialty was Baco Noir.

The trees were set up, the lights were on, but they
needed ornaments, all of which had to be pulled out of
storage at the house and carried over. She also needed
to take care of her horses for the night.

They no longer had the petting zoo, unfortunately,
but Abby could never part with her horses. Riding them
along the lake was one of her favorite ways to relax.
Her parents had given her these two colts when she was
fifteen. As she headed down to the barn and looked out
over her land, the sight always took her breath away in
any season. Today, there'd been a light snow all day long,
and it was shining like diamonds in the moonlight.

This was hers. It was home. Like her parents, she'd
love to travel more, but she'd never really wanted to live
anywhere but here.

All of the stress and work that went with it was hers,
too. Lunch with Hannah yesterday had left her with a lot
of food for thought and a lot of worry for the future.

Inside the barn she was greeted by soft, muffled wel-
comes, and she grabbed feed buckets, hay and fresh
water and took care of business, which included much
brushing and stroking.

"Hey, babes," she crooned, feeling guilty that she
hadn't done more than put them out in the field that
day. "I promise tomorrow you'll both get some good

exercise. I'll get Hannah and we'll see you both early in the morning for a nice ride."

After long moments of petting warm muzzles and feeling more relaxed than she had when she walked in, she locked the doors and said good-night, turning back toward the house. Her gaze drifted down over the landscape to the Winston property. She noted some lights on in the house, although the winery was dark. Was Reece really going to sell?

She shivered, pulled her thick wool coat tighter around her and stared at the upstairs light. Reece? In his room? Was he there alone? She shivered for a different reason.

She'd been all fired up yesterday, having fun with Hannah, but she was crazy to think she could seduce Reece into...what? Not selling his land? No doubt he would think that was very funny; she was still out of his league, always had been.

But she *was* going to talk to him. She had no idea what she'd say to try to convince him to hold off, but if he didn't rush into a sale with Keller, maybe she could help find someone who would buy in with her. It was a huge gambit, but not impossible. Not entirely. She had money saved, and she'd have to mortgage her home to the hilt, but what other choice did she have?

She had to do whatever she could to protect her home and business. Keller would ruin the entire area.

The little hamlet that had sprouted up around the wineries a few miles up the lake from the city of Ithaca offered a coffee shop, a few quaint boutiques, a gas station and a convenience store, and all of her friends were here. Unlike Reece, who had gone away as far as he

could as soon as he was able, she'd gone to college locally, at Cornell, and she went down into the city a few
times a week. They sold many of their wines in local
stores, as well as all over the region.

She wished she could go inside, open a nice bottle of
wine, make some dinner and sit in front of the fireplace
in the living room, then finish decorating her trees without it feeling like work.

It would be even nicer to not have to do it alone.

Maybe she wouldn't have to. Biting her lip, she walked
faster toward the house and didn't think too much about
what she was contemplating. If she did, she'd lose her
nerve.

Entering the warmly lit kitchen that hadn't changed
too much since she'd grown up, she went carefully down
the cellar steps to the room where they kept their private
stock and grabbed a bottle she had been saving for a
special occasion.

Back upstairs, she pulled two glasses from the shelves
and a wedge of brie and a few other goodies from the
fridge.

The trees could wait. Her talk with Reece could
not.

If she didn't do it now, she'd could lose her chance as
well as her nerve. Setting aside her doubts and worries,
she started out walking across the land between their
homes, a windy half mile, her eyes focused on the lit
windows. The snow and moon illuminated everything,
making it easy to walk, and she covered the distance
quickly. As she neared the house, her eyes focused in
on a form in the upstairs window.

Her mouth went dry and she dropped the bottle of wine, which didn't break, thank goodness, but landed softly in the snow.

She picked it up again and walked closer. It was Reece. He hadn't pulled a shade or a curtain, thinking—rightly—that no one would be looking in his windows from the field side of the house.

He was nude. Completely. Stretching his arms up over his head, and then bending at the waist, she couldn't see everything, but she saw enough to make her heart slam against her rib cage as he did something that looked very much like yoga.

He was strong. Muscled, but graceful in his movements.

Gorgeous.

She forgot to move forward, entranced, but then as she realized where she was and what she was doing, she averted her eyes—though she couldn't erase what she'd seen. How could she? The strong line of his back, the muscles of his shoulders and arms were stunning. She could imagine running her hands over him and wondered what it would be like to have those slim, strong hips settling in between her legs....

"Oh, no," she said to herself, breathless with lust, her hands trembling as she almost dropped the wine again.

She hovered for a second on the porch. Reece was home, alone and naked, and she was standing here at his front door with a bottle of wine. Her courage flagged. Maybe she should talk to him another time, like during the light of day, or at a bar with a lot of other people around.

Don't be a coward, Abby, she scolded herself. She sucked in a deep breath and pressed the doorbell before she could change her mind.

REECE STEPPED GINGERLY out of the shower, wrapping a large towel around his waist, wincing from the pain in his left leg, where pins and needles shot back and forth along his thigh, causing weakness in his stance.

Each pinprick was like an individual jab, reminding him that he couldn't get in a race car again and do the thing that he loved most. Headaches had come back earlier that afternoon as well, and he'd spent most of the day on the sofa with an ice pack.

What if this never went away? What if they never signed off on letting him race again? At this point, doctors gave him a fifty-fifty shot, but he had to be one hundred percent, his reflexes perfect, completely reliable before he could race.

The betrayal of having his own body prevent him from doing what he loved most was utterly unacceptable. He'd gotten through the worst of it, and he'd defeat this, too. There was no alternative other than…what? Staying here?

Not an option.

Crossing the hall, he walked into the guest room and dried off. His mother had long ago, with his blessing, turned his old room into a place where she did her sewing and other crafts. He came home for holidays and a few short vacations but not often enough for his parents to have preserved his room. At the moment, he was glad they hadn't. He'd been feeling strangely sentimental about the old place, and that wasn't like him. He supposed it was because of the close call with his dad. Almost losing someone—as well as almost losing your own life—made you see things differently.

He loved his family, but this was just a house, he reminded himself. A building. One he couldn't get away from fast enough when he'd been a teenager looking for something more exciting.

He started going through the stretching routine that he'd been taught by his last physical therapist to relieve the pins and needles. Focusing on his breathing, his form, he drove away unwanted thoughts. The hot shower had helped loosen him up, but it still hurt like hell at first to push through the moves and hold them, though the symptoms lessened after a few repetitions.

He felt better as he relaxed, going through the rest of his exercises for good measure. He'd talked to his neurologist earlier in the day for the umpteenth time, and he had been reassured yet again that it was all normal.

Easy for him to say.

Reece turned to grab a pair of jeans when the ring of the doorbell caught him by surprise. Who would be here now?

Surely not Charles with someone to see the house. No one had called.

Pulling on his jeans and grabbing a shirt, he rushed down the stairs and pulled open the door, unable to believe his eyes.

"Abby?"

He took in her pink cheeks and tousled hair, and stepped back, inviting her in as the frosty air nipped at his bare toes.

"C'mon in. It's freezing out there," he said.

"Thanks, it is," she said, moving quickly. Her eyes flew to his chest. He hadn't had time to completely button his shirt.

"Oh, sorry…just got out of the shower."

Her cheeks turned even pinker and she didn't meet his eyes. He wondered why she was here holding wine, two glasses and some other foods.

Reece prompted her again. "What's all this?" he asked, looking down at the stuff she still held in her arms. One glass was tenuously dangling from her fingertips.

"Let me take that for you," he offered, and reached forward to take the flute. When his fingers caught with hers around the stem, her hand jerked away and they fumbled the glass, nearly dropping the fragile crystal.

Reece frowned. "Are you okay?"

She finally smiled. "Yes, I'm fine. Sorry to intrude on your evening, but I saw your lights on and felt like some company. You said you wanted to have a drink, so…" She shrugged, holding up the bottle. "Unless this is a bad time?"

He remembered saying something about having a drink when he'd seen her at the restaurant. This wasn't exactly what he meant, but maybe it was better.

He'd had a rough day, and having a bottle of wine with a pretty woman might be exactly what he needed.

"It's a perfect time, actually. I'm really glad you decided to stop by," he said, smiling and taking the rest of the things she was holding so that she could shuck her jacket. "You walked all the way over, in the dark?"

"It wasn't that dark, with the snow and the moon.

Very nice, actually," she said lightly, handing him her coat just as she met his eyes and a spark flared as his hand touched hers.

She shifted uncomfortably, looking away and turning pink again. Reece didn't remember her being so… wait.

She'd come across the field on the side of the house where the guest room was. Where he'd been doing his stretching, with the curtains open. With no clothes on. He never closed the drapes, since no one was likely to be lurking out in the fields

Silence hung at the end of her comment, and he had to smother a smile. She had to have seen him. Reece wasn't shy and had to resist the urge to tease her about it.

So Abby was bit of a voyeur? It didn't bother him. He'd be happy to let her look all she liked, he thought, his grin breaking loose as he turned away to hang her coat.

Maybe this evening would go even better than he thought.

"Grab that bottle and we can go put the food together in the kitchen, then sit by the fire," he said casually, though he wasn't feeling casual at all. All of his worries were pushed back by a surge of unexpected lust, and it felt great. He wanted to hold on to it, ride it and see where it took him.

"Oh, that would be nice," she said, walking with him to the kitchen. Dressed in jeans and a sweater that accentuated her curves, he leaned forward and pulled something from her hair. He could swear she sucked in a breath when he did, becoming perfectly still.

Hmm.

He presented a straw of hay to her with a smile. "Been down with your horses, I take it?"

She rolled her eyes and snatched the hay from his hand, but couldn't hold back a laugh, which made her even prettier. He'd always thought she was pretty, even as a little girl, but now…she was incredible. She always looked so natural and fresh, and he wondered what her skin tasted like.

"Yes, I was closing them up for the night when I saw your lights on my way back from the barn."

"Do you still have just the two? Buttercup and Beau?"

She paused, looking surprised that he remembered. He was a little surprised, too.

"Yes. Wow, you know their names," she said bluntly, taking the plate he handed her to open the brie so they could heat it up in the small toaster oven he pointed to.

"Why so surprising? We went to the same school, rode the same bus," he said. "Must've just stuck in my mind, I guess."

"Huh. I didn't think you knew I was alive unless you were poking at me about something," she said, and it was his turn to be a little surprised.

"I always liked you. I teased you, sure, but did you feel like I picked on you? Really?" A small frown creased his lips. He didn't like thinking he had hurt Abby's feelings or been mean to her.

Taking the food, they made their way to the main room and set the dishes down on the coffee table, placing a platter with green grapes, crackers and apples and the warmed brie between them. All perfect to go with the Baco, but Reece waited for her answer before moving to the fire.

She looked him in the eye and sighed lightly. "Well, you have to admit, aside from teasing me or pulling my hair, you didn't give me reason to think you knew I existed, let alone that you would remember details of my life."

"Hmm," he said thoughtfully, rubbing his chin slowly. "I remember some things very clearly," he said with a teasing wink.

"You can't even resist now, can you?" she said accusingly, but a smile twitched at her lips.

She remembered what happened between them that night at the lake as clearly as he did, he'd bet. And, no, he wasn't sure he could resist, or wanted to. But there was time. He backed away, letting it drop for now.

"Let me put a few more logs on the fire and we can eat. Suddenly I'm starving."

He was, though he wasn't sure the food on the plate was what he had a taste for, but it would have to be enough for the moment.

They spent the next two hours eating and talking in front of the crackling fire, when Abby suddenly looked around the room.

"You don't have a tree or any Christmas decorations up," she observed.

He shrugged. "There hasn't been any time, or much point, I guess. I'm the only one here, and Charles, the real estate agent, thought it was better to show the place without a lot of decorations. Let people imagine their own lives here and all that."

"Oh," she remarked, her expression turning serious. "That's kind of what I wanted to talk to you about," she said carefully.

"Christmas decorations?"

"No, that you're selling. I was hoping—"

Reece put a hand up. "Abby, I'd be happy to sit down and talk business with you at some point. But not right now, okay?"

"But—"

"It's been kind of a tough day. I'd really like to relax, catch up with an old friend," he said.

He geniunely didn't want to talk business with Abby. He knew she'd want to convince him not to sell, or something like that, and he didn't want to discuss that with her. It was a done deal, and that conversation was sure to put a damper on the heat building between them.

She bit her lip and looked reluctant, but nodded. "I can understand that," she said, looking down at her wine. "I know things must have been hard for you this year," she said vaguely, inviting him to say more, but he didn't want to talk about any of that, either. Maybe that wasn't fair, but he needed a night off from all of it.

"Yeah," he said, and changed the subject. "But how about you? You live in the house alone now?"

Nothing like discreet fishing before you tried to seduce an old friend, he thought. Hopefully there wasn't another guy in the picture, though looking at her, it was hard to believe they weren't lined up.

She shook her head, and his relief was immediate.

"Nope, just me now. Sarah retired, and Mom and

Dad are traveling all over the world. I still have a small part-time staff, of course, to help me get things done, but I handle most of it myself."

"They don't come home for the holidays? Your parents?"

"It would be difficult. They send gifts, and we video conference on the computer a lot. Last year they were in India, helping local people build a school. This winter, they've been helping down in Haiti."

"Really? I thought they were tourists now?"

"They mix their pleasure travel with activism. It's just their way, and they have always been more like explorers than tourists."

He nodded, smiling. "I remember."

"I know what they're doing is important, and I'm a big girl. We're busy enough through the holidays that being alone at Christmas gives me a quiet day or two to relax, read, sleep in, that kind of thing."

"Your parents were always so progressive," he said admiringly, but really he was thinking about Abby sleeping in, under the covers, warm and soft, curled up in something slinky with a book. Then he imagined taking the book out of her hands and slipping the lacy bit of nothing from her shoulder....

"Reece?" she said, and he realized he had gone blank, lost in his fantasy. "Are you okay?"

She seemed worried, and it bothered him. Of all the people he didn't want worrying if he was healthy and ready to go, she was first on the list at the moment.

"Sorry. You just made me remember that summer when your parents decided to try to add selling goat cheese to the winery business, and all of the goats got loose one weekend and ate some of my dad's vines," he lied, unable to look away from her face. Her eyes had landed on the scar behind his ear—the skin graft had healed, but it was visible. Did it bother her?

The definite sparkle of interest in her eyes said no, he assumed.

She laughed then, breaking the bond. "He was pretty nice about it, considering."

Her honey-brown hair was soft and slightly curled, pushed back in a haphazard way that made him want to reach out and weave his hands into it. She didn't wear makeup, which he found refreshing. She didn't need to. Her skin was flawless, her cheeks pink and kissable. And those lips…

"Did you ever wonder?" he heard himself ask.

Her cheeks turned rosy again, her lips parting slightly, as if she knew exactly where his mind had gone.

"Wonder what?"

He paused. They'd had a nice evening, two old friends talking over high school times and getting reacquainted. Did he really want to step into other waters? He was only back for a month or so, or however long it took to sell the winery. And the faster, the better. Abby wasn't one of his pit stops.

The women he knew in Europe were aware of his commitment-free lifestyle, his focus on his racing. They knew the score. They also had their own agendas, liking to be seen with a well-known driver, having their picture show up in the next day's entertainment news.

Abby had no agenda. She was just…Abby.

He still had to ask the question.

"What it might have been like if we didn't stop that night at the lake?" he said and noted the slight catch in her breath, but she didn't look away.

"Sure, I wondered," she said simply.

"I was about to ask you out, back then, when you took off," he admitted.

"You were?"

"Yeah. I wanted to know what it would be like to be with you, for real," he said. "I always liked you, Abby. A lot."

"Oh" was her only response, sounding slightly breathless. He took that as a good sign and plunged ahead.

"Still want to find out?" he said, in spite of every bit of better judgment he had.

Her eyes widened in surprise and she stood suddenly, setting down her wine, her movements fluttering and nervous.

"I should go. We're just tired. There's the fire and the wine, and it's easy to be caught up in old times, but really…I should go," she repeated, and walked to the door.

Reece shot up, moving after her.

"I'm sorry," he said, catching her arm, turning her to him. "I didn't mean to scare you off."

He wasn't sure if he was talking about eight years ago or two minutes ago. He was sure he didn't want her walking out the door.

They were close, and she looked up at him, her eyes somber.

"Listen, Reece, as much as I might be…curious, too, it wouldn't be a good idea—"

"You're curious?" His mind selectively honed in on

the one thing he wanted to hear and he stepped closer. "About me?"

She licked her lips nervously, making his cock jerk, semihard already, against the rough fabric of his jeans. In his hurry, he hadn't even pulled on briefs, so all that held him back was a bit of thin fabric.

"I—" She had started to say something, but he saw the pulse beating hard at the base of her throat, the desire in her eyes.

"What else are you curious about, Abby? I seem to remember you liked the excitement of being there, by the hedge, in public. Are you still up for that kind of adventure?"

He remembered how aroused she had been, and it had been just as hot for him, too. Did she still want that?

Reece liked risk, too. Hell, it defined him. He also had fantasies that not all of his lovers had satisfied.

What kind of sex was Abby into? He knew about her fondness for public places. Bondage, maybe? Something more creative? Role-play, perhaps?

He wanted to find out, imagining Abby tied to his bed or dressed in black leather. What if she wanted him tied up?

He could probably live with that. He was open to anything short of real pain or multiple partners—Reece wasn't sharing Abby with anyone.

"Let's just see, Abby, what it could be like between us," he said, needing to know and pulling her to him, his hands traveling up her back and into her hair, as he'd thought about.

It was like silk. He wanted to feel it trailing over his stomach and his thighs, her mouth on him.

The thought made his kiss less introductory, less tentative, than it might have been otherwise. He took her soft lips and opened her wider, invading and rubbing his tongue against hers with a deep moan. She felt so right, like she had before, but better, the flames leaping between them.

Her arms went around his neck, and she rubbed back with her tongue, her lips and the rest of her body as she strained against him.

Green flag, he thought, but resisted accelerating, instead maintaining the steady heat of the kiss, learning her taste, her touch, until neither of them could take it any longer.

When her hands started undoing the buttons on his shirt, he walked her back against the wall by the window, pressing his hardness against her, moving his hands up to cover her breasts. She was firm and soft in his palms, the nipples budding hard.

Touching wasn't enough, he needed to taste.

Moving his hands up under her sweater, he set the flimsy lace of her bra aside and bent to take one tight, beaded nipple in his mouth. He drew on it hard, murmuring encouragingly as she arched away from the wall, her hand at the back of his head, keeping him there.

He replaced his lips with his fingers, rolling the warm buds between his thumb and forefinger as he kissed her again, wanting to be everywhere at once.

He stood back, staring down into her flushed face, her passion-drenched eyes, raising a finger to touch lips that now looked like crushed cherries.

"Abby, I want you, but…" He let the question hang. He wanted her, but he'd back off now if she wanted him to, no matter what.

"Yes, please," she said, her breathing short and hard.

She was incredibly sweet. He planned to take his time with her, he thought, and pressed her back, sliding a thigh between her legs, pinning her to the wall. He wanted to make her come as many times as he could before he got inside her, because once he was, he knew he wouldn't last long. Not this first time.

He took her lips again and massaged those pretty breasts with both hands, moving against her until she was whimpering and grinding against him. Without warning, she arched, coming hard, moaning into his mouth as she rode it out. And he didn't even get her clothes off yet, he thought with raw hunger, wanting more.

He pulled back, taking in her bemused expression, the surprised satisfaction he saw there making him swell harder.

He thought she might be shy, embarrassed, but she linked her arms around his neck and leaned in, nipping at his lower lip.

"More" was all she said as she looked him in the eye.

"Oh, honey," he choked out. "There's plenty more."

Swinging her up into his arms, he turned to take her back to the fireplace, planning to dim the lights and strip that sweater off in the warm glow of the flames, when he stopped, his gaze drawn out the window.

He stared, uncertain what had caught his eye, but a bad feeling overcame him and he let Abby slide to her feet. He walked closer to the window that looked out over the field.

"Reece? What is it?"

Sirens screamed in the distance, and the glow in the air over the field that had attracted his attention was not a figment of his imagination.

Her winery was on fire.

3

ABBY RESTED HER HEAD against Buttercup's soft neck and just thanked the heavens that the barns hadn't caught fire, too. That was something she couldn't even bear to think about.

Her house was badly damaged, unlivable after water from the hoses had ruined what fire had not, but the main rooms of the winery were reduced to cinders. The horse seemed to nuzzle her in comfort as she tried to hold her tears back, but couldn't, sobs racking her body.

What now?

The flickering light that she'd been trying to have fixed ended up being wires that the fire investigator said were probably chewed through by a mouse or squirrel in the wall. When the tree lights had been plugged in, she hadn't thought twice about it, but the circuit had been overloaded and started the fire. It had spread inside the walls before consuming the entire winery.

If she'd been home, she might have been killed if she had been sleeping or overcome with smoke, although she had detectors everywhere. On the other hand, if she had been there, she might have been able to call the fire department sooner, and maybe it wouldn't have been so bad, such a complete loss.

Instead, she'd been at Reece's, in his arms, ready to say yes to anything he asked, while her family's legacy burned to the ground.

She had to get away from the swarm of people. The firemen were still keeping watch, even though the fire was officially out, the insurance and other investigators were there, along with some neighbors, friends…and Reece. Everyone wanted to help, but she'd insisted on being alone for just a few minutes.

She needed the peace to think about what she would say to her parents, how she could tell them what happened.

Guilt assailed her. How could she explain why she hadn't been there? That she'd been so busy, and so distracted by thoughts of Reece, that she hadn't thought twice about the tree lights or the electrical problem?

She groaned, standing straight, wiping the tears away. No time for this now.

She had to get the insurance settled and cancel the wedding they'd been planning—that would be another tough phone call. The couple wouldn't likely find another venue with only weeks until the wedding, but there wasn't anything she could do about that. Abby would have to refund their deposits. That was going to hurt.

She'd see if Hannah would let her move in for a while, though it would mean driving back and forth to Ithaca daily, or maybe her insurance would pick up a room at the local inn, for a while at least.

"I thought you might be down here," a familiar voice said behind her.

"Hannah," she said, trying to sound normal, but her voice cracked under the weight of her exhaustion, being up all night, dealing with it all.

Hannah was across the barn, holding her arms out and Abby didn't hesitate.

She held on to her friend, just for a minute, but it was Reece's arms she knew she'd been seeking. Remembering how good it had been, not just the sexual part, but the way he'd held her against his hard chest later, when they'd watched the firemen work, had kept her from losing it altogether. She wanted that comfort back.

No, no, no. That was how she'd gotten into this mess, sort of.

"You okay?" Hannah asked, stepping back and smiling as two of the barn cats wound their way around her ankles.

"Yeah. I'm just so thankful the barns are far away from the house," she said, stroking Beau's silky nose. All of the animals were okay.

"That is a good thing," Hannah agreed, chuckling softly as Buttercup snorted happily in response to more scratching. "Everything else can be replaced. It was a straightforward electrical fire. The insurance agent is already on it. Things can be rebuilt."

"True, but I don't know if that will be enough," Abby said, too discouraged to be optimistic. "They can't start rebuilding until after winter, which means we're not only losing the Christmas events, but the spring wedding season and tastings as well. We lost almost all of the Riesling casks. With Reece selling, this could just be a killer blow," Abby said tightly, her throat constricting at the thought.

"How am I going to tell Mom and Dad? I feel so much like I've let them down," Abby said, sucking in more tears.

Hannah knew just what to do to drive the tears away.

"Speaking of Reece...he seemed awfully involved in helping you last night. And I couldn't help but notice when we went inside that at first his shirt wasn't buttoned up quite right. You know, like it had been put back together in a rush," she said, with mischief in her tone that made Abby's tears completely evaporate.

Abby groaned. Did everyone know where she'd been and what she was doing?

As if reading her mind, Hannah added, "He said he saw the fire from his house, got dressed and rushed down to help. Don't worry—he didn't give anything away, though I sure hope you're going to share details with your very best friend in the whole wide world, right? You know, about why Reece was really getting dressed?"

Unbelievably, Abby had to laugh. Leave it to Hannah, even in the middle of utter loss. When all Abby had left was this barn and what was in it, her friend found a way to lighten the mood.

Reece had been wonderful. He hadn't left her side until Hannah had arrived. He jumped in, talking to the firemen, police and the other people milling around, even opening up the main room of his winery for people to come in, get warm and have coffee. At some moment when she'd been talking to the fire investigator, Abby had lost track of him and assumed he had gone back home.

"Thanks, I needed that," she said, taking a breath and feeling a bit better. "And there aren't many details to share. Not really. I went down to Reece's, brought some wine, hoping to talk...one thing lead to another, but before it went too far, he noticed the fire. That was pretty much it," she said, shrugging.

"Oh, I doubt that's it. The man's interested—he couldn't take his eyes off you, especially when that hunky fireman was talking to you, and standing a little too close, by the way," Hannah said.

"You're imagining things. Reece was just helping out. We're old friends and we shared a moment—instigated by a bottle of wine. It's best forgotten. I have enough to worry about now." Abby's attention snapped to the barn doors, where outside, she heard a woman's voice, and then sharp, shrieking words. She couldn't make out what was being said, but several colorful curses punctuated the diatribe.

Abby headed out of the barn to find Sandra Towers, the Christmas bride-to-be, standing in the middle of the yard in front of the blackened mess of Abby's winery, wild-eyed and in tears. She spotted Abby then and marched across the lawn, obviously ready for a confrontation.

Great, just what she needed right now. Abby sighed. She shouldn't bothered with having quiet time in the barn. She should have been on the phone doing damage control.

Too late, she admitted, as Sandra met her, almost standing nose-to-nose, and Abby backed up slightly.

"Sandra, I am so sorry. I was about to make phone calls—"

"I saw this on the news and couldn't believe it. I had to see for myself. This is a nightmare! How could you let this happen?" the prospective bride yelled, clearly not thinking straight.

Abby tried to be patient. This was hard on everyone, and brides were under a lot of stress in general. Sandra wasn't finished, obviously.

"What am I going to do? The invitations are all sent! Everything is scheduled! How are you going to fix this?" she demanded, and Abby pulled in a deep breath, closing her eyes, reaching for patience.

"Sandra, I know it's terrible, and I wish there was better news, but I'll definitely refund all of your down payment and try to help you find another—"

"The wedding is twenty-five days away! There is *no* other place," the young woman wailed. "I know, I checked them all. We have family coming in from Europe! You had better fix this or...or...we'll *sue!*"

Abby was quite sure the normally pleasant woman was just distraught, and also was sure—mostly—that she had no basis for a lawsuit whatsoever. Still, it was hard to remain calm, and she was digging her nails into her palms in her effort to do so.

Suddenly, Reece appeared, putting his large hand on her shoulder. She looked up in surprise, noting the circles under his eyes. He was obviously exhausted, too.

"Abby, could I talk to you for a minute?" he said politely. "Excuse us for just a moment," he said to Sandra with a smile. Amazingly, the young woman didn't pitch yet another fit.

Abby walked with him to a spot about twenty feet away and wondered how she could still feel his touch when she was wearing her coat and he had put on a pair of heavy gloves. Maybe the same way she'd had a scream-worthy orgasm against his thigh—apparently clothes were not a barrier to sex with Reece Winston.

"First things first," he said, dragging her away from her thoughts and producing a steaming travel cup to her. She could smell the aroma of the hot coffee inside. She took the cup, took a sip and peered at him over the top, thanking him with a look of bliss.

"I came out to bring you that and heard the shouting. I guess you had a wedding planned soon?"

She groaned and nodded. "Two days before Christmas."

"And that is the blushing bride," he stated more than asked.

"Yes." Abby sighed. "I don't blame her for being upset, but I didn't expect her to come out here and go nuts.... Still, I can imagine it's a mess for her, too."

Reece nodded. "She's obviously missing the point that you lost a lot more than she did last night," he said in a hard tone, peering over to where Sandra stood, arms crossed, watching them.

Abby didn't say anything, but took another sip of the strong coffee so the heat would scorch away the tightening in her throat. He was sticking up for her again, just like he did when the mean boy had picked on her about her braces.

"Thanks, but I have to find some way to compensate

her. Now is as good a time as any. Then I have to find out what our exact losses are and call my parents. That is going to be so awful..." she said, and didn't dare meet his eyes, lest his sympathy weaken her resolve not to cry again.

Normally Abby never cried, not even during sappy movies, but she was overwrought and exhausted. Right now, she needed to concentrate on business.

"I have an idea," Reece said.

"If we try to lock her in the barn, I don't think anyone will believe that she's a runaway bride," Abby tried to joke, but it fell flat.

Reece smiled slightly. He tipped her chin up with his fingers, making her meet his eyes, which were sympathetic, but not in a bad way. In a silvery, soft way that made her remember his kiss.

"What?" she asked, almost panicked that amid everything, she could still lust for Reece.

"Use Winston wineries for the wedding, and for any other events you have this month. You can move your wines down to our room, and we'll feature both vineyards, if you don't mind—yours and ours. I need to clear out inventory before we sell, so it could work out for all of us."

Abby stared. Had he just offered for her to use his winery?

"But...you're selling," she said blankly. What if the place sold quickly? She'd only become reacquainted with Reece two days ago—could she trust him? She couldn't make promises that she'd break again later on.

"Don't worry about that. I can work it out so that whoever buys us, they don't close until after the wedding, at least. If it takes longer, we can figure it out as we go, but in the meanwhile, you're welcome to run your business out of our front rooms."

Abby was stunned and unsure what to say, but she couldn't think of one good reason to say no, except what had happened between them the night before. What had *almost* happened. If she and Reece were going into business together, even temporarily, she couldn't let that happen again.

"I don't know what to say…it's so generous of you," she admitted. "It would save me so much, not having to refund the deposit on this wedding. And all you want me to do is sell your wines, too?"

That wouldn't be hard; the Winstons made spectacular wines, and she had lost several barrels in the fire, so this could be the perfect solution.

As long as they could keep their hands—and wonderful, muscular thighs—to themselves, she thought silently.

"I thought you said your Realtor wanted you keeping the property empty, neutral? I'd have to decorate, and there would be people around all the time…."

Reece didn't look concerned. "I know. I'm sure he can work around it. The place is just sitting there. I already sent the staff home and was going to run the main room myself for a few weeks, but you obviously could use it."

Her heart lightened as she considered, and she felt hopeful for the first time all morning. This could save her, in more ways than one.

"We'd have to, um, keep things strictly business, though," she said, hoping he got her drift.

This would also give her the perfect opportunity to talk with Reece about selling. Maybe she could convince him there was a better way…and give her time to figure out what that was.

"Whatever you want, Abby. I'm just a friend, trying to help. No strings attached," he said, though she could tell from the heat in his eyes that he was remembering the night before, too.

Could *she* keep things "strictly business" with Reece?

"I guess I could ask Sandra," she said, though she couldn't imagine it wouldn't be an acceptable option. Winston wineries was far fancier than Abby's reception room, and with the same beautiful views.

"I could try booking rooms for the wedding party at Tandy's Inn, and I'll need one, too," she added, thinking out loud.

"We have some rooms upstairs. Mom used them more for guests, but they would work for your wedding party to dress or spend the night. You should stay at the house. You're more than welcome."

"I don't think that's a good idea," she said. "I mean, I don't want to intrude. You're being kind enough as it is."

He looked at her as if she was talking nonsense. "It's a big house, Abby, and you'd be near your barns and the winery. There's no reason to pay for a room when we have six empty ones upstairs in the house."

Abby chewed her lip, feeling like she was jumping into the frying pan after the fire, but her house wouldn't be habitable for quite some time. Staying at Tandy's, even though it was right there in the village, wouldn't be as convenient as being at Reece's.

Or as tempting.

Steeling her resolve, she nodded. *Put on your big girl panties and do this, Abby,* she mentally nudged herself. *Just be sure you keep them on.*

Ha. Like panties would matter.

"What?" he said.

She coughed, realizing she might have said that under her breath.

"Uh, nothing." She looked up at Reece. Surely last night was a fluke, the result of wine and reminiscing. They could do this. "Thank you, Reece. You have no idea what this means to me."

"It's my pleasure, Abby. Just let me know anything you need," he said.

His pleasure? Anything she needed? Ohmygod, this was a bad idea.

With another squeeze to her arm before he turned away, he walked back toward his house. Where she would be sleeping tonight.

But not with him.

Abby groaned as she went to talk to Sandra. Hannah was absolutely going to love this.

REECE STOPPED AND looked back, watched Abby walk away, her stride lighter than before. That made him feel better, too, that there was something he could do to help.

She chatted with the young woman whom he had heard yelling at the top of her spoiled, self-interested lungs when he had arrived with coffee. The two women chatted a few seconds, and the bride threw her arms around Abby. Apparently his solution worked for her.

He nodded in satisfaction, strolling the rest of the way to his place. This path over the field would get a lot of wear back and forth over the next month, he thought.

Surprisingly, suddenly, he was looking forward to Abby's company in the big house. Normally being alone didn't bother him. In fact, he preferred it, but this could work.

He hoped.

He might be losing his mind, actually, but what was done was done. It hadn't even occurred to him until he'd heard the woman yelling about suing Abby, and he'd taken in the exhaustion that bruised the pale skin under her eyes and the strain that pinched at her as she tried to maintain her composure.

How could he not offer her the use of the winery? It's what any decent neighbor, and old family friend, would do.

Right?

Right. It really wasn't an excuse to spend more time with Abby while he was here, or to hopefully have her in his bed, even though she warned him they wouldn't be mixing business with pleasure.

He hoped to change her mind on that score. Soon.

He'd have to call Charles, who wasn't going to be happy, not at all, but Reece knew his parents would agree—this was the neighborly thing to do.

Especially when his neighbor was as sexy as Abby, with lips like satin and a body that moved against his like she was made for him.

As much as he meant his promise of a no-strings arrangement, he knew she wanted him, too. He could feel it every time he touched her.

And he planned to touch her. A lot.

His cell phone started ringing as soon as he got through the door, and he saw it was his brother, Ben. Immediately concerned that something was wrong with his father, fantasies about Abby disintegrated and Reece answered the call, tense.

"Ben, what's wrong?"

"Whoa, brother, calm down. Everything's fine—but you sound upset. What's going on?" he asked sharply.

Ben had fallen in love with the game of golf when he was a kid, though he was never more than an average player. But he never gave up on his dream of being involved in the sport, and landed a graduate degree in landscape architecture, with a specialization in designing golf courses. He's spent years working with some of the best designers, building his name, and finally accumulated the backing to open his own course, his own design. Then he met his wife, Kelly, and they had two beautiful kids now. Ben had a stable, solid life.

Reece, unlike Ben, had lived a more precarious, adventure-driven existence. He'd finished college, but the business admin degree was something he'd pursued because he didn't really know what else he was going to do with his life. Reece had always bragged that he liked not knowing what was around the next corner. He never stopped moving, until recently.

"Sorry. I guess I just assumed something was wrong with Dad," Reece said.

When had his love of adventure turned into him expecting a disaster every time the phone rang? Was this part of the post-traumatic stress disorder that his neurologist had warned about—and that Reece had dismissed—that was often the result of serious car crashes?

"He's fine. Mom, too. But they're worried about you, up there, alone, especially for the holidays. I offered to come up. I can book a flight today if you want some help getting things done there, arranging the sale, the move, whatever. We could have some serious brother time," Ben said. "Go ice fishing or something."

Reece smiled. "That would be great, but I don't want to take you away from Kelly and the kids so close to the holidays. I'm good, and in fact, things have taken an interesting turn," he said, going on to explain about the fire and offering use of the winery to Abby.

Ben whistled. "Wow. Never boring for you, is it?"

Reece laughed. "Yeah, you could say that. Could you fill in Mom and Dad? I assumed they wouldn't mind."

"I'm sure they'll be fine with it. More than fine even," Ben said and Reece closed his eyes, hearing the grin in his brother's voice.

"Don't start, Ben, and don't make them think this is anything other than what it is."

"They'd just love for you to move back, whether it's to run the winery or not. And I saw Abby when we were there for Christmas last year. She filled out nice, huh?"

Reece's hackles raised, hearing his brother's frankly admiring tone. But he wasn't surprised. A man would have to be gay or dead not to notice Abby.

"Yeah, but it's not like that."

Yes, it was.

"Really? I know you, Reece. And I know you've had a thing for her ever since you were about six years old."

"How could you know that? You were only four," Reece said with a scoff.

"Yeah, well, I remember all the years after that, too. I never could figure out why you just didn't ask her out. Hell, I almost did, just to make you jealous," Ben said, laughing at his brother's expense.

And it might have worked, Reece acknowledged. But that was then. They were only kids.

And he wasn't Ben. Reece didn't do permanent with anything, not when the real love of his life was getting behind the wheel of a car and driving two hundred miles an hour for a living. He'd seen too many racers leave families behind, after they had sacrificed everything to the sport, including their lives.

"Ben, seriously, please make sure it's okay with them. I'm still planning to sell and to move back to France. I want to race again. It's all I want."

Except for Abby.

He shook his head of the thought. Sure, he *wanted* her—in his bed—but his life was still on the track, on the other side of the Atlantic.

Ben's disappointment was carefully veiled behind a general remark, but he agreed to what Reece asked. After some more discussion about the winery and its future, Reece put the phone back on the mahogany table by the window. Right there, the night before, he'd pressed Abby up against the wall with every intention of making her his.

For the night.

He still planned to do that—for a week, or a month— and he'd make sure she knew that up front, too. She'd use Winston to get through the holiday and the wedding, and they'd share some good times to make up for what they missed back in high school—or not, if Abby stuck to her guns about business only—then they would both go on with their lives. It was that simple.

Reece ignored the mocking laugh in his head as he went upstairs to get a room set up for Abby.

4

TWO DAYS LATER, Abby drove up the lake road, returning from a day of shopping. The sun hung low on the horizon, and she figured she had about an hour of dusky daylight left. Even with the shorter days, the snow helped keep things brighter longer. She turned into her driveway out of habit, forgetting that she meant to go to Reece's and unload her goods, but since she was here, figured she could check in on the horses. When she spotted the barn doors open, she froze.

Though they weren't susceptible to much crime, and though she was just across the field, she'd been worried about her horses. She'd barely had time to take care of Beau and Buttercup, having had to break her promise of a long ride and settle for leaving them out in the pasture.

But that door shouldn't be open. She knew for a fact that she'd locked it when she left that morning.

The stale scent of smoke from the fire still clung faintly to the crisp winter air as she hopped out of the car and made her way down to the barn. Slowly opening the door, she peered inside and saw no one but Shadow, their black lab, who came bounding to greet her, and Buttercup. But no Beau. The door to his stall was wide open, though it appeared undamaged.

Abby's heart fell to her feet and she stepped inside, instantly noting that Beau's tack was gone as well.

Frowning, she pulled out her cell phone.

"Hannah? Are you riding Beau?" she asked as soon as her friend picked up, though usually Hannah would let Abby know if she was coming by. Also, Hannah typically rode Buttercup, who was somewhat smaller.

"Uh, no, why would you ask?"

Abby put a hand to her forehead, closing her eyes to stave off panic, and walked back out the door to breathe in the cold air and calm down.

"Beau's not here, neither is his tack, and I've been gone all day—"

She stopped midsentence as she caught sight of a figure getting closer, down by the edge of the field. Hannah was upset, too, and told her to hang up and call the police, but a few moments later, Abby saw with a wash of relief that that wouldn't be necessary.

"It's Reece. Reece has him," she said into the phone, and then hung up as the rider and the horse came closer.

Abby had never seen Reece on horseback. She didn't even know he could ride. His family always had dogs, but never horses.

"Reece!" she called, waving, and he waved back, heading toward her.

He looked like every cowboy fantasy she'd ever had, sitting tall on Beau, his camel-colored coat and hat contrasting with the steed's dark chestnut coloring as they approached her. Beau whinnied in welcome, and Abby was so relieved he was okay she realized she was shaking.

"Hey, are you all right? What's wrong?" Reece asked as he came up next to her.

"I—I saw the door open and Beau gone… I didn't know where he was. I thought maybe someone stole him. The police told me to be careful about people poking around here, which I guess some people do when they find out about burned buildings.…" She trailed off, petting the horse's soft cheek with a sigh of relief.

"Ah, damn, Abby. Sorry about that. You left the barn keys on the counter, and I was feeling antsy. I knew you hadn't had any time to get them out for a ride, so I figured I'd do it for you," he said, clearly apologetic.

"That's so good of you, Reece. I guess I didn't think of you because I didn't even know you rode," she admitted.

"I learned in France. Haven't had the chance to ride in a while, but it felt good."

"Did you ride both of them?"

"No, I figured I'd give them both a short turn around the field, so I was just coming back for Buttercup."

Abby nodded. "Let me grab a saddle and I'll join you, if you don't mind. They can have a longer ride that way, and I could use some fresh air, too."

"Sure, that would be great," he agreed, and a little while later Abby was on Buttercup, riding alongside Reece on the lake path, more relaxed than she had been in days.

"I needed this. I'm glad you had the idea to take them

out," she said. "I feel so guilty when I can't tend to them like I always did, but it seems like the winery takes over my life sometimes."

"I hear you. I thought I would like to get some pets at home in France, but I don't want to kennel them or pay pet-sitters when I'm away, which is usually a lot."

The easy companionship between them seemed enhanced by the quiet of the trail and the rhythmic gait of the horses.

"You have a house there?" she asked.

"Yes, outside of the Talence, near the Bordeaux region. There's a lot of industry there, as well as wine and some universities. I found a house outside of the town that allowed me to go into the city if I wanted to, but to retreat when I needed to, as well. It's an older house, and I have been fixing it up slowly, when I have the opportunity."

"Bordeaux? So you left wine country to live in wine country?" she said with a soft laugh, so he knew she wasn't criticizing.

"I guess so. I did intend to study wines when I went there, and then I discovered racing."

"Funny how you had to go that far to find it, when we've lived with the Glen under our noses all our lives."

"I know. But we never really went to the races when we were kids. Ben and Dad spent more time playing golf, which I never took to. I went to a few races at the Glen, but at that point in time I was more interested in making out with whatever girl I met there instead of watching the race," he said with a self-effacing grin.

She laughed. "That's changed?"

"Mostly. I rarely date in season. I can't afford the distraction, not that there aren't plenty of offers."

"You're modest, too," she teased.

"Hey, it's true. Groupies follow racing just like any sport, and some of the guys take advantage, but it's never been my thing."

"So you don't date?"

"Not in season, not really," he said, and she considered that, leaving the subject alone for a while. She hadn't intended to turn her questions into a fishing expedition about his love life.

So he wasn't saying he didn't see women, he just didn't see them while he was driving. She guessed that made sense. She never assumed he was a saint.

"How about you?" he asked.

"What?"

"You date much?"

"Now and then, nothing serious. I've been so busy with the business since Mom and Dad left. It takes up all of my time, really."

"Lucky for me," he said, almost under his breath, and Abby blinked and shot him a look, unsure she had actually heard that. She decided not to ask for clarification, and they stopped talking for a while, making their way back up the far end of the trail, and across the fields to the barns.

"I'll get the door," she said, dismounting easily and making her way over to pull the doors open.

It was darker by the time they returned, and in the soft, golden light that spilled out of the barn, he looked even more handsome, she thought. He smiled, but there was something tight about it. He didn't dismount, and Abby wondered what the problem was.

"Are you okay?" she asked, unsure what to make of his sudden silence. Beau shifted and snorted, dancing under Reece, eager to be brushed and fed now that he'd worked off some energy.

"Yeah, I'm fine," Reece almost growled between clenched teeth, and in the next second, he swung his leg over to the ground. Abby was horrified to see that as he landed, his leg gave way and his other foot never quite made it out of the stirrup, making Beau jump sideways nervously.

"Reece, oh, no," she breathed, steadying Beau and making her way over to help him up so that he could get his foot out of the stirrup to regain his balance.

"Are you okay?" she said, looking down and stepping carefully. There was no ice.

Reece was on his feet now, his expression reflecting stifled pain, and he walked forward, taking Beau's reins as he limped into the barn without a word.

Abby frowned, following. "Reece? Are you okay?"

He paused, his posture stiff. "I'm fine, Abby. My leg just fell asleep."

"Oh. I thought it might be the injury from your accident," she said, knowing that now she *was* fishing. He knew it, too.

He rested his forehead on his hand, where it lay on Beau's back, as if he was looking for patience, or a way to escape.

Finally, he straightened and looked at her again. "It

is. It's not serious. I kept my leg in the same position for too long and it went numb. No big deal."

"It could have been a big deal if you couldn't get back up or if Beau had taken off in a panic or trampled you," she said. "Does this happen often?"

"I don't need the third degree, Abby. I just should have been more careful dismounting. Can we leave it? Okay?"

"I'm concerned," she said, refusing to feel guilty. If that had happened when he was alone, he could have been badly hurt.

"I know," he said, sounding tired. "But it's fine."

She didn't think so, but she bit back any more comments. The easy mood they'd had all evening was now replaced with tension, and she nodded, grabbing a brush and getting Buttercup set for the night.

Reece didn't say anything more, and he was still limping, if a little less severely, as he put Beau away and left, walking back to the house without another word. She would have offered to drive him, since she had to take her car back anyway, but somehow she didn't think that would help.

Obviously falling from the horse hadn't only reminded him of his injuries, it had probably dented his ego to fall in front of her. Silly, but she knew men were like that sometimes.

"I guess I stepped in it," she said to Buttercup, petting the mare's sleek coat. The horses looked at her with calm patience, and Beau snorted again.

Abby smirked at him. "Oh, sure, take his side," she said affectionately to the animal, locking the barn and making her way back to the house, as well.

THE FOLLOWING AFTERNOON, ABBY had done little more than run back and forth to Ithaca and Syracuse, dealing with insurance issues and setting up contractors. Today, she'd caught up on more personal needs, purchasing a stash of clothing to replace some basics that were ruined in the fire, taking what she could salvage to the cleaners and loading up some food for Reece's kitchen.

He hadn't really stocked the kitchen, probably because he didn't think he'd be there long, and he would probably eat out, she figured. But Abby liked to cook and she liked to eat, so food was a necessity. She also needed supplies for tastings—crackers, chocolates and cheeses. She wanted to make up for her snafu the evening before, when Reece fell. She couldn't blame him for being embarrassed, and she had been too nosy.

She planned to make him a nice dinner—it was the least she could do, given his generosity. Visiting markets in the city to find the ingredients she needed had been the first fun she'd had in days.

She'd also taken time to walk around a bit, enjoying the atmosphere and having a moment to herself. Ithaca was such a lovely little city, a neat combination of funky college town with an active arts community and working-class neighborhoods.

Set at the southern edge of Cayuga Lake, Ithaca hosted two colleges, including the famous Cornell University, her alma mater. The city also had more eateries per capita than New York City. It was surrounded by beautiful hillsides, vineyards, gorges and waterfalls, and the town had a wonderful underground mall by the Commons, the famous Moosewood restaurant and the farmer's market, where she shopped every week. She loved what every season had to offer, and the place was as woven into who she was as much as anything else in her life.

How could Reece have wanted to leave so badly? She had everything she needed here, and though everyone enjoyed a vacation away, Abby always liked coming home.

Her worries about staying at his home had been groundless—she'd been gone so much, usually working, and apparently he was busy doing things, too, so they'd barely seen each other long enough to say good morning since the horse-riding incident.

She had to walk past his room, trying not to notice the light on under the door, and continue down the hall to a large guest bedroom that looked out over the lake. The guest room was twice the size of her own bedroom in her house, and she loved the view of the lake, facing the opposite direction of her burnt buildings. She appreciated Reece being so thoughtful as to spare her the reminder.

Still, even with the beautiful view and the big bed, she hadn't slept great since the fire. It was hard to not think about everything looming over her, and she hadn't been able to contact her parents yet, which was weighing on her. Then there was the itching desire for Reece, the need to touch him, to be close to him, that she couldn't quite stop fantasizing about.

She finally finished putting everything away and left out only what she needed for dinner—a lovely pork roast, vegetables and potatoes, the perfect comfort meal for a winter evening.

She planned to make some appetizers as well, and of course, open some wine.

She paused as she started the roast—would Reece take this the wrong way? She merely wanted to do her part, to thank him for his help and to feel at home as much as she could. As much as she was tempted to give in to her fantasies, doing so would only make everything so much more complicated, and right now the last thing she needed was more complication in her life.

On second thought, maybe she shouldn't open any wine.

The phone on the wall next to her rang, and without thinking she picked it up.

"Hello?"

"Um, hello?" a heavily accented woman's voice responded, obviously confused. "I am looking for Reece?"

"He's not home. May I take a message?" Abby asked, reaching for a pen.

A heavy sigh met her request. "And who is this?" the woman asked, her "this" sounding more like "theese."

None of your bees-niss, Abby felt like saying, feeling annoyed. "I'm a friend of Reece's. May I take a message?"

"A friend, eh? You may tell him Danielle called," she said, a bit huffily, Abby thought. Maybe it was the accent.

"Danielle…last name?"

"He will know," she said with an aggravatingly sexy laugh.

"Sure."

"Be sure he receives the message, please."

"Of course," Abby said. "Goodbye."

She set the phone down, wondering why she felt so peevish. It was obviously just a friend of Reece's from Europe calling. Abby sighed, shaking it off.

She bet that Reece had *lots* of friends with sexy accents back in France. Plopping the roast into the Dutch oven a little more forcefully than she planned, she splashed stock on her shirt and shook her head.

Ridiculous to be this put out by the idea of Reece with other women. Sexier, more sophisticated, French women.

Well, she couldn't compete and didn't want to, she decided, tying on an apron to avoid further damage. Putting the woman and her snooty accent out of her mind, she turned on the radio and focused on cutting vegetables and making her appetizers.

She quickly worked her way out of her snit and was shimmying across the kitchen, singing at the top of her lungs to Mariah Carey's version of "All I Want For Christmas Is You." She was on her way to put the tray of cheese and fruit in the refrigerator, but nearly dropped it all when she met Reece's amused expression as he stood, propped in the doorway, grinning from ear to ear.

"Reece!" she said, fumbling and blushing to the roots of her hair. "How long have you been standing there?"

He pursed his lips thoughtfully. "Mmm…about from the first chorus," he said lightly, still smiling.

"Oh, God," she said, covering her face, shaking with embarrassed laughter.

"I have to admit, the apron adds a certain panache to your performance," he teased.

She looked down at the sexy apron she wore, a

Cheetah print with red ruffles and a bow at the neckline. Hannah had bought it for her birthday as a funny gift, and it had never been worn, especially since an embroidered patch on the pocket read Hot Stuff.

As if this wasn't embarrassing enough.

It was one of the few items from the kitchen pantry that didn't get ruined. She hadn't thought twice when she'd donned it, unused to an audience while cooking.

"It was a gag gift," she explained. "From Hannah."

Reece scanned her up and down appreciatively and walked over to where she stood.

"What smells so good?"

"I thought I would make us dinner, as a thank-you... and also because I like to cook. It destressed me," she said, trying to keep her voice level as he ran a finger over the edge of the bow, the tip of his finger brushing against her skin at the edge of her shirt.

"That's nice of you. I haven't had a home-cooked dinner in a while," he said sincerely, but there was a glint in his eye.

"This is every man's fantasy, you know," he said, tugging at the bow to pull her forward against him. "A sexy woman in the kitchen making him dinner after a long day."

She rolled her eyes. "Puh-leese. I can't imagine you ever having a fantasy that mundane," she said, and then shook her head.

Why was she still standing here, so close to him?

He lowered his head and nibbled at her earlobe, making her yelp.

"Reece! What are you doing?"

He chuckled against her skin. "Just having a taste,"

he said, nibbling again. "I think you splashed something on your neck. Let me get it," he offered.

It was news to her that the nerves in her earlobes were connected directly to her knees, which seemed to turn to water. She planted her hands against his chest and tried to push. The man was rock-solid.

"I have appetizers," she said breathlessly.

"Not what I'm hungry for," he said against her neck, nipping at her speeding pulse.

"Reece," she said as calmly as she could. "We agreed we had to keep things only business."

"You said that, but I only agreed out of politeness," he whispered, his breath against her lips. "I said I'd do whatever you want," he added, brushing a thumb over a very hard nipple, making her gasp, his eyes meeting hers. "You want?"

Oh, did she ever.

"It's not a good idea," she said lamely, still unable to force her feet to move. He just felt too damned good.

"Abby," he said, laughing softly, "it's just me."

That was like saying, "It's just dynamite," to her mind.

He proceeded to cover her lips with light, soft, teasing kisses that made her grab on to him, curling her fingers into his jacket as she sought more. He didn't accommodate her until she groaned and worked her hands up to his neck, holding him still as she kissed him, taking what she needed.

She was weak, but she just couldn't work up the energy to care.

"I guess you're not angry at me anymore for the other night?" she asked, breathless.

His brow wrinkled, as if he was surprised. "I never was angry with you. Just frustrated, and a little embarassed. I'm sorry if I let you think otherwise," he said. "Let me apologize properly."

Reece walked her backward as they kissed hungrily, lifting her almost without her noticing until she sat on the kitchen counter. He settled in between her thighs, deepening the kiss until breathing was unheard of and—as far as Abby was concerned—completely unnecessary.

"Nothing mundane about this fantasy from where I'm standing," he said when he broke the kiss, her face framed in his hands, his eyes devouring her.

He'd tugged the tie of the apron loose and continued to trail kisses down her throat. Slowly his hand moved down to cover her breast before pushing up the edge of her blouse, and Abby was beyond arguing. She wanted the frustrating barrier of their clothes gone and to know his touch on her bare skin.

The sheer idea made her dizzy.

He had her shirt off in a split second. She reached behind to unclasp her bra, his hands covering her, spilling over with the fullness of her bare breasts.

"Damn, babe, where were you hiding these in high school?" he said appreciatively, bending to nuzzle her intimately, her hand slipping into his hair to press him close. She wanted his mouth on her in the worst way.

"I've lost a little weight since then," she said with a chuckle, "and I guess I filled out in other areas. Late bloomer," she finished on a sigh. He'd taken her aching nipple into his mouth, sucking hard, then laving with his tongue until she was writhing on the counter.

"You're so sweet," he said, working his lips over

her stomach and taking her hand, placing it to her own breast as he watched. His eyes darkened intensely as she touched herself, tweaking and pulling as he slowly unzipped her jeans while he watched and kissed.

She stopped, and put her hand on his.

"You first. You have far too many clothes on," she said provocatively.

He nodded and stepped back, not breaking the gaze between them as he took his jacket off and threw it on the island behind him, then made quick work of his sweater.

She gasped.

He was gorgeous. Lean and muscled, his tanned skin proved he'd spent the majority of his winters in sunnier places, and she loved how his shoulders and biceps flexed as he tore the garment off.

Then she realized he'd stilled, looking at her strangely, more tensely.

"I'm sorry. I didn't think to warn you," he said, glancing down, and only then did she even notice some of the scars, remnants of a burn by his shoulder, and what looked like thin lines from surgery a little lower.

"That wasn't what I was staring at," she said, wanting nothing more than to touch him, thinking only of that. "But it doesn't bother me at all. Come here," she commanded softly.

He walked over to her and pushed his hands into her hair, pulling her up hard against him. Her breasts crushed delightfully against his hard skin, his mouth plundering hers.

She managed to retain enough focus to move her

hands to the front of his jeans, undoing the buttons, and sliding her hand down inside.

Now it was his turn to gasp, breaking the kiss. He leaned his forehead on her shoulder as he trembled beneath her touch. He was hard, thick and hot in her hand. She stroked him, loving the friction of his skin against hers.

His breathing was labored as he ground out, "No, stop." His teasing tone gone.

She froze. Had she hurt him? Done something wrong?

"What?" she asked

"I'll come," he said tensely. "It's been months, since before the accident, and this feels too good," he explained, pushing away a stray hair that had landed in her eyes.

Abby couldn't think of a single thing he could have said that would have turned her on more.

She smiled, feeling feminine, powerful.

"Seems like you're well overdue then," she said, closing in for a kiss. She continued stroking him, rubbing her thumb over the slippery head of his cock and mimicking the rubbing motion with her tongue against his.

In mere seconds he exploded, thrusting into her hand, groaning deeply into her mouth as he came. When he broke the kiss, his beautiful chest heaved with hard breaths, his cheeks flushed and his eyes were still hot as he looked at her.

"I don't think anything in my life will ever feel better than that did," he said, still catching his breath.

She smiled again. "Maybe we should go upstairs and find out."

She was more than ready to take him to bed, and she didn't want to wait. To hell with complications. Complications could feel damned good, from where she was sitting.

"What about dinner?"

"That roast has a couple hours yet. It can just simmer," she said, the last word coming out more sexually than she intended.

She would take the memory of the way he looked at her—a gaze rich with lust, gratitude and anticipation—to her grave.

The loud sound of an engine and the hissing of air brakes made her jump, and they stared at each other in confusion before she looked at the clock and realized.

"You're expecting someone?" Reece asked.

"Yes! I completely forgot—it's the trees," she said, scrambling to get her bra on and trying to find her blouse before the nursery delivery guy came to the door.

"Trees?"

"Christmas trees. I completely forgot he was bringing them today," she explained.

Reece looked bemused, but followed her lead and grabbed his shirt, buttoning up his jeans.

"You mean, tree, singular?"

"No, sixteen of them," she said, and washed her hands quickly, grabbing a coat from the hook where she had left it earlier.

"Sixteen?" he echoed.

She grinned, her lusty thoughts fading to the background. "Three for the tasting rooms, a dozen for the decorating contest and one for the house. C'mon, you can help me with them."

As they walked out into the crisp air where two men unloaded a flatbed truck loaded with trees, Abby couldn't help but feel that their arrival might just have saved her from herself. As much as she wanted Reece, and wanted to give in, it would make her life an even greater mess. Right now, that was something she didn't need. As they spent the next few hours setting up Christmas trees, she tried to convince herself she was okay with that.

5

REECE FROWNED AT THE jungle of boxes and bins that crowded the main room of his house. Even more so since there was a huge tree in the corner, by the two front windows, and then more bags of new ornaments Abby had purchased. He looked at the tree again. It had to be eight feet tall. It had taken two hours to get the trees off the truck and in place. Two hours when he could have been making love to Abby, but while he had been helping with setting up trees, she had been hauling out decorations, apparently having forgotten their moment in the kitchen.

Now he knew how much work it had been for his dad, who always brought the trees home and spent hours struggling to erect them, to get the "right side" show-ing—a tree quality that only his mother seemed able to assess.

"You really didn't have to get a tree for in here," he said, trying to be tactful. He would have skipped it, personally.

"It's your last Christmas in this house. There should

be a tree," she said, as if that was the most logical thing in the world.

Luckily, most of Abby's family ornaments and decorations had been salvageable, contained neatly in plastic bins in her basement where the water from the fire hoses hadn't damaged them.

He'd had to call his mother, but found several boxes of their own, including several that he remembered from childhood. After a fantastic dinner of succulent pork that was one of the best things he had eaten in a long time, they had opened up the boxes and pulled everything out, which created what appeared to be utter chaos to Reece's eyes.

But Abby apparently had that special, female, Christmas sense that told her what ornaments should go where, and why.

Did it really make a difference?

He could tell from the intense concentration on Abby's face and the way she bit her lip—which was sexy, as well as completely endearing—that if she had lost these bins in the fire, it would have been a terrible thing. They were clearly meaningful to her.

It wasn't that he disliked Christmas, but he'd managed to tactfully avoid it this year by staying here, alone, and now it looked like it had found him anyway. Normally he would spend most of his holiday—when he didn't come home—working, and just have dinner with friends on the day, call his family, relax. But it had been his idea to have Abby here, and so he sucked it up.

A few hours later, having strung all the lights, they were now picking through the decorations, deciding what should go where.

"The silver and white should go in the back room, for the wedding reception, and the grapes will go on the tree in the tasting room, of course," she said, pulling several boxes aside.

"Grapes? You have grape ornaments?"

"There's a little store down on the Commons, the one that sells Christmas stuff all year round—you know the one?" she said, looking at him askance.

"I don't think I was ever in there," he admitted. When he was a student, he spent more time partying than shopping, and in the years since, even when he came home, spent most of his time with his family and never went into town too much.

"Oh, they have the most unusual ornaments. All kinds of characters, food items, just…whatever. And every year we would go down to see if they had some different grape ornaments, or ones that maybe looked like tiny wine bottles—we have fewer of those. Eventually the owner just called us when he got new things in, and he would trade us ornaments for bottles of wine. We had enough to decorate one tree with them."

Reece smiled, enjoying her enthusiasm about such a simple thing. "It sounds great—I can't wait to see it."

"Well, we can do that one first then."

"Tonight?" he said, surprised.

"Yes—I don't know that we can get all four done, but I'd like to try. There aren't any tastings until Friday, thank God, but I have dozens of other things to do."

Reece hadn't been aware he was going to spend the entire evening decorating Christmas trees—he had planned on much more interesting activities, like getting Abby in his bed. But she seemed genuinely excited about the trees, and all things considered, he decided, why not?

"Okay, I'm in."

His agreement was worth the smile it elicited.

So, after all of the ornaments were separated, they hauled the boxes over to the tasting room, which in the case of Winston wineries, was completely separate from the house and a much more modern construction, with shining oak beams and plate glass windows around their sales area.

Large leather chairs were strewn around the actual tasting area, inviting guests to enjoy the view and the wine. There was a fireplace near the bar, behind which the bottles of wine were arranged. Hidden track lighting put a soft golden glow over the room, rather than anything harsh or too bright. There were double French doors at the back that led to a reception area and an outdoor deck that overlooked the lake.

"It's so pretty and spacious here. I feel like our little tasting room was about the size of your closet," Abby said with a laugh, setting down her box of ornaments with a sigh. "I hope I have enough business to justify you letting us use all this space. I'll need to run through a tour with you, too, if you don't mind, so that I can train Hannah and Carl, and we need to set up the wine displays still, and—"

Reece put both hands on her shoulders. "Abby. Stop. Right now, focus on the tree, just this tree. One thing. Tomorrow there will be time to think about the rest."

"I know, but there's so much—"

"I know there is. But we can't do it tonight, and anyway, it's been a while since I've decorated a tree, let alone four of them," he said with a grin. He leaned in to brush a kiss over her mouth when she seemed ready to argue again. "Let's enjoy it."

Taking a deep breath, her cheeks pink from the kiss— something he planned to repeat as often as possible—she nodded, smiling, too.

"Sorry. Once my mind gets rolling, I can't stop sometimes," she admitted.

"I know the feeling. I used to be like that before a race. The day before, the night before, I wouldn't be able to stop thinking of everything, double- and triple-checking every detail. But I had to learn to trust my team, and also, I needed to sleep. A tired driver isn't a good driver. By trying to do everything, I wasn't doing my job as well as I needed to."

"I know. It was easier before, when Mom and Dad were here, and Sarah, but then it seemed like it all just landed in my lap, and I got so used to thinking about it all, all the time." She cast a glance over her shoulder, back toward her burned winery, though she couldn't see it in the dark. "Now I don't know what to think."

"It will all work out," Reece said steadily. "Speaking of your mom and dad, have you talked to them yet?" He guessed that, depending on where her parents were exactly in earthquake-torn Haiti, communication could be a real challenge.

He was sorry he asked, as her face crumpled with distress. "No, I don't want to worry them with vague emails, so I certainly don't want to deliver the news to them that way. I have left messages, and I'm just waiting for them to call me back," she said, wringing her fingers together. "I'm dreading it. I hate that I let this happen. They'll be so upset," she said.

"I'm sure all that they'll care about is that you are okay. Everything else can be rebuilt. But it might be another sign you are overworked—you start trying to handle too many things, you miss important details, and that's when bad things happen."

"Like you were just saying, about racing. I know you don't like to talk about it," she said quickly, looking away as she pulled some ornaments from a box and turned toward the tree, motioning him to do the same. "But is that what happened with your accident? You were trying to do too much?"

He swallowed hard. In the middle of seducing Abby in the kitchen, Christmas tree chaos and having their wonderful dinner, he realized he hadn't thought about his accident once in several hours, maybe for the first time in a long time. He hated bringing it back up again, but he supposed it was only fair to at least answer her question.

"No, not this time. This was just one of those crazy, unfortunate things…. I actually can't remember the crash."

"You have amnesia?" she said with some surprise.

He nodded shortly. "They say it's normal in traumatic situations, like car crashes, and I had pretty serious head injuries. You probably know I was in a coma for a while," he said.

She nodded, and as they put ornaments on the tree, it was easier to share the things he didn't normally talk with anyone about, except for his doctors.

"I watched the video footage for the first time a month

ago. I blew out a tire and the roads were wet, but I don't know why I lost control so completely, and I guess I might never know. I've had tires go before and controlled it. This time…" he said, trailing off, shaking his head. "I just don't know."

Her hand was on his arm then, squeezing in a way meant to comfort, but he felt his pulse jump. Any touch from Abby seemed to make that happen.

"My dad always says the only control we have in life is self-control. We can control how we react, what we do, and that's it. You were—" she paused, catching her slip "—*are* a fantastic driver. Even if you can't remember, I'm sure you did everything you could. Like you said, sometimes things just happen."

"Your dad always was a smart guy. How would you know what kind of driver I am?" he asked, hanging his last ornament on the tree.

"Uh, um, well…" She took her hand from his arm and reached into the box for more decorations. "It stands to reason, right? You're one of the major players. They said you could be the next Clark or Stewart."

His eyes widened. "You follow racing?"

She paused, leaning into the box, and he realized she'd let on more than she meant to. It warmed him in a whole different way that she had followed his career. He never would have guessed.

"I just caught things on the news. Hometown boy makes it big in Europe, you know, and you came back and drove at the Glen that one time," she said, gathering an armful of ornaments and returning to the tree.

"Did you come to that race?" he asked. It had only

been an exhibition run, a charity event, but he'd had no idea she was there.

"Some friends wanted to go, so I tagged along."

"I see."

"You see what?"

He shrugged, unable to resist the temptation to egg her on a little. "You followed my racing, you came to my exhibition…clearly you never quite got over your crush on me," he said with a grin.

Abby's jaw dropped and she huffed something about his "intolerable ego" until she saw the barely restrained glee in his eyes.

Then her gorgeous lips quirked at the edges, too. "You really enjoy getting me worked up, don't you?"

Reece took that as his cue, and stepped around the tree to pull her up close. "You have no idea," he said, serious now as he dipped in for another kiss.

"You're wicked," she said against his mouth, a little breathless. Her cheeks were flushed, her eyes bright, and Reece couldn't seem to get enough of taking her in.

"I know," he admitted. He seemed to be having especially wicked thoughts at the moment.

"I kind of like it," she said with a grin that made his heart flip inside his chest. "But I…I've never done this," she said, looking nervous.

His eyebrows flew up. He was pretty certain that… but was he wrong? "You mean you've never, uh—"

"Oh, no! I've had sex, sure. But never when I knew it was going to end before it started. Never without at least the vague promise of something more that could happen," she said, and then broke away, looking embarrassed.

"We have a relationship, Abby. We have history, even. We're friends. That won't change."

She smiled a little. "It's already changed. We were barely friends in high school, and we've barely started a friendship now. We're leaping right into being lovers."

He knew she was right, but didn't say a word.

"I want you," she admitted. "But I don't know if I can get into this knowing you're going to sell this place and leave. I know it's stupid, and unsophisticated, but I...um, I—"

Don't want to get hurt, he finished for her in his head.

"I know, Abby. I understand," he said, though he didn't want to. He wanted Abby more than he wanted just about anything except getting back in a car, but he didn't want to hurt her, either.

She wasn't like the women he took to bed and found gone in the morning. She wasn't just using him for a thrill or some notoriety. Abby was the kind of woman you took to bed and then woke up with in the morning— every morning—for a long time.

And he wasn't that guy. Maybe someday, but not now.

"It's sweet, actually," he said, closing the gap between them and pulling her into the circle of his arms. "I can't make any promises about anything, Abby, I can only be as upfront as possible. I want you, too, a lot. But it's your choice, okay?"

She nodded against his chest, her small hands moving over his back, making him crazy, but he reined in his desire.

"Thanks, Reece. I wish I could—"

"It's okay, really. How about we finish these trees?" he said cheerfully, planting a kiss on her hair and wondering if that was the last time he'd ever have Abby in his arms.

6

Abby wrenched upward, an unfamiliar noise pulling her out of a restless dream.

The thud sounded again, and she sat up, hand to her slamming heart. Looking at the clock, she saw it was two-thirty in the morning. She'd only been sleeping for a few hours. Living alone for several years now had fine-tuned her senses to any noise in the house at night, and she listened closer.

She didn't need to wonder if she had imagined it when it was followed by a large crash, and glass breaking. She leapt from the bed, opening her door to peek down the hall toward Reece's room, but didn't see him. Had he slept through the noise? Heard it at all?

Moving on tiptoe down the hall, she stopped by his door, lifting her hand, then pausing. She couldn't knock if there was an intruder downstairs, they might hear.

She pushed Reece's door open just slightly, poking her head into the dark room.

"Reece?" she whispered as loudly as she dared.

A loud shout met her whisper, making her jump out of her skin, but also launching her inside the room and closing the door behind her. She saw immediately that the noise she'd heard hadn't been from an intruder, but from Reece, who had knocked the hurricane lamp off of his nightstand. He still appeared to be sleeping, and not well.

Venturing toward the bed, she bit her lip in concern.

"Reece, are you okay?"

He twisted in the sheets, as if trying to push them off, though he couldn't. He was murmuring, then shouting again, then whimpering in a way that told her he was in some kind of pain—or dreaming about it. She rushed to the side of the bed and put a calming hand on his shoulder, saying his name again, only to have him wrench away. He started saying things, his tone low and business-like, something with numbers and other mumbled words she couldn't understand.

Silver light shone through the window, and she could see his face was contorted in the agony of his dream and didn't know what to do. Then her eye caught sight of a small bottle on the dresser. She picked it up and held it close to the window—sleep aids. Those would knock him out and she probably didn't stand much chance of waking him up, she figured.

Still, she couldn't just leave him here like this, even if it was just a dream. Scooting into the empty space next to him, Abby knew she was playing with fire—especially when she realized he wasn't wearing anything but his briefs.

"God help me," she muttered, but settled down next to him and cuddled up behind, hoping to offer some kind of comfort. Maybe she could not let him be alone through the worst of it and then go back to her room.

Reece would never know. She rubbed his back with her palm, hoping to soothe, and after a few minutes, he did seem to quiet down. Her own body relaxed and her breathing returned to almost normal. Except that she was laying here in bed with a mostly naked, absolutely gorgeous man—still, she focused on just helping him back into a restful place.

Soon, his breathing evened, the mumbling stopped and his tight muscles softened under her hands.

"That's better," she said, intending to go back to her own room, but she was warm, comfortable and exhausted.

It didn't take much for her to drift off, too.

REECE WAS HAVING THE time of his life.

All drivers dreamed of the perfect race, and in his case, he was living the dream.

He was strapped into his Ferrari F60 so tightly that he could only just about breathe. The heat was intense, the wind bruising and the G-forces flattened him against the seat.

He was in sheer heaven—and he was in second place.

There was nothing in the universe except for his car, the road and the car in front of him. Adrenaline fueled his laserlike focus, strategy a constant clicking in his brain. Second would be his best in a World Cup race, but second wasn't good enough. Reece was pulling out all the stops and racing for first.

It had been raining. The roads were wet, but that was

nothing. He knew this car like his own body, and when he was driving it, there wasn't any difference between the two, the way he saw it.

He edged up on his competitor. Overtaking wasn't common on Formula One tracks, but he had a shot as they came around the final turn. He hit the accelerator as they rounded, positioning himself to make the most of the aerodynamics of the high-tech car he drove. The back wheel of the guy in front of him was spinning close by when Reece heard the whining noise, but he didn't catch on at first that something was wrong. He'd blown out the front driver's side tire.

He'd skipped that last pit stop. A calculated risk. A mistake.

His car could go on three tires in some conditions, but not rounding a curb, not at his speed, not on wet roads. His mind didn't anticipate the worst—he adjusted and focused on cold calculation of how to maneuver, still thinking about the win as he felt himself propel sideways, lurching hard.

Reece sometimes felt like he was flying when he drove, but something told him that for a second, he was actually airborne.

Everything was black, and then it was very, very bright.

The pain was intense, and he was trapped. He fought to get out, at least, he thought he did. He had no idea where he even was.

He couldn't seem to open his eyes, no matter how hard he tried. He wanted to speak but couldn't, and while there was noise in his head that wouldn't stop, he couldn't make out anything understandable.

Panic set in, fear clawing at him, and he tried to calm down, but it just made it worse. He lunged forward, reaching out, trying to get through the blinding brightness, the deafening noise, but he couldn't.

Was this what dying was like?

His heart felt as if it would explode from his chest when he felt something, finally. Someone touched him, and he reached, finding a hand he could grab on to. He held it like it was his only connection to life, and maybe it was.

He still couldn't speak, or hear, but he could touch.

His heartbeat slowed, the panic subsiding slightly. He was alive, connected to something.

Not alone.

For that moment, it was enough.

BEFORE SHE EVEN REALIZED IT, Abby opened her eyes to the soft, pre-dawn light, and to Reece's silver eyes watching her.

"Change your mind?" he said softly.

"Hmm?" she said, not sure what he was saying, or why he was in her bed, or… Her eyes flew open and she started to push up, but Reece's arm was over her, holding her snug against him.

"Steady," he said.

Morning brain-fog assaulted her, and she fought for words, but ended up sputtering, becoming increasingly aware of the warm, hard male body aligned with hers, both buried under the soft quilt and blankets.

"You were dreaming," she finally managed to say. "You broke your lamp. I thought you were an intruder," she explained, hoping he was awake enough to interpret her garbled, simple sentences.

As she shifted, it brought her closer to him and she knew he was *very* awake.

"You thought there was someone in the house, so you decided to crawl into bed with me?" he asked, his brow furrowed.

"No, I thought there was an intruder, but when I came to get you, I saw you had broken your lamp and were having a nightmare. Do you remember?"

He shook his head, then closed his eyes. "Vaguely. I've had it before, or other nightmares anyway. I don't know if it's the same one. I can never remember the details."

"You were thrashing around, so obviously it was... bad. I tried to wake you up, but you were out cold, so I thought maybe if I just sat with you for a while you'd be okay," she said, shrugging.

"You could have been hurt. Stepped on glass," he said, frowning.

"I was fine. You were the one hurting, apparently."

"And you helped," he said softly, looking at her strangely, like he was remembering something, but he didn't say anything, so she did.

"I meant to go back to my room, and then I guess I fell asleep."

"I see," he said, his eyes warm on her face.

"I should probably go," she said.

"Do you really want to?"

Did she?

Of course she did, but...but what?

All of her reservations seemed so flimsy. Sure, she

might get hurt, but she was a big girl. This was her chance to experience something wonderful, and there might never be another chance.

Reece would sell this winery, leave, and the odds were that she'd never see him again, except on TV.

Already, it hurt her heart a little to think about that, but so what? She'd survive, and she'd have some great memories. Maybe it was impossible to live your fantasies without some risk of being hurt. Maybe that was the price.

"No, I really don't," she said.

"Good, because I really want you to stay."

Her decision made, she smiled and slid her arm around him, too, enjoying how he pressed fully against her in a move that left her in no doubt that he wanted her—a lot.

The look of sheer hunger on his face made reason disappear. His lips were just a scant breath from hers, and she could hardly believe this was truly happening.

"Here's the thing, sweetheart," he said against her lips. "I don't care if an asteroid hits outside the window, nothing is interrupting us this time."

"Got it, no asteroids," she managed to say before he was kissing the life out of her, pushing her back until she was pinned between the warm, soft mattress and about six feet of hard, delicious man.

His mouth rubbed over hers erotically as he stopped to nip at her lower lip, his tongue darting out to lick the spot he bit before plunging deeper.

She arched into him, kissing him back with every ounce of passion she'd been holding back, tasting him as deeply as he tasted her. The faint scent of cedar, pine and smoke clung to his body from the night before, and she inhaled, loving how it mixed with his natural manly scent.

She barely recognized herself as she clung to him, wrapping a leg around his hip, arching into his hardness, rubbing and moaning into his mouth. She enjoyed sex, but she'd never felt so voracious about it. But right now, she wanted skin-on-skin, and pushed at the elastic band of the shorts between them.

He was of like mind, sliding his shorts off, then reaching for the edge of her flimsy cotton nightgown and pushing it upward until there wasn't anything hiding her from his gaze.

"Oh, sweetheart, this has been so worth waiting for," Reece said as he took her in. His hands drifted over her, learning her softness, studying her body so intently that she would have felt self-conscious if his touches weren't rendering her mindless.

"Um, I'm on birth control and I'm, you know, healthy. I haven't been with anyone in a while," she admitted, feeling a little awkward. But while they were old friends, they were new lovers, and certain things had to be said.

He nodded while nibbling at her shoulder, sending shivers everywhere.

"Me, too. Like I mentioned earlier, there's been no one since before the accident, and I've been thoroughly checked for everything with all of the time I spent in hospitals," he whispered against her ear.

She remembered how hard and urgent he'd been the day before when she'd stroked him to orgasm in the kitchen, and it was enough to make her shudder, reaching for him, wanting to make it happen again. The idea that she was his first lover after such a long time was important to her. Maybe that meant he wouldn't forget her later, either.

"Good, so we know we don't have to worry about *any* interruptions," she said with a smile.

She didn't want anything between them, and let him know by reaching down to find him, closing her fingers around him with a sigh of satisfaction. She opened her thighs and used her hand to slide him against her already slick sex, arching and then closing her legs to trap him there.

"I love how you feel next to me," she said, moving her hips against him, enjoying the slippery friction of their bodies. "But I bet it's not as good as you'd feel inside me."

"You make it tough to go slow," he said, pushing against her, sliding along the wet V of her flesh in a way that made her whimper and dig her fingers into his shoulders.

"Who wants slow?" she said, biting his shoulder. "Aren't you supposed to like speed?"

She yelped and then laughed as he found a ticklish spot and capitalized on it, then grabbed her hands and pinned them up over her head. She struggled slightly, and he could see it just excited her more when he pressed down, holding her in place.

Another little discovery about Abby.

"Now I've got you right where I want you," he said with a delicious smile. "And I plan to take my time. Maybe some guys make love like they race, but I think women and wine are more alike, they need to be savored," he said against her lips, catching her lower one between his teeth, then drawing it in and sucking before taking her whole mouth in a deep, carnal kiss. "We have time. Let's get to know each other," he said softly.

"But I want—"

"I know, me, too, and we'll get there. Promise," he said.

"You're such a tease," she accused, the last word ending on a moan as he ran his tongue along the shell of her ear, his cock still prodding and sliding along her sex, but not even coming close to where she wanted him.

"Can't help it when it comes to you," he said, moving lower to draw a nipple between his teeth, nipping lightly and making her arch, the slight pain making the drawing pleasure of his mouth a moment later even more intense.

He let her arms go and looked at her, his voice stern.

"Leave your hands there. Don't move them. I want to find out what you like, what you want," he said, his hands moving over her experimentally, lingering in places that made her react, moving on past the ones that didn't. "But if you move, I have to stop."

She nodded, moaning a little.

He was studying her body the way he must have studied a race course, or more accurately, tasting her like a good wine, she thought hazily, too immersed in sensation to argue. She'd been *done* plenty of times, but she'd never been paid attention to like this.

He dragged his lips down the inside of her thigh, and worked his way back up, nudging her legs apart with his shoulders.

His tongue found her, but only lightly, flicking at her clit, a butterfly touch that had her nearly screaming, writhing on the bed.

"Reece, please, I need you," she said, panting, but she obeyed, leaving her hands where he'd put them. It was driving her crazy, in the best possible way.

He licked her a little harder this time, and his fingers found their way inside of her—one, then two and then, making her eyes widen, another teased the other opening to her body, penetrating slightly. She tensed at the unexpected sensation, then relaxed. Her entire body shivered with the pleasure of his fingers and mouth everywhere.

"That feels so good," she said.

"And this?" he whispered against her sex, so softly she wasn't sure he really said anything before he kissed her again on pulsing, sensitive flesh.

"Yes," she said desperately, wanting more of everything, thrusting against him. "Please," she begged.

Reece was someone she'd known for so long, but she knew in that instant that she didn't know anything about him at all. He seemed to know what she fantasized about, what she wanted that maybe she didn't even know to ask for. He continued to press, to lick and to thrust until she cried out, arching off the bed, her body bent in ecstasy.

He moved back up, and levered over her, pulling her legs up over his shoulders.

"I need this so much," he said roughly, staring down into her face as he poised himself before her, rubbing and teasing her sex with his cock until both of them were mindless. When she was about to beg, he eased forward, sliding inside and filling her deeply, adjusting her legs so that he could go even deeper.

Oh, thank you, Abby thought, her entire body expressing a sigh of wonder as he started moving.

"You're so wet," he said, his jaw tight with the effort of control he was exerting. "So hot inside," he said, continuing to describe what he felt, what he wanted to do to her, in exacting detail until she wanted to just beg him to make it all real.

There was little she could do to control the pace at her angle, so she traced her hands and lips over hard lines of his chest, shoulders and hips. Every muscle was tense as he rocked into her in a steady rhythm.

She ran her fingers over his scars, exploring the different textures of his skin, then across the light hair on his chest, and over male nipples that beaded, drawing a groan from him as she pinched.

"You moved your hands," he said breathlessly.

"Do you mind?"

"Not at all."

He turned his face to the side, planting wet kisses on the side of her knee, and she whimpered as the sensation traveled all the way back down through her thighs to the eddy of pleasure between her legs.

It was all too good, but she needed more. She was so close, and reached down to touch him as he moved in and out, her fingers firm around the base of his erection.

"That's so hot, Abby," he said, watching.

She pressed on her clit then, rubbing, knowing what she needed and liking the way he watched so greedily. Hot sensation immediately coursed through her body, everything tightening, her muscles clenching down on his cock so hard it almost ached.

"Oh, yeah, Abby," he ground out, thrusting faster, deeper.

Suddenly all of the tightness melted, her climax overcoming her and drawing him along as well. Abby had never felt anything quite so pure in her life, she was sure of it.

Minutes later, Reece released her legs and fell to her side, pulling her over next to him as they both caught their breath, calming down from what Abby was sure had to be the most intense, incredible sex she'd ever had.

"I may not be able to move from this bed today," she said jokingly, though when she did try to move her leg, it felt like spaghetti. Her muscles felt as if they actually had melted.

"You'll get no arguments from me," Reece said with evil glee, propping up on one elbow at her side. He ran his finger along her sternum, down her belly, and stopped at the edge of her sex. "I thought about tying you to it at one point."

She was surprised, then she smiled.

"Maybe we could take turns."

"Sounds like a plan."

"I still can't feel my legs," she admitted, laughing.

"I'm a bit dizzy myself, but even so, I want more," he said, leaning in for a kiss.

"Me, too," she said, touching his face, running her finger along his lips. He darted his tongue out to taste her. "I want more, too."

"We can do anything," he said. "Everything. Whatever you want or need. Just say so."

In the years since her few crazy experiences in college, her lovers had been nice but uncreative men, the sex more or less vanilla, and she hadn't realized how many fantasies she had packed away. If Reece was willing to explore them with her...?

"Maybe I should write up a list, you know, like for Santa. All the things I want you to do to me, and what I'd like to do to you," she said naughtily, grinning.

"Hmm...that could be interesting. We could make it our goal to make sure every item is attended to," he said, trailing his hand over her breast, in long strokes up and down her torso, down her arm, back up again, back over her breast until she trembled.

She wanted him again, right now. Amazing.

"Roll over."

"Why?"

"Just do it," he said, commanding but gentle.

With a little shiver of pleasure, she did, snuggling down into the soft material of his comforter. It was warm and soft, smelling like sex, and she was in heaven.

Reece pushed up, balancing himself as he levered over her, straddling the backs of her thighs, and then she felt the next-best thing to sex that she could imagine as his hands slid up either side of her spine and continued to massage in slow, thorough motions.

"That feels amazing...where did you learn to give massages?" she said.

"Here and there...but giving a massage can feel as good as getting one," he responded.

As he worked her neck, she sighed. "Somehow I doubt

that," she said on another sigh, followed by a moan as he leaned forward and was inside of her again, moving in a lazy rhythm that matched the motion of his hands.

She'd never even imagined so much physical sensation being possible. He kept rubbing, moving over her and inside of her until she was clawing her fingers into the quilt and rotating her hips beneath him. It was so slow, it was torture. It was perfect.

His hands slipped down to work their magic on her derriere, massaging and squeezing. She pushed up on her elbows, thrusting back against him, seeking more. He kept up the constant gentle rhythm, a steady beat of pleasure, as if making love to her was a song. She fell to the bed again, giving herself up to him and enjoying every second of it.

He never stopped touching her, through her orgasm and then through his own. Abby drifted off to sleep later, thinking that she'd definitely given herself the best Christmas present she could have ever imagined.

REECE HADN'T FELT SO good since, well, since he couldn't remember. He'd slept some more after making love to Abby, and it had been a deep, dreamless, drugless sleep, which he hadn't known in quite some time.

When he saw the mess he'd made of the nightstand, breaking one of his mother's antique lamps, he wished he could remember the dream. The only impression he was ever left with was that of being horribly trapped, dying, until someone touched him. Abby. As if she had reached directly into his terror and made it stop.

He cleaned the mess while she was still sleeping, liking the way her foot dangled over the edge of his bed.

A silly thing to trip his heart rate, but nearly enough to make him slide his hand up the arch and crawl back in with her. He'd lived in France too long not to have developed at least a little bit of a romantic streak, he guessed, as he smiled at her pretty pink toes.

Instead, he pulled himself away and pushed through a punishing workout, especially after the wonderful but rich dinner Abby had cooked the night before.

He'd been way off the nutritional regimen that he usually adhered to during the year, but things were always a little more slack around the holidays—more sweets, more wine—and so he had to make up for it with exercise.

Racing was more punishing on the body that most people imagined, requiring a lot of strength to turn a car that was pushing down three Gs. He had to work twice as hard now.

He was feeling strong today, though. Energized. There was no numbness, no pins and needles. A second round of push-ups was interrupted by the doorbell, and he went quickly to answer, hoping not to wake Abby. Much to his surprise, Charles stood at the door, frowning through the ring of the wreath Abby had hung over the panes of glass the day before.

"What the hell is all of this?" Charles asked, looking back at the trees set up on the large front lawn as he stepped inside.

"Good morning to you, too," Reece said dryly, not offering to take Charles's coat. "To what do I owe this impromptu visit so very early in the morning?"

Charles glared. "It's not impromptu—we have an appointment with the Keller rep in a half hour, and I thought we had talked about staging? Why all the trees and lights? What's going on?"

Reece had been remiss in telling Charles about Abby moving in, and so he proceeded to do that, watching the real estate agent's face redden as he spoke. When he was done, Charles didn't say anything, but went outside, peering over across the field past the trees on the lawn to the blackened buildings on the hill before he stomped back in.

"Okay, okay, let's not panic. This could work for us."

"What do you mean?"

"Well, we'd talked about her selling, in a package deal with you, right? Maybe now that would be even more appealing—certainly more appealing than having that right in the line of view from the front door. And that barn—that alone would bring down the property value—"

Reece held up his hand. "Stop right there. The barn is fine, she keeps her horses there, and I can guarantee you there's no way she's selling. And I know she'd regret causing us any inconvenience by having her home almost burnt to the ground," he said, not bothering to hide his sarcasm, "but I'm letting her work through the end of the holiday season here, period. It's good for us, too, since I have inventory to clear out."

"So why all the trees? You selling those, too, now?"

"It's for a tasting event. They are having a tree-decorating contest and giving away a case of wine and a weekend at their inn, when it's rebuilt, to the winner."

"Cute. But we can't have this all going on while we're trying to show the place—she'll have to be willing to clear out when we're bringing prospective buyers through."

Reece pushed a hand though his hair, and didn't have time to argue as another car pulled up in front of the house, and a burly man in a black suit approached the house. He stopped and looked out over the land, and Reece could see him bulldozing just by how he surveyed the property.

Reece didn't bother to grab a jacket and the three of them walked the property, the Keller rep obviously liking what he saw. Reece liked what he saw, too. It had been a while since he'd walked the land, taking in the view of crystal blue Cayuga Lake, breathing in the clean air.

Standing among the rolling hills of vines, snow bright on the branches of trees that marked the boundaries, he wondered how he'd never noticed how similar the place was to where he lived in France. Just as beautiful, just as pristine. Showing it to the Keller sales rep was like seeing it himself for the first time.

"We'd be willing to offer you top dollar, Winston. This is a great location, driving distance to the city, and having bought it from a famous local celebrity can only add to its draw. We're thinking we could use the local vineyards as a jumping-off point, give the development a vineyard theme, all of the streets named after certain kind of grapes, maybe name the place Vineyard Hills, or something to that effect," the man said, obviously getting way ahead of himself.

"Yeah, I always wondered about that," Reece said. "Why developers come into a place, clear out all the pine trees and then name them all after what they cleared out…"

Charles glared, but the Keller rep laughed and slapped

him on the shoulder. Reece had expected some slimy sales guy, but this man was local and down-to-earth in a way a lot of central New York people were. He didn't take offense at all.

"Just the way of the business, I guess."

Reece liked him, which made it harder to think of Keller as so bad. He was a businessman looking to do business, and so why did it all irritate him so much?

"The property down the line might be for sale as well," Charles added as they stood on the front porch again, nodding down toward Abby's place. "Maybe we could work out some kind of package deal?"

"Charles—" Reece interrupted, but he didn't get far.

"I'd have to talk to the boss, but that could be a very appealing prospect," Keller agreed. "I know you want to sell, and we'd be happy to talk about some kind of package, but we're also looking at a prime piece of property over on Kueka, so we'll decide which way we want to go, but we won't wait indefinitely," he said.

Reece nodded and bit his tongue as he noticed movement inside the window. Abby was up. He wasn't going to get into this now. They shook hands with a promise to stay in contact, and the Keller guy left.

Charles looked disgusted. "He wants it, Reece, and if you know what's smart, you'll move your friend out of here as soon as possible and off-load this place, and hers, if you can get it. If not, you're going to have it shackled to your ankle for some time, or take a huge loss," he warned before walking down toward his own car.

Reece's good morning vibe evaporated, and he stood on the porch watching Charles leave. There was no way he was asking Abby to leave before the holiday season was over, and he had to hope that wouldn't get in the way of a deal. He knew he should be putting the sale first—Abby was a big girl—but he'd made a promise, and he intended to keep it.

Walking back into the house, the warmth and the scent of coffee and pine trees wrapped around him in welcome. The strong sense of being *home* was disconcerting, making him stop in the entryway and looked around the room. Maybe Charles was right about the staging. When the house was empty, his parents gone, no decorations, he could look at it as a building to be sold.

Now, with Abby's coat over the back of the chair, her bag on the table, the tree in the corner, and some boxes of ornaments still stashed by the wall, the place looked…lived in.

Was he making a mistake?

He heard her talking in the other room, on the phone, and wondered how what had been so black and white just the day before was now not clear at all.

7

ABBY AWAKENED FEELING like a cat, warm, loose-muscled and well-tuned, but the minute her feet had hit the floor, doubts had set in and chaos followed her every footstep right into the shower.

She'd slept with Reece. That seemed like a tremendous understatement. The luscious, carnal hours made her warm with arousal even now and blew her previous idea of what "good sex" could be right out of the water.

It had been *great* sex.

Still, in the very bright light of day that was glaring off the snow-covered ground, they would have to face each other and the realities between them.

The morning began with a second call for Reece from Danielle, which Abby overheard while making coffee. The woman sounded irritated as she left her message on the machine, and guilt assailed Abby for forgetting Danielle's first one.

Jealousy also kicked in, and Abby knew she couldn't afford that. It was just sex, and being jealous wasn't part of the bargain. She'd make sure he knew about Danielle's calls as soon as she saw him, which made her wonder where he was.

She looked out the front window when she heard voices and saw a black sedan parked out front, Keller Industries written in neat, white lettering on one door.

Her hands turned cold as she saw the three men round the corner of the tasting rooms and come up to the house. They stood on the porch, apparently enjoying their conversation, looking over at *her* property, once, at least, their expressions speculative.

Coffee turned to acid in her stomach as she watched Reece smile and shake hands with the guy from Keller.

Her cell phone rang, and she turned toward the table near the Christmas tree they had decorated together the night before, her mind still on Reece even as the speaker on the other end addressed her. The whole incredible evening was starting to feel like a lie, a huge mistake.

Then, what she was hearing made those concerns seem like mere annoyances, her mind snapping to attention. "What do you mean the insurance payments have been halted?" she asked, setting her cup down on the counter before she dropped it.

"The complete fire investigator's report showed that while the fire was caused by an electrical short, it came closer to the wall by where one of your trees was plugged in, not at the source of your wiring problem in the ceiling."

Abby blinked. "So?"

"There is some indication that the wires could have been tampered with when the tree was set up."

Abby's jaw dropped, and her mind blanked with disbelief.

"Are you saying you think the fire was intentionally set?"

"It's not certain, but any doubt creates the need for a larger investigation before we can pay out. We have to make sure there's no fraud concern, you understand."

He said it so politely, accusing her of setting fire to her own home, as if it was just business.

"They're bringing in another investigator to make a new report, but until then, any progress on rebuilding or payment has to be stopped. We're very sorry for the inconvenience," the insurance agent said.

"How long will this take?" Abby knew the fire was an accident, but any delay on scheduling new construction would further eat into her reopening the following year.

"The investigator will be there Monday, but the report could take a few weeks. With the holidays, everything is slowed down, but I'm sure they'll get on it as soon as possible. Can you also supply them with the names of the company that brought in the trees?"

"You think they might have tampered with my wiring? I can assure you, they didn't. No one did. This was just an accident. My family has done business with them for years. This is just some stupid misunderstanding."

"Either way, they'll be conducting interviews and getting all of the information they can."

Abby was numb as she hung up the phone and heard the front door open.

Reece.

She had to compose herself, to hide her distress. She didn't want to talk about this new mess with him right now.

But as soon as she moved, her phone rang again.

Looking down, she closed her eyes when she saw her father's name on the caller ID.

Tears stung behind her eyelids seeing her dad's name. She wished so much they were here, and at the same time, she was glad they weren't. In spite of what she had to tell them, she was relieved to hear her father's voice on the line when she picked up the call.

"Hi, Dad," she said, her voice breaking immediately even though she promised herself she'd remain stalwart. She tried, only crying a little as she told them everything, including the new trouble.

As Reece and Hannah predicted, her parents were shocked, but their first concern was her safety, and they were clearly not as worried about the property, to an extent that left Abby somewhat surprised.

"I guess I thought you'd be more upset," she said to her dad, somewhat confused. "You built this place. You devoted everything to it."

"Oh, honey, we are, but more so that you have to deal with all of this alone. Should we come home?"

"No, no, please don't. I'm not alone. I have Hannah, and Reece has been so generous," she said, wanting them to know she wasn't completely on her own, as much as she missed them. "And besides, there's not much I can do until the insurance works itself out, I guess, and they do this new investigation."

"Well, that's just absurd," her mother said, joining in the call on conference. "Dad will make a call to Harold this afternoon," her mom assured. Harold was their long-time insurance agent who had retired, but probably still would have some good advice.

"I'm glad you're taking it okay," Abby said. "I was so worried about telling you."

"Sweetheart, all we care about is that you are unhurt, and it's so good to know Beau and Buttercup and the other pets are safe. When you see the kinds of things we've seen here in Haiti, helping people rebuild when they have so little, or just getting clean water running, it tends to help straighten out priorities," her mom added, and Abby heard her father's murmured assent in the background.

"You just say the word, and we'll come back if you need us. You're our first priority and always will be," her mom said.

"I'm fine, Mom, really. I'm good here at Reece's through the season, and hopefully after that, things will be more settled. I can stay with Hannah until the house is back to rights," she added.

"I'm so impressed that Reece stepped up like that," her mother said. "Not that he wasn't always a nice young man, and I think he did have a bit of a crush on you," she said, and Abby's eyes widened as she heard the smile in her mom's voice.

"Reece? Have a crush on me? Hardly," she scoffed.

"He was a handsome boy," her mom continued. "I take it he's recovering from that awful accident? And his father is doing well?"

Abby filled her mom in on everything. Okay, not *everything,* although she had that sneaking feeling that her parents could sense something more than being neighborly was between her and Reece. She did nothing to encourage that idea—there was no point when she and Reece were clearly just having a holiday fling that would be over soon enough.

She stared at the blinking red light on the phone to her left. Danielle.

Nevermind, that. She was here, now, and some woman an ocean away was not her concern. She felt marginally better. At least telling her parents hadn't been as terrible as she thought it might be, and her parents were right.

When she hung up, Abby felt more in control of things. As her parents pointed out, there were people in the world with much bigger problems than hers. She was alive, healthy and able to deal with whatever life put in front of her.

She wished she felt so confident about her emotions concerning Reece as she heard him in the front room. Taking another deep breath, she went out to meet him. No sense in avoiding it.

She stepped through the hall and stopped in her tracks the minute their eyes met, her composure flying out the window as she remembered every single touch, kiss and more. She wanted to cross the room and throw herself up against him, to feel the warm solidity of his body and forget everything else.

His brow lowered, and he looked at her, concerned. Probably because she was just standing there like a moron.

"Abby, you okay?"

"I talked to my folks" was the first thing out of her mouth, and while she didn't move, he did, crossing the room to pull her in. He was so warm, even though he was only wearing a heavy sweater coming in from outside.

"How did it go?" he asked.

She nodded, her cheek rubbing against the rough wool that covered his chest, his warmth seeping through, comforting her.

"They took it better than I imagined. I guess they've seen so much devastation, they have a different perspective on things," she said.

This wasn't going at all as she had planned. It was wrong to feel so good being able to talk to him while he stood there, holding her. His hands were rubbing over her back, and the comfort started to turn hot as sparks of desire leapt between them.

Should they talk about the night before? What was there to say? She pushed back gently, trying to rein her reactions in.

"Um, I don't know if you noticed, but you have a message on the kitchen phone. And I forgot to tell you last night," she said, feeling her cheeks heat annoyingly.

"A woman, Danielle, called yesterday, and I picked up the phone without thinking, and I promised her I would give you the message, which she said you would know who it was, and then I forgot to let you know, with everything that…happened," she babbled, lowering her gaze to his mouth.

He had such a great mouth.

"Danielle called?" he said then, sounding pleased. Her heart sank.

"Yeah, um, I just thought you should know. I didn't know if you checked the machine, it's hard to notice that little blinking light on your parents' phone unless you are standing in there right by the sink, and so I wanted to make sure you knew," she said, babbling again in the face of her discomfort. "I'm sorry I forgot yesterday."

Was the smile on his face because of Danielle?

"No need to apologize. I miss calls on that all the time—I'm surprised she didn't call my cell, but she might not have international minutes, I guess. Thanks," he said, not elaborating. Why would he?

"Old friend?" she asked spontaneously when he didn't offer more, then bit her lip and looked away, regretting giving in to the urge.

"Yeah," Reece said easily, apparently thinking nothing of it. "Actually, her brother, Gerard, was a driver and a good friend of mine since I'd moved to Europe. He was killed in a nonracing crash a few years ago."

Abby lifted a hand to her mouth. "Oh, no, that's awful. I'm so sorry."

"Yeah, it was hard on all of us. He was a great guy, helped me get into the sport. Danielle was his only sibling, and we spent some time together after he was gone. She helped me a lot last year," he said, shaking his head, remembering.

"There were days I might not have gotten up to bother with my physical therapy if she hadn't been there, cursing me out in three languages if I whined about it," he said, laughing at the memory.

Abby was silent. And she thought they had history? How could she compete with something like that? Danielle had been with Reece day after day through a time in his life he didn't really even want to talk to Abby about. It made her feel on the outside, in spite of the closeness they'd shared just hours before.

"I'm glad you had someone there for you," she said

slowly, and she meant it, even if it cost her something to admit.

"I guess I was, too, even if at the time I didn't always like her very much for ranting at me and pushing me. I guess she figured she'd fill in for Gerard, at least, that's what Tomás told me once."

"Tomás?"

"Danielle's husband. She spent so much time at the hospital with me, he said he felt like a single parent," Reece said. "But I was grateful for her pushing. She convinced me I could do anything I wanted to do, even go back to racing. It took some of the worry off of my parents, too, knowing she was there."

Danielle's husband. The words rang in Abby's mind. She'd been thinking the sexy-sounding French woman had been a lover, picturing a svelte vixen who warmed Reece's bed when he was in Europe.

In fact, she sounded like a good friend, and a wonderful person—a much better person than Abby felt like at the moment.

"Why are you frowning?" Reece asked, watching her closely.

"I, uh…never mind," she said, not about to confess that she'd been jealous of a woman she not only didn't know but had absolutely no good reason to be jealous of.

"I saw you were meeting with the Keller rep this morning. And the man you were at the café with the other day?" she asked, changing the subject.

His mouth flattened. "Yeah, he's interested, but we're not making any deals yet."

"Yet," she echoed softly. "When?"

"They haven't made a formal offer. They're considering a couple of other properties as well."

"Including mine?" she asked.

He blinked in surprise. "Why do you say that?"

"I happened to see you all looking over there, and the man you were with pointed to my buildings. So I wondered what that was about."

Reece was notably uncomfortable. He turned, talking as he randomly reorganized some boxes that were in the path of the hallway.

"They saw it and wondered about the fire," he explained haltingly, then sighed. "But, yes, it would be more attractive to them to get both properties in a package deal. They thought that since you had the fire, you might be interested in selling, too."

"I'm not."

"I told them that," he said, making eye contact. "I know you don't want to sell. I know this affects you, too, my selling. I can't promise I'm going to sell to someone you'll approve of—"

"Keller," she said woodenly.

"Maybe. If there are options, we can talk about them."

"Okay."

"But Abby?"

"Hmm?"

"I am going back to Europe and back to racing, sooner than later if I have my way. I need you to know that."

She knew it, but she couldn't help asking what was on her mind since she'd seen him in the café. "I thought the news said, I mean, they said the doctors said..." She faltered, hating to say it out loud.

"That my injuries were too severe, I know. That I would probably never make the full recovery needed to race again," he bit out, looking away, bitterness and determination carved into every line of his face. "I know what they say." He pushed a hand through his hair.

He looked so tense, she took a step closer, trying to find something encouraging to say. "Well, you seem pretty healthy to me," she said with a smile. "What are they waiting for?"

He looked up and seemed to relax a little.

"I have relapses, numbness, some pins and needles, and my reflex time has slowed down. I can build it back up if I can get back into proper training. The longer I'm here…"

She nodded, keeping her tone neutral. "The harder it is for you to get back in."

He sighed. "I'll be easily forgotten, replaced, if I don't get back in soon. I have to show them I can do it."

"Why?" Why did he want to return to a sport that almost killed him and might not take him back?

He stared at her in surprise. "I love it. It's the one thing I have ever really loved doing, really excelled at."

She frowned, thinking back. Reece had been an excellent student and athlete.

"I find that hard to believe."

"It's true. I was good at a lot of things, but nothing was my passion. Sometimes I ever wondered if I would have one. My dad would always say how he'd had wine in his blood and he felt so connected to this place. Ben knew what he wanted to do, to design golf courses, since he stepped foot on one when he was ten. I never had that focus, that desire, until I found racing. I can't even think of what else I would do with myself," he said, sounding slightly hollow, and her heart went out to him. "It's all I know."

"I can understand that," she said, and she did. She loved her home, her business, and she couldn't imagine any other work, either.

She took a deep breath, closing her eyes, then opening them again. "Give me a week. I'm meeting with Hannah to see if there's any way for me to liquidate assets and maybe buy you out. I don't know if it's possible, but maybe we could work something out, if you're willing."

He nodded. "I'd love you to have the place, and if there's a way we can do that, I'm all for it. I know my parents would be thrilled, too. We don't want to sell to Keller, but the market is so hard now, and we can't keep this place running for long."

"I'll do what I can," she said, but hope faded as she thought about the insurance money not coming through.

It had been feasible that she could have used that as a down payment, but she didn't tell Reece that. "And if we can't, and if you have to sell to Keller, do it. Maybe you can even leave earlier, get back to your life, your training," she said, proud of how calm she sounded.

"Trying to get rid of me, Abby?" He offered a small, slanted smile, but it didn't reach his eyes.

"No, but you obviously need to get back. The sooner the better, right?" She sounded brittle to her own ears.

He stood close again, and she resisted the urge to lift a hand, to touch him. How had this become so difficult so quickly?

"And until then?"

She didn't want to talk. She didn't want to debate the options and treat what was between them like a contract, discussing the terms and what-ifs.

She wanted him, and she had the chance to spend some time with him over the holiday. She'd be too busy to deal with a broken heart later, she figured.

Reaching up, she slid her hands around his neck, linking her arms behind and pulling his mouth down to hers.

"In the meantime, we have this," she said, kissing him until talking wasn't what either of them was interested in.

8

ABBY KNEW REECE WAS avoiding her, she just didn't know why.

In the three days since their talk, their last kiss—a kiss that hadn't led to a night in his bed—they'd both been busy and preoccupied.

When she was at the house, he seemed to be gone, and she was too busy even when he was there, working in the tasting room until late hours, getting things set up, preparing for the upcoming wedding and Christmas events.

As before, she'd come home to find him already in bed, his light shining under the closed door, or in the workout room going through the punishing routine that he did two or three times a day now. She didn't want to interrupt.

She hadn't slept well for those lonely nights, and so maybe this was best. She had too much happening to lose sleep over relationship drama.

Like right now, Abby was trying to get the supplies out to the yard where the Christmas trees waited. Hannah was supposed to have come with help an hour ago, but called to say she had a bad tire and had to have it changed before she could pick up their other part-timer for the day and get out there.

So Abby was on her own. Again. She didn't like to complain—she loved her work—but so much of it had come down on her shoulders recently, she was starting to feel it more than ever.

In a short while, the yard would fill with parents and children for the Christmas tree–decorating contest. Tasting was set up for the parents, with cases of both Maple Hills and Winston Vineyard wines up for first prize, with single bottles for second and third, along with fun prizes for the kids, who could also take part in a snowball-throwing contest and a snowman build-a-thon. The first-place winner would also get a free weekend at her inn next summer as a way to promote future business, and to ensure people would know she was rebuilding.

Boxes of lights, garland and unbreakable ornaments as well as popcorn were ready to be strung, along with other creative decorations that had to be hauled out to the yard and set up. Everything had to be ready to start just past noon. She'd been running behind all morning and could have used a hand, waiting for Hannah and her other helper.

Reece's truck was over by the barn, but she hadn't seen him yet. He had come in late the night before and was probably sleeping in. Besides, he'd been clear that he didn't want to be too involved with the everyday business of the winery. He was handling the Winston inventory and sales, and answered any questions she had, but otherwise, he stayed out of it.

Now that seemed to include her, too, apparently. She didn't understand it, but something had changed after their talk. Maybe he realized he'd made a mistake, or maybe he had simply gotten what he wanted.

She had, too, right? So why did it hurt so much now? She'd gone into it with her eyes open. They hadn't made any commitments. No promises. Reece had made it clear he was still poised to leave, and she had been the one throwing herself back at him. Maybe, in his way, he had been trying to back away, but she just didn't get it. Why couldn't he just tell her so instead of avoiding her? Or maybe he had only meant it to be a one-night thing, and she had misunderstood.

She was about to pick up another full box and bring it out to the yard when she heard footsteps, Reece coming down the creaky hardwood stairs from his room. He turned the corner, pausing when he saw her. She was grateful to see him, but also worried. He looked like he hadn't slept all night, either.

"Hey," she said, unable to ignore the way the brown hair mussed, the five o'clock shadow thick on his jaw. His body was probably still warm from sleep, and the magnetic pull toward him was hard to resist. But she did. She leaned down and picked up the box instead, holding it in front of her like a barrier.

"Hey," he said back, looking toward the kitchen.

"There's still coffee if you want some," she offered.

"Thanks," he said, taking a few steps in that direction, and she noticed him wince, a hitch on his left side.

"Are you okay?"

"I'm fine," he said. "Just had a rough night."

There was no warmth in his voice, and she felt

awkward and exposed standing there, even though she was dressed in her winter coat and sweater. None of it seemed enough to keep the hurt his tone caused from penetrating into her chest.

She told herself to stop being stupid. He'd had a bad night and was tired and a little grumpy, that was all. Maybe he just needed some downtime, or some fun.

"Okay, well, we have the tree-decorating contest today. It's going to be a good time, and you're welcome to join. In fact—"

"Listen, Abby, I don't think I can do this. It's too complicated," he said wearily.

"It's just trees, Reece, we're going to—"

"I don't mean the trees," he said abruptly and shuffled off into the kitchen.

Abby took the box outside without another word, hoping the cold slap of air on her cheeks would freeze the tears stinging behind her eyes. So, he had been trying to break things off, and she hadn't understood. Now she did.

Still, did he have to be so harsh? What had she done to deserve that?

Whatever warmth was between them seemed to have evaporated. Maybe it was better. Being together like they were would only make it harder, and she couldn't say he wasn't honest about things.

Yes, this was better, she thought, her heart aching as she dropped the box by the Christmas trees and turned to get another one, pulling her coat tighter as the sun dipped behind a cloud.

Then anger set in. He might be having a hard time of it, but that was no reason to treat her badly.

Whatever was going on, she deserved better treatment from him than being so easily dismissed, she thought as she walked back in for another box and stepped past them and into the kitchen instead. She stopped in the doorway, hearing two voices, realizing Reece had turned on the speakerphone.

She should leave, she thought, but her feet didn't seem to move.

"I can do it, Joe, give me a chance to show you. Whatever little things are still bugging me, I can ignore them. It's not a big deal," Reece said, tense.

"If it were just up to me, I'd give you a shot, but it's not. Something happens to that car this early in the game, I don't have to tell you how bad that would be. I'll be out of a job, and we'll both have lawsuits landing on us. The doc says no. Sorry to say it, but you're out, Reece. It's just a shitty break."

"I don't give a damn what he says, how the hell can he know what I'm able to do?" Reece's voice rose.

The other man sighed audibly over the phone. "Reece, you need to accept reality. It can't happen. You're one lucky bastard as it is, having survived that wreck. What's still wrong with your body is enough to take you out at two hundred if something goes wrong, and you know it. Why go take a second chance at killing yourself?"

"I'd be fine. Just let me do some test drives in January, I'll show you."

Abby's heart squeezed painfully for him; he wanted this so much, and it didn't sound like things were going his way.

"I'll see what I can do, Reece. But you haven't been

cleared on the post-traumatic stress issues, either. The doctor said you stopped the counseling."

Abby froze. PTS? She'd heard more about that in the news lately, with returning soldiers, but she hadn't thought about it in terms of things like a car accident. But it made perfect sense—anytime someone almost lost their life, especially if there were violent circumstances, post-traumatic stress would be an issue.

She put a hand to her lips. Maybe that was why Reece was acting so erratically, having nightmares and so forth. Her anger melted in the face of new information.

"I'm fine. Take my word for it."

"Well, the sponsors are looking at a new guy, an up-and-comer, got a hot record so far, and…"

Abby didn't hear the rest of what the guy had to say. She watched as Reece's head fell forward in a clear expression of his frustration and unhappiness at the news.

She took a step, then another, needing to comfort him in some way, his earlier surliness forgotten. None of that mattered. All that she cared about at the moment was being there for Reece, the way he'd been there for her lately.

REECE HAD SO MANY emotions crashing together inside of him, he didn't know which one to deal with first. Anger that they wouldn't listen and that the damned doctors wouldn't clear him. Betrayal that they wouldn't trust him to do what he was so good at doing, that they were just writing him off.

Fear that he'd never get to drive again, or maybe he

was way past fear and closer to panic. Joe said the team was already lining up someone new.

When he looked up from where he had braced his hands against the counter over a cooling cup of coffee and saw Abby looking at him with her heart in her eyes, he added embarrassment to the mix.

"Joe, I have to go. See what you can do, I'll be in touch," he said, hanging up abruptly.

"Reece…" she began.

"Eavesdropping, Abby?"

"No!" She closed her eyes, blowing out a breath. "I mean, not on purpose. I came back in to talk, and you were on the phone, and I just…heard," she explained.

"I see."

He'd knew that he'd growled at her when he came downstairs, still groggy from the painkillers he was taking to help him sleep through the pain in his left leg that had been torturing him for the last few days.

He hadn't touched Abby since their conversation about the sale, and he didn't intend to. While she had come to him even after he told her it could never be more than sex, he decided to put some distance between them, to cool things off, for both of their sakes. It didn't matter that he wanted more, too. He knew they were getting in too deep, too fast, and it wouldn't be good for either of them in the end. Better to hurt her now, the way he saw it.

He hadn't counted on it, but he missed her like hell, and that pissed him off, too, unaccountably. He'd avoided emotional complications with women, and this was why.

The first two nights he'd been awake, he'd only been

able to think about her being a few yards down the hall, and how much he wanted her. He'd paced, tossed and turned, worked out and then, probably due to anxiety and lack of sleep, his left side started acting up worse than ever.

So last night he'd turned to the painkillers to smother the pain, which was now accompanied by a burning sensation that was a new kind of agony. If it kept up, he knew he'd have to go in to see the doctors, but he was determined to make it stop or to learn to ignore it. He was trying hard to ignore it.

Abby chewed her lip, watching him, looking unsure. He grabbed the coffee and then set it down, his fingers curling tightly as he fought the urge to go to her, to smooth over his harsh words.

"I'm so sorry, Reece."

"For what?"

"That they don't want you to race anymore," she said, her words soft, pained, for him.

He frowned, not wanting her sympathy. That was the last thing he wanted. "Don't waste your pity on me, Abby. I am going to drive again, and soon."

"But he said—"

"I know what he said. They might have some new hotshot lined up, but I can talk to the sponsors myself. I have a strong record, a following, and there's nothing fans like more than a comeback. I will make a hell of a lot more money for them, and get more wins, than someone green out of the gate," he said, almost convincing himself.

"What about the post-traumatic stress?"

"That's nothing. A few nightmares, some lost sleep. It will pass. The rest I can handle."

"Maybe dismissing it too easily is part of the problem," she offered.

Reece put a hand up. Abby was a good friend who meant well, he knew, but her words got his back up. He wanted to keep their friendship in place, but he also wasn't going to have this conversation with her.

"Abby, listen. I care about you, and I want us to be friends, but there's a lot you don't know about me. I know my own limitations."

"You have to talk about it with someone," she countered.

"Not you."

"Why not?"

"Abby, we slept together. That doesn't give you a free pass into my life," he said. "Besides, it's not like you don't have your own agenda. The longer I stay, the better for you, putting off the sale, right?"

He regretted the words as they passed his lips, but was unable to resist the urge to push her away.

Why? Because she was right? Was Joe right, too?

He couldn't deal with it and turned to leave, surprised when he felt her hand on his arm, pulling him back around.

She was furious, her eyes were mossy green, darkened by emotion. Her hand left his arm to settle on her hip, but he'd missed her so much that even such a quick touch left its impression.

"Are you serious? You think I am sleeping with you to stall you from selling?"

He didn't, he never thought that, but he didn't say so. If she hated his guts, things would probably work out easier for both of them. She had enough to think about without worrying about his problems, too.

She shook her head in astonishment. "I'm not sure who that is more insulting toward, me or you," she said.

"I'm sorry, Abby, it's just that I've been here before. I've been with women who think sex is more, and I know the signs."

Now her mouth was gaping at him.

"Need an ego adjustment, Reece? I have a lot going on, and yes, I don't want you selling to Keller, but I've accepted that you might. I've known from the start what we have…had…was temporary. Don't think I am hanging my future on you. My future is over there." She pointed out the window to her winery, and he saw her hand tremble. She was clearly furious, and she was right.

"I'm sorry, Abby. I just didn't want you getting the idea that I would stay, or that sleeping together means more than it does."

She shook her head, looking at him like she'd never seen him before.

"Don't worry, Reece. As far as I'm concerned, it didn't mean a damned thing."

Reece closed his eyes, wishing he knew a better way to handle this, but he was fighting on so many fronts, he didn't know what else to do. He felt as if he was fighting the whole damned world and himself, and he was tired of it.

He started to say something, he wasn't even sure

what, but she'd already started to leave the room. He stepped forward, thinking about following, but instead he grabbed his jacket from the hook by the door and went out the back door to the barn with his cold coffee.

"HEY, WHERE'S REECE?" Hannah asked Abby, smiling at a young girl who stood with her father, waiting on a paper cup of hot chocolate. "Anything interesting progressing there?" she asked slyly.

The father took a small tasting glass of Baco Noir, and Hannah marked his plastic bracelet with a second check—no one got more than three tastings in the course of an hour, even if they spat between tastings, so that they were okay to drive when they left.

Abby hadn't filled in Hannah on everything going on, but that was because she had an event to focus on, which was good. Having a couple dozen people flying in every direction and Christmas trees being decorated kept her from dwelling on what had happened that morning.

She was still furious, though maybe with herself as much as anything. How could she have been so stupid?

"Hardly. He's around here somewhere," she said vaguely. Reece hadn't left, and he hadn't been in the house the last time she went inside, sparing them both another awkward moment.

She'd heard some noises coming from one of the barns, the sounds of power tools. He must be working on something, though she didn't go to find out what. She didn't care.

Well, the sad fact was that she *did* care, but she

had to stop. The ache that had been dully thudding in the background of her heart all afternoon became so sharp as she replayed his words in her mind that she swallowed hard and pushed it back down. This was not the time.

Hannah watched father and daughter walk away, her eyes clearly focused on the man's butt, distracting Abby enough to make her smile.

"Why are all the cute ones married?" her friend sighed. "What I wouldn't give for just one night of unbelievably hot sex right now."

Abby coughed, looking around to make sure none of the children or parents had overheard Hannah's heartfelt wish.

"Weren't you dating that lawyer?"

"Yeah, that was over weeks ago. He was boring. I could hardly get through dinner on our first date without falling asleep in my spaghetti. That was enough for me."

"Oh."

"Yeah. And it's getting pretty sparse out there. I can't date the guys I work with, of course, and most of the other men our age I've known since we were kids. If I slept with one of them, everyone in town would know and my mother would have us married."

Hannah sighed, pouring herself a larger glass of the noir. "What I need is some wild, kinky sex with someone who's not local. I'd settle for just one night with a guy whose mother or friends I might not bump into the next day at the store."

Abby shook her head, grimacing. "Watch what you wish for."

"I'm willing to risk it," Hannah said. "But I take it things fizzled between you and Reece?"

"More like they imploded," she said, closing her eyes at the hitch in her voice.

"Oh, no, honey…you fell for him, didn't you?"

"Not really. Well, a little," Abby admitted. "It's not like I am madly in love with him or going to jump off a cliff, but I thought we had something. Then he—he just decided that we didn't. I didn't see it coming, not really. I knew it was temporary, but he just ended it and let me know later," she said, filling Hannah in on the gruesome details of that morning's conversation.

"Jerk."

"It's complicated for him, I know, but I can't believe he actually thought I would be so naive," she said, and told Hannah about the phone call she heard and their resulting argument.

Hannah looked thoughtful for a moment. "My Aunt had PTS after a bad car accident—she couldn't even ride in a car for a long time, let alone drive, and it can make people act very strangely, but it sounds more like Reece's ego is just too big for his body, nice as that body is. You have to watch out for yourself, too. You were just trying to help," Hannah said, giving her a hug.

"Yes, that's exactly it! He knows all about my life, he helped me with recovering from the fire, he has been there for me every step of the way, which was just… incredible," Abby said, swiping a hand at a tear that snuck out.

"But then, when I reach out to him, when I want to help, he swatted me back. Told me not to mistake sex for the right to care about him, basically," she concluded with a sniff.

"Ouch."

"Yeah."

"Well, maybe in some ass-backward male way he's trying to protect you by pushing you away," Hannah offered, shrugging.

"Yeah, maybe, but it's stupid."

"Well, he's a *guy*," Hannah said, and for the first time in hours Abby had reason to laugh.

"I guess. A lesson learned, I suppose."

"And you had some great sex, got to live out a high-school fantasy and got back in the game."

"I would hardly call it getting back in the game," Abby said. "Probably heading for another long dry spell."

They both looked over at the people happily decorating trees. She envied their simple holiday cheer.

"Oh, I don't know. I think you might be putting out the sex vibe."

"The *what?*"

Hannah grinned. "The sex vibe. It's probably phero-mones or something, but when someone is sexually active, it's like they put out a signal and attract other people who are interested, too."

"Hannah, what the heck are you talking about? Give me that wine, you've had too much," Abby said, laughing.

"See for yourself," Hannah said, holding her glass

back where Abby couldn't reach it. "A totally hot guy has been checking you out all day."

Abby had no idea what Hannah was talking about until she spotted two cute guys standing by the far edge of the crowd of half-decorated Christmas trees. One smiled at her boldly.

"Where did they come from?" Abby asked Hannah.

"They've been here the whole time, and that one hasn't been able to take his eyes off you, though you've been too distracted to notice. Good thing you have me watching out for you," Hannah said, smiling and waving back at the cute guy.

"Hannah, *don't*," Abby insisted, but then saw he was already on his way over.

"Why not? It's the perfect distraction from your troubles. Maybe his friend would be interested in doubling," Hannah said, elbowing her slightly.

Abby sent her a look that promised retribution later on, but turned to the handsome guy—whose name was Derek—and offered him a taste of the Baco.

She maintained her professional composure for the first few minutes, but Hannah was right. Derek was charming and obviously interested. Unfortunately for Hannah, his friend was already making a move on another of the event guests, and her friend winked at her, giving her an "oh well" shrug before leaving Abby alone with Derek.

He was a local business owner, too, running his own computer software shop. He was also about three years her junior, but that didn't seem to bother him any. Maybe it shouldn't bother her, either.

He *was* hot, with wavy blond hair and mischievous blue eyes, and he looked great in his jeans, but Abby didn't feel any sparks at all. For all the attraction she felt, Derek could have been her brother.

But she chatted with him, enjoying the distraction from thinking about Reece.

"I'm glad we decided to stop when we saw all the commotion," Derek said, studying the group decorating trees and stepping back to watch Abby fill tasting cups or dole out hot cocoa as people approached the booth.

"I'm glad you're enjoying yourself," she said diplomatically, wondering if there was a way to discourage him without losing a new customer or being rude. He was a nice guy, but contrary to Hannah's theories about sex vibes, Abby wasn't feeling too flirty or sexy at the moment.

"I am. I've never really been into wines. I mostly like a beer after work," he said, smiling at her in that way that surely sent many a girl into a flutter.

"I like beer, too. Many of the gourmet ones are so interesting," she responded vaguely, and that set them off talking about breweries and beer tasting, which she had to admit, was very interesting. He didn't know much about wine, but he was very knowledgeable about beer.

"It looks like the trees are almost done—I'm going to have to do some judging and hand out prizes," she said, hoping to find her exit that way.

Where had Hannah gone?

"Do you need any help?" Derek offered.

Abby was about to refuse, but then she saw Reece,

walking from the barn up to the house. He stood by the front and watched her, not moving.

She felt her annoyance kick in again and smiled brightly at Derek. "Sure. You can help me collect votes," she said, standing close to him as she explained the voting process.

Abby didn't look back, but she heard the door slam in the background and grinned.

Derek was lit up like one of the Christmas trees by her interest, and she had to stop and think while he helped her collect votes for the best tree.

What was she doing? Derek was a sweet guy, as far as she could tell, and she had absolutely no romantic interest in him at all—using him to poke at Reece was ridiculous. She just hadn't been able to help herself. Still, it wasn't fair to Derek.

She watched her new friend smiling with a group of kids as he collected their votes and laughed as he took a snowball to the shoulder from one boy. Abby smiled, wishing she could just flip her emotions off from Reece and on to Derek. But she couldn't.

"You two seemed chummy," Hannah said, appearing back at her side suddenly.

"Where were you?"

"I had to watch over the snowman-making contest," she said innocently.

"Judy is doing that," Abby said knowingly. "You left me alone with him here on purpose."

Hannah grinned. "Did he ask you out?"

"Not yet."

"You going to go?"

"I don't know."

"Then my evil plan worked."

"Reece saw us," Abby said.

Hannah smiled. "I saw him staring at something, and he nearly broke the window in the door when he went inside."

Abby shook her head. "Yeah, I think I got a little carried away and made it look like I was more interested in Derek than I am," she confessed.

Hannah grinned more widely. "Then I would say my evil plan *really* worked. Reece was fit to be tied. Only one thing would get him that worked up at seeing you with another guy."

Hope leapt in Abby's chest, but she squashed it.

"I'm not going to count on that. Nothing has changed."

Derek walked back over, and they wrapped up the contest, awarded the prizes and made sure everyone had a little something to take home with them.

It was a very successful event, in spite of her own personal challenges, and Abby felt good about pulling it off.

When Derek asked her out before he was leaving, she regretfully declined, leaving Hannah shaking her head. Derek smiled and gave her his email, just in case, writing it down on a napkin and sticking it in her pocket.

"Why couldn't I have met him a few weeks ago?" she asked Hannah as the yard turned dark, and she sat with her friend on the porch step, looking at a field filled with brightly decorated trees and a crowd of snowmen. If she had met Derek then, maybe none of this would have happened.

"Would that have made a difference, really?"

Abby sighed. "Probably not."

Whatever was between her and Reece, if anything, it wasn't easy, and it wasn't what she'd counted on. Still, she knew she wouldn't trade one second of the fun or passion they'd had, even though it blew up in her face.

"Want to spend the night at my place?" Hannah offered.

Abby shook her head. Even though it was awkward, she and Reece were in this until the end, and she'd handle it. She wasn't sure how, but she didn't really have any other choice.

9

REECE'S HANDS OPENED and closed around the leather-covered wheel. His old friend Brody Palmer, who was sitting in the passenger's seat, chuckled. Brody had come up from Florida to see family for a few days, and Reece had really enjoyed a night out with a friend, having a few beers and talking shop. It was also the first time he'd driven anything other than his dad's old, slow truck for a while, and truth be told, he didn't drive that if he could avoid it, relying on friends or public transport.

It felt good, though he was somewhat nervous. That was to be expected, right? His mind went to Abby, distracting him from his doubts. It had been a week since their argument, and they managed to move around each other without a lot of fuss, talking when they had to, but not much else. He also seen her talking with the fire investigator sent to do the second report, and the strain she'd been under was obvious. He made himself scarce, not wanting to add to it. How could they think she would have torched her own place?

He wondered where she went when she was out.

With the young stud he'd seen her flirting with at the Christmas tree contest?

He'd wanted to punch the guy in the face, but that wasn't his right. Never was. Still, it had been all he could do to keep from crossing the field and claiming Abby as his.

Which left him more confused than ever.

"Stop feeling her up and drive already," Brody said, making Reece laugh.

"Sorry. It's been a while," he said, enjoying the snug fit of the seat and the powerful purr of the engine as he hit the gas and pulled out from the restaurant where he'd met Brody for dinner. Brody had been in the NASCAR circuit for a while and was thinking about retiring, which he'd told Reece over dinner.

"It's like sex. You might be a little rusty, but it will come back to you," Brody reassured.

"You sure you trust me not to scratch her?" he asked with a hint of humor, but his nerves betrayed him.

Brody's new Dodge Charger SRT8 was a nice machine. This was the most car he'd driven since he crashed, and his hands were a bit sweaty, his heart slamming not from excitement, but apprehension.

"It's right to be nervous after a crash," Brody said, reading him. "It's normal, but if you want back in, you have to start working through it. Open her up gradually. See how it feels. You can back off if you need to."

His friend's understanding helped ease his anxiety. Brody was absolutely right—how could Reece expect to return to driving if he couldn't drive a regular road car?

He left the parking lot, and relaxed as the car started moving.

This was familiar. It felt good.

As they hit the lake road heading to the winery, Reece picked up speed, feeling his reflexes kick in, and he laughed with pure pleasure.

"Told you," Brody said, chuckling, too.

Except for when he'd been making love to Abby, he hadn't been this pumped in some time. Her face, her scent, came back to him with startling clarity, and he lost track of what he was doing for a moment, which had him backing off on the gas.

"You okay?" Brody asked.

"Yeah, sorry. I was distracted for a minute," he said, irritated. He still craved her touch, but he couldn't afford any distractions if he was going to drive, and that included women. Even Abby.

Reece focused for the rest of the drive up the side of the lake, turning into the driveway where he found a crowd of cars in the parking lot.

"I guess the party is still going, but we can head into the house, have a few beers," he said to Brody, parking the Charger and handing his buddy the keys. "Thanks for that. It felt good."

Brody stuck the keys in the pocket of the leather bomber jacket he wore, watching Reece speculatively. "I heard they were thinking of a new guy for your team," he said.

"Yeah, I heard that, too. Hope to convince them differently, but it's hard, being stuck here."

"I know a few guys at Daytona. If you want to fly in for a day, I could set up a test drive for you. We could go down there for a few times around the track, do some timed runs, if you want to see how it goes."

Reece knew he should jump at the opportunity, but the sweat broke out on his hands again. He didn't understand why he was reacting this way, and it pissed him off.

"Sure, set it up," he said evenly, though his stomach lurched as they walked up to the house.

His left leg was still bothering him. He was starting to think it might never get better, though he knew it felt worse after being locked into position while driving. Exercise and time would solve that problem, he kept telling himself.

"So what's the big event?" Brody asked, nodding toward the group of cars.

"Bachelorette party," Reece said with a laugh, shaking his head.

"Are you kidding me?"

"Nope."

Reece explained about Abby, and how she was working out of the winery. The bachelor party was at a bar in town, but Sandra had decided to have her party at the winery. Reece had overheard that conversation on his way through the house one day.

Brody stopped, rubbing his chin with his thumb and forefinger, grinning as he looked toward the reception rooms. "Should we crash?"

Reece laughed. "We're not eighteen anymore."

His friend cocked an eyebrow in his direction. "Yeah, we wouldn't have known what to do with a roomful of half-drunk chicks in the mood to party when we were eighteen," he said, making Reece laugh harder, his former tension dissolving.

"And you do now?" Reece teased back, slapping

Brody on the shoulder, but Brody was already heading toward the party. Reece followed, reluctantly.

"It's kind of Abby's thing," he hedged. "Maybe we should just stick to the house."

"Gotta get your spirit of adventure back, friend," Brody said with a grin, and Reece gave in and continued to follow. They made their way over to the tasting room, walking in the side door where it was dark in the lobby, moving like spies along the bar and cracking open the door to the reception room out back.

Reece wasn't sure what he expected to see, but it sure wasn't what he saw.

"You sure this is the *bachelorette* party?" Brody asked on a whisper, his eyes wide.

"Yeah," he answered, though he had to admit to a moment of confusion, as well.

At the far side of the room, women all gathered, and Reece had to blink a few times to believe what he was seeing. Abby had been very hush-hush about the party and changed the subject or was vague when he asked how it was going. Now he knew why.

He'd figured the party would either be a bunch of women dancing or talking, or sticking dollar bills in some young guy's jock strap, but instead, a ministage had been set up on the far end of the room, and there was a pole that braced from ceiling to floor.

And the women were taking turns dancing around it. They had their clothes on, of course. And most of them collapsed laughing as they tried to imitate classic stripper moves—some more successful than others—to songs playing so loudly all he could hear was music and shrieks of laughter, along with encouraging comments.

"Women are strange," Brody said. "Don't they usually get mad at us for going to watch this kind of thing?"

Reece laughed, edging the door open for a better view of the merriment. It was all innocent fun and games, and no one even noticed they were there, they were all enjoying themselves so much.

He naturally sought out Abby, who was standing to the side, monitoring the event and making sure all was going well. She smiled and spoke to Hannah, who stood by her side, the two women standing apart from the main action.

The song ended and Sandra, much happier than the day he'd found her screaming at Abby out in the field, took the stage. She definitely appeared to be tilting a bit, a martini sloshing dangerously in her hand.

She took a microphone and grinned at the group of women in front of her.

"This is such a blast—as you know, it's all on video, and I'll be sure to let you know which cuts make it to YouTube tomorrow," she promised. Laughter and a few playful threats ensued.

"But the martinis aren't gone and we're not done yet!" she announced to a chorus of hooting and howling.

"And not everyone has taken their turn, and we said everyone has to take a turn," she warned, turning to face Abby, who was still talking to Hannah.

The crowd cheered again as Sandra said, "Now we know Abby Harper can throw a monster bachelorette party, but can she dance?"

Abby stopped midconversation with Hannah, just then noticing the room's attention was on her. Her eyes widened and she shook her head.

"Oh, this just got interesting," Brody said, leering at Abby and Hannah. Reece elbowed him.

"The one on the right is Abby," Reece told him, but the light warning in his voice was clear.

Brody grinned. "So the one on the left is free?"

Brody was a shameless womanizer, teased in the media as to whether he had more trophies or romantic conquests. About the only thing in life he was serious about was his driving. Behind the wheel, he was all business, but out in the world, he was all play.

"Yeah, bud, go for it," Reece said, thinking it might be funny to see Brody get shot down. He'd known Hannah as long as he'd known Abby, and Hannah was as no-nonsense as they came, and she didn't suffer fools.

Abby was still vociferously protesting, even as Sandra tugged her up on stage, everyone laughing and daring her to do it.

When Abby was left alone by the pole, the crowd clapping to the beat of some bump-and-grind rock song that started playing, Abby laughed, put a hand to her face in embarrassment and rolled her eyes.

"Oh, my God, she's going to do it," Reece said, finding himself inexplicably breathless.

Abby was dressed in a very simple black dress that seemed conservative next to some of the outfits in the room, but when she kicked her heels off and grabbed the pole, Reece's cock jerked and hardened.

She slid her back up and down the pole, the simple dress sliding down off her shoulder slightly, and rising as she bent her knee to reveal a smooth expanse of thigh. When her head fell back in apparent sexual bliss, Reece heard Brody hiss a breath and elbowed him again.

When she came back up, vamping for the girls, she looked across the room and froze as she saw him.

He smiled, nodding once, and mischief sparkled in her expression. No one seemed to notice them watching but her.

Her eyes stayed on his as she started dancing again. Wrapping herself around that pole like a pro, she bent forward to show the tops of beautiful breasts as she shimmied, impressing him with flexibility that he knew he wanted to learn more about.

"*That's* your high school girlfriend?" Brody said in awe.

"No, she was just a neighbor then, a girl I knew," Reece said, not looking away.

"And now?"

"Not sure," Reece said, wanting to stop talking and focus.

Laughing, Abby held her hand out. All hell broke loose when Hannah strutted up on stage, wearing a classic wool skirt and plain white blouse, but Reece suddenly saw the smart-mouthed accountant that he knew turn into a sexy vixen. She undid a few buttons and her hair swished around her face, making those dark-rimmed glasses downright intriguing.

Brody lost all control and started whistling, catcalling for more, and the women turned, gaping, a moment of silence falling over the room, except for the heavy beat of the music still playing.

Reece wasn't sure what their reception would be, but he was poised to either apologize or make a run for it.

Brody's eyes were glued to Hannah, and he seemed to care less if they had been discovered, yelling to the women to start dancing again.

Laughter broke out, and some women came back, taking Reece and Brody by the hands, pulling them forward and insisting if they wanted to join the party, that *they* had to dance.

Reece laughed, but "over my dead body" was his silent reply to that. Brody, though, was in party form, grabbing a martini and jumping up on stage with a shocked Hannah, leading her to dance more with him, just as Reece took Abby's hand and helped her down.

"I missed you" was the first thing he said, and he realized it was true.

"I missed you, too," she admitted.

His eyes devoured her flushed cheeks and the rest of the room around them fell away.

"I don't get the dancing thing, but I sure did like it," he said in a low voice.

She grinned. "I don't know, either. It's some stripper fantasy, girl-power deal, I guess," she said, shrugging. "It was fun, though."

They both cracked up when they looked back to see Brody dancing around the pole.

Something clicked for Reece when he heard Abby laugh. He wanted to drag her off to a dark corner and take her now.

She seemed to know what he was thinking. The party had taken on a life of its own, and no one even noticed them anymore.

Before she could find some reason to change her mind, he took her by the hand and led her out of the room, into the tasting room, behind the bar. It was mostly dark, and no one else was there, though everyone was about twenty feet away at the party.

He backed her up against the wall, silencing anything she might say with a kiss that made his need clear. She moaned into his mouth, and as he slipped his hand up under the skirt of her dress, he found her slick, as aroused as he was.

"It's not the hedges, but it will do," he said roughly into her neck, need clawing at him as he picked up the scent of her sweat and sex, her skin hot from dancing and arousal.

"Someone might come out, they could see," she said, but he knew from her tone it was exciting her more... and she didn't ask him to stop.

"Yeah, they could, so we'd better hurry," he agreed, freeing his erection from his jeans and lifting her hips, cradling her butt in his hands so that she could wrap her legs around him.

Reece wasted no time getting inside of her, pushing deep and hard, taking her in short, quick thrusts that made her arch against him. She muffled a cry of pleasure as she dug her fingers into his shoulders, hanging on. She was hot and tight around him, and he didn't care if someone did come out and catch them, he needed her too much.

He didn't think he'd ever been this aroused. He was starving for her. In fact, he never would have risked this kind of public exposure given his responsibilities to the team and his sponsors, but right now, he didn't have to worry about that.

He leaned down, bracing Abby against the wall so that he could suck a nipple through the fabric of her dress. That sent her over the edge. She sank her teeth into his shoulder as she came, holding on tight and trying to hold back the scream that became a low keening against his neck.

He couldn't stop, either, and found her mouth, plundering it with a deep kiss as he exploded inside of her, the orgasm making his legs weak, but he rode it out, taking every last bit of pleasure she offered him.

When the moment passed, they were both sweaty, sticky and breathless. Reece heard voices coming toward them and they quickly ducked down behind the bar. Abby was illuminated in a sliver of light that angled down from the front windows, her eyes wide and sparkling, hair tousled. She covered her mouth to smother a giggle.

He pulled her in close, wrapping his arms around her as the voices came closer.

It was Brody and—if he was correct—Hannah.

He felt Abby shift in his arms, she must have realized, too, and reached to see. He held her still, putting a finger to her lips until their friends moved on, and Reece heard the grumbling engine of the Charger rev to life.

"Sounds like Hannah is taking home a little Christmas cheer," Abby said, chuckling, and Reece grinned as they both stood up, surveying the area as they fixed their clothes and emerged into the other room.

"Who was that, anyway?" she asked, threading fingers through her hair to smooth it down.

He ran his eyes over her and wanted to mess it right back up again.

"My friend Brody. Palmer," he added.

"Like, *the* Brody Palmer?" she asked. "Are you telling me my best friend just left with *Brody Palmer?* The one whose fan site has a poll keeping track of whether he's ridden more cars or women?"

Reece winced and opted for being straightforward.

"Yeah, that would be the one."

Abby groaned. "I don't know whether I should call her to warn her off or congratulate her," she said.

"You can't believe everything you hear in the media," Reece said, chuckling.

Abby eyed him doubtfully, and he caved.

"Well, okay, when it comes to Brody, most of that is kind of true, but he's a good guy, I promise. She'll be okay with him," he insisted.

"If you say so," she commented, smiling, and pressed in close. She kept Hannah's comments about wishing she could find a hot guy to use for sex to herself. It looked like her friend's wish had come true.

"How about you?"

"What?" he asked, playing dumb.

"More cars or women?" she asked with a grin.

"I don't have anyone running polls, but I'm pretty sure I can say cars," he answered, nuzzling her neck. "I'm not a saint, but I'm no Brody Palmer."

"Thank heavens," she said, laughing and wrapping her arms around his neck, sighing.

Bright lights flicked on and they flew apart to find a grinning, soused bride-to-be facing them. Sandra stared at them for a minute, still smiling.

"Sandra, are you okay?"

"I'm *won-fer-dul*," she said, lurching forward to wrap her arms around Abby in a drunken hug. Abby sagged under the slack weight of the woman, who mumbled praise about the best party ever and being so sorry she had threatened to "shoe" Abby after the fire.

"It's okay, Sandra. I knew you were just upset, and wouldn't really sue me," Abby comforted, trying to support her weight and looking over Sandra's shoulder for help.

Reece came to her rescue, slinging one of Sandra's arms over his shoulder, bracing most of the weight as they got her to one of the fireplace chairs and gently deposited her in it.

"What are you doing with the not-so-blushing bride?" he asked with a grin.

Abby sighed. "I can find out which of her friends or sisters is most sober, and see if they can get her upstairs to her room. I have all of their car keys over at the house, so no one is going anywhere tonight. Big sleepover," she said, chuckling, and Reece relaxed. "They have a group brunch planned for tomorrow morning, so once I get them set tonight, I'm done."

"What can I do to help?" he asked, and she looked at him in surprise.

"You can't take care of all of this alone, and Hannah is gone for the night," Reece pointed out.

"You're sure?" she said, and he saw the doubt in her eyes. He didn't blame her.

But now that he'd had her in his arms again, he knew that he didn't want to let her go one minute sooner than he had to.

"Absolutely. Abby, I'm sorry I was an ass last week. I guess I thought it would be easier if I put some distance between us, but it wasn't."

"Reece," she said on a sigh, leaning her forehead against him.

"That guy, at the Christmas tree event…did you go out with him?"

God, he felt sixteen, but he had to know.

"No. I was just trying to tick you off."

"It worked," he said with a grin, but then became serious again. "I didn't mean to hurt you. I just…I don't know," he admitted, feeling foolish. "I was messed up."

She pressed a kiss to the corner of his lips. "I know. Me, too."

Suddenly the world seemed a little more right again, and Reece blew out a breath, looking at his watch.

"You can go see what's what. I can start cleaning up, if you want," he said.

"Thanks. I appreciate it. I'll be right back."

He watched her walk away, all female grace and strength, and knew he couldn't fight what he felt for her anymore, but he had no idea where it was heading, either. Nothing had changed—and everything had changed.

"Abby?" he called out, before she disappeared back into the reception room.

She turned. "Hmm?"

"Maybe we should leave that pole up, though, just for a night or two," he said, imagining he'd like a show for one.

The sexy, mischievous look in her eyes as she smiled told him she agreed.

10

ABBY WAS GETTING USED to her life on a roller coaster, and when it meant she was able to wake up in Reece's bed, that was definitely okay with her.

She wasn't interested in fighting it anymore, releasing all the doubt and worry. They were good together. She wanted him, and apparently he wanted her. She shivered, thinking about the wonderful, desperate way he'd taken her the night before, standing up, behind the wine bar. The sex had been fast, a little awkward and… spectacular.

They'd worked side-by-side the rest of the evening, some understanding hammered out even though they didn't talk very much at all.

As much as she wanted him again, they'd both crashed as soon as they hit the mattress, exhausted and wrapped around each other. She remembered feeling a deep satisfaction that he seemed to have missed her as much as she missed him.

Maybe that was foolish, but she didn't care.

She stared at the empty pillow beside her—he'd probably gotten up early to work out. Her cell phone rang, interrupting her thoughts. Hannah.

"Hey," Abby said cheerfully. "I didn't expect to hear from you today, you wild woman," she teased her friend.

"You know me, I'm an early bird," Hannah said, her voice practically singing with I-had-a-night-of-wild-sex energy. "Even when I was up very, very late."

"Do tell."

"Later, promise. Right now, we were wondering if you'd be interested in brunch."

"We?"

"Brody and I. We're calling for both of you, but if you want, you could just come yourself."

Abby detected the unspoken question in Hannah's voice—she must have seen them leave together, and wondered what had happened.

"I'm sure Reece will want to come, too."

Hannah laughed knowingly. "So your cold spell is over," she said happily.

"Most definitely," Abby said with a smile. "Where should we meet you?"

They named a time and place, and Abby got up, taking off what little she had on and padding to the bathroom, where she had just heard the water turn on. Losing her robe, she smiled, pulling the door open to find Reece waiting.

"I was hoping the noise might wake you up," he said with an unabashed grin, holding out a hand to her.

"Wow," she said, not hiding her awe. He was using the master bath, and she had been using the guest bath attached to her room. Hers was very nice, she had no complaints, but this was just…sinful.

The entire space was composed of granite with specks of gold, black and dark red lending a warm touch, textured on the floor so as to avoid being slippery, and smooth, but with a matte finish, on the sides. Plants lined a window that set a few feet above them, draping down, obviously loving the high humidity and light. Abby felt like she was stepping into a hidden cave with a waterfall.

There were five jets at different heights, and a bench seat that ran almost the entire length of the shower, with a shelf of soaps, shampoos, body oils, sponges, loofahs and pretty much anything else you could think of. You could even adjust the lighting, bright or soft, and the controls for the water temperature were digital so you could set the degree—no guessing.

"This isn't a shower. This is shower heaven," she said.

"Yeah, it's extreme. My dad always called it 'The Lagoon,'" he said with a laugh.

"That's it exactly."

"It was my mom's pet project. She set out to create the perfect bathroom one year. It actually was featured in a home décor magazine. She was on top of the world."

"She nailed it," Abby agreed breathlessly, and he laughed as she went into his arms under the hot spray.

His hands covered and massaged her breasts as they kissed, and he added, "Now *this* is shower heaven."

"Mmm-hmm," she agreed, her hands dipping low to stroke his ready erection, making him groan. She was intrigued when he trembled as she reached lower, stroking a finger over his balls and petting the soft skin deep between his thighs.

"Come here," he said as he sat on the bench and pulled her on to his lap, angled slightly so she could kiss him as the water poured over them from seemingly everywhere.

She started to turn to face him, to straddle him, but he shook his head. "You'll punish your knees on the stone. Like this," he said, stretching out his legs straight and moving her over him.

"Oh…*oh*," she gasped as he slid deep inside.

He held her there against him, kissing her ears, her neck. His hands covered her breasts, plucking and rolling hard, wet nipples between his fingers until she was writhing.

She had a feeling he'd planned that, and she liked a man who thought ahead. The throbbing of the hot water against her flesh and the sensation of him buried deep inside had her moaning as an easy orgasm rolled over her. Reece whispered hot, raw things in her ear as she came, and then came again.

Breathless and panting, she pushed forward, still poised against him, bracing her hands on his knees, looking back with a sexy wink.

"I like this," she said, enjoying how his hands covered her bottom, his fingers digging in a little as he brought her down the way that he needed.

"Me, too."

She moved her right hand from his knee to stroke herself as she took him deep and ground against him in a way that had him yelling her name, arching up and pushing even deeper as they came together.

She relaxed back against him, turning her face into the strong column of his neck.

"That was so good. It's always good with you," she said, wrapping her fingers in his as the water washed over them.

"I'm glad you think so."

"I do."

He helped her up and stood with her, grabbing a soft natural sponge and some soap. He washed her carefully, tenderly, and she nearly purred. She'd never felt this cared for, and the intimacy was stunning as he bent before her, washing her legs and between them, planting kisses where the shower washed away the soap. She was feeling sparks again before he was back at eye level.

"Do you like games, Abby?"

A flicker of anticipation teased her.

"Like Monopoly?" she asked innocently.

He smiled, and pulled her closer, whispering in her ear. Her breath hitched. How was it that her fantasies seemed to be his?

"I love those kinds of games," she said, finding it hard to breathe.

"Come here then," he said, pulling her upright.

He positioned her by the edge of the spray, and she looked up, seeing the two ties that hung limply from the shower rod. Realization dawned.

"Oh. I thought you had just left your laundry in here," she said, her heart stuttering as he lifted her arm and pulled one tie down to her wrist.

"Make sure the ties won't give," she said, daringly, and saw his eyes darken as they met hers.

"Is this comfortable?" he asked, securing the tie.

She wiggled her fingers, and pulled. The knots were solid. A slight edge of apprehension rose, but curiosity and excitement outweighed it.

"I'm good," she said, watching him step back and look at her.

"We're going to do what I told you, and you're okay with it? My rules?"

"Yes," she said, as submissively as she could.

"Good," he said, his eyes dark and passionate on hers as he stroked himself to semihardness.

She watched, fascinated, unable to take her eyes away from him. She'd never watched a man pleasure himself, and felt herself get wet from more than the shower.

"You'd like to watch me finish this, wouldn't you?"

She struggled, flexing her fingers, wanting to touch, to go to him, but he was out of reach. And if she couldn't touch him, she wanted to touch herself, suddenly craving release again.

"I'd like that very much," she admitted. "But there's a problem."

"What?"

"I want to come again, too."

"Well," he said, teasingly, softly, "we'll both get there, eventually."

She frowned. "Eventually?"

He walked over to her, leaning in to nuzzle her neck, and she whimpered, needing the touch.

"You'll see."

He kissed her sweetly, then moved down her body in a string of butterfly kisses, leaving sparks of heat everywhere, but not giving her anything near what she needed. He brushed his thumbs and then his lips over her nipples, lightly, teasing some more, until she was almost limp and begging.

Then he went down farther, and she braced for his kiss between her legs, but he only ran his hands up and down her legs, kissing and nibbling at the insides of her thighs. She opened herself as much as she could, trying to show him what she needed.

"You want my mouth on you, Abby?"

"Please, yes," she said weakly. Desire was a hot weight in her abdomen, a bomb needing to explode.

He nodded and whispered, "Okay," against her skin, then used both hands to spread her slick flesh, but rather than planting his mouth against her, he flicked his tongue against her clit, the sensations intense but fleeting, not constant enough to push her over. She tried to press against him, to find the pressure she needed to come, but he would move and she cried out in lust and need.

"Please, Reece. I don't think I want to play anymore," she said.

He stood, his jaw tight, his eyes dark. "Abby, I'm hard as rock, ready to explode—again. I haven't felt need like this in years. I want to pull you up and fuck you until we both dissolve under the water," he said, and his raw language only excited her more.

"Do it," she urged, wanting exactly that. "Just think how good it would be, Reece. You could take me any way you want…and I want you to," she tempted, trying to break him. "Whatever you want, however you want me," she whispered.

By the look on his face and the way his cock jerked at her words, it was working.

He came up close to her, and she cheered inside her mind, celebrating her win.

He smiled and then did something she never expected, bringing his hand down on her bottom in a stinging swat. "Stop that. We both have to wait. Those are the rules."

The sting from the swat turned to heat on her skin, and she found she craved more, anything that would relieve the torturous pressure of arousal inside of her. They'd just made love minutes before, but it had been too long, and her body was on fire for more.

He rubbed his hand over the spot where he had spanked her, and brushed his lips against hers, then kissed her more deeply.

Their bodies were hardly touching, though their mouths tried to make up for it, mating furiously.

"Reece, I need you," she said, breaking the kiss to breathe.

"I need you, too, Abby," he said roughly. "So much."

He reached up past her, the length of his body touching hers, making her shudder, and she heard a noise. One arm fell free, then the other.

She looked down at her wrists, and he reached over to shut off the water.

She stared at him, stunned. "You really mean it, don't you? You're going to make us both wait?"

He nodded, stepping away and coming back with a heated towel that he wrapped around her. She was dizzy with arousal, and he pulled her up close, rubbing her back soothingly.

"That's right. That's the game."

"What if I don't want to wait?"

"You already agreed to play," he said, pulling her

behind him and grabbing a towel for himself. "Don't worry. I'm just as hot as you are, and you'll have your turn later," he promised. "Didn't you say we have to go meet Brody and Hannah for breakfast."

She almost groaned in dismay. She'd almost forgotten. How was she going to get through brunch with friends, as wound up as she was? She couldn't even think straight, she was so turned on.

It was wonderful.

She was tuned into him more closely than she had ever been to anything in her life, as if she was aware of every movement, every breath. She rubbed her wrists.

"You okay?" he asked, clearly concerned.

"Yes. I liked how it felt. I wanted it to last longer," she admitted, starting to calm down a little. She was on edge, certain that so much as a touch from him might send her into climax, but now…now she also wanted to see how long they could last. How crazy they could make each other before they gave in.

And she was very much looking forward to her turn to push Reece to his limit.

He smiled at her, as if he'd read every thought. It was incredibly intimate, linking them together in a way she hadn't experienced with anyone else, ever.

As they got dressed, he leaned in and planted a kiss on her lips, whispering, "It's going to be worth every second we wait, I promise," he said.

She believed it.

REECE SHIFTED IN HIS chair at the table, dealing with an on-and-off hard-on all through brunch. Abby was a clever lover—and a little mean—he thought with a smile.

When he'd told her he wanted to tie her up and tease her until she begged, she'd been all for it. When he told her he was going to leave them both on edge, not give in, she'd doubted him, but it was perfect. The constant potential for satisfaction—or not—was like live electricity crackling between them.

He'd read about extended sexual seduction practices. They included but also went beyond Tantra to create arousal that lasted for days, resulting in climax for both partners that was off the scale—but he'd never been with anyone he desired enough to actually try it. He imagined him and Abby seducing each other with baths, massages, meals and light sexual teasing for days before having sex. He'd always wondered what that would be like.

Now he knew.

She became adept at the game very quickly.

Small touches to his knee or his thigh were bad enough, but the way she innocently worked bondage references into her conversation taunted him, reminding him of how incredibly erotic she had looked hours ago, and how close he had come to taking her again.

But this was better. The play was demonical, but fun.

His focus was on her hand as she appeared to absently rub her wrist as they ate and chatted—not because it hurt, but because she knew, the little minx, that it would be driving him out of his mind to think about tying her up again. The first time had been an experiment, and way too brief.

"So anyway," Brody said, stretching back in his chair,

grinning and eyeing Reece speculatively as Brody's hand landed on Hannah's nape.

It was an oddly possessive gesture, Reece thought. He'd been surprised enough that Brody was at a brunch with a woman he slept with. It might be a first. Reece certainly didn't know the details of Brody's love life, except that most of his stories of the women he met included a hasty exit before morning light.

Hannah seemed quite happy with herself this morning, too. Interesting.

"Anyway," Brody started again, "I talked with a friend down at Daytona this morning. If you're interested, we could fly there later today, do a test run tomorrow, see how it feels, get your legs back under you," Brody announced.

Reece hadn't seen that coming, either. Brody was full of surprises. He knew he'd told him to set it up, but he thought it would probably be weeks, not hours.

"Wow, that was fast," was all he could say.

"Strike while the iron is hot," Brody said, chugging back his orange juice. "We'd have to leave later today, but I can get us down there. Friend of mine has a private plane and pilot here that he's willing to loan out."

Reece was dumbstruck, and he knew his response should have been immediate. Brody's eyes narrowed as he watched him, but he didn't say anything else.

Reece was dealing with the fact that his first response had not been *hell, yeah,* but that he didn't want to leave Abby, not when they had just found their footing again.

Which was ridiculous. He'd be back after a day or so. She'd still be here, right?

"Reece, you have to get back behind the wheel before they're even going to look at you for the new season. You have to get your mojo," Brody added.

Reece knew he shouldn't need arm-twisting, and jumped when he felt Abby's hand cover his in a visible show of support.

"You should go," she said, her voice sure.

He looked at her and she didn't waver, just gave him a single nod before squeezing his hand and returning to her breakfast.

He wasn't sure how to respond to that, either—was she able to let him go so easily? Why did that bother him? He'd done nothing but tell her that he was leaving since they first met.

"You should come with me," he said to her, the words leaving his lips almost before the idea had fully formed in his brain. It made sense though. For one thing, he felt better when he had Abby with him—he'd slept peacefully for the first time last night, and his legs or arm weren't bothering him at all this morning.

Maybe it was the sex, the release, the stimulation or just her personal magic, but she made him feel good. And he needed to feel good if he was going to get into a car and hit a track at one-eighty plus for the first time in months.

"Oh, I don't know...." she said, frowning. "The wedding is only ten days off—"

"You have most of that prepped," Hannah interrupted. "Anything else is up to the families, except for the decorating, but you don't need to do that now. I checked the schedule, and the next thing you have is the Christmas and Chocolate party this Friday night. You can manage to take a few days off. C'mon Abby, let's take a little vacation," Hannah urged.

"You're both going?" Reece asked, looking at Brody with even more surprise.

"Yeah. Hannah says she wants some excitement, and I can't think of anything more exciting than being at the track. So she's coming with me for a month of preseason."

Abby and Reece were both struck silent with surprise. Hannah's cheeks were warm, but her eyes were bright with pure joy.

"I hope that's okay, Abby, I was going to talk to you before Brody decided to just leap in and volunteer the information," she said, sliding him an affectionate look. "But January is always slow, and you can take my apartment while you're working on getting things done with the winery, I mean, you know, if you're still not at Reece's after the New Year," Hannah said.

Abby nodded, and didn't appear to know what to say. Reece put his hand on hers this time and squeezed, turning to her so that they were only looking at each other.

"I'd really like it if you could come with me," he said. "It would mean a lot, but I also understand if you can't."

Abby, looking slightly cornered, shook her head, as if trying to clear her thoughts. She turned her hand over to hold Reece's, an encouraging sign.

"Hannah is right. I can close for a few days, not much happening on weekdays now anyway. I'll have Judy come by to look in on the horses and animals. She's done that for me before," she said.

"So you'll come?" Reece asked, feeling far too hopeful.

She paused for another moment, then smiled. "Yes, it'll be fun," she replied. "And I want to be there for you."

"Great! I'll make the flight arrangements right now," Brody, their man of action, said, planting a quick kiss on Hannah's mouth. He pulled his cell phone from his pocket and stood up from the table.

Reece leaned in to kiss Abby's cheek. "Thank you. This will be a lot less nerve-racking with you there."

She was obviously surprised at his unvarnished admission, and he was, too, but it was the truth. He was developing emotions that amounted to far more than lust for Abby. He had a need for her that went beyond the physical.

She was different than any woman he'd ever known, and he didn't want to lose whatever was growing between them.

What they would do about that, long-term, he had no idea, but for now, he would just take the curves as they came.

Hannah was grinning at them, all dewey-eyed.

"I'm so glad you guys made up," she said.

Reece straightened in his chair, realizing Abby would have, of course, told her about their fight, and no doubt what a jerk he was. But the way she looked right now, happy and hopeful, made him a bit twitchy. He was willing to admit that he had some serious feelings for Abby, but he wasn't entirely comfortable having assumptions made about them as a couple.

"So you're going to hang out with Brody at the track for a month?" he said to Hannah, changing the topic.

"I need some adventure. This sounds…adventurous."

"You follow racing?" Reece asked.

"No, not at all. But I guess I'll learn," she said with a goofy smile, picking apart a croissant.

Reece liked Brody. He was a good friend, and a great driver. But somehow, he felt like he had to say something to Hannah.

"I hope you're not putting too much stock into this, Hannah. Just so you know. He's a good man, but, well, you know what I'm trying to say. I'm surprised he was even here for breakfast," Reece said bluntly, drawing a shocked look from Abby, but Hannah just stared, and then burst out laughing.

"Thanks, Reece, but Brody made it quite clear that he's not interested in anything permanent. That's perfect, because all I want is a month of hot sex and something new in my life before I come back to my routine," she said, making Reece choke on his coffee.

"You two should be perfect together, then," he agreed, laughing.

Abby was uncharacteristically quiet, focused on the remainder of her breakfast, but he could practically hear the wheels spinning in her mind. Right now though, all he cared about was that she would be with him.

They'd have a few days in sunny Florida to go to the track, and to hopefully continue their fun and games.

As much as some excitement had filtered through about the prospect of getting back into a car, it was disconcerting to know that the second item excited him the most.

11

ABBY SQUINTED AS SHE DEPLANED, walking down the short course of steps onto the tarmac. She hadn't flown anywhere in quite some time, and never in a private jet. It had been a lot of fun. She'd forgotten how much she enjoyed the speed and thrill of takeoffs, checking out the landscape below as she flew by and the joy of setting feet to ground again. They'd had a smooth flight, and it was only early evening, the weather clear and warm.

She was also starving and, frankly, so horny she could hardly stand it. The close quarters of the plane had given them plenty of time to play their secret game, with quick touches and teasing talk or glances. She figured she might help him relax once they got to their condo, a place Brody owned right by the track.

But there was more than sex going on between them. Reece had thanked her about ten times since brunch, and it warmed her to know that her presence here meant so much to him. She could also detect the fine tension in him. She knew this was a big deal for him, and she was perhaps more nervous for him than he was for himself.

She didn't want to think about where it was all leading. They had something new, some kind of deeper connection, an intimacy that had blossomed quickly and almost without her realizing it. It was as if, after the argument, they had come back together more deeply than before.

Or maybe it was just her. Somehow, regardless of all of the external circumstances and doubts, she knew she could trust Reece, and she wanted to be with him, no matter what the future held.

She was dying to talk to Hannah about her arrangement with Brody, and what had happened to make her friend take off on such a wild lark. She seized the opportunity as they crossed the terminal to a large SUV that was waiting for them. Brody had thought of everything. The men walked ahead, and she slowed down, hanging back with Hannah.

"So…a month with Brody?" she asked, opening the door for Hannah to elaborate.

"Yeah, it's crazy, I know," Hannah said, shaking her head, her strawberry-blond hair swinging over her shoulders. "I wanted to talk to you privately first, since I know this affects you, too, with the winery, but Brody, well, he's kind of a force of nature," she said with a grin.

Abby smiled. "Yeah, that's the perfect description," she agreed. "Must have been some night you had with him, but are you sure a month is going to work out? It's a long time with someone you barely know," Abby said.

"Well, I can always come back early if I don't like it, or if things aren't good. But, Abby, he's amazing. If the month with him is anything like the other night, I'm not sure a month would be enough. I could get addicted."

Abby frowned. "That's another problem altogether. What Reece was talking about. These guys…some of them settle down, but not Reece. Not Brody. I don't want you getting heartbroken," Abby said.

Do as I say, but not as I do, she thought to herself. She wanted to save her friend some pain, if she could.

"I won't. I have no interest in love," Hannah continued. "I just want to be free for a while, to get out of my routine and live a little before I come back and probably end up marrying some nice, safe, dependable man and raising our two-point-eight."

Abby couldn't begrudge her friend that, in fact, she understood all too well. She loved their small-town life on the lake, on the vineyards, but it was a relatively ordinary life. Reece and Brody were extraordinary men.

But it was even more seductive for Hannah, Abby imagined. While she and Reece had grown up on the vineyards with parents who were successful enough to provide some of the extras like college and vacations, Hannah hadn't.

Her parents owned a local farm that had become defunct. Most of Hannah's youth had been beyond difficult, her father working too hard and dying of a heart attack when she was only ten. Her mom had had to work constantly after that to keep the house, and they had eventually sold and lived in an apartment in Ithaca.

Hannah had lost her dad and her home, and yet she'd never moaned and felt sorry for herself, which is something Abby admired so much. Hannah had spent many nights and weekends at Abby's house when they were kids, and she felt more like her sister than her friend.

Hannah's mother did better now, but that was largely

due to Hannah working her way through state college on loans and scholarships, and making life better for both of them.

Abby knew it was no accident that Hannah had studied accounting and that she worked like a dog. Hannah applied the same logic to her love life—she wouldn't marry a man who risked her security. So Abby knew that Brody really was just a wild fling, and if anyone deserved some fun and time away, it was Hannah.

Her friend's sexy brashness made her smile to herself, and she sighed as they were almost to the car.

"Yeah, that's what I thought with Reece at the beginning. Just be careful."

"You two seem more serious now, I take it?" Hannah queried.

"I'm not sure. The other night was…I don't know what it was," she said honestly, with another sigh. "I care about him. I think he cares about me. But as far as I know, nothing has changed. That's why we're here, right? So he can get one step closer to leaving."

"Aw, hon," Hannah said, slinging an arm around her. "Just have faith. If you two are supposed to work out, you will find a way."

Abby didn't want to think about it, really, and she also didn't want to rain on Hannah's fun, so she just smiled and nodded.

Right now, she was just focusing on the moment.

Hannah grinned, nudging her in the side as she ogled the guys' backsides. "They sure are a couple of hotties, though, huh?"

Abby had to grin, taking a long peek at how well Reece wore his jeans as they approached the SUV.

"You said it," she agreed, and they laughed the rest of the way to the car, the guys watching them curiously as they opened doors, climbed in and headed to the track.

THE CONDO WAS SPACIOUS and modern, with a huge picture window that looked out over the racetrack. Abby was thrilled that she had come along on the trip, not only to be with Reece and Hannah, but also because she had never been to a track except for Watkins Glen, which was a great racetrack, but with it being almost in her backyard didn't have the same kind of excitement.

Like some people enjoyed the beauty of baseball parks or tennis greens, she felt a zing of excitement run down her spine as she scrutinized the raceway. The track wasn't completely empty, though the stands were, but workers were getting ready for preseason events, and she'd seen one driver out on a test drive earlier that morning.

She couldn't help but shiver, watching. She enjoyed the thrill of the speed and the noise, but it had all been so distant before. Now it was real, and it would be Reece in that car, speeding around the curves.

"You're like a kid in a candy shop," Reece said, smiling as he slipped his hands over her shoulders, enjoying her excitement at being involved in his world. This wasn't Formula One, but people who were in racing and who really enjoyed the sport had to respect both circuits, regardless of the debates that always raged among fans about which was superior.

"It's pretty amazing," she said, snuggling back against him. "I'm glad I came."

"Me, too," he murmured.

The night before, they'd gone for a late dinner with Hannah and Brody and then out to walk around the town, as neither Hannah nor Abby had ever been to the area.

It was quite an experience, as they ate in a restaurant that had Brody's picture on the wall, and as they were interrupted by fans of both drivers for pictures and autographs. Both men were gracious and friendly, and Abby had watched in wonder, seeing a whole new side to Reece. He was a well-known public figure. She knew that, but it had never really hit her until now how famous he actually was in this world. And he was here, with her.

It was hard for her to get her mind around it, but she was learning not to second-guess everything.

Brody's condo was huge and, luckily, provided three large, separate sleeping quarters, which Brody often lent to visiting friends and family, or his team. It was immaculate, but not homey, obviously more of a practical investment for Brody than a place he had any emotional attachment to.

"Shouldn't you be at the track with Brody?" she asked, not wanting him to leave, but also wanting to support him, not become a distraction.

Reece seemed to have other ideas, sliding his hands over her hips and up her stomach to cover her breasts, and she couldn't deny the wave of lust that shook her to her toes as they stood before the large window.

They weren't very likely being watched by anyone. The scattering of people who were on the track were busy with their own concerns. Still, the idea of being here, so visible, turned her on.

"You have to drive today," she said on a groan as he nibbled her earlobe.

"I know, and I'm kind of on edge. I need to relax, burn off some energy. You have any ideas?"

She had nothing but ideas.

"What about our game?"

"We can just let off steam, maybe," he said, nipping at her neck and easing her shirt up, sliding his hands beneath as he pressed his hardness against her bottom.

"Oh, okay, then," she said, happy to pursue the satisfaction that had been keeping her in a constant state of wanting. The night before, she had done to him as he had to her, kissing him everywhere, taking him into her mouth and bringing him to the edge, but not finishing. They'd come back down to earth with kisses, eventually falling into an exhausted sleep.

In a strange way, she liked it. What had been frustration turned to something else, a kind of constant promise of intimacy that she had never imagined.

She turned in his arms, pulling his head down for a kiss, after he got rid of her shirt and undid her bra. "One of us has too many clothes on," she said, reaching for the buckle of his belt and undoing it.

Things were getting hot quickly, and she didn't recognize the sound filling the room, but then realized it was her phone.

"Let it go to message," Reece said, drawing on her breast so sweetly she gasped.

"I can't," she said breathlessly, pulling away gently. "I'll see what's up and be right back," she promised.

When she grabbed her phone, she saw it was her insurance agent. She answered immediately.

"Ms. Harper?"

"Yes?" Her heart was in her throat and she couldn't say more.

"Good news. The second fire inspector deemed the fire accidental. We can continue with paying the claim, as planned."

Relief made her hands tremble, and she felt tears sting her eyes. "Oh, thank you so much. Really, I appreciate you doing this so quickly," she said, her voice thick.

"You're very welcome—we do try to do the best for our clients, and a call from your father's friend helped me speed things along," he said with a smile. "Merry Christmas, Miss Harper. We'll be in touch."

She put the phone down and tried to compose herself before she turned back to Reece, but he was already there, turning her to him, taking in her tears. "What is it? What happened?"

She bit her lip and told him everything. He looked surprised, concerned and confused.

"Abby, why didn't you talk to me about this? It has to have been worrying you sick," he said, pulling her in next to him, his chin resting on her head as he rubbed her shoulders.

"I just never could. The timing was always wrong. I worried, at the start, that you might go ahead and sell to Keller if you thought that I wouldn't be financially viable, and then we had our blowup, and now we're just back together, and it's all been crazy," she said, hoping he understood.

He tipped her face up to meet his gaze.

"I guess I can understand why you'd think that, before,

but I hope you trust me with more than your body by now. I wouldn't do anything to hurt you, Abby, ever."

"I know. It's just been…intense. But when they pay out, I might be able to use the funds as a down payment on your property. It'll take everything I have, but if you're willing to work with me, I could do it," she said, holding her breath again.

He nodded, though there was a strange glint in his eye that she couldn't quite read. "I'd like nothing better than for you to have that land. I'll do whatever it takes to sell Winston Vineyards to you," he said. "But what about your own property?"

"At some point I'll repair our house, go back to living there. It's my home, but I won't build new tasting rooms. Yours are so much larger and nicer. If it's okay with you, I thought I might change your house into a bed-and-breakfast," she said, gauging his reaction. "That way it maintains the house, and puts it to good use."

He nodded. "That's smart."

"I'm glad you approve," she said with a smile, feeling lighter by the second. "I would keep your family's vines, too, though I would probably slowly transition the entire operation over to organic."

"Mom and Dad will love hearing that," he said.

The lightness of having things worked out made her dizzy. Reece was going to sell to her. It was going to be okay.

It would be financially tight for many years, but she'd be able to keep her legacy—and his—in place. That was worth everything.

"So, where were we?" she said, sliding her hands up under his shirt, and watching his eyes darken with desire. "I think we were loosening you up for your drive this afternoon?"

He groaned, looking at the clock. "I really do have to meet Brody. I suppose we'll have to…wait."

She smiled, kissing him again. "That's okay. It can be our celebration after you finish your drive."

Her heartbeat raced as she said the words, determined to be supportive and appreciate what they had, for now. The good news from the agent didn't reduce her anxiety about Reece driving, or about him eventually leaving. After all, that was why he was here—to get a second chance at his old life, even if she couldn't be part of it. She was with him now, so she shut out the rest and focused on that as he erased her thoughts with one more scorching kiss before he left.

REECE RAN HIS HAND OVER the hood of the car—it was a beauty, and he was anxious to get out on the track, his nerves banished. He felt great.

The stock car was heavier and built out far differently than those he drove for Formula One, not as low or aerodynamic, but it was a powerful beast, and it would put him to the test.

He knew he could do this. He was ready.

"Feeling good?" Brody asked, walking up beside him, handing him a helmet.

"Yeah. Yeah, I am."

"Let's go then," his buddy said with a slap on his shoulder. "They have everything set up and won't time the first run, so you can get a feel for it, but we'll time a second and third."

He tried to pretend this was as informal as Brody

said, but Reece knew a couple of reporters had caught wind of this drive, and asked to come on site. He'd allowed it. It was risky, but he had nothing to lose at this point.

"Sounds good," Reece said, pulling the helmet on, adjusting and testing the microphone as he prepared to slide himself into the tight spot, the men suddenly gathered around him ready to strap him to the seat.

Before he did so, however, he glanced up and saw Abby, waiting just beyond the perimeter with Hannah and a few other onlookers.

He waved, and she blew him a kiss back.

"You ready, Romeo?" Brody teased and Reece slid into the seat and got prepped.

Minutes later, all systems checked and ready, it was up to him now. Reece had driven this track once or twice before, never officially, but as he looked ahead, everything fell into place.

The world outside of the car dropped away as he pulled forward and got a feel for the smooth, powerful growl of the engine. Something very close to arousal flowed through him, and he became completely focused as he started a first lap, taking it slow at first, getting into the groove.

"God, this feels good," he said with gusto into the mic.

"You're looking good," he heard Brody respond with a knowing laugh.

Closing one lap, Reece got serious and picked up speed, moving the tach up to about 7000 rpms. He took the next corner perfectly, smiling.

This was right. This was where he belonged.

He did a few more laps and pulled in, signaling that he was ready for a timed run.

A short while later, he was off again, punching up the speed, testing the car, his reflexes and his body.

All seemed in working order, and he pulled in a few seconds later, listening over the radio for his time.

"I can do better," he said, to himself as much as to the guys on the other side.

This time, he went for it, watching the yellow light come on that told him he was pushing into the higher area of speeds that could disqualify a driver from a win, but he wasn't competing with anyone but himself and the clock.

He pushed it a little more, coming into the last lap, and caught his breath, cursing as a sharp pain shot up his calf to his knee, causing him to lose focus slightly, and the car wavered on the track.

Cold sweat broke out as he controlled the car, fishtailing slightly, trying to ignore the pain.

"Again," he ground out over the mic, even though Brody was saying no.

"One more."

He managed one more set of laps, clocking a decent time, though slower than he'd have liked.

But he had to stop, he knew, because the pins and needles were so intense, he couldn't feel the accelerator with his foot.

The frustration was more painful, but he swallowed it as he unbuckled himself and was pulled out. When he was set on his feet, his left leg faltered slightly, and he caught it in time to save himself public humiliation.

Brody noticed, and did him the favor of distracting those who were watching.

Abby noticed, too. She was as white as a sheet, staring at him with dark eyes.

A second later, she launched herself at him, and if not for the car behind him they would have both gone down.

"You were wonderful," she said, but she was trembling from head to toe.

"Hey, what's wrong?" he asked. "You're crying."

"I'm so happy for you, and that you are here again. I thought you were going to crash when you fishtailed—it scared me," she said. "But you didn't. You did it," she said, hugging him tightly again.

"My leg went buzzy on me," he said, disgusted with himself, adrenaline still surging through him, his own hands shaking. "I needed to do better."

He figured this was it. He'd made the drive, but his warble was going to be the thing everyone focused on. The thing that would convince the sponsors not to take a chance on him.

"It was respectable, considering," Brody interrupted. "What happened?"

"Lost feeling in my leg—or rather, pins and needles were too intense for me to apply as much pressure as I should. I lost focus for a moment," Reece admitted.

"You controlled it, and your time was decent. Still, your cars and tracks are a lot different, more unpredictable," Brody said, sliding one arm around Hannah and the other rubbing the back of his neck in an obviously nervous gesture. "Maybe if you rest one more season and let your body heal, you'll be in better shape next—"

"I can't do that, Brody, and you know it," Reece said. His leg was a little better now that he was out of his cramped position, but it still bothered him. "This will either convince them or not," he said, thanking his friend and shaking his hand. The chance to prove himself was was all he could ask for, but even Reece knew the drive hadn't gone as well as he needed it to. Not well enough for sponsors to risk millions of dollars on him.

Still, he had done it, and he was going to celebrate, like he had promised Abby.

"Hannah and I have plans tonight—you two are okay on your own?" Brody asked as they left the track.

"Yeah, we'll be fine. You guys have fun—we fly out early?"

"Yeah, see you in the morning."

They parted ways out in the lot after Reece had changed and met Abby where she waited for him outside.

"So, you want to go out and celebrate that I didn't completely wipe out?" he said with humor he wasn't completely feeling.

She touched his face, her eyes fierce. "You did better than that—you had one lapse, and I've seen drivers do a lot worse. We should celebrate because you did *well*."

Reece pulled her in, hugging her tight to his chest, a feeling of warmth and a tangle of other emotions washing over him. To keep himself from thinking about it, he found her mouth, nibbled at it, then kissed her more deeply, soaking up her warmth and her taste and everything that was Abby.

He wanted to hold on to her forever. He loved her, he thought, gazing beyond the open track. The realization didn't come as a surprise, more of a relief. He'd been struggling with his emotions for days, and it felt good to just set them free. He didn't know if he had room for both loves in his life, but he wanted to try.

12

BACK AT THE ROOM, Abby was relieved that her stomach had settled and her hands had finally stopped shaking. She hadn't realized how afraid she'd been for Reece until he actually started to drive.

As she watched the bright blue car covered with logos make laps, she'd relaxed and cheered him on, and when he'd lost control for that handful of seconds, her heart thudded in her chest, and she'd found herself propped up by Hannah.

All she could think of was him dying in that car, and it had flattened her.

The thought of life without him was suddenly impossible.

She loved him. It was a mistake, but she knew it clear down to her bones in the second that the car had fishtailed, and she knew she couldn't stand the idea of losing him, or of him being hurt again.

Lost in her thoughts as they entered the condo, she wandered into the bedroom with the idea of freshening up and maybe taking a nap, and saw several large boxes, all wrapped in bright Christmas wrapping, waiting on the bed.

"What's all this?" she asked Reece, who stood just behind her.

"For you. Open them. This one first," he said, handing her a large, flat box.

"But…it's not even Christmas yet, and I didn't buy anything for you," she objected.

"Just open it, Abby," he said, giving her a patient look.

She did, and set the box down, pulling out the most lovely emerald-green silk dress she had ever seen. A modest scooped bodice was held by lacy spaghetti straps, nipping in at the waist and flaring out around the knee in an ultrafeminine way.

"Reece, it's gorgeous," she breathed, and she sucked her breath back in, coughing as she saw the name of the designer. "Oh, no…this is too much."

"It's what I wanted to buy you. I saw it when we were out yesterday, and I knew it would be perfect on you. And it's warm enough to wear it down here," he said.

"Now?"

"We're going out tonight," he said. "On a date. We haven't had time for that. We need to make time."

"Oh. Reece, I'm so—I'm so…" She tried to find words, but she put the dress down and didn't know what to say. She didn't know what this meant, and she hated the confused rush of thoughts, hopes and doubts that crowded her mind.

"Open the others," he said, pushing her back to the pile of boxes.

"It's too much. The dress is enough."

"What, are you wearing it barefoot or with your boots?" he teased.

She noticed the size of one of the boxes was perfect for shoes, and leapt on it. She couldn't resist shoes, and he was right, she had to have something for the dress.

When she pulled out the sexy, strappy black stilettos, she groaned. "I think I am in lust," she said, petting the soft leather.

"I can't wait to see them on you." He handed her another smaller box, grinning devlishly.

Seeing that he was enjoying her opening the gifts as much as she was enjoying receiving them, she unwrapped the next one, and paused. The box itself was made from black leather with the word *Naughty* embossed on the top.

Taking the lid off, she saw a pair of shiny new handcuffs.

Her heart began to race.

"I want you to wear those tonight, too," he said. "Later," he corrected, his eyes burning hot.

She looked up at him. "I can do that."

The last box, also black leather, said *Nice* on top.

She smiled. "How can nice be as fun as naughty?"

"Open it and see."

She did, and saw a small bottle of cinnamon massage oil—edible—and she smiled. She lifted it, opening the bottle, the spicy scent greeting her, and she put a dab on her finger, then tasted it, meeting Reece's eyes.

"That is nice," she said, drawing her finger out from between her lips in a sexy gesture, watching his jaw become tense with desire.

But there was one more thing in the box, and she pulled out a small black satin bag, from which a sparkling silver chain fell out into her palm. She lifted it with shaking fingers, a flawless emerald teardrop winking at her in the low light of the room.

"It's beautiful, but I can't possibly accept this, Reece," she said, looking up at him.

He pulled her to her feet, and into his arms for a tight hug followed by a deep kiss.

"Please, I want you to. I want to see you in that dress and the necklace, and then we're coming back here, and it will be my turn to unwrap you," he said, trailing his tongue down her neck, making her shiver.

REECE KNEW HE WAS PLAYING with fire. It'd be hours before he could go back to the room and enjoy Abby's body in every way he imagined.

They sat at a private table at the back of one of his favorite restaurants, the lush bougainvillea and palms surrounding them, a half-finished bottle of wine on the table between them.

Abby was beyond gorgeous in the dress he'd picked out for her when he had snuck out earlier in the day, his plan in place. Hannah had been his coconspirator, and he felt a serious wave of pride and possession as he and Abby had entered the restaurant. He knew every man there envied him, and rightfully so.

Her eyes were as bright as the emerald that lay against her skin, and he got hard every time he thought about their using his other gifts.

"Would you like to dance?" he asked, as the band started to play a slow romantic tune.

She smiled, her eyes soft with the effects of wine and their relaxing time together.

Though she kept silent, he stood. "Dance with me, Abby," he said, his heart hammering in his chest. He wanted to give her everything, which was the source of his dilemma.

She put her hand in his, and it was like a fantasy as they walked onto the dance floor. Amid other couples who swayed together under the Christmas lights hung round the room, they danced to a sexy jazz version of "Have Yourself A Merry Little Christmas."

He pulled her close, pressing his lower body against her and letting her feel how aroused he was. He smiled into her neck as he felt her fingers curl into his jacket.

The dress was a mere scrap between them—another reason he'd picked it out, and he felt her nipples bead under the thin fabric. He moved to the music, letting his chest brush against them, and felt her shudder.

"Reece," she breathed, burying her face against his chest, sounding like she was barely holding on.

It was the sexiest moment of his life. They were in the middle of a crowd of people, and he discreetly leaned in to kiss the curve of her neck, while letting his hand brush her pebbled nipple. She came apart in his arms as they danced.

He captured her surprised gasp with a kiss, the shock of sensation moving through her as she moaned into his mouth, the music offering some disguise. He nearly lost control himself, but somehow managed to hold on.

Later, he thought, smiling at the idea of peeling this dress away, using the handcuffs and the oil. However, he wanted her to leave the necklace and stilettos on.

"Reece, that was…" She paused, looking up at him with smoky eyes and flushed cheeks.

"I know," he murmured, dipping to catch her mouth in another kiss, and keeping her in his arms for several more turns around the dance floor.

He really didn't want this to end—ever—and that was where the danger lay.

The day had been one he wouldn't soon forget—the drive, even though he had had a lapse, was more or less successful, but it was Abby's support that made it shine for him. She made him feel like he could do anything.

She knew he had to leave, that he would go back to racing, and yet she gave herself to him completely, and supported him completely, as well.

He loved her, and he wanted it all—he wanted to race, and he wanted Abby, for good.

He barely noticed the music had stopped, until light applause from the group shook him out of his deep thoughts.

"This has been wonderful," Abby said, looking up at him. "But can we go back to the condo now? Please?"

Her sexy plea shook him with desire, and he nodded, retrieving her shawl and paying the bill. She was the only Christmas gift he ever wanted.

REECE SET FORTH, paying great attention to every aspect of Abby's body. He loved how he could find some new spot that would make her whimper or gasp and when she insistently wove her fingers into his hair, directing him as to what she needed.

She was beautiful but real, smart but modest, sexier

than hell and everything he could ever imagine wanting in a woman.

Limp from his intimate kissing, he carried her to the bed. Slowly he took the sexy shoes off, kissing her ankles and massaging her feet, still sifting through his emotions as he stood to take his own clothes off and join her on the bed.

"No talking," she said, putting a finger against his lips. "Just make love to me, okay?" He was glad to oblige, covering her completely as he drove deep inside. Bodies moving in harmony, their patience and seduction paid off in a series of powerful orgasms that left them both breathless and hanging on to each other.

"I love you, Abby," he said, feeling the truth of what he told her as much as anything he had ever known in his life.

She studied him, as if wondering if she had heard correctly.

"Reece," she said, sighing. "I love you, too."

He had not realized how he'd been holding his breath.

Joy coursed through him. "I've loved you forever, Abby, it just took me a long time to realize it," he said, leaning in to kiss her softly, tenderly, trying to communicate everything he was feeling. It seemed impossible. "Come back with me. To France. Please."

His question hung in the dark between them, and he knew her answer before she even said it.

"I can't…you know that. I mean, I could visit, I could come to see you, but I can't leave the vineyards."

Everything inside of him sank. "You can. We can make it work."

They parted, and pushed back on the pillows, facing each other. He had to convince her, somehow.

"Reece, you know how you said racing was your passion, the thing you loved?"

"Mmm-hmm."

She shrugged her shoulder slightly. "That's what the vineyards are for me. I love it there. It's my home, but it's also my passion, and it feels important to preserve that legacy. My parents left me the business they spent their lives building. I can't just abandon that."

"We could work it out. You could get a manager, and we could come back as often as we needed to—" he said, but she interrupted.

"And what would I do in Europe? Follow you around to the races? As much as I want to be with you, that's not a life I want. And…I don't know if I could do it. It was hard, watching you drive today. I was proud of you, happy for you, but I don't think I could stand there and watch if something bad happened again. I just… couldn't."

He pulled her in, not wanting her to see how disappointed he was, though he knew she was right. He shouldn't ask her to make this sacrifice for him.

"It's selfish of me to want you to come with me, you're right, and I suppose it's time I face facts. They aren't going to take me back," he said, weaving his fingers through hers and not wanting to let go. "Maybe Brody is right, maybe another year, or maybe not. Maybe it's time for me to move on to other things."

"Do you mean…are you saying…?"

"I'll stay. I want to be with you, Abby, and I think today proved that it's the right choice for me to make."

She was quiet in his arms, and he wanted to see her face.

"You okay? I thought you would be happier."

"I am," she said, looking at him closely. "I just don't want you giving up on your dreams for me."

"Maybe it's just time I learn to chase a new dream, don't you think? One you and I could share together?"

She smiled then, and reached up to kiss him.

Reece let the passion rise again, losing himself in Abby, and setting his doubts aside. He loved her. He was making the right decision. He had to be.

13

ABBY PANICKED WHEN she walked out of Reece's kitchen, the scent of fire meeting her nose. Following it, she found Reece down behind the lower barn on his property, a fire burning in an area he cleared, and some contraption built above that held a wine barrel in place.

"I wondered what you were up to," Abby said. He'd spent most of his time here since they had gotten back from Daytona the day before. She'd been constantly busy, too busy to investigate before now.

"It's a wine barrel," Reece said, grinning.

"I see that. I knew your Dad was a cooper, but I didn't know you were."

"I'm not," Reece clarified, rubbing his hands together and leaning in for a kiss before he nodded to her to follow him into the barn. "Dad always tried to get me into it, but I was never interested. I forgot he had this workshop. I figured I'd see what I could remember, and looked up the rest on the Internet." He checked the steaming barrel suspended above the fire. "That's my first one. We'll see what happens."

"Wow, I am impressed. You are a man of many talents," she said, reaching up to kiss him again and loving the smoky, earthy scents that surrounded them.

Still, something was off, and she'd felt it in the four days since they had returned. Since he had told her he was staying, she knew. It was what she wanted. She loved him, and she wanted him here, but some undefinable layer of tension seemed to run underneath them now, and while she thought it was good for Reece to get back in touch with his family's history and pursuits, he himself had said this was never his passion.

Driving was his passion, and he was giving it up, for her.

So she had made a few calls herself, namely, one to Joe, the man Reece had been talking with before. His number was left on Reece's phone, and Abby called, and talked to him, to find out if Reece really was out of the sport.

As it turned out, just the opposite.

News of Reece's test run had spread and, true to form, fans were cheering him on, wanting him back. Joe knew it, and sponsors knew it, and they were willing to give him some test runs in Europe, to see how things went.

They wanted him there soon, and they had been going to call him, when Abby had taken the tiger by the tail and contacted them.

Her chest tightened as she pulled back from Reece's increasingly passionate kiss.

"I have something to tell you," she said, trying to sound normal, but her heart hurt a little, even though she knew this was the right thing to do. She loved him, and that meant not having him just walk away from his dream for her.

"Yeah, can it wait?" Reece said teasingly, dipping in for another kiss.

She laughed, evading him, and putting a hand on either shoulder, she made him listen as she told him about her phone call to Joe.

Everything from confusion to disbelief to excitement passed across his face, and finally, he shook his head and pulled her in closer.

"I can't believe you did that," he said huskily against her hair.

"I didn't do anything. They were going to call you anyway. And you know you have to go. Reece, you have to."

He didn't say anything, but she'd seen the light, the hope, in his face. She wouldn't let him stay here and give it all up.

"So what do we do, then? I don't want to lose you," he said, the emotion in his voice sincere.

"I guess we'll just have to see what happens. Maybe we can visit each other, definitely we'll talk on the phone," she said. She feared her tone betrayed her, that maintaining a relationship that way probably wasn't re-alistic. "It'll only be for another few years, and then we could make some decisions about being together for good, right?"

REECE HELD HER TIGHT, his mind spinning with the news. They wanted him back! But he also wanted to be with Abby. Conflicted, he didn't know how to answer her question.

He was on the circuit for months at a time. Some of the guys' families did stay home, especially when there were kids and other considerations. Not all of the wives traveled with their husbands, but a few did.

Still, those couples had the deeper connection of years together, a marriage to return to. He didn't know if what he had with Abby was too new, too tenuous to endure that kind of separation. The realization hit him like a ton of bricks, and he lifted her face up to his, kissing her.

"Aw, Abby, don't cry."

"I can't help it. I love you, and you love me, but I can't see how we can make this work," she said, her voice tight and pained. "I want to, but…"

He held her tight, unable to stand that she was suffering, even a little, because of him.

He knew how to make it right. They could make it work—and they would. He was going back to Europe, and he had no idea what the future held, but he knew two things for sure: he had to at least try to get back to racing, and he couldn't lose Abby.

The answer to both seemed clear.

"Abby?" he asked, his heart thundering.

"Yeah?"

"Will you marry me?"

ABBY WAS UP TO HER EARS in satin, flowers and bridesmaids.

Two days before Christmas, the winery was decorated, and everything was ready for the wedding reception. She'd been working overtime—an understatement—to make sure it was all perfect.

Looking around at the young women in beautiful,

deep red satin Christmas gowns, it put to rest the notion that bridesmaids wore ugly dresses. These were chic and stylish, and Abby thought of the beautiful silk dress Reece had given her. It was far too light to wear, even indoors, in this climate, but she felt very proper back in her basic black business dress.

She lifted her hand to the emerald that lay against her throat. She hadn't taken it off since Reece had put it on for her that night in Florida.

The winery looked magical. Christmas lights were strung everywhere along the reception-room ceiling and through the entryway. He'd helped her string them before he left. It had only been four days and it felt like so much longer.

A fire crackled in the fireplace. The tables were set with fine white china, the glasses were sparkling crystal and Christmas bouquets of holly, poinsettias and white roses decorated each table.

The small band the bride and groom had hired was setting up in the reception room. Specialty bottles of different varieties of both Winston and Maple Hills wines, uniquely labeled for the bridal couple's special day, looked elegant on the tables, ready for each guest to take one home.

All they needed now was the bride and groom, who were taking a little longer arriving, so the bridesmaids and some of the groomsmen—also handsome in gray tuxedos with deep red cumberbuns—milled around, tasting appetizers and enjoying some drinks.

Abby felt incredibly alone even though she was in a roomful of people. Her throat tightened with emotions she had been fighting off since Reece had left for France.

He'd had to go. She wanted him to go. His sponsors were asking him to come back. No promises, but they were giving him a chance. It was exactly as Reece had predicted—everyone loved a comeback.

She wasn't about to stand in his way, and she made that clear by refusing his proposal. It had been the hardest thing she'd ever done. He wasn't angry, but he also told her he intended to keep on asking.

She figured he would, maybe, for a while. Then his life would take over, and he would know they'd made the right decision. Maybe, in a few years, things would be different, she thought, but found it hard to believe. So many things could happen in that time.

On top of that, Hannah was gone, too, staying in Florida with Brody. She had offered to come back, but Abby had released her from that responsibility. Abby was glad to take it on by herself, to have so much work to do that maybe she wouldn't think too much.

That would come to an end after the wedding, when she would close down through New Year's.

And do what? With whom?

Well, she thought, she had Beau and Buttercup.

She couldn't even move forward on plans for the reconstruction, since the city more or less closed down between Christmas and New Year's.

Reece had asked her to come to France for Christmas and stay the week. She was tempted. She'd never seen France, but would it just be extending the torture for both of them?

She didn't know if she'd be able to leave if she went there to be with him.

The fact was, though they loved each other, they had both chosen their individual passions over being together. Who was going to budge? Who should give up what they loved? What kind of foundation was that for a marriage? And how could they even think of getting married when they had only been lovers for less than a month? It was so unfair. It went against every grain of common sense she had, and at the same time, she knew he was the only one for her.

She was shaken from her reverie as applause scattered around her, growing louder with hoots and whistles as the bridal couple arrived, and Abby joined in. Sandra looked absolutely gorgeous, and as the party started, she took her place with the caterers and other party organizers, making sure all went well.

Seeing Sandra and her new husband so happy filled Abby with doubt—had she made the wrong choice?

Was being here more important than being with Reece, and supporting him as he made his way back onto the circuit? He would only be racing for another few years at most, and then they could open their own winery, wherever they wanted. Everyone else in her life was gone, out living their lives, but this was her life, her dream—wasn't it?

She didn't know anymore. What was the right thing to do? She had so many plans to revive this place, and at the very least, she needed to be here during the rebuilding to see that through.

Her heart was heavy, and she was exhausted as the hours wore on. Late in the evening, the caterers gone, the party was still lasting long past her ability to stay. She needed to be alone, to go off and lick her wounds in private.

As she started back toward the house, she saw head-lights turn into the drive. It was very late for anyone to be arriving—a late wedding guest maybe?

The car came closer, and her heart leapt as she rec-ognized the driver. She ran toward the car as the door opened, feeling happy for the first time in days.

"Oh, Mom, Dad! I'm so happy you're here!"

Her parents had no idea what to do when she launched herself at them and broke down in tears.

THEY WANTED HIM BACK.

While the younger guy who had been in line to re-place him had been close to doing just that, the media coverage of Reece's trial in Florida, coupled with an interview that hit the French and U.S. papers, had fans insisting they wanted Reece back on the track. The re-sponse was overwhelming, especially online, and Reece had as hard a time believing it as anyone.

He should have been thrilled.

Snow was falling in Paris as he sat in a conference room with his manager, the car's owner, the sponsor reps and God knew who else. They had been talking incessantly about new acupuncture methods, hiring him a personal physical therapist and doing whatever was necessary to get him back in a car, winning races.

It was what he wanted, so why was he sitting here thinking about what Abby was doing? Today was the wedding, and she was probably so busy she hadn't even thought of him. He'd sent her an e-mail, left her a phone message earlier, but hadn't heard back.

He still couldn't believe she had made that call—she hadn't set any of this in motion, of course, but the fact that she had been willing to let him go, to put his dreams first, still stunned him. If it was possible, he loved her more every time he thought about her.

He didn't know how he was going to manage it, but he wasn't going to lose her. She'd said no this time, and that was fine. She was right, again. It was too soon, maybe he had proposed for the wrong reasons. He had been desperately trying to find a way to make it all work, but he knew he really did want her, and only her, in his life. Maybe she'd say yes the next time, or the time after that.

He didn't plan on giving up.

"Reece? Can you be in Italy in two days? You can start training now. We want you back in shape and ready to go as soon as possible," his manager said. Tony was a good guy, but Reece swore he saw dollar signs flashing in his eyes for a moment.

Reece wasn't a person—an actual human being—to anyone gathered in this room. He was a commodity, a product.

He listened as they discussed liability issues, if the car would be covered, how much they stood to lose if he crashed again, what the risks were with insurance if anyone thought he wasn't up to racing in the first place.

He was. Even with his problems at Daytona, he knew he could do it. No more cold hands or nerves at the thought of getting behind the wheel, but what if the worst happened?

He could care less about the car, or anything else. His doubts weren't borne of fear of dying, but of fear of never seeing Abby again. Could he live with that?

No.

"Reece?" Tony asked again, sounding irritated. "I hope your focus is better when you get back in a car," he said.

Some muffled laughter and commentary met the remark, and Reece smiled. He couldn't believe what he was about to do.

"Two days from now? That's Christmas day," he said, sparking off a round of confused glances around the conference table.

"So what? You need to be on this ASAP and 24/7 if it's going to work. The docs will clear you, but only if you sign a contract and follow the physical regimen to the letter."

Reece looked out the window at the snow, thinking, of all things, about Abby's pork roast. That was certainly not going to be part of his training. He'd invited her to come see him next week—but now he would be in training, out of touch twelve to eighteen hours a day, every day.

He wouldn't ask her to do that. No way would he say she had to come all the way over here and then form her life around his crazy racing schedule, content to see him in whatever cracks of time he had left.

It was why he'd never gotten into relationships in the first place.

"Reece, what the—"

"I'm sorry, Tony, I can't do it this week. I have other plans for Christmas," he said, amazed at how easy it was. Abby had given him the gift of going after his dreams, after what he really wanted, and that was what he was going to do.

"You...you *what?*"

"Listen, I appreciate this. I thought it was what I wanted, but I need to be home for Christmas."

"Home? Reece, you are home. This is home."

He grinned again, feeling incredibly giddy as he torpedoed his racing career for good.

"No, home is where Abby is."

"WHY DID YOU DECIDE to come back?" Abby asked, wrapped up in a blanket that smelled like Reece, having a very late-night cup of hot chocolate with her parents.

Her mom and dad shared a somewhat guilty look, and Abby peered at them over her mug. "Tell me."

"Well, to be completely honest," her mother began, "Hannah called us."

Abby groaned. "I'm sorry, she shouldn't have done that. I'm fine."

Her mom looked at her, and Abby felt like she was ten again.

"She told us Reece proposed."

Abby groaned a second time, closing her eyes and planning what she would do to her friend the next time she saw her. It wouldn't be pretty.

"We had no idea you and Reece were an item, let alone so serious," her dad said.

"We...it's complicated. He has his life, I have mine. The two don't match up so well."

"Why is that?"

"He has to be in Europe, racing, hopefully, and I have to be here, rebuilding and running the vineyards."

"Is that really what you want, honey?" her mom asked, as if seeing right through her. "It's clear just by the look on your face, and how you cried your heart out a little while ago, that you love him. So why aren't you in France with an engagement ring on your finger for Christmas?"

Abby opened her mouth, gaped, started to say something. "Mom," she began, "I love it here, and I have responsibilities, and—"

"They sound more like excuses than reasons, Abigail," her father said.

"Wait," she said, putting her hand up. "You know how much work this is, and it's even more so now with the fire and the reorganizing. I have to be here…right? And besides…" she said, but didn't finish her thought.

"Besides, what?"

"I don't know. There was this moment, when Reece lost control of the car for a minute, down in Daytona."

"We saw it on the news. He pulled it back."

"I know. But it scared me to death. What if he hadn't? What if he died, right there in front of me? I don't know if I can handle that."

"Would you rather it happens when you're not there? When you're not the last person he sees before he races? The person he woke up with that morning? I'm sorry to be harsh, honey, but your father and I have seen a lot of pain and suffering in the last few months, and one thing I can tell you is that you can't avoid it. If Reece crashed, would your pain be any less for staying here?

Would it be better not to have married him and had that time together?"

Abby gaped, wordless in response to her parents' questions. That Reece could crash, could get hurt or worse, knowing that she hadn't wanted to be with him, had said no to marrying him. Had let him go...

And what about when he won? When he wanted to celebrate and enjoy life? Didn't she want to share that with him, too? The good and the bad?

"Oh, Mom," she said, a fresh batch of new tears at the realization flooding her eyes.

"It's hard to figure out on your own sometimes, I know," her mom said.

"But if I go...what about here? What about the wineries, and the rebuilding?"

"Well, that was kind of the miracle of Hannah's call. She gave us an excuse to come back."

"She...what? I thought you loved your travel and your work?"

"Oh, we did. It was wonderful, but it made us also realize how precious home was, and how long we had been away. We wanted to come back, to come back to running the vineyard, but we didn't want you to feel like we were intruding or suggesting you weren't doing just fine. When Hannah called, we knew it was the right time to come back. For us, and for you."

"You want to run the vineyard again?"

"Yes, and we have a bit more money in investments set aside, so we can, we think, with the insurance, probably buy Reece out, instead of you doing that and going broke trying." Her mother shook her head. "Really, Abby, didn't we teach you better about leading a balanced life?"

Abby fought the urge to smile. "Hannah really did tell you everything, huh?"

"Yes."

"Remind me to thank her."

Her parents' grins broke out wide, and so did hers. "We'll do that. But you have to get ready."

"Ready? For what?"

Her parents chuckled conspiratorially and her father handed her an envelope with a red ribbon on it.

"You have a morning flight to Paris. Our Christmas gift to you. Go pack."

REECE TURNED INTO the driveway of the house and parked at the edge, party-goers apparently still sleeping from the wedding reception. It was Christmas Eve morning; he had made it home, just in time.

He couldn't wait to sneak in and wake Abby up—he fully intended to make love to her until she agreed to wear the ring he had in his pocket. It was his mission, he thought with a smile.

As he climbed the steps to the porch, he paused, looking out over the snowy fields down toward the grapes. All of the trees Abby had put in the yard sparkled and were lit, and Christmas was in the air. He never really understood what people meant when they said that, but he could feel it, right now, and he knew. Some of her Christmas magic must have rubbed off on him, he guessed.

He heard the door open behind him and spun, expecting to see Abby, but found himself facing an older man instead.

"Uh, hi," Reece said, peering at the man more closely. He looked familiar. "I'm Reece, I live—"

"Oh, I know who you are," the man said, letting out a belting laugh. He was then was joined by an older woman, whose eyes went wide.

Reece's did, too. He could see Abby in her mother's face and laughed as well.

"Mr. and Mrs. Harper! What a surprise," he said. It *was* a surprise. His sneaky seduction of Abby would have to wait, he supposed. "It's so nice you made it here for Christmas, and not to be rude, but where is Abby?"

CHRISTMAS AT HANCOCK INTERNATIONAL AIRPORT wasn't exactly what Abby had counted on, but she was going to wait out this flight delay no matter what. It would figure. She had nearly killed herself getting here, unable to fly out of the smaller, Ithaca airport, and now her flight was delayed for weather.

She was going to call Reece and let him know she was coming, but then she thought she would make it a surprise instead—hopefully a happy one. He had invited her, so she hoped he'd be glad to see her.

So, she gave up her seat to a young mother carrying a baby, and paced in front of the gate, willing the delay to be lifted. She couldn't sit still anyway, in spite of getting no sleep, she was wired and eager to get going. The place was crowded, flooded with holiday travelers, and she felt sorry for the mom with the crying baby, and for kids napping against the posts and harried parents.

She paced to the vending machine and looked over the candy selection, and grabbed a chocolate bar, then headed to the Starbucks to get another double-shot expresso.

Her phone rang, and she looked.

Reece.

Her heart trip-hammered in her chest, and her hand shook as she clicked the talk button, though it could have been from the caffeine.

Right.

"Abby, it's Reece," he said.

She laughed. "I know."

"Oh, right. Listen, I just wanted to let you know I've had a change in plans, and I won't be able to meet you in France for the week."

She paused. "What do you mean?"

"Listen, I know you probably weren't planning to come anyway, but I have to be somewhere else, and I didn't want you coming here and ending up finding me gone."

Her heart sank. She looked at the lines of people suddenly in motion as they flooded the gate. The flight was boarding.

Of course it was.

She took a deep breath and got a grip.

"So, where will you be? I'll meet you there. Wherever," she said, determined to make this work.

"Really? You'd meet me anywhere?"

"Yes. Reece, I have a lot to tell you, but things have changed, and…I want to spend Christmas with you, and tell you everything that's happened. I don't care where you are, I just want to be with you."

"I can't wait," he said, but this time the sound of his voice didn't come from the phone, but from right behind her.

She turned, and found herself nose-to-nose with him, and let out a screech that stopped just about everyone around them in their tracks. Throwing herself at him, they nearly both fell over until he got his balance and set her on her feet, saying nothing until he kissed her thoroughly.

"Hi, sweetheart."

"When did you come home? How did you know…?"

He smiled. "I didn't. I was at the house, and your parents said you were taking a flight. I couldn't believe it. I was breaking land-speed records getting here, I think, because I thought I would miss you," he explained.

"You mean…at our house?" she asked, slowly putting two and two together.

"Yeah. I'm back. I didn't want to go through Christmas—or my life—without you."

She was stunned, and lack of breathing threatened to steal words from her, the emotions hitting her too hard, the questions all rising too quickly.

"Breathe, Abby," he said, kissing her again, and making sure she did.

"It was all happening, just as I hoped for," he explained, "but none of it felt right. It wasn't like before. I didn't feel like I was home or happy or doing what I wanted to be doing. I didn't expect it. They were offering me everything I wanted, and all I could think of was that I wanted you. I wanted to be here. I wanted to wake up in bed with you Christmas morning, for the rest of our lives."

Abby almost wondered if she had fallen asleep and was dreaming all of this. She must have said so, because he assured her he was real.

"I love you, Abby," he said, his voice low and full of emotion. "I'm yours, if you want me."

"I love you, too, Reece. And Christmas in bed sounds perfect to me," she whispered, sliding into his arms once and for all.

Epilogue

ABBY BUSTLED AROUND the kitchen, making Reece the most amazing anniversary dinner he could imagine. They ate out at restaurants so often when they were on the road with the new team that she wanted to do something special, and something private. Her parents had gone on a vacation to the house in Talence, leaving Abby and Reece home to watch over the vineyard and enjoy their first anniversary alone together. With that amazing bathroom, she thought with a grin.

She loved the house, and their new life following the races around the U.S. and traveling and working the vineyard in between. Reece and Brody were co-owners of a new racing team now, and they were often surrounded by crowds and people, which was fun and exciting, but Abby wanted her husband to herself tonight. The team was doing very well, and Brody was in charge while Reece took the week off.

It was their first anniversary, after all, and she looked out the kitchen window at the pristine summer countryside. She loved Christmas, but was happy they had waited for a summer wedding. The vineyards were so lovely, and they had been married out among them, over-looking the lake.

She had plans for her husband, who had been teasing her mercilessly for a week, keeping her on edge, dol-ing out his seductions with practiced patience. She was intent on doing whatever was necessary to make him give in to her tonight.

The thought put a sly smile on her face. She didn't think he'd mind. They'd honed the practice of extended sex play and seduction to a fine art.

She checked all of the food, and took another peep at the delectable pastry in the refrigerator that was one of her favorites.

Her plan started now.

Shucking her clothes, she grabbed the sexy apron he'd caught her in that first Christmas and donned only that, taking her coat from the hook and heading down to the workshop Reece had remodeled to continue per-fecting his cooperage. The craft had created a new bond between Reece and his father, as well, which both of them enjoyed, and now many of the barrels in which they aged their wine were made on premises.

She walked into the workshop, which smelled of oak and the delicious scents of wine and burnt wood, and she had come to find the aroma incredibly erotic. Reece was bent over an almost finished cask, cauterizing the opening through which the wine would be poured. She waited for him to finish, enjoying watching him, ap-preciating every sexy muscle in his body as he leaned into his work.

When he finished, he looked up and was unsurprised to find her there.

"Hey," he said, taking off his safety glasses and

crossing to a sink to take off his gloves and wash his hands before he crossed to her, kissing her soundly. "How long have you been there?" he asked.

"Just a minute," she said, love filling her just looking at him. "Dinner is almost done."

"Do we have a few minutes?"

"Sure."

"Isn't it a little hot for a coat?" he said, his eyes drifting down over her bare legs.

She smiled and wiggled her eyebrows. "I didn't think you'd want me walking down from the house in only this," she said as she dropped the coat and watched his eyes darken with lust. "So what did you have in mind?" she asked innocently, raising an eyebrow at some ties attached to a beam that had been put to very good use the evening before.

"I have an anniversary gift for you," he said, his voice a little raspy.

She smiled. "I have one for you, too, back at the house—but it's something we'll want to use there," she said, sending him a sexy look.

"Mmm. Maybe we can come back for yours then," he said, grabbing her by the waist and pulling her up close, where she could feel the extent of his excitement.

"Nope, I'd like mine now, please," she said, poking him in the chest playfully.

"Okay, vixen, come with me," he said, bringing her to a set of newly finished barrels. He opened one bottle and drew two glasses from the tap, a rich Baco that he sniffed, swirled and tasted, then handed hers to her.

"It's perfect, just like you," he said, toying with the apron tie at her neck.

She sipped the rich, fruity wine and groaned in

appreciation as the flavors washed over her. "I don't think I have ever had a wine this complex—how did you get those sorts of sweet, smoky notes in there?"

It was a sexy, sensual wine, and she took another sip, feeling the tie at her neck pull loose.

"I've been experimenting with the barrels. This wine is ours. Like your mom and dad always did, I named it for us, too. Our story," he said. "Happy Anniversary."

"Oh, Reece. This is lovely. What did you name it?"

He put his glass down and pulled her in close as the apron fell away completely.

"Christmas in Bed."

She smiled, so much in love she didn't think she could ever express it, so she just let herself be carried away by his kiss, because Reece was right. It was perfect.

* * * * *

Join Britain's BIGGEST Romance Book Club

- **EXCLUSIVE offers every month**

- **FREE delivery direc to your door**

- **NEVER MISS a title**

- **EARN Bonus Book points**

Call Customer Services
0844 844 1358*

or visit
millsandboon.co.uk/subscriptior

* This call will cost you 7 pence per minute plus your phone company's price per minute access charge.

BKCB3